Heart of Stone

Rock Star Fairy Tales

Heart of Stone

Rock Star Fairy Tales

JM Paquette

4 Horsemen
Publications, Inc.

Dedication

To everyone tired of waiting on the One

Fenton
Shellbrook
Rutvik
Mer
Warman
Keswick
Dunlop
Gibs
Eston
Fufallon
Ter
Vedum
Hidesfont
Stettler
Saro
Yens
Talberg
Pemberton
Lidon
Boult
Biskra
Sorne
Arillo
Bettant
Pomiss
Ancy

Depaw
Curtis
Leland
Slaton
Orland
ille
town
Akkoy
Nerva
Armav
Tunica
as
Karacay
Tortom
Taflah
Kocarli
Genc
Sivas
Mineo
Bacoli
Altino
Dikmen
Yarma
Vada
Denham Island

STONE DRAGONS

HEART OF STONE TOUR SCHEDULE

DECEMBER

21	22	23	24	25	26
				Lemke Bowl Sorne, Arillo	
30	31 Todd Hall Stettler, Yens				

JANUARY

Sunday	Monday	Tuesday	Wednesday	Thursday	Friday	Saturday
				1	2 Beat Arena Eston Yens	3
4 The Omni Dunlop Warman	5 Mirage Dome Fenton Warman	6	7 Cedar Pt. Place Keswick Warman	8	9 The Jane Center Shellbroook Warman	10 The Jane Center Shellbroook Warman
11	12	13	14 Hannah House Pemberton Yens	15	16 Crone Park Saro Hidesfont	17
18	19 Arman Stadium Vedum Hidesfont	20 Arman Stadium Vedum Hidesfont	21	22	23 Mira Castle Rutvik Hidesfont	24
25 Allon Center Fufallon Hidesfont	26	27 Red Wine Castle Talberg Hidesfont	28	29	30	31

FEBRUARY

Sunday	Monday	Tuesday	Wednesday	Thursday	Friday	Saturday
1 Slate Theatre Boult Arillo	2	3 Dockside Theatre Bettant Arillo	4	5 Tidwell Centre Pomiss Arillo	6	7
8	9 Millay Stadium Ancy Arillo	10	11	12	13 Orion Center Velines Arillo	14 Orion Center Velines Arillo
15	16	17	18 Revel Coliseum Kerva Armav	19	20	21 EcoDome Akkoy Genc
22	23 The Hive Sivas Genc	24	25 Jupiter Arena Mineo Bacoli	26	27 Riverside Theatre Altino Bacoli	28

Sunday	Monday	Tuesday	Wednesday	Thursday	Friday	Saturday
1	2 Thessaly Stadium Vada, Bacoli	3 Thessaly Stadium Vada, Bacoli	4	5	6 Dikmen Palace Dikmen Genc	7
8 The Yama Bowl Yama Genc	9	10	11	12 Carli Amphitheatre Kocarli, Genc	13	14 Willis Center at Beau Lake Taflah, Genc
15 Fan Gala The Aerie Taflah, Genc	16 Willis Center at Beau Lake Taflah, Genc	17	18	19 The Red Wing Denham Island	20 The Red Wing Denham Island	21 The Red Wing Denham Island
22	23	24	25	26 Kinsem Park Tortum Genc	27	28 Bright Star Amphitheatre Karakay, Genc
29	30	31 Ward Stadium Slaton Leland				

Sunday	Monday	Tuesday	Wednesday	Thursday	Friday	Saturday
			1	2 The Humble Hold Orland, Leland	3 The Humble Hold Orland, Leland	4
5 Brockew Arena Curtis Leland	6	7 Freya Hall Depaw Leland	8	9 Longshanks Castle Merlin, Leland	10	11
12	13 DoUrden Dome Gibsonton Leland	14	15 Zylas Room Tero Yens	16	17 Chamberlin Bowl Twille Yens	18
19 Mackie Park Minetown Yens	20	21 Savage Center Lidon Yens	22	23 Lance Arena Bikstra Arillo	24 Lance Arena Bikstra Arillo	25
26	27	28	29	30		

ENTER THE LAIR

STONE DRAGONS

SATURDAY, FEB 21ST	MONDAY, FEB 23RD	WEDS, FEB 25TH
AKKOY	**SIVAS**	**MINEO**
ECODOME	THE HIVE	JUPITER ARENA
FRIDAY, FEB 27TH	MONDAY, MAR 2ND	TUESDAY, MAR 3RD
ALTINO	**VADA**	**VADA**
RIVERSIDE THEATRE	THESSALY STADIUM	THESSALY STADIUM
FRIDAY, MAR 6TH	SUNDAY, MAR 8TH	THURS, MAR 12TH
DIKMEN	**YAMA**	**KOCARLI**
DIKMEN PALACE	THE YAMA BOWL	CARLI AMPHITHEATRE
SATURDAY, MAR 14TH	SUNDAY, MAR 15TH	MONDAY, MAR 16TH
TAFLAH	**FAN GALA**	**TAFLAH**
WILLIS CENTER AT BEAU LAKE	THE AERIE	WILLIS CENTER AT BEAU LAKE

ENTER THE LAIR

GENC AND BACOLI

Chapter 1

Stone Dragons at the Revel Coliseum

Night, Wednesday, February 18th
at the Revel Coliseum in Kerva, Armav

"Where's my blue Nibson?" Nik shouted. "Baby Go! Why isn't it here?"

Through the narrow opening into the back room, beyond the recessed bunks along the sides of the luxury RV, Margot, also known as Baby Go when the band shouted at her, could see Nik weaving back and forth, scanning the rows of instruments on the back wall for his beloved guitar. She rolled her eyes at her cousin and finished the last of her iced tea, gathering up her paper plate from where she sat at the small table across from the kitchen and putting both in the trash can under the sink.

The luxury RV was much bigger than her converted TW bus. It had two cushy seats in front of a long couch that ended at the small kitchen table. Beyond the kitchen, the Party Bus, as Nik had dubbed this RV, contained four oversized bunk beds for the members of Stone Dragons. For this road tour, they spent most of their time here lounging between shows. Earlier tonight, the band had been sitting on the couch watching TV while Nik absently strummed his guitar—which still sat on the couch.

She picked up the battered Aniphone and walked back to where he stood, shaggy dark hair wet from his post-show shower. "It's packed with the rest of the show gear," she reminded him, tapping his shoulder with her free hand. "Because you don't take the fancy guitar to the afterparty, Niklaus." When he turned, she handed him the dark brown guitar. "You take the ancient Hummingbird when you show off for all the ladies." After a pause, she added, "Since you like to leave your instruments behind for your adoring fans."

He took the guitar, giving her a conspiratorial smile. "What if I want to show off for you instead?" he asked, a teasing glint in his eye.

Margot gave him a solid push toward the door. "Take your guitar and go," she ordered. "I know you too well for you to show off for me."

"You know you love it when I sing," he crooned but started walking toward the door, snagging a t-shirt from atop his bunk and sliding the small privacy curtain closed, sealing off his space until he returned. Standing in the small hallway, he dragged the green shirt over his head, managing to shove his arms through the sleeves without losing the guitar in the process, a display of back muscles and tattoos that Margot could appreciate on a certain level. Niklaus Hodges was a beautiful man: dark eyes, tousled brown hair, the taut forearms of a guitarist.

If he wasn't her cousin, she might have responded to his charm. Then she saw that he was wearing yet another of his t-shirts emblazoned with a picture of himself—playing drums—in high school. She sighed, shaking her head.

"Again with the shirt?" she asked, knowing he did it to annoy Timothy, the actual drummer of Stone Dragons.

He grinned at her. "Chicks dig it."

"I don't know how you manage to get laid at all," she commented but didn't mean it. The number of groupies surrounding the band had grown the last year. Even though they were doing an actual road tour, no airplanes and no hotels—much to the delight of their manager Cayla, who thought they were all crazy but wasn't going to stop them if they wanted to drive across the country—the number of wild fans the band continued to pick up was starting to be a nuisance.

Margot could understand why the people were drawn to Stone Dragons. Rock star status aside, all of the members were beautiful, blessed with an unearthly presence that called followers to them in droves. They sang like angels—or demons—depending on the song. In addition to playing lead guitar, Nik was backup vocals and chorus, but he was working on songs of his own. He liked to entertain the ladies at the afterparty with his works in progress.

Margot blew him a kiss when he turned at the RV's door. "Knock 'em dead," she told him.

"You coming?" He took the first step down and patted his pockets to make sure he had his phone.

"Later," she assured him. "I still have a few things to do. Some of us work when you're not on stage."

Nik gave her a look, knowing that Margot's "later" often meant "never."

"Timothy is heading over," he told her. "And I saw Ash..."

"I know," she said quickly. "I saw."

Margot hated the sharp jab of jealousy that always surfaced at the lead singer's name. Though she tried not to, she pictured the long line of sexy women who were waiting for Ash Stonewall as he exited what they called the Entertaining Bus, the RV with the actual bedroom in the back. He would stroll out like the rock god he was, long dark hair aching for a smoothing touch, hazel eyes sparkling as he considered his options. Wearing his afterparty clothes—jeans and a faded band shirt (she predicted tonight would have the Blue Giants logo), he might grab a hoodie if the air turned chilly. Ash didn't have to worry about looking good; he had rolled out of bed dripping with sex appeal since Margot first met him years ago. All of the scantily clad women waiting for him were eager to parade about on his arm or jump into his bed—women who could stand on spike heels and pull off leather miniskirts—despite the brisk winter air in Armav. Margot glanced down at her sweaty band shirt and jeans, dirty from the grime she acquired setting up for the show.

Nik frowned, then gave her an understanding smile. "It doesn't matter," he said, lingering on the bottom step. "*They* don't matter."

"Right," she sighed, wishing her little crush wasn't quite so obvious to everyone around her. Ash had certainly talked to her, hired her as their stage manager for the tour, and he was always warm enough when they spoke to one another, but he had never looked at her in *that* way.

Margot wanted more. She wanted what all those other women wanted, and it was embarrassing. She'd known Ash for years now, and though she'd been starstruck from that first moment, then 18-year-old Ash Stonewall hadn't looked at the 15-year-old Margot as anything more than a helpful acquaintance who was his friend's cousin. Ash and Timothy had come to live with Margot's aunt Maddie only a few months before Margot herself arrived—distant relatives on Nik's dad side.

Margot had been shellshocked from the death of her mother and the end of the carefree life she had always known back in Belsune, but the boys—especially Nik— had done their best to make Margot feel at home in Ardon, helping her learn to live on the new continent. They had explained the little things—like driving on the right side of the road instead of the left—and Margot had always felt that Ash and Timothy were sometimes as lost as she was, adrift in a new place unlike their home, though they were only from Yens, the province north of their home in Arillo. One thing Margot had learned by traveling this continent by bus—things varied immensely from province to province: food, language, customs. She had always thought Ash understood how she felt in a new place, their shared ignorance of local customs something that should bring them together. They may be closer eight years later, and clearly Ash valued her assistance since he'd brought her on tour the last two years, yet Margot still longed for the day he would look at her as something—anything—more, but she was always going to be "Baby Go" to him—never Margot the Woman.

At least Nik and Timothy could appreciate that she had grown up. Both were always encouraging her to find herself a man for the evening.

"You're the oddest 23-year-old woman I've ever known," Nik would tell her. "Who goes on a worldwide tour with a rock band and stays in her bus reading all night long?"

"Ardon is not the world. There's a whole other continent out there, and I come to the parties!" she would argue.

"Yeah, to stare at the god himself, sigh a few times, then wander back to your bus and disappear into a book."

"Sometimes I watch TV," she would defend. Lamely.

"You're young. We're young. And we're on tour. Have some damned fun, Margot! Let loose a little."

She never took his advice, but thinking of the line of women waiting to touch Ash, she let out a long breath, something in her shifting. Maybe it was time to do something else.

"You said Timothy was already there?" she asked Nik, tugging off her sneakers and sliding off her socks, already running through the clean clothes she had that would work for the party tonight.

Nik watched her curiously. "Yeah?"

"And you're going now?" She yanked her t-shirt over her head, glancing down at her tank top. She could probably still wear it, she decided, tucking the clothes and shoes under one arm.

Nik nodded, still not following where she was going with the questions.

"Good. We're stopping by my bus on the way there. I need to change. Ten minutes."

Nik's face lit up. "Baby Go is coming out with the boys?"

"Margot," she emphasized, "is going to the afterparty and is going to have a good time."

"Margot should meet someone sexy and have a very good time," Nik agreed, stepping aside so she could exit the trailer ahead of him.

"Who knows?" she asked, stepping onto the still-warm asphalt of the lot behind the coliseum. "Maybe tonight's my lucky night."

Chapter 2

Lessons Learned at Parties

Late Night, Wednesday, February 18th
at the Euphoria in Kerva, Armav

Margot had been at the party for a total of ten minutes when she decided it was a terrible idea. Nik had disappeared, her cousin easily distracted by the catcalls and gestures of a group of women sprawled on the couches cleverly spaced along the VIP floor of the Euphoria nightclub. The bouncer had taken one look at her plain button-down green dress and black boots, and she knew he had been about to dismiss her, but a word from Nik had changed his mind.

"Go's with the band," Nik announced as he breezed through. "She gets everything we get."

Margot watched the other women in the club for a moment, their high heels and slinky dresses, their dark smokey eye makeup and perfectly messy hair, then shook her head and headed for the bar, tugging out her ponytail and smoothing her mass of dark hair into a tight bun atop her head. The bun flopped forward, skewing to one side, and she paused to slowly redo it before she settled onto a stool.

The bartender wandered over, a tiny woman with short blonde spiky hair who gave Margot an expectant look. "What would you like?"

Margot considered the bottles lining the back of the bar. She wasn't a drinker, but tonight seemed to call for something a little more than her usual soda water. "Rum and cola," she told the bartender, hoping that she wouldn't taste the rum too much. The woman nodded, turned around to grab a bottle from the shelf and filled a glass with ice. She topped off an alarming amount of amber liquid with a spray of cola from the hose, then slid the drink across the bar without a word. Margot wondered if she would ask her to pay, but the bartender headed down the line to help other customers.

There were definitely some perks when traveling with rock stars.

She took a sip, winced, then took a deep breath and forced herself to swallow a third of the glass. Slamming the cup down with a *thunk* that disappeared into the background music, Margot paused, hearing the low electronic beat with eerie singing. She listened for a moment, trying to pick out the words. Was it a foreign language? It seemed familiar, but just out of reach, like something heard in a dream. She knew a few words of Armavian, the Ardon dialect not that different from her native Belsune, but it wasn't that.

"I didn't think to find you at the bar, Margot." The voice startled her back into the moment, and she turned around to smile at Timothy. His tone was kind, like his eyes, but as the oldest member of Stone Dragons,

Timothy made Margot feel like she was ten years old again. Though he was only a few years older, certainly on her side of thirty, something about his bearing spoke of long experience—and Margot thought he always seemed slightly sad. Wistful even.

She took another long sip, grimaced, and looked up at Timothy through teary eyes. "It's that kind of day," she said, trying to stop her gaze from drifting over to the cluster of couches that held Ash and Nik and their spellbound harem. Timothy followed her look and sighed, eyes coming back to rest on her with something like sympathy.

"Ash is young," he said quietly. Despite the noise of the music and the crowd, Margot heard him easily, as if his words were for her ears alone. "He'll learn better. Eventually."

"He's not that much younger than you," she snapped, the alcohol sharpening her tongue. "Did you learn better?"

"Eventually," Timothy said and smiled.

Something in the way he said it made Margot pry in a way she normally wouldn't. She could appreciate how handsome he was. Not for her, not her kind of man, but definitely a heartthrob for the right woman. That shaggy brown hair begged for fingers to twist through it, and his mouth promised a good time. He didn't have the cool distance she found in Ash's attention when they had a real conversation. She always felt Ash was listening to her intently, but that part of him was longing to get away from her—and he only stayed to be polite. She tried to keep her communication brief, her words pointed so he didn't have to linger in her presence. But he did linger, asking more questions, probing her mind to get beneath the surface.

"Did you learn in time?" she probed.

Timothy's smile devolved into a smirk, and he winked at her. "No. You think I'd be trekking around the world with you lot if I was smart?"

"We're not that awful," Margot defended. "Are we?" She gave him her best ingratiating smile.

Timothy relented. "You are perfectly delightful, Margot. They—" he nodded over his shoulder at the group on the couch, "need polishing."

Margot saw that two women were currently jockeying for position to be behind Ash on the arm of the couch. Their movements were subtle, nothing obvious like elbowing the other aside, but Margot could feel the tension escalating between them. Ash, however, seemed to enjoy the competition, occasionally glancing at one or the other in encouragement.

"So get to work," she told Timothy. "Polish away!"

"Oh no," Timothy laughed. "It's not my help they need."

He gave her a long appraising look, and Margot felt a whisper of something against her skin, not quite a chill, but not far off. She sniffed, rubbing her upper arms, and glanced around the bar, thinking she may be able to pinpoint the source. Her gaze skated over a tall man heading to the bar, paused, then settled on him. He was lovely—and Margot was surrounded by handsome men—slightly too long white-blond hair, pale skin, high cheekbones, and thin lips that curled into a charming smile as he stepped near.

Margot's focus wasn't so diverted that she didn't see Timothy notice the direction of her gaze, seem about to say something, then shake his head, adjusting his jacket and scanning the room, as if keeping quiet track of who was in it. He always did that—Margot always assumed he was just paying attention—but part of her wondered if he was looking for someone specific.

"Be careful, little Margot," he warned, a hand touching her shoulder for a moment and breaking her free from the spell of the newcomer. "You will attract a great deal of attention in this place."

"Maybe it's time I had some attention," she told him.

He glanced over at Ash quickly and shook his head again.

"You are right," he agreed. "You deserve to have your own fun." He paused, letting go of her shoulder. "Just be careful. These are dangerous waters."

"I can take care of myself," she insisted, taking another long sip of her drink, steeling herself for a conversation with a sexy stranger.

"I have no doubt," Timothy said and walked away, leaving her alone at the bar.

Margot finished her drink and slammed the ice-filled glass on the bar with more vigor than she intended.

"Want another?" a honey voice asked from behind her.

"Maybe," she said, turning to face the stranger. He smelled nice, and her body responded to something unspoken between them. "Why don't you have a seat and we can talk about it?"

Chapter 3

Strangers and Back Rooms

After Midnight, Thursday, February 19th
at the Euphoria in Kerva, Armav

Two hours later, Margot and the stranger had worked their way through a row of glasses, the evidence clearly displayed on the bar before them, and they were laughing loudly, the sound lost in the general cacophony of the club. The stranger—his name was Tobin—hadn't pressured her to drink, but Margot wanted to let go, to give herself permission to cut loose for just one night.

"You know," she giggled, putting her hand on Tobin's arm, loving the slight thrill that ran through her body at the touch, "I wasn't even going to come out tonight."

"What a loss that would have been!" he said, his warm hand covering hers. "I am very glad to have met you, Margot."

He leaned down to look into her eyes, his face at first blurry, then crystallizing in her mind. Margot couldn't say what motivated her in that moment, but she tipped forward, closing the distance between them, and kissed him. He seemed surprised for a second, lips flat beneath her mouth, then rallied and tilted his head, moving his mouth against hers in a way that sent shivers across her skin. His hands found her shoulders, pulling her close. Margot reached out awkwardly, not sure what to touch, and she pushed against his stomach. She heard him chuckle, and their mouths separated a few inches.

"I..." she managed, too shocked at her forward behavior to finish the thought. Rum really did give her liquid courage. She met Tobin's eyes boldly. "I think we should get out of here?"

She meant to say it as a statement, but it came out as a question. She didn't know much about him, other than he was visiting the province and avoiding the trouble to the south, conducting business on behalf of someone else. She knew he made her laugh easily. For tonight, that was enough. Normally, she let men come on to her, offering their place for the night. Margot's bunk on her bus was too small for entertaining.

Tobin glanced around, and Margot followed his gaze to the VIP couch where Ash and Nik had been joined by Timothy, the drummer having maneuvered his way through the harem to sit on the couch next to Ash. None of them seemed to notice Margot at the bar with her new friend.

"Your friends won't mind if I steal you?" Tobin asked quietly, and Margot grinned at the teasing tone in his voice.

"I'm my own person," she informed him. "Maybe I want to be stolen tonight."

Tobin took the hint, grabbing her hand and lifting her to her feet. The world tilted a little as Margot stood.

She was definitely tipsy, but not enough to not know her own mind. She looked at Tobin, studying his face.

I want to kiss you again, she thought, turning to look around the club. *But where can we go?* Maybe a dark corner to make out would work for the immediate future.

"I have an idea," Tobin said, raising an eyebrow. "You up for an adventure?"

"Oh yeah," she replied, gripping his hand more solidly. "Lead the way."

Tobin headed away from the bar, tugging her along in his wake as they passed through the rope marking the VIP area. Instead of heading down the stairs to where she could hear other voices, Tobin turned to the right, leading her swiftly up the stairs. At the top, he lifted her, giggling, over another rope with a sign in a language Margot couldn't read—she wasn't as fluent in Armavian as she was in other languages—but the warning of Employees Only looked the same in any language. For a moment, Margot hesitated, debating the wisdom of breaking the rules in a province with a brewing civil war in the south, then decided she didn't care. She wanted to kiss Tobin again, and if they got caught and got in trouble, she would deal with it then. They ducked under a dark curtain into a small back room. Tobin released her hand, taking in their new surroundings, and Margot made out the dim shapes of stacked tables and chairs.

"Come here often?" she asked, a giggle escaping. "This where you bring all the girls?" She peered at him, sure the alcohol was affecting her vision since he seemed to glow slightly in the dim light, his features standing out in the darkness, bright eyes and pale skin beneath all that white-blond hair. She wanted to touch him, to run her fingers through his hair, to yank him close to her, claiming him and never letting him go.

"No one else is like you," Tobin replied, moving closer to her as he seemed to know exactly what she wanted. This time he kissed her, and Margot let herself melt into him, her mouth eager as her hands began to wander, one sliding up the hard line of his shoulder and curling around his neck. His silky hair brushed the back of her hand, and she twisted it, suddenly yanking hard and tugging his face away from hers. His eyes opened wide, the pupils huge, and the surprise was replaced by excitement as he looked down at her.

"No one else is like me," she echoed, pushing onto her tiptoes so she could reach his face and kiss him again, harder this time. Pausing for breath, she whispered into his mouth, "No one else will be like me ... for you." She didn't know why she said it, wasn't normally one for talking in the middle of making out, but something inside screamed that the words were right. That she needed him to understand just what she was to him.

And what are you? The thought was distant. *A drunken hookup in the back of a bar?*

No, the voice inside replied. *This is more.*

"I want more," she mumbled, losing herself in the kiss again. Tobin, hearing her words for the invitation they were, moved his hands down her body, sliding along her thighs and beneath her dress to the bare skin. She released his hair, softening her touch and pressing herself into his embrace.

"You want more?" Tobin whispered against her lips. "Tell me what you want."

"I want you," she panted, body moving so his hands could gain more access under her dress. She wanted to pause, to remember that public sex, especially in Armavian territory where they were strict about such things, was probably a bad idea, but Tobin's kisses made her delirious, and his hand knew exactly how to touch her. Part of her resisted, knowing that while the man in front of her was sexy and turning her on in all the right ways, he wasn't the one she truly wanted.

You can't have the one you want, she told herself coldly, shutting down the line of thought. *But you can have this. You can have him.*

"I am yours," Tobin said, hand moving faster now, sending streaks of delight through her body. "All yours, Margot."

Her name on his lips was the final touch, pushing her over the edge until she came apart in his arms. She wasn't Baby Go to Tobin; she was Margot, and she was shuddering against him, mouth eagerly working against his as the pleasure washed over her.

Caught between gasps and echoes of pleasure, Margot realized something else was happening. She expected to feel Tobin against her eager hands, to press against the hardness she knew was eagerly waiting for her touch. But instead, something was happening to her back. She stepped away, awkward on one foot as his hand still held her close, slick against her thigh.

"I—" she managed and collapsed forward into his arms as an explosion of pleasure and agony streaked through her body. She fell to her knees, bringing Tobin to the floor with her, and drew him close, not understanding what was happening through the haze. There was a bright light and a flash of something skittering along the skin of her back, and then the sound of something ripping.

When she came back to herself, Margot was on the floor, straddling Tobin's hips as his arms wrapped around her. There was something odd about the way he was holding her, one arm tight against her ass and the other clutching her neck and pressing her face into his chest. When the moment passed, he slowly eased his grip, peering down to study her face. "Margot?" he whispered, fear and excitement blending in his voice. "My Lady?"

"What was that?" she replied, looking down at her body, trying to see what was different. She could feel something new, a shift in her weight. "What just happened?"

"You've been Awakened," Tobin said in a formal voice.

Margot frowned at him, trying to sit back and get some space. His arm released her shoulder, but the one around her ass stayed firm, holding her on his lap. "Look," she told him, not liking his tone, "I've had an orgasm before. This was something else."

Tobin bit his lip. "Definitely something else," he agreed, his gaze leaving her face to examine something over her right shoulder. Margot turned her head to follow his look, caught a glimpse of shimmering iridescence, and her body froze.

"Tobin," she said quietly, "why the hell do I have wings?"

Chapter 4

Fae Awakenings

"Because many fae have wings?" Tobin replied, though the words were more like a question.

Margot pushed away from him, not liking the sound of the word "fae"—like the stories her mother had told as Margot grew up—but Tobin held her firm, not letting her slide off his lap.

"Careful," he ordered. "You'll hurt yourself."

"Let me go!" she squealed, fear streaking through her as she took in more of the thin material hovering over both shoulders. "What did you do to me?" She tried to scramble back, but something caught on her new wings, and she stopped at the painful tugging in the center of her back.

"I told you," he said, his voice way too calm for the situation. "You've been Awakened." He canted his head. "Surely they have told you of such things?"

"I'm wide awake," she insisted, moving more slowly to untangle herself from him. This time the bottom of her other wing caught on the top of her boot, and she shrieked at the jolt, arms pinwheeling as she fell forward again—right into Tobin's waiting arms.

"Easy," he said. "The first time is always painful."

"This is not my first time," Margot gritted, words pouring out at the suggestion of her virtue, not wanting to think about what he really meant. She looked up at him, meeting that bright gaze, and something sparked deep inside—a connection she didn't want to explore. "I don't understand," she murmured, fear fading as a sense of rightness filled her body. Feeling calmer, she narrowed her eyes at him. "What do you mean by Awakened?"

"How do you feel?" Tobin purred, leaning close, his eyes darker.

Biting her lip, Margot tried to sense her body. She felt … light. Filled with air and satisfaction. The new wings were silk against her bare skin, and she realized that her dress must have ripped when they came out of her body. "I liked this dress," she managed to say.

"I like you better without it," Tobin whispered, mouth closing the distance between them. Margot allowed herself to be kissed, shivering as his hands slid along the new wings, her body a riot of sensation. It was easier to lose herself than face the situation anyway.

Kissing Tobin made everything better, and she surrendered to the feelings—both physical and emotional—that rushed over her. She could ignore the rest, though there was a quiet litany of confusion and shock in the back of her mind, just waiting for the moment to burst free. Margot pushed it down, twining her fingers into Tobin's hair and devouring his mouth.

Familiar. Comforting. Safe.

"Take your hands off of her right now," a cold voice snarled, "and I might let you walk out of this room."

Margot's head snapped up, breaking the kiss, and she twisted to see who had entered the back room with them. She recognized the voice, sort of, but she didn't believe the words had come from Ash Stonewall until she saw the expression on his face. His eyes were wide, his jaw set, his mouth turned down in a frown. Margot barely recognized the man she knew.

"Ash?" she asked, very aware of how she was sprawled on Tobin's lap, his arms still around her body. Ash may not ever want her, but she didn't want him to see her atop another man. She pulled her fingers out of Tobin's hair.

Just in case.

"Let. Her. Go," Ash repeated.

Tobin did not release her, his gaze sliding back to study Margot's face. "I don't hear her complaining," Tobin said finally. "Do you want to go, Margot?"

"I..." Margot tried, but words failed her. What could she say to Ash, the man she had longed for since she started wanting anyone? He was looking at her like she had betrayed him. Tobin's words sank in, and she jerked her head down to look at him instead. His smirk was all male, clearly thinking he had won some kind of competition.

"Seriously?" she said, glaring at him, then tried to stand up, tripping in her haste. Tobin released her immediately, hands moving to help her, but Ash was faster, stepping across the space between them. He put his hands beneath her armpits and lifted her easily to her feet, but paused when he set her down, not letting her go until she found her new balance with the wings.

Margot frowned, reaching back to touch the new part of her body. Her wings were soft, silky diaphanous swaths of many colors: brown where she could see over her shoulder, brightening to white and blue at the bottom that brushed the back of her knees. Deciding she could stare at the new wings when she stood before a proper mirror, she settled into her new center of gravity and stood firm, gaze flicking from the man still sitting on the floor to the man standing next to her.

"So," she said, her voice sturdier than she expected, "who is going to tell me what is going on?" Her heart rate was steady, likely a result of the alcohol slowing her reactions.

"You've been Awakened," another voice said, and Margot looked up to see Timothy had entered the room and was standing near the doorway.

"So I hear," she retorted. "Want to tell me what that means?"

"You're fae," Ash whispered. "Your powers have Manifested." He looked at her, and Margot wished she could read his expression, his blank face perfectly neutral, the rage from earlier vanished. He sounded both wistful and excited at the same time.

Margot scoffed. "Like a fairy in a story?" Both Ash and Tobin nodded, though Tobin's grin suggested he was far more thrilled about her new status than Ash or Timothy. "Wait," she said, glaring at all three men as suspicion snaked through her. "How do you know this? Are you fae or whatever?"

Tobin hopped to his feet and tugged his shirt over his head. Margot was almost too distracted by the sudden sight of his bare chest, abs she had been feeling as they pressed close, but then there was a quick flash of light, and a pair of black and silver wings like her own appeared from his back. Margot's mouth opened to say something, but no sound came out, and she simply took in the glory that was Tobin.

Tobin smiled, blew her a kiss, then cut his gaze to Ash, the gesture clear.

Your turn.

Margot turned to Ash. "Do you have freaking wings?"

Ash shook his head. "No. I have ... other gifts."

Margot's eyes widened. The insanity of the situation was too much, so she focused on the nearest thing. "So what makes you ... fae? Like, how can people tell?"

Ash gave Tobin a dark glare. "They can't." He shook his head. "Put those away, vassal. Someone might see, and we are among mixed company here."

"Vassal?" Margot echoed, thinking of knights and armor.

"You know who I am?" Tobin asked, a challenge in the question. A flash of light pulsed and then his wings were gone, though his glorious bare chest remained. Margot tried not to stare at him, remembering her hands on his body.

"I know you," Ash confirmed, then with a look at Margot, he added, "and clearly you know who we are."

"Why don't you show her?" Tobin prompted, shirt held loosely in one hand. "She'd love to see you in all your glory. We all would, my Lord."

"I am no Lord," Ash snapped, putting a hand to his forehead the way he did when he was contemplating a difficult problem. Margot had seen that motion often back when he helped her rebuild the battered TW bus that her mother had left behind, the two of them carefully working together to make it livable again. Hand falling to his side, he glanced at Margot, whose wings were still out for all to see.

"Go," he said, and for a moment, she thought he was dismissing her, but it was just her name. "Close your eyes and concentrate on willing the wings away. You can do it."

Nodding, Margot closed her eyes, glad that the distraction of Tobin was hidden, and thought about her wings, glad to have something specific to do.

Go away please, she thought clearly, and to her surprise, she could feel a pulse of heat along her back, a burst of light against her closed eyelids, and then her balance shifted again. She could feel the air on her bare back through the holes in her dress. "Oh," she said, wonder infusing her voice. "That was easy."

Ash nodded. "We ... have much to discuss."

"You're telling me," she agreed, then remembered Timothy by the door. "Are you one of them, too?"

Timothy bent into a courtly bow, a faint smile on his lips. "At your service, Lady Margot."

"Don't," Ash barked, but Timothy ignored him, already reaching out to gently take Margot's hand.

"Allow me to be the first to congratulate you on your Awakening," Timothy continued, placing a delicate kiss on the back of her hand before releasing her.

"She hasn't Awakened," Ash insisted, continuing despite the two men giving him incredulous looks. "She just has wings. That's minor. It doesn't mean—"

"Apparently, it means that you have forgotten your manners entirely," Timothy interrupted. He gave the lead singer a hard look, and shame flooded Ash's face. "Margot is fae, only just revealed. She deserves your respect."

Ash frowned, then sighed heavily. He took a step toward her, taking her hand formally and leaning down to kiss it. Margot snatched her hand back, not wanting Ash to go through the motions of civility when he clearly didn't want to. Jamming her hands into her dress pockets, which remained mostly intact despite the destruction of the back of her clothing, she glared at Ash. "Someone please tell me what the hell is going on."

Ash's eyes were wide as he stared at her hidden hands, realizing she had rejected his touch.

Tobin was the first to speak, stepping quickly in front of Ash, and putting himself close to her. "Ask me anything, Margot. I will tell you everything."

Timothy's head moved quickly, shock flitting across his features at Tobin's declaration, but then the look was gone. Ash tried to step between them, but Tobin only moved closer, gently touching Margot to keep her next to him.

"Well," she began, "how about Awakening?"

Chapter 5
The Fae Power Scale

"It has many names," Tobin explained. "The Awakening, the Manifestation." He glanced at Timothy. "It means your fae abilities have been triggered, and you are no longer what you were before."

What was I before? The thought was fleeting, her scattered mind trying to keep up with her new reality. Again, she latched onto one word he had said. "Abilities?" Margot echoed. "As in plural? What else is going to happen to me?"

Tobin shrugged, way too nonchalant for the situation. "Time will tell. You have wings, so you may be a high order fae."

"Not necessarily," Ash interrupted, but Tobin ignored him.

"You can fly, obviously, but your other abilities will appear soon." At the look on her face at his casual mention of the ability to fly, he added, "Do not fear, Margot." With a pointed glance at Ash, he continued, "I will be here to guide you every step of the way."

Margot nodded, reassured despite herself. He seemed quite casual about everything. "Does this ... happen often? People Manifesting?" Questions swarmed through her mind, and she snagged onto a random one. "Are there a lot of fae?"

"Some," Tobin replied vaguely. "It depends on where you are. For instance, this bar has several fae, drawn by the presence of such fascinating ... rock stars."

"Do they know?" she pressed, wanting to blame Ash's magnetism on his fae nature. She glanced around the room, scanning their faces in turn: Ash, Tobin, Timothy. "Do you all know one another?"

Ash's voice was brutal. "No, they do not know. And they *will* not." There was no mistaking the threat in the words. "Not all of us are as brazen as he."

"Still going to play the game, then?" Tobin asked, judgment clear in his tone. "Still pretending to be human?" He paused, adding, "No doubt your father must be very proud."

Ash moved, but suddenly Timothy was in front of him, placing his body between Ash and Tobin, defusing the situation. He gave Ash a long look, communicating something Margot didn't catch, and Ash was calm again. "You should not speak of things you do not know," the lead singer said finally.

"You don't know what I know." Tobin smirked.

"Stop it," Margot said, not liking the way Tobin was taunting Ash. "You're not helping by being a jerk about whatever this is." She gestured between the two men. "I'm sensing some tension here, but right now, I don't care what your issues are. Not to be a bitch about it, but can this be about me right now? I need to know more."

This time it was Ash who spoke, clearly wanting to one-up Tobin with his sudden forthrightness. "What do you want to know, Go?"

Margot winced at his use of her nickname, hearing echoes of their teenage yells when they first met, "Baby Go is on the loose! Baby Go is going to get even for that one! Baby Go is feisty tonight!" Ignoring the memories of their teasing, she focused on what she knew. "Okay, so you don't all know one another. Can you sense another fae? Like, is there a way you guys can tell? Without wings?"

"Some fae have horns. That's pretty clear," Tobin added helpfully.

"Yes and no," Ash replied, and before she could frown at the non-answer, he continued, "Strong fae can usually sense weaker fae. Some fae can hide their presence entirely from others if they wish, but weaker fae are almost always able to be found."

"Do strong fae hide themselves often? Is that common? Why?" Head spinning as she tried to take it all in, Margot wondered how she had lived her entire life without knowing any of this.

Ash shrugged. "I don't know."

"Sure you don't," Tobin quipped.

"Which are you?" she asked, looking at Tobin. "Are you stronger or weaker fae?"

Ash frowned, clearly not wanting to answer what Margot realized was probably a rude question. But Tobin replied, "Strength of magic doesn't always mean strong. Power is a complicated thing."

"Clearly." Margot sniffed, thinking. She shifted to her other foot, the memory of wings altering her balance. "So, what do wings mean? Where does that fall on the fae strength gauge, if that's a thing?"

"That's not a thing," Tobin answered with a grin, "but I take your meaning. Often, wings are found on weaker fae—one of the most common abilities we have."

"Oh," she said, heart falling as she realized what that likely meant. "Figures." She was a fae, like Ash, finally on his level, but she was only a weaker fae. *Still beneath him.*

"Wings are only one of your abilities, Margot," Tobin continued. "I have no doubt that you have others. I look forward to seeing what they are."

"What are the options? I mean, what can you do?"

This time, Tobin's face closed, the friendly demeanor slipping for a moment. She could tell he didn't want to answer her.

"There are many abilities," Ash answered instead. "Flying, obviously, but glamours are common enough. Magically altering one's appearance. Not true shape-shifting, of course," here he gave Tobin a sharp glance, "but close enough. Superior physical abilities, like strength or speed are also normal." He paused, considering. "Manipulating the elements is less common but still possible. Telepathy. Telekinesis, that sort of thing. Very strong fae can teleport and control others, and some can manipulate emotions."

"They can make people feel things that aren't real?" Margot asked, latching onto the last item on his list of possibilities. "That sounds awful. No respect for free will at all." She scoffed. "What do you think is likely for me?"

Tobin pursed his lips. "That depends on your parents. What could they do?"

Margot frowned. "My parents? They could ... get sick and die?" A flash of her mother at the very end filled her mind, and she closed her eyes, not wanting to remember her that way. Her father had never been part of her life, though her mother had always spoken fondly of him. Margot got the impression her parents had loved one another very much—but something kept them apart. "I'm sorry. That wasn't fair." She shook her head. "I don't know what they could do. I didn't know they were fae."

"Penelope, your mother, was fae," Ash said quietly with a quick look at Tobin. "She could fly, and she had some elemental control. Air was her specialty."

Margot had another flash of memory, a younger self giggling as the wind played with her hair, her mother smiling as they soaked up the sunshine on an afternoon on a beach in Belsune long ago. She stared at Ash, surprised he knew so much about her mother. "How do you know that?"

"Your aunt," Timothy said. "She too was … fae. They shared similar abilities, though Maddie's specialty was water." Margot thought of that first summer at her aunt Maddie's house, the first time she had met her cousin Nik, and Timothy—and Ash.

"If my mom was a fae, why did she get sick? Why did she die?" The words came out before she could stop them, and Ash put a soothing hand on her forearm, his palm warm against her skin.

"She was fae. Not immortal. We can all die."

"Oh," Margot said, deflated. Part of her had thought that becoming some kind of supernatural creature automatically made her impervious to harm—like the movies. It had been a silly assumption to make, one she only thought because she was overwhelmed.

"And what of your father?" Tobin prompted.

Margot frowned, her mother's wistful expression coalescing in her memory. "No one of consequence," she replied quickly. "He left before I was born."

"A human?" Tobin pressed, looking at Ash.

Ash nodded. "So Penelope told her sister Maddie."

"Does this make me a middle-road fae? More powerful than some but weaker than others?" Ash and Timothy shared another of those long looks that Margot couldn't read. "What did I say?" she asked. "Why do you keep doing that?"

"She needs to know," Timothy said. "She needs to prepare."

"Prepare for what?" Margot asked, a cold feeling pooling in her gut at their expressions.

Chapter 6

The Claiming

"In our world," Timothy began, his face carefully neutral, "there is a ... hierarchy. Everyone has a place."

"That's not exclusive to you," Margot declared. "That happens everywhere."

"Not like this," Ash added. "You will need to find and accept your place." He looked away, clearly wanting that to be the end of the discussion.

"What the hell does that mean?" she snapped, not liking the sound of it at all.

Tobin broke the awkward silence, his words blunt. "It means someone will Claim you, and you have to serve them."

"Serve them?" she echoed, hearing him but not understanding.

"And you no doubt will take servants of your own, given your likely standing," he added helpfully.

"I'm not taking servants!" Margot yelled. "That's ridiculous!" She whirled on Ash. "And what does he mean that someone will Claim me?"

Ash's reluctance was palpable. Margot was tiring of his hot and cold approach to the situation: one second all caring concern, the next coldly distant. When he acted like this, she was so sure he was into her, and just as sure he barely tolerated her.

"Everyone in our world owes fealty to someone else," Tobin explained. "We all have our place."

"And where do you belong?" she asked, turning on him. "Who Claimed you?"

"Lord Rebinus," Tobin replied immediately, and Ash glared at him, eyes dark with old anger and a long-festering sore.

"Oh," she said simply, not knowing who that was. "Wait. That's why you called him vassal earlier. He's a vassal to that lord. Regulus."

"Rebinus," Tobin corrected gently.

"Whatever!" she snapped. She turned her gaze to Ash and Timothy. "And you?"

Ash opened his mouth to speak, then closed it again. Timothy seemed to wait another moment to see if he would try again, but when he didn't, Timothy said, "We cannot say. We do not have such liberties with our situation."

"I have no idea what that means," Margot deadpanned but moved on. "Okay, so how does this Claiming work? Do I get a letter in the mail or what?"

Tobin snorted, then covered his mouth. "Not quite. Your Claiming will likely be more ... dramatic."

She narrowed her eyes at him, not liking the tone. "Dramatic how? What happened to you with your Reginald?"

"Rebinus," Tobin corrected again. "And mine was different. I was claimed as a child. There was a small ceremony when I was taken into his household. As I said, your situation is different."

Margot shook her head, too tired to think much more. She'd had a long day getting the show ready, and while her night had started out good, she was ready for it to be over. "Look, as long as I don't have to sleep with a stranger, I can work this out."

Ash's face blanched, and Timothy looked quickly away. Tobin alone continued to stare at her, his face waiting for her to figure it out. As she stared at him, he slowly raised a delicate eyebrow, chin dipping lower.

"No fucking way," she whispered, then turned to Ash and Tobin, who both refused to meet her gaze.

"It is expected for such a late manifestation to be claimed in the old ways," Tobin explained, voice soothing.

"And what if I don't want to be Claimed? What if I want my freedom?" she asked.

Tobin shrugged, but there was little sympathy in his expression. "We all want such things, Margot, but there is a price to this new power of yours."

"The price is my body?" she asked. "Fuck that. No."

"The price is your free will," Ash said quietly. "After that, no doubt you will not care so much about your body."

"And who fucked you?" she demanded, whirling on Timothy as the easiest target.

Tobin chuckled. "She sees you well, Timothy," he commented, "assuming you would be Claimed and not the other way around."

Timothy's expression was bland as he looked at Tobin, then returned his attention to Margot. "I was very young when I was Claimed," he explained, jerking his chin at Tobin. "Like him, there was a ceremony."

"And you didn't object?"

"I did not object," Timothy said quietly. "I am happy to serve."

Margot looked at Ash. "And you?" she asked. "Who owns you?"

Ash stared at her, face blank, but he said nothing. "Whatever," she grumbled, turning back to Timothy. "There has to be a way…" she began, but he shook his head.

"We all answer to someone, Margot," the drummer said. "It is the way of the world."

"No," Margot said, determination filling her. "Not my world. There is no way I am going to let some strange fae come in here and steal me away. What is this—a fairy tale?"

"A rock star fairy tale," Tobin said, smirking at Ash and Timothy.

"How can you be so calm about this?" she asked him, glad to find an easier aim for her anger.

Tobin shrugged, pushing a strand of white-blond hair behind his ear—which Margot now saw was slightly elongated. "You will be just fine, Margot," he said. "No need to worry."

"How will this be fine? You just said some stranger is going to kidnap me!"

"It's not like that," Tobin explained. "You will be courted… mostly." He frowned, possibilities moving across his expression. "Probably." Cocking his head to the side, he added, "It doesn't have to be a stranger," Tobin said, then glanced at Ash. "He could do it."

Margot sputtered. "What?!"

"It's easy enough. Before another arrives to Claim your new powers, Ash can Claim you as his own. We all know he's strong enough for it." Tobin raised an eyebrow.

"And I'd wager neither of you would mind the physical part of the ceremony."

A burst of hope shot through her at Tobin's words. She tried to think of the important things—her free will, her freedom, her bodily autonomy—but that faded before the incredibly wicked image she had of Ash standing before her, shirtless. She'd seen his chest before, of course, plenty of times on stage, especially when he launched into their hit "Heart of Stone" at the end of the show. But this was an older memory, Ash back when he'd helped her fix the TW bus, the two of them both comfortable and awkward in turns as they used the common goal to focus their attention. Margot still didn't know if he had helped her out of obligation, something about taking care of her since her mother had died, or if he legitimately wanted to. Her mind snagged on the random detail, and she stared at Ash.

"You don't have to," she blurted, trying to quell the heat she could feel rising in her face. "You don't owe me anything."

"He owes you protection," Timothy supplied helpfully, giving Ash an appraising look. "We both do."

"What does that mean?"

"We promised your aunt Maddie when you first arrived that we would always look out for you," Timothy volunteered. Margot glanced at Ash and quickly away. She assumed it was something like that. They didn't really want to be around her. She was an obligation, a burden. But Timothy was still speaking. "We will not abandon you, Margot. Not when you need us."

"That's curious," Tobin commented, looking Timothy up and down. "I mean, you could technically Claim her, but then you'd expose yourself to those who no doubt seek you and your master. And for what?" He frowned. "The next fae would only Claim you both." He narrowed his eyes at Ash. "He has to be the one, and we all know it. What will it be then, Ash Stonewall? Rock star or the fae I know you to be?"

"You have no idea who I am," Ash replied, voice distant, aloof, and suddenly authoritative, like when he threw himself into the chorus and made the audience members swoon, wishing for his touch. "You walk in here, Awaken my Go, and think I will jump to take your suggestions?" He scoffed. "You may be here by the leave of your Lord, but I answer to a different power, and I will not be bullied into a foolish Connection."

Margot frowned. It was one thing to be a burden, an obligation, but worse to be seen as a foolish connection. She took a step away from them, clutching her dress to her chest, not wanting to hear any more.

But he said you were his Go! Margot ignored the small voice, the ridiculous obsession she hadn't been able to dismiss in all the years since she'd first met him. *It doesn't matter. He will never want me the way I want him.*

Something broke inside of her, a part that had been slowly shattering for a long time. She felt it crack, the pieces tumbling free, and suddenly she was angry. Heat flooded her chest and face.

"Stop," she said, voice quiet but powerful, and all three men looked over at her, seeming to notice that she had moved away. She pierced Ash with her glare. "Don't do me any favors," she told him. "I would never want to be one of your *foolish connections*." She hissed the last words, then turned to Timothy. "And no more about promising Maddie you'd protect me. I'm fine. I'll be fine." Before he could speak, flashing that charming smile that disarmed her so, she cut Tobin off, "And you. Obviously you have an agenda here. So here's what's going to happen: I'm going back to my bus, and you're all going to leave me alone."

When Tobin opened his mouth, she continued, "Alone. And I don't want to hear anything else about fae or powers or Claiming bullshit." She looked at Ash and Timothy in turn. "You know where I'll be. If you want anything, send Nik to ask. At least I can trust him not to lie to me."

Without waiting for a reply, she turned and walked out of the room. Very aware of her torn dress, she hurried down the stairs and over the rope blocking off the Employees Only area. The hour was late, and the bar had emptied, especially since Ash was no longer entertaining his harem on the couches. She could see a few women lingering, hopeful as they glanced around. A few of them spotted her quick exit from the stairwell and glared, their eyes hot with jealousy.

You wish, she thought, knowing they all wanted to be tangled in a rock star's arms for the night, and pushed open the door to the outside, glad her home on wheels wasn't too far away.

No, I wish. *And I need to stop.*

Chapter 7

There's No Place like Home

Early AM, Thursday, February 19th in Margot's Bus in the back lot of the Revel Coliseum

Margot sat on the modified bucket set, swiveling aimlessly as she stared at the ceiling of the converted bus she called home. The space was small but comforting. Familiar. Even though it wasn't the same configuration she had grown up in with her mother as they traveled the other continent, the bus was the same.

The old bus interior had a small kitchen and mini fridge on one side, a tiny toilet tucked to the other side, and a bed filling the back against the doors. At night, they would pull down a plank and tuck it above the bed, making Margot's bunk. She had felt so safe there, sleeping above her mom, secure in the passenger seat as they drove from place to place. Showering outside on cold days had never been her favorite, and Margot still relished a hot shower, but those days had been easier somehow. Simpler.

Then her mom had gotten sick, and Margot barely recalled the days between sleeping in the hospital and being shuttled across the world to live with a stranger. Maddie had been a good aunt, showering Margot with the love and affection her niece needed and giving her a predictable place in the new world, but from the start, Margot only had eyes for Ash. Though she was only 15, and he a "worldly" 18-year-old, she would never forget the first time she saw him, stumbling into the bar late one night with her cousin Niklaus, both of them shushing the other as they tried to creep back into bed. Sometimes, Margot wondered if the reason she had latched onto Ash so strongly was because she had just lost her mother, and his cool distance was a solid replacement—unattainable, just like her mother now was. She could pine after Ash like a painting of an angel or a photograph of her mom laughing on a distant beach.

When she turned 17, the old bus had shown up. A stranger had driven it right up to the bar one day. They had been closed, Margot still repainting the trim while the others had gone into town to get dinner, and the man had simply walked inside and smiled at Margot as though recognizing her immediately, despite her bedraggled paint-smeared presentation.

"Margot Tanner," he had said, his voice friendly, and Margot thought she should know that sound, recognize the man. Then he was handing her the keys with gentle warm hands. "This is yours, of course. I'm sorry it took a while to get it over here."

"Wait—" she had called after him, but he left immediately, saying nothing else. She had dropped the paintbrush and followed him outside, but he was gone. Her mother's TW bus was parked off the side of the parking lot, next to where Maddie parked her truck. She had gone inside, sat on her mother's bed, and sobbed her heart out.

It had been Ash who had comforted her then. Gently. Distantly. He had coaxed her out of the bus that night and into her room, even wiping her face free of paint as she sat listlessly on her bed. Over the next month, he had found her in the bus often, never saying anything, and when she started talking to him about her life with her mother, he listened. When she said she couldn't stand the bus this way, couldn't stand the memories but was conflicted about ignoring such a huge part of her past, he had left her, returning later with Niklaus and Timothy, and they were the ones who suggested the remodel. A project, Nik called it. A new start, Timothy said. They had redone the entire bus, this time updating the features and adding Margot's favorite treat: a shower.

Glancing at the back where the beds used to be, she smiled, seeing the small sink and stove to the right of the green wall that hid the toilet and shower. It had taken some magical thinking to redesign the space, but having the water in the back actually worked out, and they were able to raise her bed in a bunk along the side of the van, butting up against the wall of the shower. A low counter beneath her bunk served as a desk so she had workspace and storage available. Her spinning chair was specially designed to sit flat on the floor near the head of the bed, though she could also fold it down into a foot stool or lift it up to sit a third passenger. With it open, she could splay her legs straight toward the small kitchen at the back of the bus, though now, as she spun around, staring up at the white plank edging her bed with each rotation, she sat crosslegged, her knees easily clearing the desk where her small laptop perched.

Along the still-original green back wall below the bottom of her bunk was a small row of windows, interrupted by three framed pictures: one of her mom on a beach in Belsune, her hair wild around her face as she laughed; one containing both of them, Margot around ten years old, standing next to her mom among a forest of huge redwood trees, both of them smiling; and the final picture much newer: Margot, Nik, Ash, and Timothy at the lake, all of them young and goofy as aunt Maddie yelled at them to smile.

Behind her bed was a tiny closet with shelves holding randomly colored bins of her clothes, and then the driver's seat. Though the drivers were typically on the left side here on Ardon, the bus was from Belsune, so it had the driver on the right. The dislocation felt by those who normally drove in Ardon was part of the reason why Margot didn't let anyone else drive her bus—a lesson learned early when Ash had tried to move her bus from one side of the parking lot to the other when they first started the demolition—and nearly tipped it into the ditch at the edge of the lot. He wasn't used to thinking about the space the bus occupied from that side, but they still gave him crap for that day. He hadn't been allowed to drive anything for months—everyone jostling him out of the driver's seat if he tried to claim it, grumbling about how they wanted to get to their destination—not end up in a ditch somewhere.

The driver's seat was a regular configuration, but the passenger seat next to it was able to spin around, though not like her desk chair. It had to be road-safe and only flipped around with a handle. Nik usually sat there when he visited her, though he sometimes complained about the clothes she had dangling from the small rod across the top. She may abuse their fancier RVs for the washing machine, but most of her clothes she hung up to air dry.

The bus was small, her bed just big enough for her to sleep comfortably, still covered by the t-shirt quilt her mom made the summer before she died, the two of them laughing about their horde of shirts from all the places they had been. The bed was surrounded by a few precious books tucked along the walls, but Margot was home. It was still the bus she grew up in, but now it was hers, the ghost of her mother finally put to rest.

A knock on the door interrupted her thoughts, and she sighed, letting her spin glide to a stop. She faced the side door and glared through the window at the top of Nik's head.

"It's open," she grumbled, then started spinning again, not eager to face this newest betrayal.

Chapter 8

One of the Boys

Her cousin had the decency to look bashful as he pulled the door open and promptly stumbled as he encountered her discarded boots in the small footwell. "C'mon!" he groaned, regaining his balance. "You didn't have to boobytrap me."

"My boots were here before you," Margot snapped. "Deal with it."

"It's like that, is it?" he asked, opening her small fridge and retrieving a can of soda. He glanced over at where she sat. "Want anything?" he asked. "You know," he added, tapping her foot, "since I'm already in the kitchen."

"Jerk," she said, but the old joke made her smile. In Maddie's house behind the bar, they had always played the "While you're up..." game, and though Margot could easily reach anything in her tiny home, Nik teased her, knowing it made her smile.

"Tea," she told him, and he plucked a bottle of iced tea from the door, handing it to her before shutting the fridge. He made noises as he pushed her few hanging shirts aside to sit in the passenger seat.

"Seriously," he said, "you're not making this easy on me."

Margot turned to face him directly. She dead-eyed him as she opened her tea, took a swallow from the bottle, capped it again, and put it on the desk beside her. "You knew." She didn't have to say anything else. The guilt on his face was enough.

"I..." He opened his soda, took a sip, then tried again. "I couldn't."

"Couldn't?" she pushed. "Or wouldn't?"

"They didn't know if you would ever ... you know," he defended. "They couldn't tell you unless you were one of them, and there was no way to know!"

"But you knew," she argued, "and you're not one of them."

"I am different," he said, taking a hasty sip of his soda and leaning back in the chair, suddenly finding the ceiling above his seat very intriguing.

"Because you're one of the boys, right?" Margot asked, bitterness seeping into her tone. "Because they want you with them."

"We all want you with us, Margot," Nik said, abandoning his study and leaning forward.

"Yeah," she griped, spinning her chair again, "because Maddie made you promise or something."

"My mom," Nik began, then took another sip before setting his nearly empty can down on the floor beside her closet door. "She worried about you, about all of us, but more about you. Your mom—"

"I know," Margot replied. "My mom was the wild card, running around strange countries with strange men."

"Your mom never said who your father was. Maddie thought he was human, so there was a chance you were too. As a human, you would never have to deal with any of this." He reached out to stop her spinning. "And if you were human, you were vulnerable, and we needed to look out for you."

"Now that I'm not human?" she pressed. "It seems like I'm more vulnerable than ever. Did you know about this Claiming bullshit?"

Nik frowned. "I've heard of it."

"And you? Are you Claimed?" she asked.

"I'm not fae," he said. "That doesn't apply to me."

"But you knew!" she repeated. "Why would they tell you if you weren't one of them?" She corrected, "One of *us*, apparently?"

"It's ... complicated."

"Oh, Nik," she sighed, leaning back to study him. "You always make everything complicated."

"I don't make things any way," he said. "Things just sort of happen to me."

"What, like stumbling into fairy secrets? Did your mom tell you because she was one?"

"Fae," he corrected. "They hate the word fairy. Something about some playwright misrepresenting them hundreds of years ago. And no, my mother didn't tell me," he said, and for a moment, she thought he would say something else, but he stopped himself. "Look—it's not important right now. Tonight is about you. Isn't that what you wanted—for everyone to focus on what you needed?"

She glared at him. "Ash and Timothy told you everything that happened?" When Nik nodded, she asked, "Was Tobin with them?"

"The new guy?" he asked. "No. I don't know where he went."

"You don't know him?"

Nik shrugged. "Never saw him before. Why?"

"He seemed to know who Ash and Timothy were. I assumed he knew you too."

"I don't know," Nik said. "This is the guy at the bar, right? The one you were so friendly with?"

"Watching over me, are you, Nik?"

He sighed. "C'mon, Go. You know I always have your back. You seemed to be having a great time talking to him. I was—am—happy for you."

"Even though whatever he did caused wings to pop out of my back, and now I'm apparently fair game for any wandering fae?"

Nik cracked a grin. "I heard about that. Can I see them sometime? Ash and Tim never show me any fae stuff. You'd think they were in hiding or something. I only know because it came out when—" He stopped abruptly, his familiarity and ease with his cousin causing him to be careless. "Look," he said, "I know this is scary. Navigating new abilities is terrifying. But it's going to be okay."

"How do you know?" she asked, resting the cold tea bottle over her forehead where a small headache was building.

"Trust me," Nik said. "I know. And as long as you have someone to help you, it's not so bad."

"Who is going to help me?" she asked. "You?"

"Nah." He shook his head. "I don't know much about fae powers."

"Then who? Ash made it pretty clear he wants nothing to do with me. Timothy, I guess?"

"What about New Guy?" Nik asked. "He Awakened you. You must have a Connection."

"What do you mean?"

Nik shrugged, grabbing his can and emptying it before tossing it the length of the van into the small garbage can tethered to the front of her sink.

"Score!" they yelled simultaneously, years of habits hard to break. Margot turned to him. "No, seriously, what do you mean?"

Nik shrugged again. "Like I said, it's not really my area of expertise, but I always thought Awakenings happened when there was a deep Connection of some kind between two fae."

She glared at him. "What kind of connection?"

He scoffed. "Please. It's not always about sex, Go. Just a closeness, a comfort, I think. Maybe it's magic." He gave her a wry grin. "Apparently, a connection you did not share with Ben or Thomas."

Margot reached out to shove him, Nik landing back in the chair with a laugh. "Shut up!" she snapped, embarrassed and annoyed that he would mention the two boys she had dated during high school. "At least I remember their names!"

"We both do," Nik said, "and if Ash knew, they'd both wish he didn't."

It was Margot's turn to scoff. "As if he would care." She sighed, turning a soulful gaze onto her cousin. "You didn't see him, Nik. The idea of being with me, Claiming me, whatever that means, disgusted him. Like totally and completely repulsed." She put her head in her hands, the weight of this newest rejection sinking in. "I'm such an idiot."

Nik's hands were warm on her shoulders, offering comfort. "You're not an idiot, Go." He rubbed between her shoulders, ruffling her long hair the way he always did when trying to cheer her up. "You may aim a bit high, but you're not an idiot for falling in love."

"Is it love?" she asked, fingers over her eyes as the tears began to fall. "I don't think I know what this is any-more... except pathetic."

"Ash is fantastic," Nik said. "Hell, if I went that way, I'd be into him too, but he has a lot going on."

Margot snorted, regaining her composure. "Of course you would defend him. His rock star life is complicated? Whatever."

"Not that," Nik said quickly. He reached down to lift her face, pushing her hair behind her ears and wiping her eyes. "Look, I think Ash has a lot more going on than he tells any of us."

"Like what?" she asked, wiping her nose and taking a shuddering breath. "Like fairy—I mean—fae stuff?"

Nik cocked his head, pursing his lips in contempla-tion. "Yeah, that for sure, and the band stuff, but there's something else."

"What?"

"I don't know," he admitted, breath exploding out of him, "but it's definitely growing." He gave her a long worried look. "It's not new, and it's getting worse." He ran a hand through his hair, then smiled at her. "I'm so glad I can finally talk to you about this now."

Margot sat up, eager to hear what worried her cousin. Despite herself, a small voice whispered: *It doesn't matter. I will always keep Ash safe.*

Chapter 9

Fae Powers

Nik cocked his head, leaning forward like he always did when he shared gossip. "Okay, so you know a little bit about fae powers, right? Useful stuff, most of the time: glamours, mind wipes, elemental control, but Ash? He does none of it. None. Dude lives like a human."

"He has a harem," Margot observed dryly. "That's fae power stuff."

Nik laughed. "Go, that's rock star stuff." He gestured at himself with a supremely arrogant smirk. "No fae glamour here, and I get plenty of action just being nearby." He shook his head. "But Ash—and Timothy too—they never do anything remotely supernatural. I'm starting to think that they don't want anyone to notice them that way. Being rock stars is one thing, but they are the most rock star-ish rock stars I've ever seen. Like, they're every stereotype you can imagine, like they're trying to fill a role."

"Why?" she asked, intrigued. She thought about Ash's behavior: the groupies, the parties, the occasional drugs, though she knew the boys rarely went there. The elusive lead singer smolder could be a cover for something bigger. "What do you think?"

"I said it earlier, though joking." He gave her a hard look. "I think they're hiding from someone."

Margot nodded, recalling snippets of the conversation between Tobin and Ash, hints that Ash and Timothy were recognized as something more than members of Stone Dragons. "Who?"

Nik shrugged. "No idea. But with you Manifesting, it's sure to bring attention this way—attention neither of the guys want."

Margot frowned. "Wait. So if they never do anything … supernatural … as you put it, how did you know they were fae?"

Nik shook his head. "Long story, Go. Too long for tonight, but I do promise that I will tell you all of it. Soon. But not now. This is enough to worry about."

"I always worry about you, Nik," she told him. "This is nothing new."

"No need, Go," he assured her with a wink. "I have you to look after me."

She smiled, a soft laugh escaping her, and sniffed a final time, finding her center again. "Thanks, Nik. You always know what to say, even if it isn't anything I don't already know."

"Glad I can help." He pursed his lips. "So, am I staying here tonight, or do you want to be alone?" It was rare, but sometimes Nik would spend the night in her bus, on the floor with her swivel chair as a pillow or sprawled in the passenger seat with a pillow between him and the door.

Margot shook her head. "You're all parked nearby. I'll be fine." She took a deep breath, then finished her tea. Giving Nik a challenging look, she tossed it toward the can, the bottle bouncing off the edge and rolling on the floor along the bottom of the cabinet. "Damn," she sighed. "Guess sprouting wings didn't help my aim."

"Your aim is fine, Go," Nik assured her. "It's been a wild night. Take some time to think." He paused, then added, "You need to be ready for what comes next."

"The Claiming bullshit?" she asked. "That's not happening. I will drive this bus to the other side of the continent if I have to."

"Not that," he said quickly, though she couldn't ignore the shadow crossing his face. "Your abilities. They will Manifest soon."

"Oh yeah," she said. "That part." She leaned back, running a hand through her long hair, gathering it up and tossing it over her shoulder so it hung down her back. "You really think New Guy would help me?"

"He seemed pretty into you. And no doubt he felt that Connection too." He frowned. "Why? You think he's gonna disappear on you?"

Margot recalled Tobin's face when he had seen her power: his lust, his excitement, his eagerness. "No," she admitted, "but I would be surprised if Ash and Timothy let him near me. There was definitely some tension there."

Nik's frown deepened, but he sighed, standing up and offering her a hand. "Ash wants what is best for you," he said, "and if that's the New Guy—"

"Tobin," Margot said, not wanting to call him New Guy lest the nickname stick.

"Tobin," Nik repeated. "If he's the one who Awakened you, then they have to let him help. I know enough about fae laws to know that they cannot actually deny him access to you, nor you to him. Not until you're officially Claimed, that is. Until then, he's your … teacher."

"Some teacher," Margot snorted and stood, a flash of Tobin's mouth on hers making her shiver and the hair stand up on her arms.

Nik gave her a knowing look, eyebrow raised. "Hot for teacher, are we?" he teased.

"Shut up," she mumbled, then turned him around to face the door. "Good night, Niklaus."

"Good night, Baby Go," he said, opening the door. "I should probably stop calling you that, huh? Are you Lady Margot now?"

"Good night!" she said, pushing him between the shoulder blades.

"As you wish, my Lady!" he yelled, hopping down. He grinned at her before shutting the door, and Margot smiled as she pushed the lock button. She grabbed the empty bottle on the floor and tucked it into the garbage can, then stood in the center of her bus, willing herself to do the next part.

"Just do it!" she ordered herself. "Time to see these wings." A long mirror mounted on the bathroom door showed her reflection. She had changed into soft pajama pants and a tank top after returning home, then spent the shower thinking about her wings, but thankfully, they didn't pop out while she was in the small space. Alone, she tugged the tank top over her head, tugged her hair out of the way, and angled her body so she could see her bare back in the mirror. At first, nothing visible showed, but then she noticed a patch of lighter skin between her shoulder blades. Grabbing her phone, she arched and clicked pictures until she found the right angle. Bringing the phone closer to her face, she tried to find the different skin, but her camera didn't seem to notice any difference.

Maybe it's a magic mark?

Margot twisted around and around, eventually identifying a small, stylized set of slightly raised soft pink lines across her skin. The mark was small, only a few inches across, but Margot knew it had not been there before. She pushed her hair behind her shoulders, seeing that the end of her hair rested just above the new mark.

"Damn," she whispered. She had hoped her hair might hide it if she ever lost her shirt. She shook her head, dark hair moving around like snakes. "Lose your shirt?" she asked her reflection over her shoulder. "What are you thinking?" Frowning, she nodded, hoping the pain she recalled that first time had more to do with her wings tearing through her dress than actual pain each time she called them. "Okay, then. Just do it."

Closing her eyes, she thought about her wings. *Please come out,* she thought. A flash of light against her eyelids, images painting the inside in a riot of color, and she could feel them. Opening her eyes, she studied her back.

The wings were big, but not huge, the width just beyond her elbows with her arms held out at shoulder height. In the small space, she had one hand against her bed and the other against the top of the door, and her wings fit easily in the space between. They were longer than they were wide, the tops of each wing peeking a few inches above her shoulders and ending just below the back of her knees. The color was glorious, a wash of browns and blues, and Margot stared at herself for a long time, moving this way and that, getting a sense of how she could make the wings move too. The feeling was odd, but also completely natural, like making a fist or wiggling her toes. Her body simply knew how to move them.

"Can I ... fly?" she whispered, then moved the wings in the way that made sense. Her feet left the floor of the bus, and she rose a few inches in the air. Margot lifted her arms up, stopping her flight before she crashed into the roof, and her feet landed on the polished wooden floor with a thump. "Oh crap," she cursed, then closed her eyes, willing the wings away. That flash of light, and she was herself again, standing topless in the middle of her home.

Too much, she decided. *Time for bed.*

Margot moved to hop up to her bed by stepping on her desk but realized she didn't need to. Her body felt so light she simply rose into the air. She rolled into the bunk the way she always did, pretending to ignore the ease with which she had moved—the same lightness she had felt when Tobin had asked her how she was feeling right after she Manifested.

Right before he kissed her in a way that made her toes curl in memory.

Nope. Stop that, she told herself. *It's been a day. Go to sleep. You can think about it again tomorrow.*

Turning on her music and closing her eyes, Margot settled in bed. She knew she would dream of Tobin's hands on her body and his voice in her ear, saying, *Tell me what you want.*

Chapter 10
Glamour in the Morning

Morning, Thursday, February 19th in
Margot's Bus in the back lot of the Revel Coliseum

Margot didn't notice her new ability had manifested until she was brushing her teeth the next morning. She was bleary-eyed, waking up as much as the shower would allow without her dose of coffee, and it was only after she swiped her hand across the foggy mirror that she realized the face staring back at her was not her own.

Her first thought was that she was somehow seeing the reflection of an intruder—triangular face, swath of blonde hair, pixie nose—but she dismissed it immediately, knowing no one could be standing behind her in the tiny bathroom stall. She pushed the door open anyway, startled, and the rush of cold air made her skin pebble with goosebumps. Grabbing her towel, she glanced down at her body, still recognizing the familiar lines of herself, and took a calming breath. Still a bit unsettled, she walked away from the mirror, spending the next few minutes making herself a hot cup of coffee, lingering over the small dollop of sugar and stirring slowly with her spoon. She took the first glorious sip, relishing the heat swirling through her body and the coherence waking her brain.

"Okay," she announced to the empty room, eyes lingering on the back window and the empty lot beyond. She could see a copse of trees beyond the fencing, the firs of northern Armav still green despite the winter chill. "I think I'm ready to face this. Whatever this is." She reached up to run her hands through her normally long hair, glad to feel it was still there, and turned to face the mirror. Her mouth fell open as the reflection showed a different woman with short blonde hair staring back at her—though her mouth was also hanging open. The woman wore the same blue towel, but her face was completely different. Margot flexed her fingers in her hair, watching transfixed as her reflection's fingers seemed to brush against short spikes when she could clearly feel the soft length of her still damp hair.

"Glamour," she said to her reflection, as though her heart weren't hammering away in her chest at the disconnect. "Good morning to you, too." Closing her eyes, she concentrated for a moment. "Can I have my face back, please?" She felt something echo through her body, a quiet pulse, and she carefully opened one reluctant eye, peering at her reflection nervously. Her familiar face met her in the mirror and she sighed in relief, sagging back against her kitchen sink. She stood, breathing deeply, trying to recall everything the guys had said the previous night.

Glamours were a common gift, she recalled. Something all fae could do. *But only in appearance,* she thought, remembering Ash's side glance at Tobin. *Not in reality. That's why my hair still feels like my hair even though it looks different. Okay then. I can deal with this.*

She dressed quickly in yoga pants, a tank top, and a hoodie, tucking her dark hair up in a messy bun, then settled on the floor before the mirror with her steaming coffee beside her, ready to experiment. She had time this morning. The band always gave themselves a recovery day after a show before traveling to the next gig. If things were normal, she wouldn't expect to see any of them until the crack of two pm. Margot was a morning person, often up with the sun, and she enjoyed her quiet mornings alone. That said, the odd occasion where she attended an afterparty would let her sleep a bit later—like today. It was already 10.

By noon, she had enough control to adjust her face, altering her nose and eyes, redoing her hair and adding accessories. Her favorite new look was the pixie blonde with librarian glasses and striking green eyes, though she could also manage to make her face appear as Ash, Nik, Timothy, and Tobin. She had stared at the latter for a long time, tweaking details as she recalled his appearance before returning to the new favorite face.

The pixie blonde with glasses was so removed from her own average looks. Her dark hair and brown eyes had her blending in with many of the women who screamed the lyrics to "Heart of Stone" and went home alone.

Maybe if I looked like this, she thought bitterly, *Ash might want me.*

She stopped the thought, not allowing herself to go down that road. It was familiar, but she had other things to worry about—like her growling stomach. She let the glamour fall, staring at herself for a moment before standing and putting her empty mug in the sink. She almost left it there, but then she sighed, not knowing if the boys would end up wanting to move when they woke up. She washed the cup and started making herself a small lunch. Routine helped settle her nerves, though she couldn't stop the thought, *One day and I already have a new ability. Is that good or bad? Does this mean someone will come to Claim me sooner?*

She wasn't excited about going outside, something she normally enjoyed, but she finally opened her door and emerged from her safe place. The sun hid behind thick clouds. She stretched, glancing around. She could see three tour buses parked on the far side of the lot behind the coliseum, sleek black lines against the mountain range around them. The near RV, what Nik called the Party Bus, would hold the band, their normal home on the road, each member claiming a bunk along the sides. The middle RV, which Nik dubbed the Entertaining Bus, was more traditional with a kitchen, dining room, and bedroom. That's where they took their eager fans, though Margot never quite figured out what guy code they used to know when it was available. The farthest bus was not nearly as fancy or as new, and it carried the crew for the trip: Travis, Dustin, John, and Benjamin. She grinned at the thought. Her fling with Ben had been years ago, both of them fumbling teenagers. He would always hold a special place in her heart, but they were just friends now. Comfortable enough, but not close anymore. Travis was an older man with a handlebar mustache, a traditional roadie who knew how to make the amplifiers sound heavenly. Dustin and John were younger, newer to the game, both polite enough. They all called her Margot, none of that ridiculous Baby Go nonsense from the band, and alternated driving their bus. There was a constantly shifting pool of drivers who dealt with the equipment trucks—which she saw had already left, likely heading to Akkoy for their next show.

She frowned, wondering if she would see Jeff or Alex, the two drivers of the other buses. They usually slept during the day, making it easier to drive the bus to the new location overnight.

I bet they're vampires, she thought suddenly. *Perfect cover.*

If the world contained fae, why couldn't it have vampires? Margot tried to recall if she had seen either of them in the day, then wondered why she assumed that vampires in the real world would follow the rules established by television and novels. She glanced nervously at the sky, wondering if some creature was going to fly down and steal her.

"Oh fuck," she said out loud, hand covering her mouth.

"Good morning to you too," a voice said, and Margot whirled to see Tobin leaning casually against the passenger door, his white-blond hair shining despite the lack of sun. His voice was exactly as she remembered, sending shivers down her back as it had the night before.

"You ready for some flying lessons?"

Chapter 11

A Question of Firsts

Early afternoon, Thursday, February 19th
outside in the back lot at the Revel Coliseum

Tobin wasn't alone. Standing next to him at the front of her bus was Timothy, the drummer's face serious as his eyes flicked back and forth between her and Tobin.

"Good morning," Margot said, out of habit. "Or afternoon, actually." She bit her lip, not sure what to say to either of them.

"And a lovely day to you as well, my lady," Tobin said formally, though he winked at her. Margot couldn't help the smile that crossed her lips. Tobin may be the reason for her current situation, but he was always so charming. She couldn't help herself. His cheer was much more welcome than Ash's gloomy dismissal. She wondered where Ash was, then forced herself to stop.

Timothy frowned at Tobin's greeting, though Margot couldn't tell if it was the wink or the words. "How are you, Margot?" he asked.

She began to nod automatically, then paused, changing her mind to shake it. "Okay. Ish. I mean, I figured out how to glamour this morning, so that's something, right?"

"What do you mean, how to glamour?" Timothy echoed in surprise.

Margot closed her eyes and thought of the pixie blonde hair, the high cheekbones, the bright eyes. She heard their intake of breath, and both of their eyes were wide when she looked at them. "I'm guessing this isn't expected," she said, reaching up to touch the messy bun of her real hair. "How does this look to you right now?" she asked, hand still touching her bun. "Are my hands just floating?" She pictured a movie with bad CGI, characters obviously interacting with nothing.

Tobin shook his head slightly, eyes squinting. "The magic accounts for things like that. We—" He paused, glancing over at Timothy. "I see you playing with your short blonde hair. Very interesting look, but I prefer the truth, if I'm honest."

Margot glared at him, not liking his casual dismissal of her alter appearance.

"As if you could recognize the truth," another voice said.

Margot turned to see Ash had joined them, walking around the back of her bus, the lead singer casual in jeans, blue t-shirt, and unzipped hoodie. A pair of sunglasses shielded his eyes and a ballcap covered his head—what Margot called his "Blending In" look. Since Stone Dragons had hit the top 100 list two years ago, Ash had a tendency of getting swarmed in public when they hit the bigger cities. He was staring at her new face, and she couldn't tell if he liked the look or not. The need for his approval grated on her nerves.

Before Tobin could reply, Margot had a thought. "Wait," she said, gesturing at Ash's disguise. "Why do you do this if you can just change your face?"

Ash glared at Timothy. "You taught her how to glamour?"

"I taught myself, thank you very much," she snapped. "While you were all sleeping."

"That ... isn't great news," Ash said.

"Why?" she pushed. "You don't want me to learn new abilities?"

"It's not that," Ash said. "It's just ... fast. Too fast."

"Too fast for what?" she asked. "For you?"

"You remember what we said about power last night?" At her nod, he continued, "Gaining abilities this quickly means you may be more powerful than we thought. Someone will notice."

Margot glanced around, seeing only the three men around her bus. She hugged herself. "Here?"

Timothy shook his head. "Not here, no. We're in Armavian territory. Other fae are avoiding this area... until things are decided."

Margot nodded, knowing he spoke of the civil unrest to the south of them. There was a reason Cayla had only scheduled one show in the province, and far to the north to avoid any chances of them getting caught up in anything. "I heard Jeff and Alex saying they would head to the border tonight if they could, get into Genc early, and spend their day off there." She took a deep breath. "So fae avoid human politics?"

All three men exchanged a look, but it was Tobin who spoke. "No. We won't interfere in wars here until it's over one way or the other—but then the Lords will be right back to meddling.”

“Ah.” Margot nodded, trying to recall what had been said about fae Lords and why Tobin would have said “we” like he was one of them. Deciding to ask about it later and focus on the moment, she scanned the empty lot, then glanced at Timothy. “No Nik yet? He still sleeping off last night?”

“He left this morning,” Timothy said. “He’ll be back soon enough.”

Margot considered the city they were in. Kerva wasn’t a tiny town, but it was hardly a city where Niklaus would wake up early to explore. “Wait, he knows someone here, doesn’t he? I remember him going away for long weekends over this way when I first arrived at Maddie’s.” She searched her memory for the name of Nik’s Armavian friend. “Paul?” she guessed.

“Tomas,” Ash corrected.

“Yeah, that’s it,” Margot agreed. “They were friends and he moved away?” She looked at Ash. “Did you know him?”

Ash smirked. “I know him, but trust me when I say he has no interest in seeing me. Especially not now.”

“Is Tomas okay, you think, with everything going on?” Margot hadn’t paid close attention, not wanting to make herself paranoid while they were in Armav, but she knew the cities in the south had started a small rebellion against the government in the capital city. What had begun as a small group of disgruntled citizens had spread far and wide, and the capitol sent troops to quell the disturbance. Margot still followed a few Armavian social accounts, but she had decided not to check them until she was safely across the border into Genc. Cayla knew that the EcoDome at Akkoy was small, only 3,000 people—nothing compared to the 20,000 they had seen at the Coliseum the night before—but she had said the band (and Margot) would need the intimate show to settle their nerves.

"Tom will be just fine," Ash assured her. "He has a way of surviving anything."

"I wonder how he'd deal with wings bursting out of his back one night," Margot commented.

"Did you practice with your wings?" Ash asked. "Last night?"

"No," Margot insisted, not considering her slow study of her new appendages anything akin to practice. "Why?"

"Using abilities tends to bring on others."

"Well, I don't know about that. I talked with Nik last night—nice move, by the way, sending him in with the white flag—and at some point I'm going to ask how he knew about you when I didn't—but not right now. After he left, I went to bed. Then when I woke up and saw my reflection this morning, I had a different face." She sniffed, then resettled her messy bun, using the motion to calm her suddenly jangled nerves. "I'm fine, by the way. Totally not completely freaked out."

"I said I would teach you," Tobin said, but Ash was already shaking his head.

"You aren't doing anything," he ordered. "You've done quite enough already."

"Don't blame him," Margot defended, the words out before she could stop them.

"But this is his fault!" Ash cried.

"This is my parents' fault," she corrected him. "And it was always going to happen. The least you could have done—especially since you promised my aunt you would look after me—the very least you could have managed would be to tell me." As she said it, she knew she was being unfair.

"How could we tell you?" Timothy spoke for the first time in a while. "What could we say?"

"I don't know," she moaned. "But something. A hint. A clue. Not just leave me to Manifest one night in a bar."

Ash looked down, face reddening. "I did not realize that he was your first—"

"Oh fuck no," Margot interrupted him, seeing where this was going. "You are not talking about virginity, are you?" She scoffed. "I'm twenty-three years old, Ashton Stonewall. I've been having sex for years." She glanced over at Tobin. "And not with him."

Not yet, she thought.

Chapter 12

Secrets Revealed

Ash furrowed his brow, glancing back and forth between her and Tobin, a number of emotions crossing his face: anger, annoyance, relief, a hint of guilt, and finally, a tiny glimpse of jealousy. "But to Manifest, there needs to be ... a Connection."

Margot rolled her eyes. "Nik said that too." She cut her gaze to Tobin, and he grinned at her. The sight caused something in her chest to lighten, stressed muscles unlocking deep inside. "What do you think, Tobin?"

"I would be happy to pursue further Connections, Margot," Tobin said.

Ash growled, moving toward the stranger, but again Timothy stepped between them, the grit of the parking lot loud beneath his feet as he shifted quickly to defuse the situation.

"If you have something to say, my Lord," Tobin said, standing down but continuing to push with his words, "now is the time. Your follower has Manifested. Claim her and provide for her safety."

Ash glowered, kicking a random stone and sending it deeper into the lot. "I cannot."

"Then step aside," Tobin insisted, "and let me do what needs to be done. Margot is powerful—or will be. I can sense it. She needs training if she is to have any say in her Claiming."

"Wait," Margot said. "You mean, I can have a choice?" She whirled on Ash. "You made it seem like it was a done deal—that I was at a stranger's mercy! Is that not how it is? Can I ... fight?"

"Of course you can fight," Ash said. "It just..."

"No," Margot said. "Don't finish that sentence. I don't care." She turned to Tobin. "You're willing to teach me?"

He nodded, tucking a piece of hair behind his ear, the motion somehow endearing. "Happy to, Margot. You know I want to spend more time with you."

"But how? We're in the middle of a tour. We need to be in Akkoy in two days."

"Genc is lovely this time of year," Tobin said. "Slightly chillier than here, of course, but still lovely. There will likely be snow on the ground."

"I've been to Genc before," she told him, reminding him that this wasn't her first tour. "I've been all over." She glanced at Ash and Timothy, knowing she had them to thank for bringing her on their trips, though she definitely earned her keep as stage manager chasing after them and getting them on stage in time. "I've seen snow before."

"Have you seen the mountains from the Aerie in Taflah?" Tobin asked.

Margot frowned. She had heard of the exclusive high-end club called the Aerie, nestled high in the mountains and only accessible by a special lift. They had a big fan gala planned there after the show at the Willis Center in March, but Margot had never been there before. "Of course not," she said, shaking her head. "I'm a roadie, not a rock star." Margot had never stated the distinction between her and the band so clearly before. As their stage manager, she was always with the guys—but not part of the band. And she liked it that way. She belonged backstage.

Tobin glanced at Ash and Timothy. "Do you not take her with you to your afterparties?"

Ash looked down and Timothy shrugged. "Margot rarely chooses to attend. She generally prefers her bus to parties," Timothy said.

"Huh," Tobin considered. "And yet last night, you released her into the wilds all alone? And here in Kerva of all places?"

Margot bristled at his suggestion. "They don't *release* me to go anywhere," she snapped. "I do what I want."

"And yet of all nights, you decided to go last night ... to the very bar where I would be." He glanced over at Ash again, an unspoken implication in the look. "How interesting."

Margot followed his gaze to Ash who still wouldn't look at her. "What does he mean?" she asked the lead singer. "Tobin is making it sound like you wanted me there so I could meet him."

"Didn't he?" Tobin asked, eyebrow raised as he watched Ash. "A troublesome problem for one in his situation, no doubt. An unknown quantity, a possible fae in his company, and yet he is in no position to offer his protection should she come into her powers." He winked at him. "It seems like you needed me, my Lord."

"I don't need you," Ash gritted.

"Okay, time out," Margot said, making the universal symbol with her hands. "What the hell is going on between you two? I know you're pretending you don't know him, Ash, but he knows you, so what gives?"

Ash said nothing, and Tobin scoffed. "You wish me to tell her, then?" Tobin purred. "Of course you do. No doubt you plan to use me for all of the things you cannot say."

"Don't."

The word was a whisper, a hint of a word, a breath. Margot waited for Ash to say more, but he didn't, staring across the empty parking lot at the fir trees and the mountains beyond. Tobin was also staring at the lead singer, waiting, letting the moment drag out. Finally, he sighed. When he spoke, his voice wasn't the jovial tease Margot expected.

"Last chance," he said. "You can stop this."

Ash's lip twitched, but the rest of his face remained impassive. Slowly, he turned his head back to look at Margot—a long assessing look—and she felt his appraisal, the subtle touch of something she hadn't been able to sense before.

Is this some kind of fae magic? She wondered, feeling the light brush of sensation against the skin of her cheeks, the top of her ear, the backs of her hands. Finally, Ash shook his head, frowning, and looked away, this time seeing Tobin. There was no anger in the look, only a passive acceptance. He gestured with his chin, a small movement, as if to say *Go on then.* Timothy grabbed his shoulder, about to speak, but Ash only shook his head again, the movement a decisive and regal judgment.

"Very well," Tobin said. "But remember that you had a choice, Ashton Stonewall. I gave you a choice."

"I will," Ash replied coldly, eyes skipping to Margot's confused face and away again. "I will never forgive you for it."

"As you wish." Tobin bowed then, executing a formal gesture with hands out in supplication—clearly a familiar motion.

I'm going to need to read up on curtseying, Margot thought frantically. Apparently, fae could be super formal.

Tobin dismissed Ash then, focusing his full attention on Margot—and it was dazzling. He was handsome, but she spent a lot of time around handsome men. It shouldn't be affecting her this way. But she could feel the response in her belly, the heat flushing her face and neck, her body's instant response to his presence and attention.

A connection, she thought dazedly. *Yes. Definitely need to learn more about that.*

"My Lady Margot," Tobin began, "allow me to introduce myself. Once the first-born son of Lord Novus Stonewall," he emphasized the last name, "and now Tobin Fetch, vassal to Lord Rebinus."

"Stonewall," Margot echoed. "You're related to Ash?"

"He was my brother," Ash said quietly. "A long time ago."

"Half-brother," Tobin corrected, and Margot heard the rage behind the word.

"What happened?" she asked, speaking softly in the hopes they would actually answer her.

"Our father sent him away," Tobin explained. "Sent him here, to live among the humans. To hide himself in *safety and anonymity.*" He sneered the last few words.

"But he's a rock star," Margot argued. "That's hardly anonymous."

"To the fae Lords, being a rock star is trivial," Timothy explained. "They do not concern themselves with such things."

"So you're in hiding," Margot said. "But why? Is your family in danger in some way?"

Tobin chuckled. "Powerful fae are always in danger," he said, "especially ones who come into their power early and are not protected before another Claims them."

Margot paused, putting the pieces together. "You were Claimed by this Lord Rebinald—"

"Rebinus."

"That guy—when you were young. And rather than risk his other son," she looked at Ash, "your father sent you away to hide." She nodded. "I can see how that might generate some ... resentment."

Chapter 13
To Try

"He was always the favorite," Tobin sneered. "The chosen one. The perfect son."

Ash scoffed. "Hardly perfect. You know better."

"I certainly know how much he preferred your mother to mine," Tobin snapped. Margot tried to see the family resemblance between the two brothers. Tobin was pale, silvery while Ash was tan and dark-haired, but Margot could see they shared a similar facial structure—high cheekbones, pointed chin, and wicked smiles.

"What happened to your mothers?" Margot asked, trying to defuse the tension.

"My mother went into exile," Tobin snarled, "while his moved into her rooms in the palace."

Okay, Margot thought, *that failed utterly.*

"I am not responsible for your Claiming," Ash told Tobin quietly. "Nor am I to blame for what happened with your mother."

"Wait." Margot held out a hand, trying to stem the flood of information. She looked at Tobin. "So your mom was married to your dad when she had you, but then he met someone else, and they what? Divorced? Is that a thing among fae?"

"Separation is a possibility," Timothy answered. "Marriages are sometimes abandoned."

"What about Claiming, though? Husbands and wives don't Claim one another? I thought that was permanent."

"It is," Tobin assured her.

"But not all couples are part of a Claimed relationship," Timothy added, gesturing to Tobin and Ash. "Their father is a fae Lord, beholden to no one but himself now that his father has passed. Lady Sylvia, Tobin's mother, belonged to Lady Drina." At Margot's confused expression, he added, "Drina is not a Lord, though Fae Lords can be any gender—it's about power. And Claiming can occur between anyone."

"Anyone? So can powerful fae just Claim one another?" Margot asked, still seeking an out.

Tobin frowned. "They could, but it's against our laws to deprive the Lords of a new fae like that. Ultimately everyone needs to fall under one of them."

"Oh," Margot said, trying to keep it straight. "Wait, you said your father isn't Claimed?"

"That's why he's a Lord," Tobin explained. "Those who remain Unclaimed eventually become Lords." Tobin glanced at Ash, and Margot followed the suggestion—if Ash remained Unclaimed, as she suspected he was—he could become a Lord.

"But Lady Drina?" Margot asked.

"Ultimately she's with Lord Kristoff, but he allows her a great deal of freedom. And she is a forgiving mistress," Timothy said, "so when Lady Sylvia wished to depart her ex-husband's home, she permitted her to return to her household."

"Under her protection, perhaps," Tobin said, "but not part of the household. She was shamed, exiled, spurned. You both know that."

Timothy shrugged. "I was younger then, so I only know the rumors. But I understood Lady Sylvia to be content in her new place."

"As if any of you noticed she was gone," Tobin snapped. "No doubt thrilled that Father no longer had to provide for her needs."

"You know our father was devastated," Ash said quietly. "Even my mother couldn't truly soothe him. After you left—"

"Taken," Tobin corrected. "Unwillingly."

"Yes, after what happened to you—it was a terrible year."

"I'm sure you were drowning in your sorrows at the loss of your pathetic elder brother," Tobin said sarcastically.

Ash glanced up quickly, a flash of hurt in his eyes, there and gone in an instant. "You are my brother," he said quietly. "I missed you."

"Whatever," Tobin scoffed, rolling his eyes. He looked at Margot. "Last I heard, his parents are quite happy together."

Ash made an involuntary sound, but it was Timothy who spoke. "Then you have not been listening recently. Lady Abigail has ... departed."

"She's dead?" Tobin asked, shock making the question harsh with disbelief.

"She's gone," Ash corrected.

"Oh," Tobin said, forehead creasing in concern. "I did not know." He paused, then added, "I am sorry for your loss."

It was Ash's turn to scoff. "Of course you are."

"Your dad sent you here," Margot said to Ash, trying to shift the subject. "But why? What does it mean to hide among the humans?"

Timothy put a hand on Ash's shoulder. "It means I get to keep this one out of trouble while we tour the land of Ardon, making music with our friends." He pointed at Margot. "That includes you, Margot. You're one of us."

"Thanks, Timothy," Margot said, feeling a rush of warmth at his words. At least he enjoyed her company.

"If she's one of you, then give her the protection she needs," Tobin said, bringing the conversation back around.

"Not that again," Ash grumbled. "Let it go, Tobin."

"Forgive me if I cannot," Tobin said. "As someone who was Claimed against my will, I have strong feelings about the possibility for anyone else."

"If you cared about anyone else, you wouldn't be here," Ash said, stepping closer to Tobin. Timothy's hand fell from his shoulder.

"What is that supposed to mean?" Tobin snapped.

"It means you shouldn't have Awakened her in the first place!" Ash shouted, and Margot flinched at the rage in his voice, suddenly visible in his expression. She'd seen Ash get emotional on stage—lost in the words, face transfixed with the feeling of the song—but she'd never seen him lose his temper like this and certainly not over her. She glanced around, glad to see no one else had come outside into the back lot to see them.

"It was bound to happen," Tobin said. "You're being careless and you know it. You assume if you wait long enough, she will become someone else's problem."

"I am no one's problem," Margot stated, but they ignored her.

"Thanks to you, soon everyone will know about her and try to Claim her. That problem is your fault!" Ash continued, voice raised but not the angry shout from before.

"Then let me help her, at least!" Tobin shouted back, getting in his half-brother's face.

"I think you've helped quite enough!" Ash retorted. "Any more help and she'll be bound to you!"

"Better me than the others!" Tobin argued.

"Is that an option?" Margot asked. The brothers ignored her, still bickering, but Timothy cocked his head, considering.

"Possibly," he answered. "Tobin isn't a minor fae. He's Lord Novus's son and powerful in his own right. He is Lord Rebinus's vassal, though, so him Claiming you would ultimately make you Rebinus's."

"You say that like it's not a good thing," she observed.

"Lord Rebinus has a certain reputation for cruelty," Timothy told her. "He is powerful and cunning, but I wouldn't want anyone I know joining his household."

Margot nodded. "So even if Tobin Claimed me, I would still be in danger."

Timothy frowned. "Yes."

"But Ash—" she started.

"Ash is very powerful," Timothy admitted, "but he is under very specific orders." He sighed. "I cannot say any more about it, except that I know he would Claim you if he could."

Margot gave him a sad look. "A sympathy Claiming? Ugh. No, thank you." She turned her attention back to the still arguing brothers.

Timothy grabbed her arm. "He would Claim you, Margot. In an instant. If he could."

She raised her eyebrows at him, glancing over at Ash, who was still yelling back and forth with Tobin, years of frustrated sibling rivalry finally out in the open. "I hear you, Timothy," she said, "but I doubt it. He's never wanted me."

Before the drummer could continue, Margot stepped away, not wanting to hear more.

"—if you'd just give me the chance," Tobin was saying. "I could teach her things! She could defend herself!"

"What can she learn that will matter in the end?" Ash asked. "You would only give her false hopes of freedom."

"So you'd condemn her to servitude without even a chance of resistance?" Tobin pushed.

"Of course not!" Ash snapped. "But we need to be reasonable. How could she withstand someone powerful?"

"I have learned a great many things since leaving home," Tobin said ominously. "I could prepare her. She could stay Unclaimed for a while yet."

Ash sighed, glancing around. "You know as well as I that the only reason we aren't fending off fae is because we're in Armav. The moment we enter Genc, they will sense her."

"Then we need to give her a basic skillset before we enter Genc," Tobin argued. He looked at Margot, seeing her approach. "She's already mastered the glamour on her own. With more training, who knows what other abilities she may possess? You said her mother could control air and her aunt water. Those gifts are powerful if harnessed properly."

"You think air and water can fend off someone like Lord Rebinus?" Ash snarled.

"I think she can pull the air from a Lord's lungs and evaporate the water in a Lord's body," Tobin replied, his voice cold.

Margot's skin prickled at the words, at the idea that she could—or would ever—do such things.

"You've been living among the humans for a long time," Tobin said, looking at Ash. "And before that, you were sheltered at home. There are things we can do, tricks we can show her, that may preserve her freedom."

Ash nodded slowly, Tobin's words breaking through his denial. "I believe that you can, but at what cost? Would you have her tainted by darkness if she had such gifts, to use them that way? You know how that ends," he said sadly. "And what use is all of that when we all know where it leads anyway?"

"We all die in the end," Margot interrupted, remembering her mother. "But that doesn't mean we shouldn't live in the meantime." She glanced nervously at both faces—Tobin flushed with excitement and promise, Ash withdrawn and serious. "I want to try," she told them. Glancing at Tobin, she said, "If you can teach me something to keep me free, I want to try." She turned her gaze to Ash. "Please, let him try."

At her plea, something in Ash's determination shattered, and he closed his eyes. Taking a deep breath, he stared down at her as if she were every problem and every solution at the same time.

"All right, Margot," he said finally. "We can try."

Chapter 14

Driver Chooses the Music

Twenty minutes later, Timothy was still arguing with Ash.

"No," the drummer repeated, "I am not leaving you here to ride to Akkoy with Margot." He pointed to himself. "Bodyguard, remember?"

"We will be fine," Ash insisted. "Go get Nik and head into Genc. He'll need you tonight." He gave his friend a meaningful look, clearly trying to guilt him by mentioning Nik. "You know how he gets."

Margot watched them, standing outside yet another unspoken conversation about her cousin. Whatever Nik's secret was, both Ash and Timothy were in on it, the three of them working together to keep it safe.

"And after that, what? I watch you get arrested for smuggling a criminal across the border?" Timothy asked, glancing again at Tobin.

"Hey!" Tobin exclaimed. "I'm not a criminal!"

"We are not smuggling anyone across the border," Ash repeated. He gave his half-brother a stern look. "Tobin will find his own way into Genc. In the meantime—"

"In the meantime, the two of you will teach Margot how to protect herself—as much as she can," Timothy summarized. He slumped, hands finding the pockets of his jacket and settling there as he considered his options.

"It's only a day," Ash insisted. "There is very little danger."

"No, no danger at all being away from your guard with your estranged bitter half-brother while you try to upend the very foundation of our society." Timothy let out the long-suffering sound of the badgered best friend and studied Ash's face. "You will not move on this, will you?"

"Nope," Ash replied, shaking his head, then poked his friend in the side. "You know I won't."

"Fine," Timothy finally agreed. "But I hate it." He glanced at Margot. "No offense, Margot. I want you to be happy. But this is dangerous."

"I know," she said, feeling awkward and burdensome as they planned how they would help her. "Thank you for doing this. For letting him do this."

Timothy turned away, rolling his eyes and shaking his head. "I know I'm going to regret this." He glanced back one more time to pierce Tobin with his glare. "And you! He is your brother—"

"Half—"

"*Brother*," Timothy emphasized. "And brothers watch each other's backs. I'm trusting you to keep him safe."

There was a long awkward silence, then Tobin nodded, wilting under Timothy's expectant look. "I will," he said finally.

"Good." Timothy studied all three of them. "I want to give you all a long list of warnings, but I know you're just going to ignore me, so I won't bother." He saluted them, heading off to the Party Bus. "See you all in Akkoy in two days!" he shouted over his shoulder. "Don't die before then!"

Ash gave him a two fingered salute from the forehead, but Timothy didn't turn around to see it. They watched him walk away.

"So..." Margot began awkwardly. "How does this work?"

"I think we should begin with flying," Tobin said. Margot glanced up at the clear blue sky, excited and nervous at the prospect of actually using her new wings.

"Of course you'd say that," Ash complained. "Just can't wait to get her out of her shirt again." Margot felt her cheeks flush as she recalled her ruined dress and bare back, then grew hotter as she thought of Tobin's hands on her body, under her dress.

"This has nothing to do with her shirt," Tobin defended. "Though I wouldn't mind at all," he added with a wink, seeming to read her mind. "But I did come prepared." He shrugged off the backpack he wore and began rummaging inside, eventually pulling out a black swath of clothing he held out to Margot. She accepted it, then took a moment turning it this way and that to figure out how it worked. "Oh!" she said when she finally got the angle right. It was a long-sleeved shirt but cut very low in the back to leave room for her wings. She glanced around the back lot. "Are we just doing this here?"

"No," Ash said, reaching for the door to her bus. "We'll go to Kerva Point Park. It should be easy enough to find an out of the way place to practice."

Margot glanced at the woods beyond the lot. Kerva Point Park was about half an hour away, into the mountains. It was a good place to practice her new gifts without being seen. Afterward, they could continue through the park over the mountains and to the border crossing into Genc. They hadn't come this far north on their last tour and part of Margot was excited to see the mountains up close. Her lust for travel and new experiences was one of the main reasons she agreed to join Stone Dragons on tour—well, that and Ash. But now she got to enjoy looking at both.

And Tobin.

"Okay," she agreed, stepping past Ash to enter her bus. For a moment, she wondered if she had left too many things lying around, nervous what Ash would think of her bus after not seeing it for so long. Luckily, Margot didn't have many belongings, and she was neat with the ones she did have—mostly a result of living in a small space but also because of her nature. Even living at Maddie's, she hadn't acquired a lot of stuff, content with a few books and her laptop. Hell, her kitchen only contained two mugs, two plates, two bowls, a small pan, and one pot. Margot wasn't set up to entertain. Her space was free of clutter. Satisfied that Ash wasn't going to walk in to see her panties anywhere, she stepped aside, moving out of the way so he could enter behind her. She turned around just in time to see Ash step inside, and Tobin move closer to the doorway outside.

Ash spun immediately, still standing on the step. "You can get yourself there," he told Tobin, taking another step inside. He reached past his brother's head for the door. "Good flying practice for you. See you in a bit." He slammed the bus door in Tobin's face.

Margot let out a breath. "Seriously?" Shaking her head, she reached down to grab a bottle of water from the fridge, then did a slightly awkward dance to get around where Ash stood to sit in the driver's seat. He flattened himself against the door as she passed, arms up at his shoulders, but she still brushed against him, very aware of his presence in her space. Putting him behind her, she settled herself into the driver's seat, trying to ignore the excitement she felt at having Ash in her home.

Ash slid her few shirts and dresses aside, revealing the passenger seat, then spun it around easily to face the window. Margot sometimes forgot that he had rebuilt the bus with her—he knew how everything worked.

"Driver chooses the music," she said, buckling in and reaching for the radio.

"Passenger shuts his piehole," Ash replied automatically, the old rule bringing them both back to early days when the band was still practicing in Maddie's old barn and they fought over the radio in her old truck when they drove into town. He buckled his seatbelt and held his hands out. "I would never presume to touch your radio, Margot."

"Uh huh," she said, narrowing her eyes at him as she selected her "Sing Along Driving Music" playlist. The first notes of a guitar riff echoed through her speakers, followed by a slow drumbeat. She put the bus into drive, bobbing her head in time with the music as she pulled slowly out of the venue backlot, heading into the nearby mountains.

Ash sang along, his haunting voice soothing her nerves.

Chapter 15

Playing with Fire

Afternoon, Thursday, February 19th
in Kerva Point Park in Kerva, Armav

"This feels so weird," Margot said, stepping down from the bus onto the grassy space in the park. They were near the top of the mountain in a secluded spot away from prying eyes. Ash cocked his head, taking in the backless shirt she wore as she twisted a little. Margot frowned. "Please don't tell me I put this on wrong."

Ash shook his head. "No, it's right. I just haven't seen anyone wear those in a very long time."

Margot glanced around. They were alone. Tobin would find them soon enough, Ash had assured her, but not yet. "How long?" she pressed. "Since before you came to Maddie's?"

Ash shrugged one shoulder but said nothing. He had left his hat and glasses inside her bus, disguise forgotten now that they were in no danger of spectators, and she enjoyed seeing the breeze play with his hair, tendrils sweeping this way and that.

"You weren't there that long before I arrived, were you?" she asked quietly. She recalled the night she had arrived. The boys hadn't been there—Maddie said they were at a friend's house. She had snuck out of her new room and was sitting in the bar, not drinking, but trying to imagine how her mom would have looked in the space. She had always known she had an aunt who owned a bar over in Ardon, but sitting in that bar after her mom's death had been surreal, everything somehow warped with her grief and disconnected. She heard the boys before they came in, drunken giggles and high-pitched whispering, and she had quickly ducked behind the bar, not wanting to be seen with tears streaking her face. Nik came first, her cousin bleary-eyed and stumbling as he made his way to the back stairway. She'd seen old pictures of him, so she recognized his face. The other two boys were strangers, though Maddie had told her to expect them—distant cousins who had come to stay with her. The one on the right was dark-haired and serious, though he too swayed a bit as he held up his companion. Crouched behind the bar, barely peeking over the top to see, Margot would never forget her first sight of Ashton Stonewall, his messy brown hair, his tan skin, his long limbs, and perfect voice as he too whispered nonsense to his friend.

That one, she had decided, something inside of her bursting alive and scorching her soul. *Him.*

Of course, her beautiful soulmate had turned to the side and vomited, hitting Timothy with most of it, and the two had squealed and scuffled their way back outside to find the hose, Nik grumbling after them that they were making too much noise.

Margot came out of the memory as if waking from a dream to find a much older and more serious Ash staring at her. He studied her face, seeking something Margot thought he may never find.

"No," he said finally. "I came to live with the Hodges about six months before you did."

"Why them?" she asked, deciding to take her openings where she found them. "Did your family know them?"

He nodded. "I'm not sure exactly, but Maddie welcomed me. Us. Timothy came with me from my father's house."

"Was Marcus still alive then?" she asked, recalling the photos of Maddie's husband and Nik's father in the hallway of the old house.

"No," Ash said. "He'd died about a year before. I think maybe that's why we went there. Maddie and Nik were all alone." He paused, then added, "It used to be a tavern, back in the day. You knew that, right? That's why there's so much living space above the bar. I think they used to rent out the rooms before Nik was born."

Margot nodded, recalling fumbling moments in the dark rooms above the bar, Ben's awkward kisses, their teenage bodies doing things her mother would not have approved. Margot was lucky no one had ever caught them, though Nik always seemed to know the next day. "But Maddie was fae, like my mom. So Marcus was human then?"

Ash nodded. "Yeah. I'm sorry I never got to meet him. From what Nik has told me, he sounds pretty amazing. A really great dad."

Margot nodded. No doubt Ash was comparing Nik's wonderful, loving, dad to his own—a man who had lost one son and hidden another. She knew Nik's dad had died in a car accident. Nik had told her once, after hearing her talk about how happy her own mother had been, that his mom used to be like that before the accident. The Maddie Margot had known, warm, loving, soothing, no nonsense Aunt Maddie, was not the same woman who had raised Nik. In a way, he had mourned both of his parents after the accident. And two years ago, Maddie had also died—another car accident. It was a miracle Nik even agreed to touring on the road like this.

"But Nik—" she began, wanting to discover more about her cousin's odd not-human/not-fae status, but the wind blew, cold and biting, pushing Margot's hair off her bare back, and she shivered. Ash moved immediately, hands already glowing with some kind of magic, and he wrapped an arm around her shoulder. Warmth spilled over her, and she sighed into him, allowing herself a moment to appreciate the strength of his arm as she glanced over at the hand on her bicep. A slight red haze shimmered above it, and Margot felt something deep inside her respond to the power, like a minor chord in one of Stone Dragons' ballads.

I will keep you warm, my love... with the fire that burns deep inside...

The words to "Dragonfire" drifted through her mind. "How do you do that?" she murmured, tilting her head to look up at him. His face was very close to her, and she bit her lip, not wanting to do anything stupid. He always smelled so good, like cinnamon and woodsmoke. He watched her for a moment too long, then a corner of his mouth turned up, and he moved his hand so she could see it, still holding her close to his heat.

"It's fire," he explained, flipping his hand palm up, and a small flame exploded in his palm, fierce and glowing. The fire spread out to his fingers, then rushed back to the center of his hand before going out. Margot gasped, then grabbed his hand, inspecting it for damage.

His palm was smooth and unblemished, though she could feel the calloused tips of his fingers, a guitarist's hand. "How?" she blurted, still holding him. She felt him shrug behind her. "Can I do that?"

"Maybe," he said, the word brushing against the back of her ear, and she shivered again, unable to stop herself.

"Can you teach me?" she asked, letting herself lean back into him a hint more, wanting to feel his breath on her skin, her bare back pressed against his sweatshirt.

"Yes," he said, the word a promise and more.

She turned around in the circle of his arm, very aware that he did not let her go—his hand remaining on her upper arm and the other snaking around her hip and keeping their bodies pressed close together. "Ash," she whispered, not used to being so close to him, to feeling the full power of his seductive gaze. Sure, sometimes he looked at her like he wanted nothing more in the world than to devour her, but he always seemed to remember something, pulling himself back from some invisible ledge. He would be distant, a stranger, the Ash she glimpsed vanishing yet again.

He's with you now, a quiet voice said. *Just enjoy the moment.*

No, a stronger voice replied. *I will not settle for moments. If I can't have all of him, then I don't want any of him.*

Keep telling yourself that.

Margot steeled herself, very aware that his eyes had moved from her own to glance at her lips. *No,* she decided. *Not like this.* She reached up, and Ash leaned closer, clearly thinking she meant to cup his chin, his face, as their lips met, but instead, she put both hands flat on his chest and gently pushed him away.

"I'm fine now," she said, stepping away as Ash's expression cycled through shock at her refusal, then embarrassment, and finally settled into guilt as he released her. The cold wind seared her back, and Margot closed her eyes.

Wings, please come out now, she thought, seeing that starburst of light through her eyelids, and then she was stumbling, the wind catching a wing and tugging her backward.

"Whoa!" Ash said, grabbing her forearm with steely fingers and holding her steady. He glanced around. "Maybe we're up too high. It's too windy."

"It's fine here," another voice said, and Margot whirled away from Ash to see Tobin floating down to where they stood. He was bare-chested, wings fully engaged, and she had another moment where she was floored by his otherworldly beauty. She swallowed it down, trying to see how he was flying. His wings barely moved in the breeze, seeming to catch the current and use it to lower himself. "I'll teach you to use the wind," he promised, nodding at where Ash still held her forearm. "Assuming he lets you go, of course."

Chapter 16
Seeing the Wind

Four hours later, the sun was setting and Margot was absolutely done with her would-be tutors. Tobin's advice was practical and quite hands-on as he guided her through the basics of hovering, rising, flying, and what Margot considered the most important skill—landing. The fae was quick to touch her, correcting her posture here, adjusting the angle of her wing there, and Margot couldn't deny the frisson of excitement that jolted through her at the feel of his hands on her body. Tobin was with her—excited to be there, eager to help—and he seemed to understand her struggle before she could articulate it.

Ash, on the other hand, spent the afternoon on the ground, watching them both with a critical gaze—and eyes that seemed to spark fiery red each time Tobin touched her. His advice was more theoretical since he didn't actually have wings. He did seem to know a lot about flying theory, telling her how to sense the wind in a way that made Tobin give him more than a few dirty looks.

Flying was exhilarating, especially once she realized that Tobin wouldn't let her fall. He didn't hold onto her as Ash had, but he hovered near. She could hear the wind in his wings as he flew beside her, laughing with her as they flew higher, reassuring her as she watched her bus and Ash growing smaller beneath them. They repeated a similar process for each flight—gently rising, circling in slowly widening rotations as they moved higher into the sky, the wind growing colder and more insistent the higher they went.

Margot ignored the barbs the brothers traded easily enough, focusing on getting a handle on her new skill, but this last round had turned uglier than normal, and she was tired of both of them.

It started with a comment about the wind, Ash telling her to close her eyes and focus, sensing where the air would take her. A gust came from out of nowhere, catching her wing, and she landed hard on the ground, her knee banging painfully into the rock surface.

"I'm not my mother!" she snapped, angrily rubbing her knee. "I can't control the air. I can't see it. I don't know why you think I can!"

"Perhaps because he forgets that others can't see the wind as he can," Tobin observed, and Ash's fairly calm expression twisted into something ugly. Margot didn't understand how, but Tobin had poked a deep wound.

"I cannot see the wind," Ash insisted.

"Keep telling yourself that," Tobin snapped. "Perhaps one day it will be true."

"You will not," Ash said in a low, dangerous voice, advancing on his brother, "insult my mother again."

Margot got to her feet and put her hands between them, keeping the distance. "Hold up," she demanded. "Saying someone can see the wind is insulting their mother?"

"No," Tobin said, "but only dragonborn can actually see the wind."

Margot frowned, staring at Ash, remembering the ease with which he had controlled fire to warm her. "Dragons, huh? Is that a fae thing?"

"No," Ash said. "Dragons are not fae." He gave Tobin a harsh stare. "And my father was not a dragonborn."

"Of course," Tobin agreed, though mockingly. "You simply have the look of your mother entirely." Margot glanced at the brothers, trying to see the similarities between them. They were very different in appearance, Tobin pale and silvery with that shock of white hair and Ash tan with his mop of messy dark hair. Ash was still angry, hands fisted as he took long slow breaths, while Tobin stood there, a smug smirk on his lips. Their mouths really were quite similar.

Margot grimaced. "Tobin, stop being a jerk about this."

Tobin put a hand to his chest, affronted. "My father replaces my mother a year after I'm born with a woman who can't even be true to him, and I'm the one being unreasonable?"

"You don't believe that," Margot told him. "Because if you did, you wouldn't care at all. You certainly wouldn't claim him as your half-brother, even to me."

"He hasn't Claimed me," Ash interrupted.

"You know what I mean," Margot said, annoyed at both of them for rehashing years of family trauma when they were supposed to be helping her master her abilities.

She turned to Tobin. "Stop punishing him for what happened to you."

"I didn't know you were a therapist, Margot," Tobin snapped, and she flushed. It was the first time Tobin had turned his barbed tongue her way, and she didn't like it. Brother issues were one thing—dragging her into them was another. Then again, she had stuck her nose between them.

"I call it when I see it," she said. "Look—I get it. You're mad. Ash got to hide while you had what I imagine is an awful experience. That sucks. But right now, I'm about to have that same experience with some stranger, so if you could put this aside for the moment and help me, I'd really appreciate it." She sighed, glancing at the sky, seeing the darkness creeping over the trees on the mountainside below them. "Though I think I'm done flying for the day. I'm not sure about flying at night."

Both brothers shook their heads. "Not yet," Ash said, at the same time Tobin said, "Soon though."

She stretched, closed her eyes, then thought, *You can go away now, please.* The flash of light popped inside her eyelids, and a cold breeze raked across her bare back. She opened her eyes, wrapping her arms around herself to stay warm, the protection from her wings gone. She frowned at both of them. "What now? More glamour practice? Should I see if I have another gift?"

Ash shook his head. "Now you rest," he declared. "I know you don't feel it yet, but flying can be exhausting, especially at the beginning."

"How do you know?" she asked, not wanting to be bitchy but genuinely curious.

Ash shrugged. "I read up on fae abilities when I was young." He glanced at Tobin. "Our father insisted I know as much as I could." He paused, then added, "There was a time when we studied together."

"That time is long gone," Tobin said.

"I know," Ash agreed. "But for Margot's sake, can we call a truce for the moment? Just until she learns ... enough?"

"I thought you said it would never be enough," Tobin reminded him. "That this was a fool's mission guaranteed to give her false hope. One day of watching her fly and you've changed your mind?"

"I want to be wrong," Ash admitted, and Margot tried not to notice how adorable his smile was. "And she's a natural, obviously."

"I am?" Margot asked, cheeks heating even as she stepped back toward the bus to cut the wind freezing her skin.

"Most fae take weeks or even months to do what you did this afternoon. You are truly gifted, Margot," Ash told her. She nodded, and her teeth clacked together as she started shivering. "Oh!" he said, stepping forward to put an arm around her waist, drawing her near, that red shimmer bathing her in warmth again. "She should go inside." She saw Tobin's eyes track the location of Ash's hand, and his smirk was back.

"Of course, now you're here," Tobin said. "No doubt you plan to keep her warm all night long."

Ash's hand casually resting against her waist froze, the gentle touch becoming awkward. "I only—"

"Don't let me stop you," Tobin said, stepping away. "You'll save me the trouble of all this training."

Margot frowned at him, not thrilled about being a burden. "You don't have to—"

"Oh, I know, Margot," Tobin said, face melting again and piercing her with that same direct focus she enjoyed. "I want to help you. I'm all in with you on this." He paused, glancing at Ash. "But don't forget that he could make all this unnecessary quite easily."

"I cannot C—" Ash began, but Margot interrupted him, her hand resting atop his on her waist, feeling his warm skin relax against hers.

"I know," she said. "No Claiming. And it's fine," she insisted, glaring at Tobin. "You keep bringing this up, Tobin. You sure you can't Claim me and also make this unnecessary?"

Tobin met her eyes for a long time, and for a moment, she thought she saw something else there, a desire, there and quickly hidden, but then the fae looked away. "If I could..." he began.

"Yeah," Margot agreed, sighing heavily. "Apparently that's a common refrain around here." She assessed the darkness pooling around them. "Where will you go for the night, then?"

He raised an eyebrow. "You concerned for my safety and wellbeing, darling?" he asked. "Or just jealous?"

She narrowed her eyes at him. "You want it to be both, of course." Shaking her head, she let go of Ash's hand, stepping out of his grip. The cold sliced through her, the mountain wind unforgiving as the light faded, but she took the few steps toward Tobin, enjoying the way his body reacted to her approach, the excitement in his eyes glowing as she drew near. "Thank you," she said formally, grabbing both of his hands and bringing each to her lips for a gentle kiss. "I appreciate everything you are doing for me. I know you don't have to, that it's not your responsibility. So just ... thank you."

"You want me to stay?" Tobin asked quietly. "Or do you want to be alone ... with him?" She didn't turn around to see what Ash was doing, not wanting him to know they were talking about him.

"No," she replied, just as softly. "I think you two need time apart. But seriously... thank you for today."

Tobin nodded, leaning down to kiss her cheek. Heat flooded her at the contact, and for a moment, she wished he would kiss her properly, the way he had in the night-club, igniting every cell in her body. "Guard your heart, Margot," he whispered. "Or he will break it again."

"I know," she said, giving him a quick hug before stepping back. Despite the cold, his bare chest was still warm, no doubt the result of his own fae powers. "Tomorrow then?" she asked. "Across the border in Akkoy? We're at the EcoDome. The show isn't until Saturday."

Tobin nodded. "I know." Margot couldn't help the shiver that ran through her at the casual way he said it, how he knew where she would be. It was impossible to think she had only met him last night. She had never felt such an instant connection, an immediate bond. "But I might not be there until Saturday night," he said. "After your show. We can see what other abilities you have by then."

"Be careful," she said suddenly worried he would do something foolish before she saw him again. "Come back to me."

"I will, Margot," he promised. "You're not getting rid of me that easy." He nodded over her shoulder to Ash, then lifted skyward.

Margot didn't hear Ash step close to her, but she felt his hand on her shoulder, the bottom of his palm touching the bare skin below the edge of the shirt, heat flooding her again. She didn't look away from Tobin's retreating form, watching until the white spot faded into the night sky, becoming yet another star in the distance.

Chapter 17

Grilled Cheese Sandwiches

Evening, Thursday, February 19th
in Margot's Bus in Kerva Point Park in
Kerva, Armav

She stood there for a long time, feeling Ash's palm on her body, hating herself for the wave of gratitude she felt at the idea of him touching her willingly. Finally, she turned around to face him. He was watching her carefully, the emotional drain of the day spent bickering with his brother evident in his eyes. He was waiting for her to say something, and by the look on his face, he was not expecting her to be kind. Sighing, she stepped past him, opening the door to her home and stepping inside.

When he didn't immediately follow, she stuck her head out and gestured for him to follow. "Get in here," she said. "It's chilly out there."

"You don't have to," Ash said, pausing at the threshold. "I can stay out here. Give you your privacy."

Margot shook her head. "Ash, my privacy has been shot to hell since last night. Get your butt inside."

A small smile touching his lips, Ash obeyed, tugging the door shut behind him. He glanced around the small space, then reached over to spin the passenger seat, settling himself down and pushing her clothes to the side again so they didn't hang in his face.

"Want something to eat?" she offered, kicking off her sneakers and tucking them on the step next to her boots.

"Sure," Ash agreed, "though I don't think they deliver up here. We can go back into town to get—"

"I can cook, remember?" Margot told him. "Grilled cheese and bacon?" she said, recalling many days in Maddie's house where they alternated who cooked the grilled cheese and who decided how crispy the bacon got.

"Sure," he agreed.

She removed the small pan from its hook along the back wall and turned on the burner of her stovetop. While it heated, she pulled the bacon from the fridge, settling a few strips on the metal pan in her small convection oven. She recalled Ash liked three strips on his sandwich, while she preferred only two. Glad she always had basic food supplies on hand, Margot pulled enough for two sandwiches each. Sometimes she cooked more elaborate food for herself, but for now, the simplicity of her motions helped soothe her. There was comfort in working in her kitchen, in her space. She was aware of Ash watching her, very aware of her bare back when pieces of her hair, escaping from her bun, managed to touch her skin, but she didn't turn around.

When the bacon was ready, she began assembling sandwiches, the routine easy enough. When all four sandwiches were ready, she turned to face him, finding him sitting in the same position. He took the plate she offered, and she plopped her plate down on the low desk beneath her bed. Kneeling before the fridge, she opened the door, then glanced at Ash. "Tea or bubbles?" she asked him, knowing his preference for both iced tea and seltzer.

"Bubbles," he answered. "Do you have the lime ones?"

"Of course," she told him, plucking out a can and tossing it his way. He caught it easily in one hand, a move that only made her wonder what else those hands could do, and she reached back in for a tea, trying to focus. Just as she was about to shut the door, Ash leaned forward, body easily covering the small space between his seat and the fridge, and peered inside.

"Wait," he said, head close to her chest. "Is that...?" He glanced at her. "Aunt Maddie gave you a bottle of her wine?"

Slightly embarrassed, Margot nodded, reaching deep inside to retrieve the oddly shaped bottle in question. "Yeah, a long time ago. She said I'd want it one day... when I really needed answers."

Ash sat back, studying the bottle from a distance. "I didn't know any of it was left."

Margot swirled the bottle, tinted glass making the liquid inside a dark purple, almost black. It had no label, just a handmade wax seal over the opening. "Was it a special pressing or something?" she asked. "I don't remember seeing any others like this at the bar."

"No way she would share it," Ash said, taking a bite of his grilled cheese and sighing in contentment. He chewed for a moment, contemplating, then swallowed. "That's way too precious for just anyone to have."

"The good stuff, huh?" Margot asked. "I'm not much of a drinker and definitely not wine. I think I forgot about it back there." She put it on the floor between them, the overhead light casting a dark shadow through the glass and onto the wooden floor. Margot stared at it as she began to eat her sandwich. At first, she was convinced there was something off about the shadow, like the haze that shimmered over Ash's hand as he warmed her, but then cheese and bacon and salty goodness exploded on her tongue, and she closed her eyes, relishing a good sandwich. She had moved on to her second sandwich and finished most of her iced tea before she slowed down enough to return her attention to the bottle.

"Have you had this before? Is it any good?"

Ash took a swig of his lime seltzer, peering at the bottle on the floor. "I have," he answered slowly, "and yes, it's quite good. Potent."

Margot narrowed her eyes. "I'm sensing some hesitation," she offered. "Did you get drunk on Aunt Maddie's special wine, Ashton Stonewall?"

He smiled in response to her flirtatious tone and nodded, a bit of red creeping up his neck. "Not one of my finer moments," he recalled. "Though Nik and Timothy were no better off."

"Nice," Margot judged, taking her last bite of sandwich. "No wonder she gave me the last bottle. Apparently I know how to be responsible." She was about to stand up, but Ash beat her to it, collecting her plate and stepping to the sink. He turned on the water and quickly washed up, hanging up her frying pan and putting the plates back on their shelf. The bacon pan took a little bit more effort, and she enjoyed watching him from behind as he moved, scrubbing the grease away in small bursts, careful to conserve her water supply. They'd both lived in RVs long enough to be careful of water usage.

As he finished, drying his hands on her small blue towel, she tilted her head. "Any idea what she meant by that wine giving answers? Did you get visions or something when you drank it?"

Ash chuckled. "Not exactly," he admitted. "I got really sloppy drunk."

Margot frowned. "It must have been a long time ago then. I've seen you drink, and you don't get sloppy drunk, Ash."

He shrugged. "I've had some nights."

Margot looked away, seeing the line of desperate women who always surrounded him, wondering if she wanted to hear more about Ash's nights.

"Not like this, though," he said, walking back to where she sat. He leaned down to pick up the bottle, seemed to contemplate something, then shook his head, putting it back into the fridge.

"Like what? Stuck in a tiny bus on a mountainside?" Margot asked, hating the bitterness she could hear in her voice.

"Margot," he said, and she looked up, not used to him calling her by her full name. "I am not stuck with you. I am here because I choose to be here."

"But you wouldn't be," she said, unable to stop talking. "If Tobin hadn't forced you, you would be somewhere else."

With someone else.

Ash bit his lip, but he didn't say anything, something hiding behind his eyes.

"I'll say it again, damn it, since you keep giving me that look. You don't have to be here. Just go." She took a deep breath, then finished her drink with a too-long swallow that stole her breath.

"I want to be here," he said again. "With you."

Margot coughed at the words she had longed to hear him say. When she finally stopped choking, she gasped, "Why?"

Ash knelt by her side, waiting for her to wipe her teary eyes and gather herself. When he saw he had her full attention, he said, "Because I like you, Go. Don't you know that by now?"

Chapter 18

The Last Woman
in the World

"But not enough," she said, bold now that he was on her level. "Not enough to protect me."

"I cannot," he repeated.

"Tell me why," she dared. "I'll believe you."

Ash reached out to brush a stray lock of hair behind her ear, his touch trailing little fires across her skin. "I would," he said softly, moving closer, "if I could."

"Why can't you?" she pressed, needing to know.

"I..." His mouth moved, words trying to force their way out, but then he was shaking his head, defeated, lips together in a hard line.

"Is it someone else?" she asked quietly.

"Isn't it always?" he asked sadly.

His words cut deep, and Margot leaned away from him, suddenly too close and too overwhelmed by his presence.

Someone else, she reminded herself. *It's always someone else.*

"Then go," she insisted, then recalled they were alone in the mountain park after dark. It wasn't like he could walk across the parking lot to his RV. "I mean, we can go. I don't want to keep you from them."

"From who?" Ash asked, confused by her sudden shift in mood. Realization crossed his face a second later. "Wait—no. Go, it's not like that."

"It never is," she retorted, scooting back into her chair.

Ash caught her shoulder, preventing her from spinning away from him. "Listen to me, Go. It's not like that at all." He looked deep into her eyes, a look he had no doubt given to hundreds of eager women over the tour. Margot knew better, but it didn't stop her for her from falling. "There isn't someone else like that."

"Then what did you mean?" she pushed. "Why can't you Claim me?" She frowned. "It doesn't have to be sex, you know. It can just be a connection. Don't we have a connection, Ash?" She hated the words as they came out, but she knew she had to ask them, had to pull off the bandage and deal with this wound. When Ash said nothing, only kept staring at her intensely, she added, "Do you feel nothing for me, then?"

"I feel for you, Go," he finally said.

"Gee, thanks," she muttered, getting to her feet. "Don't do me any favors." She remembered that she was wearing the silly shirt and reached for a bin of clothes tucked in her closet behind the driver's seat. Yanking a t-shirt from the top, she stepped carefully around the lead singer in her bus and into her small bathroom, sliding the door shut behind her with a bang. It was a dumb move. The room was too small to properly stretch her arms over her head and remove the weird shirt, and she ended up nearly strangling herself in the process.

Her elbow thumped the wall loudly, and she heard Ash ask from outside, "You okay in there?"

"I'm fine," she huffed, both arms twisted around her middle and the neckband tight around the back of her neck. "This shirt is stupid."

"You need help?" His voice was just on the other side of the door. Margot huffed, looking down at her tangled arms.

"You say that to all the girls?" she retorted, still annoyed with him.

"Only the ones trying to take off a wing-friendly halter top," he said, and she could feel his charm through the door. "I've seen plenty of people get tangled up in them." A pause, then, "Seriously, Go, let me help you. I've watched someone nearly strangle themselves getting one off." Another pause, then, "I need a sign of life out here, Go."

Margot couldn't help the smile across her lips. She took as deep a breath as she could manage with the shirt twisted up tight around her, then slid the door open with her foot, staring up at Ash with a grimace. "Don't you dare laugh at me," she snapped. She stepped out of the bathroom, clutching her t-shirt in one hand, then stood in front of Ash, turning so her back faced him.

He chuckled, said, "Arms up."

She tucked the new shirt between her knees by folding her upper body down and thrust her arms overhead, allowing Ash to untangle the fabric from her raised arms, finally untwisting the band from around her neck and pulling the whole thing off. Her hair slid through the final piece and landed against the bare skin of her back, hair tie lost in the shuffle.

Ash let out a little gasp.

"What?" she asked, pulling up the t-shirt and starting to slide it over her arms.

"Did you always have that?" he asked.

"Have what?" she asked, shirt pressed against her front, ready to go over her head.

"That mark on your back," he said.

"Oh!" she exclaimed, remembering her attempt to study it in the mirror and then on her phone. The magical mark that wouldn't photograph. "No, that's new. Any idea what it means?"

Ash moved away, and she quickly tugged the shirt over her head. Snagging a new hair tie from the bathroom sink, she pulled her hair through and took a moment to redo her bun, twisting her hair back into place. She had so much hair. Ash had stepped away to the far end of the bus, the death trap shirt forgotten in his hands. Wary, she stepped closer but didn't reach out to touch him.

"Oh, Go," he whispered, the lines of his body nearly vibrating with distress, "I should have known."

Margot's hand reached out of its own accord, hesitated, poised between them only a few feet, but so much more than that. Margot was very aware of the gap yawning between them, keeping them apart. She had thought for a brief moment that her being fae might have narrowed the distance, but she'd been wrong. Ash was as unattainable now as he ever was.

It didn't matter. It never had. She still wanted to touch him, to help him, to ease the pain she could feel radiating off him.

She heard Tobin's voice echo in her memory: *Guard your heart, Margot, or he will break it.*

I am an idiot, she told herself, then let her hand finish the journey to touch his back.

"Ash?" she whispered. "What is it?"

He turned around, moving fast and tugging her close, cocooning her in the circle of his arms. Margot stood perfectly still. Ash had hugged her before over the years, but not often, and definitely never like this, not like he thought someone was about to steal her away from him forever. Though the bus was warm enough, she felt heat spool over them both, and when she cracked her eyes open, she could see the red haze covering them. It was warm, but not uncomfortably so, and she closed her eyes again, relishing the feeling of being in his embrace. She knew she would not be the last woman to enjoy his arms, but she would take what she could get, though that same small part of her hated how grateful she was that he would touch her.

She sank into his embrace, letting him hold her like she was the last woman in the world.

Chapter 19

In Vino Veritas

Margot realized that Ash was trying to speak, his mouth making empty sounds, his breath tickling her hair. She leaned back, looking up into his face. "Ash?" she asked.

His mouth moved, but again no sound came out. The heat around them flared, and she gasped. It wasn't painful but quickly moving away from comforting warmth into uncomfortable hot. "Ash," she said, "calm down." When he only stared at her, she reached up to touch his face, closing his open mouth and ending his strangled attempts to speak. "Don't burn down my bus," she told him clearly. "Cool it."

She could feel it, that brush of something against her skin—magic, she realized—as Ash slowly pulled it back, the heat retreating with it.

Ash seemed to return to himself, closing his eyes, and she felt the air temperature cool, suddenly aware of the sweat beading on her skin. "Good," she soothed, a hand brushing his hair away from his face, a movement she had longed to do and wasn't going to miss now that she was in his arms. No doubt other women had done the same, and Margot decided that at that moment, she didn't care. She would take her moment as so many had before, and she would enjoy it.

When he had settled and her bus was a reasonable temperature again, she cocked her head. "You want to tell me what brought this on?"

He nodded, opened his mouth, but she shut it, gently pushing his chin up, silencing any words he managed to say. It was clear that something happened to him any time he tried to tell her whatever was going on right now. Margot didn't know much about fae magic, but the way the lead singer couldn't make sounds pass his throat suggested this was more than normal hesitation. Ash could sing like a god, his voice divine even when he wasn't trying. Something choking his words could only be magical.

"But you can't tell me, can you? It's all connected: the Claiming, your family, the reason you're here at all..." She frowned. "Is it magic?"

He nodded again, eyes closed, then he sighed, his entire body shifting and moving her with him. He leaned his head down atop hers, resting his chin on her crown and drawing her close again. Margot stood there for a moment, recalling what she had learned in the last day about magic as she let him hold her, and then a thought popped into her mind.

When you need answers.

"You think getting really drunk would help?" she asked, her lips brushing his shirt as she spoke. "I mean, you said it was magic wine."

Ash released her slowly, eyes wide as he looked at her. He found his voice again, apparently able to answer her on this point. "Are you sure, Margot? Perhaps these are answers you do not want to hear."

"I think the time for what I want or don't want has come and gone," she told him. "I think it's what I need."

"What do you need, Go?" he asked, his voice husky as his eyes skipped down to her lips.

You.

The thought was instant, familiar, consuming, but she knew better than to say it. *Not yet,* she told herself. *Not now.*

Why the hell not? A part of her demanded answers while another just wanted him to keep looking at her like she was the only woman in the world for him, the only one he wanted to touch.

Because I know better, she reminded herself. She had seen the groupies who stalked him afterward, the ones who grew desperate in their need to bask in his attention one more time, the emptiness in their eyes as they slowly realized he would never look at them again. *I will not become one of them.*

She wondered how much of his sex appeal was due to his fae nature. She wondered if being with him was like some kind of fae drug, his magic somehow stealing a part of his partners' soul, sparking their need for him. She had worked with the police on more than one stalking case, filing restraining orders as his groupies became too determined to see him again. Both Timothy and Nik had their share of stalkers, but none so frenzied as Ash's former partners.

"I need more," she said finally.

"More what?" he asked, still giving her that hungry look.

She slowly lifted his arms from her body, stepping away from him. "More than you can give," she said simply. "And I want to know why." She moved quickly, not wanting to see his reaction to her words, ignoring the tingle of frustration that spilled from him.

Leaning down, she opened the small fridge and retrieved the bottle from the back. She stepped over to the back wall of her kitchen, and while she didn't have any wine glasses—or any glasses at all, actually—she did have two coffee mugs, and she handed one to Ash, settling herself cross-legged on the floor with the bottle before her.

"Okay," she said, studying the wax seal. "Is there a trick to this or what?"

Ash mimicked her position on the floor, then set the blue mug down next to the bottle. "Are you sure about this?" he asked. "Last time, it got ... intense."

"I am," she said, lifting the bottle to the light. "Are you?"

He nodded.

"Good," she said, then used the edge of her nail to break the seal, folding up the wax and opening the bottle. A glorious scent filled the air, sweet and seductive but without the bitter undertone she associated with wine. She poured a small amount into his mug, then the same into her own. She set the bottle on the floor, then raised her mug to his. As they clinked, she said, "To answers."

The first few sips were divine, and soon, Margot forgot why she was slowing herself down, refilling both her and Ash's mugs without thought.

"I guess," she pondered after a long sip, "I just never had good wine before?"

"This isn't ordinary wine," Ash told her. "This is powerful stuff." He took another sip, then cocked his head at her. "You've really never had a wine you enjoyed?"

Margot shook her head. "Not at all." She sighed, recalling the long nights spent sitting at bars, surreptitiously watching Ash in the mirror, waiting for him to leave with his companions before she headed back to her bus, alone. Well, she didn't always leave alone—but usually. "I tried a few and settled on rum and soda."

Ash's eyes widened in shock and surprise. "How boring, Go! Next time we're at the bar, I'll get you some drinks. We'll find something you like."

Margot held up her almost empty mug. "It won't matter. Nothing will ever be as good as this, will it?"

Ash looked at her for a long time, weighing her words, and she refused to look away. "Nothing," he said finally, the words coming out thick and purposeful, as though he had to pull them from his throat, "will ever be as good as you, Margot."

"I'm not that good," she replied, assuming he was referring to her "good girl" status when compared to the debauchery of the rest of the band.

"No," he agreed. "You're perfect. I hate that I can't be with you."

"Why can't you be with me?" she asked, the question she kept asking escaping yet again.

Ash hesitated, took another sip that drained his mug, and set it on the ground. Margot refilled it, waiting for him to find his words.

"I am under a spell," he said, the words coming easily, and a huge grin split his face. He reached for the mug anew, taking another sip. He looked up to the roof of the bus and held the mug out as if in salute. "Thank you, Aunt Maddie."

Margot smiled at the mention of her aunt. Though she wasn't actually Ash or Timothy's blood relative,

Maddie had taken them in and accepted them both as her own—as she had done for her niece.

"What kind of spell?" Margot prompted, not sure how long the magic would let him speak and eager to get as much information as she could.

"A family oath," he replied, eyes alight as the words came easily. "When they took Tobin, my father made me swear fealty to him alone, so it couldn't happen to me."

"He Claimed you then?"

Ash shook his head. "No. Parents cannot Claim their children. There's loyalty there, of course, but Claiming is something else."

"And oaths? How do they play into this?"

Ash sighed, clearly organizing his thoughts. "Claiming is a life-long commitment, a promise to obey an individual and actively promote their agenda in all things. It's like getting your dream job and doing everything you can to keep it, to keep your boss or whatever powers that be, happy with your work."

"That doesn't sound awful," Margot said. She thought of the way Tobin spoke of his Lord, distantly respectful. But Tobin was definitely vocal about his dislike of Claiming in general. Margot wondered how much freedom was allowed within the bond.

"You can't ever break the connection," Ash told her. "And you won't want to. That's what makes it so awful. You lose your free will. You forget you ever wanted anything else."

Margot frowned. "You say that like you've seen it happen," she observed. "Tobin?"

He nodded. "Before he was taken, Tobin and I were close. We both swore we'd find a way to avoid the Claiming, often joking we'd just Claim each other if that meant nothing would change. It's illegal, of course, to create a household of two, but we were already loyal to one another." He took a deep breath, running a hand through his shaggy hair. "But after he was Claimed by Rebinus... he was different."

"It made him loyal to Rebinus?"

"Yes, but that wasn't what made it terrible. He didn't *mind* that he was Claimed by Rebinus. The brother I knew would have fought back."

Margot nodded, knowing that much was true. Tobin didn't seem to mind his Claim that much. It was her getting Claimed that he disliked—if it wasn't by Ash. She peered at the lead singer in her bus. "So you saw him again after he was taken?"

Ash nodded. "He may tell you he was kidnapped or taken, words implying violence or even legal recourse in this world, but in our world, he had been fairly captured. Our father had been careless and left him vulnerable—a mistake he would not make again as you can see. But there was a ceremony, and I was permitted to attend. The brother I saw before the Claiming and after were not the same person."

"I'm sorry," Margot whispered, trying not to think of how much her mother had changed in those last months when the sickness really got its claws in her, how the mom she had known faded into a memory. "That must have been terrible."

"I don't want your pity, Go," he insisted. "It is Tobin who deserves compassion for what he suffered."

"I'm still confused," Margot said, focusing on the oath instead. "How does this oath protect you and prevent you from Claiming someone?" Margot took another sip, refilling their mugs again. She knew she ought to slow down, but the flood of information was too tantalizing. She had longed for Ash to give her straight answers since the day they met. Sure, he would tease her and offer comfort in extremity, but he had never been so open, so willing to share himself with her.

"A family oath ensures that my loyalty remains with my father. It limits my focus, meaning..." His voice trailed off as he gave her a long look.

"Meaning you can't be devoted to anyone else," she finished for him. "Does that mean you *can't* Claim anyone or you *shouldn't* Claim anyone?"

He tilted his head. "Being sworn to my father—and hidden among the humans—makes it very unlikely that another fae would try to Claim me—if I even can be Claimed." He looked surprised as the last few words came out, then glanced at the mug in his hand and put it carefully on the ground.

"Putting a pin in that possibility," Margot said, mirroring him and putting her own mug down. She let him shift the focus, address the rest of what he had said. "Why is it unlikely another would try? I get the impression your father is powerful—and you. Why wouldn't someone try to get you?"

"My father is quite powerful in our world. That's why Tobin was taken. He certainly has abilities that Rebinus has found useful. But anyone who tried to Claim me would earn my father's anger, first, but also, if they weren't much stronger than I am, they wouldn't be able to countermand the oath."

"So other fae must do this oath thing, then, right?" Margot pried, trying to understand.

"Only the truly powerful among us. It wouldn't matter for a lesser fae. It may bind them in some ways, but the Lord would only overcome it in the Claiming."

"A powerful fae … like you," she repeated. "Ash, what can you do?"

"I can make you smile," he said quickly, and Margot felt her cheeks warm as she returned his grin. "See?"

"I'm being serious," she said, slapping at his arm. Her voice sounded a bit off to her ears, a tiny bit like a radio warbling in and out or range. She knew there were other questions she should be asking, but she stared at him instead. "Can you fly?"

He nodded.

"But you don't have wings."

"Not like this, I don't," he said, moving his arms and shoulders as he looked down at his body. At the words, he slapped his hand over his mouth, eyes wide as he stared at her. Margot wasn't going to let him go, not when he was finally so vulnerable before her.

"How do you fly, Ash?"

His hands moved a tiny bit, his mouth visible between his splayed fingers. The words kept spilling out. "When I transform, I can fly. But in truth I don't need to. I can simply will myself other places."

Margot decided to ignore the idea of willing herself from one spot to another for the moment and sat up on her knees, leaning closer to him, focusing on the other thing he had said. "Transform into what, Ash?"

Chapter 20
Love and Seduction

When it seemed like he actually wouldn't answer, eyes wide as some deep-seated secret inside struggled to remain hidden, a surge of guilt rushed over Margot. Here she was forcing him to tell her things he clearly didn't want shared. She was fine with using the wine to loosen his words about things she needed to know—the Claiming, her abilities, his fae world—but his secrets weren't hers to pillage. His lips moved, but she slammed her hand over his mouth, blocking him from speaking.

"I don't want to know things you don't want to tell me," she insisted. "Tell me what you can't tell me without magic wine, and the rest is yours. You have the right to your secrets."

"I've never told anyone," he whispered when she removed her hand. "Even Timothy doesn't know."

"Tell me about Timothy, then," she encouraged, shifting the conversation to safer ground. "He's some kind of bodyguard?"

"He's mine," Ash said simply.

"Yours? What does that mean?"

"I Claimed him when we were children. He's always been with my family."

"Wait." Margot held up her hands. "You already Claimed someone?"

"Years ago, yes. Before I was in hiding. Before the oath. Before Rebinus took Tobin and everything changed." Margot nodded, but her face still showed her confusion. "Go," Ash said, raising an elegant eyebrow, "you didn't think we could only Claim one person, did you?"

Margot paused, realizing that she had thought exactly that. The math of it all made her brain fizzle under the effect of the wine. "Shh," she told him, embarrassed. "I realize what you're saying. Of course you would all Claim more than one person, especially those Lords you talked about. They must be at the top of the food chain. Pyramid." She paused, images of the food pyramid in a textbook her mom had used to teach her suddenly filling her mind. "Pyramid scheme," she muttered, the wine starting to kick, and she shook her head, willing the effects of the liquor away as her mind skipped ahead to another topic. "Has your father Claimed many people?"

"The household, mostly, are under his protection, and a few lesser fae here and there."

"But no one Claims him, your father, I mean?"

"He's a Lord," Ash explained. "To be a Lord, you remain Unclaimed."

"How many Lords are there?"

"Right now?" Ash thought about it. "When I left, there were five." He held up his first finger. "My father, Lord Novus." Another two fingers—ring finger and pinky. "Lord Alick and Lord Kristoff. They give us the most trouble." Another finger—the thumb this time.

"Lord Tennere. He's not as involved, or he wasn't a few years ago. Generally kept to himself." A final finger— the middle one now. "And Lord Rebinus. He's trouble. He keeps building his power, Claiming new talents. He would have tried to Claim me, were it not too risky as a direct act against my father. He may have subdued a ten-year-old Tobin, but he would find me a bit more challenging. Especially now."

Margot nodded. "I want to ask you about that, but I won't. I will accept that you are strong and have secrets of your own. That's your business. My business is what I'm supposed to do now that I've Manifested or what-ever." She paused, staring into space, seeing Tobin's worried face from last night. "I think that's what Tobin is afraid of—that Rebinus will Claim me." She frowned. "Is he really that bad?"

Ash clearly wanted to say yes, but he held back. She could see the effect of the wine in his expression, the loose grin on his lips, the way his eyes occasionally slid from her face to her body. "Lord Rebinus Claimed Tobin—and Tobin's still alive."

"How encouraging," Margot commented.

Ash reached out to touch her hand, pulling it close to his body. "It is encouraging. He may not be the boy I knew, but Tobin is powerful now. Respected. Safe. He would do what he could for you."

"While his weird power-hungry Lord rapes me," Margot said sadly, the enormity of the Claiming sinking in.

"It wouldn't be ... rape," Ash argued. "You... you wouldn't mind."

"I wouldn't?" she echoed. A hot flare of anger spiked in her chest. "You presume to tell me what I want?"

"It's magic, Go," he defended. "It's not like some stranger grabbing you in an alley." He frowned, looking down at her hand in his. She could feel the calluses on his fingertips against her palm. "He will seduce you. That's how he works." He sighed, stroking her hand. "He's quite good at it."

"Maybe I won't be seduced," she insisted. "Maybe I don't want some stranger."

"You want Tobin," he said bluntly, eyes lifting from her hand to her face. "He's a stranger."

"Is he, though?" She pursed her lips. Tobin was Claimed by Lord Rebinus, so anything he did or said would be in the Lord's best interest. She knew it probably meant he was helping her to gain favor for his master, but she didn't care. Tobin sparked something deep inside, something she wasn't willing to dismiss easily—even if he did have shady motives. "He seems so familiar to me, Ash. Does that mean something?"

"Could mean a lot of things," Ash admitted, voice deepening. "We have many magical possibilities: a spell, a kinship, a Connection. Perhaps he's your soulmate."

She smacked him with her other hand, and he caught that hand too, adding it to his lap as he tugged her closer. "Why does it have to be magic?" she asked. "Maybe I just like him because I like him."

"That's also possible," Ash admitted, giving her hands another soft tug, and she leaned into him, her feet nearly kicking over the mugs and bottle as she climbed onto his lap. "I like that option."

"That I just like Tobin without magic?" she echoed. "Why do you like that one?"

"Because it means I have a chance, Go," he said, wrapping her in his arms. She settled her legs around his hips, hooking her feet behind his back to secure herself atop him.

"A chance for what?" she pressed, looking directly into his eyes. Ash wasn't much taller but sitting like this on his lap gave her enough height to see eye-to-eye.

"To change your mind," he said, hand abandoning her back to slide along her cheek.

"Change my mind to what?" she asked, a little breathless, the wine making her body warm, and his touch making her hot.

"To me," he said and leaned down to kiss her. Margot stopped him, putting her hand between their lips.

"Don't you dare, Ashton Stonewall," she hissed, leaning back and regaining her senses.

"Dare to kiss you?" he asked. "I've been longing to do this for years, Go." He leaned in again, confident her obvious attraction would overwhelm her refusal.

"No," she said, and he stopped at the word. "Don't you dare pretend you don't know how I feel about you."

"How do you feel about me?" he asked.

Margot felt the wine surge in her, but she didn't need the magical aid to confess. "I love you," she admitted. "I've loved you since I first saw you—and you know it, so don't pretend you're some lovesick boy now. I know better."

Ash narrowed his eyes, then he grabbed both of her hands in one of his and held them above her head, trapping her on his lap. She started to move, to unwrap herself from him, but his other hand was touching her face again, cupping her cheek. "But I am a lovesick boy," he insisted. "I've wanted you for a long time." He leaned forward, resting his face against her neck, moving her shirt aside to leave a gentle kiss on her collarbone.

"Liar," she moaned. "I bet you say that to all the girls."

He jerked her hands up, and she opened her eyes to look at him. His stare was intense. "I never lie about love," he said fiercely. "And I never lie to you, Margot."

"So what then? You saying you love me?" she challenged.

"Of course I love you," he replied. "I just can't have you."

Chapter 21

Accidental Claimings

Margot wanted nothing more than to dissolve into Ash's embrace, to taste what she had been longing for, but something held her back. She still needed answers.

"You can't have me," she repeated, "because you think Claiming me would break your oath and move your loyalty away from your family—"

"To you," he emphasized.

"And leave you open for those other Lords to Claim instead."

Ash sobered, his immediate ardor doused by her clinical summary of his situation, and he lowered her arms, his strong hand still clutching both of hers between their bodies. He seemed to debate for a moment, but it wasn't the wine in him—though that was still very much present. She could see it in his flushed cheeks and red lips.

"I don't know if I can be Claimed, Margot," he said, staring at her hands in his. "If it were just me, I would be willing to risk it to be with you, to protect you." He slowly lifted her hands again, easily moving her off his lap, a display of physical strength that sent a surge of heat into Margot's belly. "I'm strong now, and while the oath does protect me, it's more for my father." He looked at her, imploring as he let her down, though he didn't release her hands, tugging both over his head and behind his neck so she held him between her arms now. "With my mother gone, my father is all alone. He has allies, but I cannot abandon him."

"Where is your mother?" she asked, fingers playing with the small curls at the base of his neck, losing herself in the silky tendrils she had always longed to caress. "Do you know?"

"I think she might have gone home," he said wistfully.

"Where is she from? Not your home?"

"Denham Island," he answered.

"We'll be there next month," she said, recalling the tour schedule. "I didn't think a fae Queen could be from Ardon," she mused. "Or is it fae Lady?"

"Queen," he confirmed. "Lady is what we call someone who Claims those beneath her."

Margot tried to keep the terminology straight, but it was blurring in her wine-haze. She wanted to ask what they called the male fae who Claimed others but were in turn Claimed but decided it didn't matter. Ash had told her what he hadn't been able to. She may get more answers tonight, but the important part was the reason Ash couldn't and wouldn't Claim her. The hardest part was that she understood his reason, respected it. It didn't make her heart hurt less, though. She let her mind wander, wondering what Ash's mother was like.

"You think she'll come see you? Does she know where you are and what you are doing?"

"I think so?" he guessed. "But I'm not sure, and my father never told me."

She nodded. "I get family loyalty," she said. "I understand that. And though it took magic wine for you to tell me, I'm glad you did."

"I couldn't tell you," he insisted. "The magic will not let me say the words. I can't write it down or communicate it in any way." His face darkened. "And I can't be made to reveal it. The others know I am protected by powerful magic. They don't know what kind of magic, or they would be hard at work to break it. This way, I am protected and hidden until my father calls for me."

"When do you think he will call?" she asked, a sharp pain cutting deep inside at the idea of Ash going home one day, disappearing without a trace back to his own world.

He shrugged, body moving beneath her in a delicious display of hard muscles and soft skin. Margot was very aware of the heat of him touching her.

"Where is your home?" she asked. "Are all fae in Ardon?"

He shook his head. "No, we live in a parallel world: Lorellon. There are connection points between the two worlds, hence the fae who wander this world with the other creatures here."

"Other creatures?" she asked, tilting her head as she considered the possibilities.

"Oh yes," he said, giving her a wicked grin. "This world is mostly humans, but also shifters, vampires, demons, witches, and other unspeakable creatures I'd rather not mention."

"Oh. Great. Like I didn't have enough to worry about."

"You're fae, Margot. They would not dare."

"I'm weak fae," she grumbled. "Apparently, I'm a target for everyone."

Ash caught her face, lifting her chin so she looked at him. "You are not weak, Margot. You are new, but you are most definitely not weak."

"How are you so sure?" she snapped, tugging his hand from her face.

"You learned how to fly in one day. You figured out your glamour on your own."

"So what? You said yourself that it's not enough. That some Lord will show up and Claim me, and it won't matter what I learn to do."

"I want you to fight, Go," he said earnestly. "I want you to have a choice."

"And I can't choose you," she said wistfully. He opened his mouth, but she put her finger over his lips. She reached behind her to where the abandoned wine bottle still sat on the floor. Pulling it over, she took a long drink from the bottle, then offered it to him. He accepted, drinking straight from the bottle as she had before setting it on the desk.

"Tell me," she said, "what do you think my odds are of avoiding a Claiming?"

"Don't ask me that," he said, leaning down to rest his head on her shoulder. "I want you to have a choice," he said again.

"Do you love me?" she asked against his hair. "Is that the truth?"

He looked up, eyes soulful and everything she had always wanted. "You know it is."

"I'm glad," she said, "that you told me. Was that the wine too? You couldn't say it before?"

He shook his head. "I probably could have said it," he admitted. "But why would I? It would only hurt you."

"And this doesn't hurt me? Telling me you love me but can't be with me?" She leaned down, her forehead touching his. "I wonder if it was easier to just want you from a distance and not know any better."

"You still do not know any better, Go," he whispered. "Surely you knew how I felt before now? The only thing you've learned tonight is why I couldn't act on it."

"I didn't know," she told him. "I wished and I hoped, but I didn't know." She sighed, hands sliding down his arms and back up again to rest on his shoulders, feeling the lines of his body through his shirt. "Yet you're here," she said. "Shouldn't we ... not be this close?"

"Why?" he asked, his hands trailing down her sides to cup her hips. "You feel so good to me, Go."

"You said that Claiming didn't have to be about sex," she blurted, the wine giving her courage, "though for someone my age, it probably would be."

"With Lord Rebinus, it would be," Ash corrected.

"Is it something that happens spontaneously? Like, could you accidentally Claim someone?"

Ash's gaze snapped up. "No," he said seriously. "Claiming is quite intentional."

"So there's no chance of you Claiming me if you didn't want to?" Margot asked, needing to know how far she could push this.

Ash did not miss her intention, eyes flicking to her lips again as his hands tightened on her hips. "No," he said. "I cannot accidentally Claim you."

"Good," she said, then leaned forward to kiss him, claiming his mouth as she had longed to do for so long.

Chapter 22

New Uses for an Old Bed

Ash Stonewall was an amazing kisser, but Margot had expected that. He wouldn't have a devoted following of women hoping for another chance if he wasn't. Still, the touch of his mouth on hers, finally, stole her breath and curled her toes in all the best ways.

"Margot," he moaned against her mouth when they paused. "Where did you learn to kiss like that?"

"I told you I'm not a virgin," she told him, hand curling in his hair and jerking his mouth back down to hers.

He broke the kiss, mouth moving as if to ask the question, "Who?" but she stopped him. "You want to talk about other people right now, Ash?"

"No," he agreed, leaning back in to kiss her. She was surprised by his strength when he moved beneath her, easily climbing to his feet as she wrapped her legs around his waist. He glanced around the small bus, clearly trying to figure out where to put her. "Go," he said, head moving from side to side as he considered the options; small fridge and tiny counter on his right where the door was, her bunk bed and the bathroom to his left, the small counter that served as her desk and storage area splitting the space below. He even turned around, glancing down at where her chair swiveled in the floor and over to the reversed passenger seat. "Where do you bring people?"

"Not here," she admitted. "I go to their place."

He raised an eyebrow, a challenge in his voice. "You've never brought anyone back to your trailer?"

"Not since high school," she told him, and his eyes narrowed.

"Who were you fooling around with in high school?" he demanded. At her raised eyebrow, he broke off, shaking his head. "Nevermind." He glanced at the door, then shook his head. "It's too damn cold outside."

"You can't keep us warm?" she teased.

"I could," he said, "but I don't want to be distracted by anything else right now."

"Oh, so making fireballs is not something you can do on autopilot?" she asked, laughing as he spun and rested her upper back against the side rail of her bed.

"It does require a tiny amount of concentration," he said, bracing his hips beneath her.

Margot ran her hands through his hair, hooking her feet at the ankles and relaxing into his hold. "Then don't," she said. "I want all of your concentration tonight."

She kissed him again, loving the freedom of it.

"Are you sure?" he asked her, eyes dark and wide as the words caressed her lips. "You want me?"

"I've always wanted you, Ash," she assured him.

"But I can't—"

"I know," she said quickly. "No more about that." She caught his mouth again, hungry, hands sliding deep into his hair and around his back, greedy fingers starting to slide his shirt up. "We can have this," she insisted. "Just this."

"Just this," he agreed, then leaned back and, balancing her against the bed, grabbed the collar of his shirt, tugging it over his head. His skin was warm and tan, his arms covered in tattoos of dragons inked in red and black and a swirl of fire. She traced the lines, studying the art close up in a way she never had before.

"Why dragons?" she asked suddenly.

"What?" he asked, leaning over to tug on her shirt. Margot leaned back, giving him access, and sat forward as the shirt slid up her back.

"Dragons," she repeated. "Why not some other mythical creature? I hear centaurs are pretty hot right now. Or even fae…"

He paused, peering down at her, leaving her shirt where it was bunched up under her breasts. "Margot," he said sternly, "centaurs are not hot. Ever."

She laughed, wondering what centaur stories he could tell her, but she was recalling something else Tobin had said about Ash's mother, about dragons, about Denham Island in particular. "Dragons," she said again, the lust haze fading for a moment. "Ash, are you—?"

He didn't let her finish, lifting her up and sliding her onto her bed, her back secure on the mattress while he held her lower body in space. "See, this I can work with," he said, then grabbed her waist, fingers catching the edge of her yoga pants. He slid them down slowly, deliberately, pausing to rest each foot on his shoulder as he tugged them free of her legs. Margot leaned up on her elbows, the high ceiling of the bus giving her enough room to maneuver, then looked down her half-naked body at him.

She narrowed her eyes as he tossed her pants aside and stepped closer, her knees bending over his shoulders. "This seems like avoiding the question, Ash—" she began, emphasizing his fiery name, but he stopped her words with a long kiss, fingers working magic in ways that had her squirming immediately. "That's cheating," she moaned, gripping the edge of the bed as he chuckled, his movements growing more determined. When she was close, he lifted his face, fingers still moving, and grinned up at her. "You want me to stop?" he asked.

"No," she moaned.

"You don't want your answers?" he pressed, leaning down to kiss her again. She shuddered, his guitarist's fingers strumming every note in her body.

"I—" she managed, but he was between her legs again, and all coherent thought fragmented into a wave of pleasure that buried her beneath it.

When Margot returned to herself, she opened one eye to look down at where Ash still stood between her thighs. "I—" she started, then tried again. "I can't believe I never thought to use this bed like this."

Ash grinned at her, raising an eyebrow. "I thought you didn't bring anyone back here," he reminded her, hands slowly beginning to move again. "Now who has secrets?"

"Secrets are fine," she allowed, closing her eyes again as the pleasure built. She managed to open her eyes and look down at him. "But no lies," she demanded, shuddering again.

"No lies," he agreed, his breath warm on her sensitive skin. Her leg jerked, a muscle spasm catching her off guard, and she stretched her body, releasing tight muscles.

"I have to move," she told him. Up on her elbows, she considered. "You coming up here or am I coming down there?"

"I always wondered how much room you had up there," he said, helping her slide fully onto the bed and twist so she was laying in the right direction. He hopped up after her, shoulders hunched as his feet hit the wall of the bathroom and his head nearly hit the wall of her small closet at the head of the bed. "Hmm," he considered. "I don't know about this. My bunk is much bigger."

"The rock star can't figure it out?" she teased. "Let me help you think it over." She reached down to find the waist of his pants and began working the button and zipper. The jeans let go immediately, and she reached inside, happy to find only Ash. "Of course," she sighed. "You would be perfect in every way."

They spent the next few minutes giggling as they twisted on the small bed, Margot finally freeing Ash of his pants and getting him to lay on his back. They tossed her pillow to the floor and discovered if Ash reclined with his head a few inches from the wall, he could lay flat with his feet reaching the wall on the far side. "Margot," he said, eyes half-lidded as she touched his body, "you really need a bigger bed."

"Why?" she asked. "It's normally just me in here." She playfully smacked his hip, her other hand working slowly up and down.

"It's a bit ... cramped."

"You want to leave?" she prompted, leaning down to take him in her mouth. He groaned, eyes closed as he bit his lip. Margot smiled, returning to her task with renewed vigor.

"Fuck!" he yelled a few minutes later, grabbing her head to keep her steady. "You need to stop that—"

"Or what?" she goaded, her breath misting his wet skin. He shuddered.

"Or I'm going to have to do this," he said, pushing her up the bed and onto her back as he flipped over onto his knees. His elbow hit the ceiling, and he cursed, but then situated himself between her legs, hands on either side of her waist. He looked down at her tenderly and kissed her, pressing his body close to hers. Margot wrapped her legs around his hips, loving the contradictions of hard muscle and soft skin against her body. When he finally pushed into her, she groaned, biting his lip as the passion built between them, the heat of their skin scorching as he moved. They held one another close, making love with sweet words and muffled curses as they shifted and bumped into walls. The attraction that pulled them together finally realized, Margot lost herself in his arms, his mouth, his body, and Ash seemed to savor each gasp, every groan, memorizing the lines of her body.

Hours later, he lay on his back again, Margot tucked neatly under his arm as the faint light of the morning sun slipped into the bus. His hand was idly tracing symbols on her bare back, and she shifted, adjusting so she rested her chin on her hands as she looked up at him.

"Ash," she said, mind clear and full of questions again, "what does the symbol on my back mean?"

Chapter 23
Family Ties

Morning, Friday, February 20th

Morning, Friday, February 20th
in Margot's Bus in Kerva Point Park in
Kerva, Armav

Ash sighed, arms moving awkwardly in the small space. "I hoped you wouldn't ask," he admitted, and she heard the last of the wine in his voice.

"But that's what started all of this. Tonight." She grinned. "Last night, I mean." He shifted beneath her, and she moved with him like a ship on familiar seas. She didn't look away from his face, needing to hear all of it.

I can take it, she assured herself. *I've taken in a lot of changes without breaking—even the possible loss of my free will. This will be one more detail to add to the pile.* She took a deep breath, relishing the feel of his body beneath her, finally hers to explore as she wanted. "Tell me."

His hand slid up her back to trace the curve of her head. "It's a family mark," he said bluntly. "For Lord

Tennere." He glanced down at her small kitchen. "You want coffee? I want coffee." He moved out from beneath her, sliding out of bed and hopping down to the floor. She remained where she was, enjoying the sight of his bare bottom as he walked over to her small kettle and began filling it from the water jug beneath the sink.

He ducked into her bathroom for a minute, and Margot climbed out of bed with less grace than she usually managed, abused muscles protesting as she moved. She grabbed a long t-shirt from the small bin at the base of her tiny closet, sliding it over her head and trying to subdue her love-tangled hair. There was a soft thump from the bathroom followed by a low curse, and she smiled. Her bathroom was small, even for someone her size—but it was hers and it worked just fine. She had enough room to stand in front of the toilet and enjoy the shower.

As long as my wings never pop out when I'm in there, she thought. *That could get awkward.* She yawned, and when the door opened, she and Ash exchanged places, him leaning down to kiss the top of her head as she passed, the gesture familiar and exciting in ways Margot knew better than to get used to.

As she closed the bathroom door, she reminded herself of all the reasons she had never truly pursued Ashton Stonewall. He was a manwhore, for one, sleeping with different women, and some men, in every city. He was a rock star. He may have said he loved her—*He loves me!*—but it didn't really matter. She was still not good enough for him. Not enough for him. She could hear him in her kitchen, opening the little cupboard to set up the coffee in the pour-over carafe. Of course he knew where everything was—he'd helped her set up this place years ago. Before he was the lead singer of Stone Dragons. Back when he was just Ash and everything she wanted in life.

That seems like a lot, she told herself. *Is he really everything you want in life?*

I don't know. Yes. And no.

She shook her head, running a brush through her hair and quickly brushing her teeth before stepping back into the living space.

Ash had two mugs ready for the brewing coffee, the liquid slowly sieving through the cloth filter. He had put on his pants, and she missed the familiarity of his naked body. "Thanks," she said, nodding at the coffee, very aware that she wasn't wearing pants and he wasn't wearing a shirt. As if sensing her mood, Ash gently tugged her close, wrapping her in his arms as he leaned against the edge of the sink.

"I'm not hungover," she commented, noting the relaxed and content feel of her body in his arms.

"Me either," Ash agreed.

"I thought you got sloppy drunk the last time you drank Maddie's wine?" she prompted.

"I did. But I was very young then. Maybe it's just not meant for teenagers."

Margot recalled seeing them stumble back into the bar, Ash throwing up on his friends. "Did you tell Nik?" she asked. "Did the wine let you tell him the truth?"

He nodded. "But Nik was already ... different. He needed to know."

She sighed. "And I didn't." Before he could say anything, she hugged him tighter. "It's fine. I get it." They said nothing for a moment, his hands sliding lower until they moved beneath the shirt to caress her back, eventually hitting the spot where her new mark was.

"It wasn't there before," she said, recalling their conversation. She had a bad feeling about where this was going, but like everything that had happened since wings first popped out of her back, she couldn't stop it. She added, "It's not like I always had a birthmark."

"I know," he said. "I've seen you in a bathing suit, Margot." His hand slid over the space between her shoulder blades where the mark was—the same place where her wings sprouted when she called them. She shivered, trying not to think of her skeleton, the way her body shifted with magic, defying the laws of physics and gravity and biology.

"I didn't think you were looking," she told him.

"I am always looking," he declared, then he leaned down to kiss her. A few long breathless moments later, they finished dressing their coffee—sugar for her, a splash of milk for him—and moved to sit down. She sat in her normal swivel chair, and Ash sat on the floor before her, his mug on the ground beside his knee.

"Why is the mark here now?" she asked, continuing the conversation.

"It appeared when you Manifested," he explained, taking a sip of his coffee. He looked a little embarrassed, and added, "So everyone knew where you should go ... until..."

"Yeah, yeah," she said, reaching for her own mug. "We know that's not happening. I'm not running to some fae to hide. I'm staying right here." She took another sip. "Does it help—going to a family? Does it prevent Claiming?"

Ash shrugged. "Depending on the family, perhaps, but it's not a long-term solution. Just long enough to get one's affairs in order, say any goodbyes…"

"Tobin and Timothy were Claimed as children. Is that common? Or does it happen later in life like me? Can a person have a normal life and have to leave it behind when they Manifest?" The idea was shocking that a society could function that way.

"Young Claimings are more common," Ash explained, sipping his coffee, "or arranged Claimings. But yes, sometimes people don't Manifest until later, after they have some life established."

"Do some fae just not Manifest at all?"

He nodded. "Yes. Not everyone is officially Claimed but those who aren't generally don't have much power in our world. They usually serve a Lord anyway, though without the magic."

"Such a weird concept," Margot mused. "Everyone having a specific place." She thought of her own life, mostly wandering with her mother, seeing new places but never calling one home—besides the bus.

The caffeine and conversation cleared some of the morning-after haze from her brain, and Margot moved slowly side to side in the chair, her thinking movement. She spied the wine bottle, mostly empty, abandoned on her desk, and grabbed it. She handed it to Ash.

"Do we keep it?" she asked as he shook the bottle to reveal the few remaining inches at the bottom.

"Can't hurt," he said, rolling up a cloth napkin as a makeshift stopper before he put it back in her fridge. Margot frowned, legs pushing her this way and that as she tried to recall what he had told her the night before.

"Tennere," she repeated, then held out her thumb, mimicking his motion. "He was the odd man out, the distant one. The not-threatening one."

"Lord Tennere is plenty threatening," Ash warned. "But he poses no threat to you." He chuckled. "Not many can claim that honor—to be safe from Tennere."

"Not you?" she asked.

"Meh," he said. "I'm definitely not topping his list of enemies—my family, I mean. But we're not allies either. Tennere and my father have sparred often enough."

"So my mother and Maddie—they were part of the Tennere family?"

"No. Your mother was an Atherton."

Margot frowned, recalling the names. She looked at the ceiling, as if they were written there, lifting a finger for each. "Your father, Lord Novus?" At his nod she continued, "Alick and Kristoff, the troublemakers of the moment. Tennere, the odd man out." She pursed her lips. "Then the bad one, Renulus." A pause, then she tried again, "Rebulus."

"Rebinus," he corrected.

"Yeah, that one," she agreed, pleased that her magic wine-addled brain had remembered most of it. *I suppose when people want to kidnap you and claim you, you pay attention to the details.* She frowned. "But you didn't mention a Lord Atherton?" She paused, realization sinking in as she contemplated the logistics. "Duh," she said. "Of course there would be more families—all of them nestled somewhere in the hierarchy below those five you mentioned, right? Five CEOs with everyone working for them somewhere along the line." She took in a deep breath, preparing for another hit of bad news. "So where are the Athertons?"

Ash moved his hand from side to side. "Middle. Last I knew, they served under Lord Kristoff."

"Uh oh, he's one of the bad ones." She narrowed her eyes. "So why am I marked for Tennere if my mom was one of Kristoff's? Did something shift while you've been gone?"

"No." When she didn't seem to understand, Ash looked at her carefully. He put his mug down, reaching out to cradle her face with both hands. "Your father, Margot," Ash said, his eyes sad. "Lord Tennere is your father."

Chapter 24

Catastrophic
Emotional Outbursts

Afternoon, Friday, February 20th
in Margot's Bus in Northeast Armav

Hours later, Margot stared at the road through the windshield, eyes squinting in the bright sunshine, part of her still not willing to accept what Ash had said. They had dressed quietly, neither speaking beyond necessity, the comfortable morning glow abating as Margot's spiral intensified. Ash held her for a bit, offering comfort when she stopped moving, suddenly losing her entire focus. She knew she had an idea of the next step, the next move, but suddenly, her mind was blank, everything forgotten.

It was not the first time she had lost herself this way. Ash had been there for her then, when he helped her demolish the returned bus and rebuild it. He had been the one to hand her the sledgehammer, seeming to understand her need to vent some rage in physical destruction. He had also been the one to hold her when she fell apart, allowing her time to grieve and accept her new reality in her own time.

He didn't speak, offering his bodily comfort as she needed—and obliging eagerly when she had reached up to kiss him, losing herself in him again. For all the obstacles that lay between them, Ash understood the silent longing inside Margot, giving what she needed without needing to ask.

Is that why it took a magic bottle of wine for us to actually get together? she wondered, stealing a glance at Ash who sat in the passenger seat, face blank as he watched the road ahead. *We needed words to finally admit how we feel? Words neither of us can say.*

Now that the effects of the wine had passed, she was wondering if the forthright Ash she had known last night would vanish into the distant, silent one she recalled. He hadn't seemed to mind her invitation that morning, meeting her lust with a passion that allowed her to forget everything. She let herself recall the details, the touch of Ash's lips on her skin, his warm hands pressed hard against her back, her fingers twined in his hair while the other hand clutched his hip as she moved.

"Go!" he shouted, and she opened her eyes—not realizing she had shut them—and brought the bus back onto the road. She had only closed her eyes for a second, but it was long enough for the bus to find the road's shoulder as the highway twisted back down the mountainside, closing the distance to the Genc border.

"Sorry," she blurted.

"You okay?" he pressed. "I can drive."

"As if. I'm okay," she insisted. Part of her wanted to take him up on the offer so she could close her eyes again, recall the feel of his kiss, the press of his body beneath hers—to forget everything else he had told her and remember only the way he could make her body feel. But she knew better, knew she couldn't bury herself in her desire for Ash and ignore the truths he had revealed. And no one drove her bus but her.

"You want to talk?" he prompted.

She bit her lip, not sure how to reply. Talking had started this whole thing, hadn't it? She longed to share her confusion, to find out more, to understand this new world and her place in it.

"I don't know," she replied honestly. "I don't know what I want to say."

"What can I do?" he asked, and the openness of the question broke her.

"You can—" Margot began, tears flooding her eyes. "You—" she blinked rapidly, trying to clear her vision, but the gate had been opened, and she couldn't stop. She took her foot off the gas pedal, letting the bus slow to a stop on the side of the road. As soon as she pulled up the parking brake, Ash was there, unbuckling her seat belt and pulling her into his lap, holding her tightly as she sobbed.

Margot wasn't sure exactly why she was crying—only that if she didn't let it out, she was going to explode. Maybe it was for the loss of the life she had known, being thrust into this new threatening world; maybe it was the overwhelming knowledge that the world she had known had never been what she thought, and she had been so wrong about everything. Maybe it was finally being with

Ash—and the knowledge that he would never be hers—not really.

Amid the flood of her tears and her emotions, Margot felt something growing within her, a dazzling power that threatened to burst through her skin, and with a gasp, she sat up, knees pressed into the seat alongside Ash's thighs as she faced the back of her bus, and flung her arms out to the side as her back arched. Her right arm hit the passenger window with a loud bang at the same moment lightning cracked the sky, immediately followed by a huge crash of thunder.

Rain poured from the sky.

Margot's body heaved, and she took in a gasping breath, feeling like she had just run at top speed for long minutes. She blinked, limbs heavy, and her arms slowly fell to her sides. Ash caught her hand, the one that had hit the window, and he cradled it, keeping it from hitting anything else as she slumped down into his arms, head collapsing on his shoulder. The rain pounded on the roof of the bus, a settling sound, and for a time, Margot might have slept, lulled into comfort by the sound.

"Go," Ash said, his quiet voice creeping into her dream.

"Mmm?" she asked, still lost in a vision where she lay cradled with Ash's arms around her body, holding her possessively. She snuggled closer to him, loving how their bodies fit together.

"Margot," he said again, this time louder.

"Hmm?" she managed, slowly groping her way back to wakefulness. "What?"

"You need to stop," he said gently, one hand gently caressing the back of her head. "Let it go, baby."

"Let what go?" she mumbled, her brain slowly catching up. *Did Ash just call me baby?*

"Let it go," he repeated, hands sliding down to rub her upper arms. "Just ... stop."

"What?" she demanded, annoyed now. "What are you talking about?" She sat up, looking down at him with a scowl.

"The rain," he said slowly. "Margot, you have to stop the rain."

She glanced out the window where sheets of rain were sliding across the glass. Another bang of thunder accompanied a flash of lightning. Margot cocked her head—the storm must be right on top of them if the lightning and thunder were simultaneous. "It's just a storm," she said, weariness sneaking through her body. There was a gust of wind, and she felt the entire bus shift. Ash's hold on her became firm. "Margot," he said, sharp now. "Stop."

"I'm not doing anything!" she told him.

He reached up to grab her chin, making her look at him. His face danced and shimmered in her vision. "You ... need ... to ... stop," he said, each word clipped, her hearing dipping in and out, "or ... you ... will ... kill ... us ... both." A dark haze was encroaching on the edges of her eyesight, a low buzz beginning in her ears. She reached out to touch Ash, her palm landing solidly in the center of his chest as she tilted dangerously. "Let go," he said again, then reached out to kiss her.

His touch was soft, lips gentle, and as her mouth moved against his, she could feel the sense of draining slow down, a trickle of energy that eased and finally stopped. She shuddered against him, then sagged, all of her strength gone, and his hand guided her head back to his shoulder.

"Good," he said in the same soothing voice. "You did good." Hands patted her back as the sound of the storm outside abated, the pounding water diminishing to a summer drizzle, and then nothing.

"Rest, Margot," Ash said, tucking her close on his lap. "I've got you."

Chapter 25

Proper Hydration

Late Afternoon, Friday February 20th
in Margot's Bus in Northeast Armav

When Margot opened her eyes, every part of her body ached. She was confused for a moment, finding herself in bed and staring at the familiar ceiling of her bus. Margot could still see light filtering into the bus from outside, but it was much later in the day. She must have fallen asleep, and Ash had moved her to the bed. She was still wearing her clothes, but her blanket covered her body. A quick glance to her right showed Ash sitting on the floor below, legs crossed as he sipped from a mug.

"You're awake," he said, leaning over to open her fridge. He pulled out a bottle of water, then hopped to his feet and handed it to her. "Drink."

"Okay," she said, rolling to her side and lifting up on one elbow. "You say that like an order."

"It is an order," he said. "What you did expended a crazy amount of energy. You need water, sugar, and a load of vitamins." He gestured at the bottle. "Drink."

Margot obeyed, the water soothing her parched throat, and without realizing it, she had finished the entire bottle. She handed the empty to Ash, wiping her mouth. "What the hell?"

"Magic like that takes a lot of energy." He held out his hands. "You want to come down?"

She narrowed her eyes at him in annoyance. "I am perfectly capable of getting out of—" she started, sliding over the edge as she did every single day, when she wasn't sharing the tiny space with Ash, of course. Instead of her sturdy legs easily landing on the floor, they folded like rubber, and if Ash hadn't caught her by the hips, she would have fallen. He set her down gently in her chair.

Margot slapped her barely functioning legs. "What is wrong with me?"

"Magic overexertion," Ash said. "Conjuring a monsoon will do that. Usually it takes a dozen fae to change the weather."

"A monsoon?" she echoed, taking the can of sugary soda he held out, devouring it just as quickly. She recalled the storm in snippets, vaguely, sensing Ash's growing concern as she grew sleepy. "You think I made it rain?"

"I know you created a massive storm," he said. He gestured out the window, and Margot followed his gaze, seeing the battered landscape. She finished the soda, abandoning the can on the desk behind her, then slid forward, trying to stand but settling for shuffling on her knees as she tried to see outside.

"But it was sunny…" she said. Ash reached over and opened the door, revealing the devastated environment outside the bus. Tree branches and rocks littered the road. Part of the shoulder had been washed away entirely. Margot covered her mouth with her hands, body weaving as the enormity of the destruction set in. Ash's hand quickly settled on her shoulder, keeping her steady. "Oh wow," she managed. "I did this?" She looked at Ash. "How big was it?"

He shrugged. "I'm not sure. For a minute, I thought you'd take down the whole mountainside. Including us."

"I remember." She nodded, eyes wide as she studied the rocks thrown by fierce wind, the surviving trees along the side of the road, white where branches had been torn off. She remembered the feeling, the power rushing out of her, destroying everything in its path. "You said I would kill us both."

Ash nodded. "You nearly did."

"So what does this mean? When I get sad or mad, I cause freaking hurricanes?" Her voice rose. The idea terrified her, but thankfully, nothing stirred outside. Whatever power she had was gone, used up by the storm she had apparently conjured. Part of her heard what Tobin would have said, had he been there: *They call them typhoons here, Margot.* The idea was soothing, his imagined perspective slowing her pulse.

"No," Ash told her, leaning down to put his head next to her face. "This means you can control the weather, a very powerful gift. You just have to practice."

"This seems like a bit more than practice," she grumbled, swallowing hard. "This is too much."

"Yesterday, you taught yourself to control the glamour, and you learned to fly. I think a little storm control is minor in comparison."

Margot glanced at him, face creased in worry. "You think so? I don't want to destroy an entire ecosystem."

"You won't," he assured her, then tilted his head at her, expression gentle. "But maybe next time, you should try opening up before you explode. Just a thought."

"It's been a very stressful few days," she snapped, rubbing her face with her hands. "And you have a show tomorrow night. We need to get to Akkoy." She glanced again at the wreckage outside. She recalled feeling the bus move in the wind and not caring, knowing she was safe in Ash's arms, knowing he would protect her.

Did I really do all this? It was just a moment, she reminded herself. *I deserve to get upset for a moment. But what happens the next time I get upset?*

"Am I safe?" she asked, imagining the destruction she could cause in an open-air theatre, like the Yama Bowl in Genc or Mackie Park over in Yens. *I could kill the fans,* she thought, *without even realizing it.* She grabbed Ash's hand, needing the reassurance.

"Of course," Ash assured her, his touch gentle but firm on her shoulder. "No one will hurt you here."

"No," she said, turning to face him. "I mean, am I safe to be around people? What happens if I get frustrated with one of the crew and set off another hurricane?"

"In that case, it would likely be a tornado, especially if it's Travis," he joked, trying to lighten her mood. "You know he loves to get under your skin. A storm would definitely keep him inside the building."

"He just kills me with those smoke breaks!" she griped, appreciating the distraction, the reminder of the ordinary things in her life. "We would get set up so much faster if he could just wait until after we're done."

"Says the non-smoker," Ash observed.

Margot sighed, her bruised hand reaching out for his. "What am I going to do?" she asked.

Ash gently pulled her so she was leaning against him, supporting her weight and relieving her strained muscles. "You're going to drink this," he said, thrusting yet another drink—this one a blended green smoothie he pulled from her fridge—into her other hand. Margot wondered what she had in her fridge with which to make a drink that color, then decided not to think about it.

"So it's going to be torture by bathroom," Margot guessed, taking a sip and wincing at the overwhelming sense of green that flooded her mouth. She didn't love the taste, but her body seemed to crave whatever was in the shake, so she drank it, feeling strength steal back into her abused muscles. She held the smoothie out, tapping the cold side against her forehead as she did when she was thinking hard. "Seriously, Ash. This is too much. I don't know if I can handle it."

Ash took her hand, Margot's eyes watching as he brought it up to his mouth, kissing her palm, then gestured at her to keep drinking. "You can do this, Go," he assured her, watching as she drank the smoothie. "I know you can."

Chapter 26

Roadside Encounters

Late Afternoon, Friday, February 20th
in Margot's Bus in Northeast Armav

By the time Margot felt sturdy on her feet again, the afternoon light was waning. They had inspected the bus, making sure it hadn't sustained serious damage from the storm, but aside from a few dents in the roof—nothing new there—the bus was ready to drive again. Margot had been even more disturbed by the level of devastation surrounding them: downed trees, swaths of asphalt torn away, replaced by rivulets of dark sand, the volcanic rock sliding down the mountain.

"I feel like I should donate to the road repair crew," Margot said, settling into the driver's seat again. "This will cost a fortune to fix. I'm shocked there's even a road left to drive on."

Ash nodded but gave her a reassuring look. "That's what taxes are for, Margot. Storms affect roadways all the time. This isn't a new thing."

"No, but I literally caused it." She started the bus and checked her mirrors. Even though she was the only one who ever drove her bus, she always checked her mirrors every time she sat down in the driver's seat, a habit learned from her mother who drilled road safety into her as they traveled the other continent. "Isn't one of the reasons for the southern resistance about taxes?"

"Yeah, taxes on imports from Genc and even Arillo keep increasing, even though they mostly come via the port in Tunica. The rebels say someone in the southern government is pocketing all the extra," he explained, settling into his seat as Margot carefully pulled onto the road. Even though it wasn't yet dark, she turned on her headlights, staying well below the limit as she drove around scattered debris.

"You think we'll have any trouble at the border?" she asked. They normally crossed between provinces in Ardon without much more than showing ID cards, but Margot didn't know if the unrest had changed the normal customs.

"I doubt it," Ash said. "Tim and Nik crossed easily enough. They're already at the venue. There's a big pre-show party tonight at the Uptown Olive."

Margot gave him a quick side glance. "I'm sorry," she said.

"Why are you sorry?"

"Because you should be with them. Now all my crap is fucking up the tour." She frowned, squinting through the windshield as she followed a curve and headed sharply downhill. They seemed to be reaching the edge of the storm field. Margot was relieved—it had only covered a few miles, with her bus at the center.

"It's fine, Go. I don't love those parties anyway."

She scoffed, flipping on her bright lights since there was no one else on the road. She finished the curve to the right and turned left, continuing downhill. "Liar," she declared. "You love those things." She started to add her next thought—that Ash met most of his women at the parties both before and after their shows—but stopped speaking, squinting again as something appeared in the middle of the road ahead. "Is that—is that a person?" she asked, slowing down.

"Margot," Ash's voice was deadly quiet, "don't stop."

"What?" she asked, foot lifting from the brake but not completely, the bus still slowing as they drew near to the figure. It was tall, and wearing some kind of dark cloak, definitely not the kind of clothing to wear while standing in the middle of the road in the deepening gloom. The fading light behind it seemed to glow, the stranger soaking it up in a spot of darkness. "But we're in the middle of nowhere. We can't just leave someone stranded—"

"Margot," he insisted, "don't stop. Hit it."

"What?!" she shrieked, slamming on the brake as she turned to gawk at him. "I am not running someone over!" she declared, offended he would suggest such a thing. "Not in my bus!" she added, the afterthought the least of her reasons, but still in the list.

The bus came to a stop about fifty feet away from the figure.

"It's not a someone," Ash said. "Not anymore."

"What are you talking about?" she demanded.

"Look at it," Ash said. "Centaur's Balls, Go—That is not a person!"

Margot glanced at it again, seeing the dark cloak that had begun to flap in the non-existent wind. A cold feeling crept up her arm. "Is it a fae?" she whispered, not sure why she suddenly wanted to hide.

"It was, but not anymore. It's a faeng." Ash's voice was low and he moved slowly, unbuckling his seat belt.

"What the hell does that mean?" Margot asked, fear slicing through her chest in a cold arc.

"It means you stay here," he ordered, reaching for the door handle. She grabbed his hand. The bus lurched forward as her foot left the brake pedal, and she whirled, jamming it into park. The creature, which had been taking a slow step toward them, hesitated.

"Are you kidding me?" she asked. "Seriously, have you never seen a horror movie? Do not go out there!"

"We don't want it in here," he said reasonably. "Better to fight it out there. I don't want to wreck your bus."

"Why are you fighting it? What is happening right now?" she demanded, anger replacing her fear.

"Because otherwise it will try to Claim you, and I don't think you want that." He lifted her hand to his mouth, gave it a quick kiss, and opened the door. At her shocked expression, he repeated, "Stay here."

Feeling like an idiot, Margot watched him get out of the bus and shut the door. He strode confidently down the road in front of the creature like a dark avenging comic book hero. She had a heated debate where her hand moved to open the door and follow him and froze on the door handle.

"You have no business here, faeng," Ash said to the creature. In the eerie quiet of the last light of day, she could hear him easily through the window.

"Give us the girl," the creature hissed, its voice a mix of whisper and gravel.

"She is not for you," Ash insisted. "You know better."

"She is Unclaimed," the creature declared. "We will have her." Margot scanned the road, wondering why the creature would use the plural. Maybe it was like the royal *we*, she thought, but glimpsed movement in her mirror, a darker splotch approaching the bus from behind. She didn't hesitate, hopping out of her seat and clambering into the back of the bus, crouching next to the side door.

"She is spoken for," Ash said.

The creature made a sound that Margot recognized eventually as a laugh.

"And who are you, little one, to speak for one such as she?" the faeng asked. The faded light outside the window in the back rear window darkened, and Margot flung the door open, slamming it into the other creature who was creeping alongside the bus. There was a screech, and then the door was slammed shut, nearly hitting her in the process, the force making the entire bus rock dangerously on its wheels. Margot flailed to catch her balance and settled on the balls of her feet, waiting for the door to swing open and the other creature to come for her.

"She is ours!" the first creature shrieked, and she caught movement through the windshield. She didn't look, focusing on her own problems. A quick survey of her surroundings reminded her of the metal baseball bat she kept in the corner, a last ditch safety net if someone should get rowdy in the parking lot. Margot snatched it, teeing up for a swing when the door opened. She didn't know what a faeng was, but she imagined it wouldn't enjoy a bat to the face. She heard the scraping of nails— *Oh fuck, are those claws?*—on the outside of the door and metal thunking as it fumbled with the handle. She waited, adjusting her grip on the bat, accounting for the small space, recalling those days with the boys when they played the occasional baseball game—except back then it had been Benjamin who had sidled close to her, showing her how to hold the bat to have the strongest swing.

Okay, she thought, *I'm ready to hit one out of the park.*

Chapter 27

Dressing Monsters

There was an awful wrenching noise, and the door opened, slowly this time as the monster stayed behind it. Margot held her position, bat ready, waiting for the creature to reveal itself. There was a noise from the front of the bus where Ash was, but she ignored it, waiting for her own foe to materialize.

It's waiting for me to come out, she thought. *Like I'm an idiot.* A long moment passed, and there were several more loud noises from the front of the bus. She wanted to look, but something told her that the creature could see her somehow, sense her, and it was waiting for her to be distracted. *Ash is fine,* she told herself. *He's some uber fae prince. He's got this. Me, on the other hand...*

She ran through her newfound fae skills: wings—not super useful at the moment, glamour—pretty sure it knew what she was, and the storm—that had exhausted her. And while she wanted to destroy the creatures, especially after hearing the mangling of her poor bus, she was rethinking her decision not to run the first one over. Not yet anyway. She recalled Tobin's comment about sucking water out of bodies and wished suddenly that she had an idea how to do that—if she even could.

Another moment passed. There was a loud thump as something hit the front of the bus, and she forced herself to stare out the open door instead, not checking the front window to see who it had been.

"Oh, come on," she said finally. "You just going to hide out there? Scared of a little girl in a bus? You don't deserve to Claim me!"

There was a screech, and the creature materialized in the open door. Margot got a good look at it: the cracked and ruined remains of skin that covered what must have been a human face, the bedraggled remains of hair flowing from clumps on its skull and hanging over what appeared to be rotten clothing under a worn black cloak. It was every monster she had run from in every nightmare. A strange feeling slid up her skin, a dark push of power, and she could feel her will to fight back slipping away.

For a split second, she froze, panic seizing her muscles, but then her sweaty hands slipped a fraction on the metal bat, and she came back to herself, recalling her plan. She swung the bat, twisting her hips as much as possible in the small space, aiming for the creature's face, and was rewarded by an awful wet snapping sound as she connected. The creature tried to shriek, but she must have damaged its nose because the sound was muffled. The cloak flowed up, clearly trying to protect its head. Margot wound up and swung again, this time not as hard but glancing off the cheek as the cloak deflected her attack.

"Seriously with the magic cloak!" she yelped, using the bat as a crutch as she kicked at the creature. It hadn't expected a blow from her foot and actually moved a step away from the door. Margot winced, pain radiating up her ankle and knee. It had been like kicking the side of the bus. Ignoring the pain, she swung the bat again, not wanting the thing to get inside. Its hands were tipped with long claws, and once it gathered its senses, it wouldn't take much to slice her to pieces.

She was holding her own, but it wouldn't last. "Ash!" she squealed, kicking at the creature again as it lunged at her, a claw catching her hip and dragging a line of fire across her body. She screamed, unable to stop, and almost dropped the bat. It remained in front of her body, luckily in the right position for her to deflect the other claw as it swiped at her. "Ash," she managed, the name only a puff of air instead of a sound. Her left hand fell to her hip, pressing against the hot line as a wave of warm heat flooded down her leg.

Do something, she ordered herself, willing another power to manifest. *You're the daughter of a fae Lord— that has to mean something!* Despite her pleas to the power within, nothing happened. The faeng reeled back, winding up for another blow, and Margot turned to the side, hoping to make a smaller target, the bat held vertically before her unwounded right side. The claw swung at the space where she had been, and she stumbled back, deeper inside the van, landing hard on her swivel seat. She poked the bat at the creature still in the doorway, a futile gesture, and it climbed inside, sinewy limbs first moving onto the step, then a hand gripping the wall on its left.

"Mine," it hissed, and Margot tried to hit it with the bat. It knocked the weapon away, her fingers going numb with the force of the blow. Her hand flailed, reaching for anything she could use as a weapon, and settled on the bin of clothes tucked in the bottom of her closet. Without thinking, she clutched a handful of fabric and flung it at the creature.

A pink tank top hit it square in the head, then slid down to hang awkwardly on one clawed hand. The faeng paused, as shocked as she was, then growled and swiped the shirt away.

"Fu—" Margot managed, but an arm appeared around the faeng's neck, wrapping it in a chokehold. The body was yanked roughly from the bus, claws scraping the doorframe as it was forced away. There was another horrible screech, a crash, and then nothing.

Margot sat in stunned silence, hand still pressed against the slash on her hip, waiting for movement. When she heard more sounds of battle from the front of the bus, she staggered to her feet, using the desk for leverage, then hopped awkwardly to the doorway, hanging onto the twisted doorframe for balance. Her hip was aching fire, but she needed to know that Ash was alright.

"Ash?" she asked, leaning out to see what was going on. The pile of what had been her faeng lay a few feet away, unmoving. She looked to her right, surprised to find Ash slumped halfway down the passenger door.

"Ash!" she yelled and scrambled down, forgetting her hip as she slid to a halt next to him. He was a mess—his face swollen and streaked with blood, his light blue shirt shredded and dark with patches of blood. Another shriek made her jerk her head up, searching for what had made the sound. Hadn't Ash just saved her? Wouldn't he have finished with his faeng first?

Her questions were answered as she took in the scene before her bus. The original creature was still alive, but barely, its limbs flailing weakly in the grip of the other fae who held it aloft.

"Die," Tobin ordered, shaking the faeng once more with a force that disconnected several joints in its body. He let it drop to a pile, shaking his hand as if ridding himself of the creature's filth. Margot stared at his back, the man she recognized, knowing him deep inside somehow, and yet he was also a stranger—a terrifying fae who had held that creature up with one hand and literally shaken it to death. Her chest heaved, and she realized she had stopped breathing.

It's just Tobin, she reminded herself. *He's on your side. Thank the fucking gods,* she added.

Chapter 28

You are an Idiot

Margot closed her mouth and reminded herself to breathe. It took a second with her eyes closed to concentrate on getting air back into her body. When she exhaled a long, shaky breath, she turned her gaze to Ash.

His battered face looked up at her. "I'm so sorry," he mumbled, mouth swollen and bleeding. "I couldn't... can't..."

"Shh," she said, hands running over his shirt, trying to find the worst of the bleeding and press on it. "It's fine. We're fine."

"You are not fine," Tobin said, the fae walking over to stand next to them. "What the hell are you playing at?" he snapped, more angry than Margot had ever seen him—not that she had seen a lot of him. He scowled and knelt at Ash's side. "It would serve you right if I left you here bleeding," Tobin ranted. "Trying to take on two faeng with human means—What kind of idiot are you? Getting laid addled your mind!"

"I didn't know what else to do," Margot defended, hurt that he would attack her methods. "I got in two hits."

Tobin scanned her quickly, eyes lingering on the bloody mess of her hip and leg. "I'm not talking to you," he said quickly and returned his attention to Ash. "I'm talking to my imp-brained brother who nearly let the both of you get killed by rogues."

"I told her to run it over," Ash mumbled, eyes struggling to stay open as Tobin's hands moved over his body.

"She is a brand new fae," Tobin said, "and this bus is a classic." Margot snorted, unable to stop the sound. The hand she brought to her mouth ached in ways she didn't know possible. "You know how long it would take to get a new windshield?" Tobin touched Ash's right shoulder, and Ash groaned. "Why didn't you just use your magic, you idiot?" A soft glow encased Tobin's hand as he gripped Ash's shoulder. As Margot watched, the ragged edges of the wound slowly closed and faded, replaced by fresh skin. "You trying to show off for our girl?" Ash moaned, wincing in pain as Tobin continued to work. As soon as the shoulder wound was closed, he moved down, finding a deep gash on Ash's side and repeating the process. "You know that whole fire thing is way more impressive than getting yourself sliced into ribbons, right? The ladies love it."

He glanced at Margot as he said it. "Pardon my saying so," he said with a grin, completely ignoring Ash's obvious pain as the healing magic closed yet another wound, "but this idiot knows better."

"I ... had ... it," Ash wheezed.

"You had it," Tobin echoed mockingly. He glanced down, resting his hand on what appeared to be the last big wound on Ash's thigh. "You were doing a wonderful job bleeding out while Margot over there was fighting for her life." He shook his head, finishing the last wound and smacking Ash's leg. "If I hadn't gotten here when I did, you'd both be dead. What the hell is wrong with you?" he barked.

"Can't ... use ... powers," Ash wheezed, leaning back with his eyes closed. "Hiding."

Tobin rolled his eyes, stood up, and reached a hand out to Margot. "Let's get you fixed up," he said.

Margot eyed him suspiciously. "With your ... magic?"

Tobin shrugged. "I mean, we can use your first aid kit if you prefer, but I think magic is faster." He paused. "Though it does hurt."

"A lot," Ash said helpfully from the ground.

Margot glanced down at her hip. The bleeding had slowed, but it still burned fiercely. She knew it would start shrieking when she moved again. "I guess so?" she said weakly.

He gestured with his hand. "I need you to stand up," he said. "It wraps around most of your leg, and I can't reach it with you sitting like that." He stepped over Ash as if his brother wasn't lying on the ground wheezing. "Come, I've got you." Margot recalled seeing him lift the creature with one arm, and part of her wanted to recoil from his touch, from that kind of dangerous power.

But it's Tobin, she reminded herself. *Your side, remember?*

"Why are you helping me?" she asked bluntly.

"Because I like you," he replied immediately. "And you seem to need my help."

She glanced at Ash, who hadn't moved, and whose eyes were watching their exchange carefully. "That's not enough," she said, wincing as Tobin lifted her smoothly to her feet, holding her uninjured hand. He did it quickly, careful not to jar her leg, but it made the wound sing with pain. Margot closed her eyes, gritting her teeth. "Do it," she ordered, not wanting to lose her nerve.

"Forgive me," Tobin said, and his hand was on her hip.

Fire exploded along the line of the slash, and Margot whimpered, biting her lip hard enough to draw blood. She could feel Tobin's magic sinking into her, knitting the torn skin and muscle of her hip and leg together. It hurt as much, maybe more, than the original wound. When the healing was over, the pain replaced by a cool numbness over her waist, she sagged, and Tobin caught her easily. He reached for her wounded hand, but she jerked it back.

"It's fine," she told him, deciding that letting her hand heal on its own would probably hurt less.

Tobin sighed, but he didn't push. "I imagine I'll be driving then?"

Margot opened her mouth to tell him that no one drove her bus but her and stopped. She was in no shape for driving. Ash may be healed, but he was still heaving.

I just need a few minutes, she decided, *then I can drive again.* She shook her head at Tobin and gestured weakly in the direction of the bus. "I'll be okay in a minute."

"Wonderful," Tobin said, "but we have to hurry." Keeping Margot steady in the circle of his arm, he gave Ash another dirty look. "You should have known to leave immediately after she called the storm. You knew others would come."

"Couldn't ... go," Ash managed. "She ... collapsed."

"You could have driven this thing," Tobin accused. "No doubt she slept for several hours. You just sat here like a fool waiting for their arrival!" With Margot held in his steady arms, he shook his head. "She didn't know any better," he said finally. "You, on the other hand, are determined to be a prize idiot. Are you trying to get yourselves killed?"

"She … needed … to see," Ash insisted, struggling to get his hands under his body and stand up.

"Whatever," Tobin sneered.

"And," Ash added, voice steadier now, "no one … drives Margot's bus … but her." Tobin took a long-suffering breath, anger fading into annoyance. "You would know that … if you knew her at all."

"I know her enough," Tobin said, glancing down at the still unsteady Margot in his arms. "Unless you'd like to get off your ass and get her cleaned up?"

Ash struggled again, managed to get a knee beneath his body, but slid down to the ground again.

"You healed him," Margot said, putting a hand against Tobin's distractingly muscled side and standing up straighter. "Why isn't he better?"

"I healed his wounds," Tobin explained, holding out his arm so she could steady herself without danger of falling. "Idiot lost a third of his blood pretending to not have powers. My healing can't help that. I'm not a phlebotomist." At her alarmed expression, he added, "He'll be fine. It will just take a bit." He cocked his head. "Your show is tomorrow night?" At Ash's quick nod, Tobin curled his lip, contemplating. "You'll probably be fine to sing. Definitely if you can get a transfusion before then. Maybe if I can get you to Akkoy alive, we can pop by the hospital." He paused suggestively and added, "I know a guy."

"I bet … you do," Ash quipped, then surrendered, body slumping as he stopped trying to move. He gestured with his chin. "Get her inside and let her clean up. I can get myself inside."

"As if," Tobin snorted, but he stepped up and helped Margot inside the bus. "Shower," he told her. "Clean yourself. You'll feel better."

Margot nodded, feeling her lip start to tremble as the last events caught up to her, the shakes setting in as the adrenaline left her system. "Easy now," Tobin assured her, leaning in to give her a hug. "You're alright. Ash is fine. You're both fine."

"How ... did you find us?" she mumbled into his shoulder, startled tears falling as she let the panic wash over her.

"I can always find you, Margot," he said, whispering into her hair. "I won't let anything happen to you."

"You saved us," she said, slowly regaining control of herself. "Thank you."

"Don't thank me," Tobin said, allowing her to end the hug when she was ready. "Like I said, I'm happy to help."

"Thank you," she repeated, sniffing and wiping her nose. She glanced around for something to wipe her face, and her eyes caught on the remains of her pink tank top in a pile on the floor. She couldn't help the burst of laughter that escaped at the sight, recalling the faeng's shocked expression as she threw clothing at it. Tobin followed her gaze and bent down to retrieve the cloth. Holding it out, he examined it, finally holding it in the right direction and studying the cuts, understanding what had happened. "Pink, huh?" he asked. "Definitely not the faeng's favorite color."

"No," she giggled. "Definitely not."

"Get cleaned up," he told her. "I'll deal with Ash."

She nodded, wanting to thank him again, but he shooed her toward the bathroom. It was awkward getting undressed in the small space, but when the hot water hit her skin, Margot was glad for the chance to shower. Tobin was right. Getting clean made everything a little bit better.

Chapter 29

Border Guards

Evening, Friday, February 20th
in Margot's Bus in Northeast Armav

"So," Margot said, watching Ash slide a clean shirt over his head. The cloth covered a chest that was still lined with red marks, though not open wounds. Margot still had a vivid red line across her hip and down her leg, but it didn't hurt when she touched it. Washing her hair with one hand had been challenging, though.

Tobin seemed to have everything they needed in his backpack, retrieving new clothes for Ash, jeans and a green shirt that said "Village Idiot" on the front. There had been some back and forth about clean underwear, but Margot wasn't sure of the outcome, more focused on studying the damage done to her bus and debating how and when she would get it fixed. The door still shut, mostly, if she yanked it hard enough. Hopefully, she could find a body shop between Akkoy and Sivas that could do something, or maybe on the longer stretch from Sivas down to Mineo since they had a few more days between shows. She didn't want to think about explaining the damage to the border guards when they crossed, especially now that Tobin was with them. "Are we going to talk about what just happened?"

Tobin watched Ash step slowly over and into the passenger seat, chest still heaving slightly. "Definitely," Tobin said, "but let's talk and drive." He glanced out the front window from the swivel seat, now raised to a normal seat height and locked in place. "We've already lingered too long."

"Thanks," Margot said again, settling into the driver's seat and checking her mirrors.

"Stop thanking me," Tobin insisted. "I said I was here for you and I meant it."

Ash let out a snort, and Tobin glared at him. "No noise from you right now. Besides, you need all the air you can get."

Margot turned on her headlights and started driving again, avoiding the mound that had been a creature as she headed down the mountain. She scanned the horizon, looking for dark shapes against the night sky as she picked up speed, the road clear beyond the storm debris.

"What was that—faeng thing?" she asked. "Some kind of fae monster? With a magic cloak?"

"They used to be fae," Ash explained, head leaning back on the seat as he too scanned the horizon for threats.

"What happened to them?" she prompted.

"Dark magic," Tobin volunteered. "We don't like to talk about it, but there are abilities that poison the soul. Fae who have such powers must control them, or the darkness controls them."

Margot frowned. "That sounds awful. What kind of abilities could do that?"

"The ones that affect free will," Ash offered.

"Like Claiming? Is that an ability?"

Ash shook his head slowly. "No, Claiming is a ceremony, a spell. Any fae can Claim another, so long as the Claimer is stronger. Faengs use other powers."

"Like mind control stuff?" she prompted, slowing down to take yet another curve though it seemed like they were nearing the bottom of the mountain.

"Yes," Tobin confirmed, "though the minor stuff usually takes a really long time to have an effect. You know—making someone look left instead of right so they don't see a thing, or convincing someone they don't recognize you. But the faeng are fae who forced others to do their will, completely violating another's volition, often wiping their memories and replacing them with falsehoods. The more they use their power to upset the balance within others, the more the darkness they unleash builds in them, eventually resulting in what you saw. Just wraiths, really, burning with the need for a new fae to abuse, to fill their need for more darkness."

"Why are they called faengs?" she asked, remembering that push of power she had felt urging her to surrender when the faeng first appeared before her door.

"Fae who have fangs," Tobin offered. "As they continue to abuse their power, their fangs grow. It's one of the earlier physical symptoms of corruption." At his words, he smiled at her, displaying a wide row of perfectly ordinary white teeth.

Margot grinned back, unable to stop herself, then asked, "How did they find us? Was it really the storm?"

"You certainly know how to make an entrance, Margot," Tobin commented. "There weren't many fae in northern Armav. Anyone who cares is south, closer to the conflict. These faeng were hiding here, so it was easy enough for them to feel your call. But others will come too, now that they know a powerful new Unclaimed fae is in the area."

"I didn't call anyone!" she insisted, taking a corner slightly too fast and slowing down, aware that her frustration was spilling into her driving. "I don't even know how I did it."

Tobin nodded. "No worries, darling. We'll work on that as we work on everything else. It's a matter of focusing your emotions, using them to change the world around you."

"Can you do it?" she asked, glancing over at him. "Make storms?"

"I can do many things," Tobin said mysteriously, and Ash scoffed again. "At least I'm willing to teach her," Tobin snapped. "I won't leave her defenseless."

"You know I already said I would help her," Ash defended. "I'm sorry if my years of never seeing anyone escape Claiming has poisoned my optimism."

"But fae Lords are Unclaimed," Margot reminded him. "Why not be one of them?"

"She says it as if it is a simple thing." Ash laughed. "Margot, there is so much you don't know." He glanced at Tobin, head bouncing as the bus went over a bump in the road. "You think Tobin would have let himself be Claimed if there was a choice?"

"But you have a choice," Margot reminded him. "Your father can't be the only one who did this. I mean, oaths are common enough among humans—"

"Go!" Ash snapped, and Margot shut her mouth, wondering what she had said. Ash's face said she had betrayed a secret, and she recalled that he hadn't been able to tell her about the oath's power without the magic wine to loosen his tongue. She bit her lip, not sure what to say.

Tobin nodded, lips pursed. "Interesting," he said finally, cool eyes assessing his half-brother. "So many secrets coming to light."

There was silence as Margot finished driving down the mountain, silently kicking herself for her stupidity. It was Tobin, she decided, his familiarity and comforting presence that made it easy to say things in front of him, to tell him things. She knew, somehow, that he understood.

Though she had been welcomed by her aunt and cousin, taken in as part of the gang with Ash and Timothy, even made stage manager on the tour, Margot never forgot her isolation, her loneliness. Something deep within her responded to Tobin, recognizing something in him that echoed her own needs.

She glanced at him, a niggling question surfacing. "Why did they want me ... and not Ash? I mean, he's Unclaimed too."

"In hiding," Tobin explained. "If he doesn't use his powers, they can't sense his presence. You're the beacon, darling."

"Great," Margot said, and they drove in silence for a time with only the music on the radio. Ash's fire and heat magic must not be enough magic for anyone to notice, she thought, mind whirling as the road spooled out before her.

When they passed a sign for the border ahead, Margot turned to Tobin again. "Do you have ID?" she asked suddenly. "I am not hiding you in my bathroom."

"Of course I have ID," Tobin said, offended.

"Are you allowed into Genc?" she pushed.

"I'm not a criminal," Tobin defended. "No matter what Ash might think."

"You just work for one," Ash commented.

"As you said, I didn't have much choice in the matter. And I know you don't believe it, but Lord Rebinus is actually not a terrible Lord."

"See?" Ash asked Margot. "That's the magic talking. He can't help himself."

"You don't know what you're talking about," Tobin said. "You aren't Claimed. You just don't understand."

"It can't be that wonderful if you're so determined that Margot not be Claimed," Ash observed.

"I want Margot to make her own choices," Tobin said fiercely. "Someone should get to do what they want around here." He paused, slipping in, "Or does that only apply to you?"

"I don't do what I want," Ash grumbled, but he looked out the passenger window, not catching Margot's glance.

"Please," Tobin drawled. "You mean to say that you dislike your rock star lifestyle? The poor lonely misunderstood musician?" He snorted. "As if you won't go right back to your parties and your companions tomorrow night, leaving Margot alone and undefended."

"I'm not alone," Margot argued. "And I think I'm learning to defend myself—"

"Of course!" Tobin interrupted. "He can't even be bothered to risk his cozy disguise to save your life—or his own." He leaned over to Margot. "For future reference, fire is the way to kill faengs. They flee from it at the very least, and their cloaks are quite flammable."

"But you didn't use fire," she commented, voice quiet. "You just … shook it to death." At this, Ash's head whirled around to face his brother. Margot had forgotten that he hadn't seen how Tobin killed the creatures—he had been bleeding and near unconscious on the ground.

"Humph," Ash grunted. "Looks like I'm not the only one with secrets here."

"So I'm stronger now," Tobin said. "My Lord grants me certain gifts." He reached out to smack Ash's leg. "Besides, the last time we actually sparred, I was a child. No doubt you've grown in strength as well."

"No doubt," Ash repeated.

Chapter 30

Rabid Fans

Evening, Friday, February 20th
in Margot's Bus at the Border of Armav and Genc

They continued in silence through the countryside, eventually leaving the mountains and rejoining traffic on the highway. As they approached the border crossing, Margot felt herself tensing. She knew better. Crossing the border was easy enough, and she had never had a problem before, but she hadn't been trying to leave Armav since the fighting started. Nor had she been transporting a possibly sketchy traveling companion. Margot knew her and Ash's IDs would be approved right away—and despite Tobin's insistence that he wasn't a criminal, she couldn't quell the doubt in her gut. They filed into a lane to the left, following the guard who waved them over, then parked in the spot indicated. Margot rolled down her window. A guard from the right lane walked over, taking in her foreign bus with the driver's seat on the right side.

"Good evening, ma'am," the border guard greeted, a bored-looking middle-aged man with a mustache. He peeked inside the bus, studying the steering wheel. "An '05 TW? I haven't seen one of these in a long time."

"It's a classic," Margot said, patting the dashboard. "Still got plenty of life in her."

The guard nodded. "Definitely. What brings you to Genc?"

"Business," Margot replied. "I'm with a rock band tour. Our next show is in Akkoy."

The guard nodded, as if he had heard this before. "IDs?" he asked, holding out his hand. Margot slid hers out of her small purple wallet, then held out a hand for Ash and Tobin to deposit theirs. Ash's plastic card was the same as Margot's—marked with the blue seal of Arillo—but Tobin's ID was completely white, his picture and name clearly displayed above the word "DIPLOMAT" in gold lettering across the bottom. Margot's eyes widened as she saw it, but she rearranged her expression as she handed it over to the guard.

She had heard of diplomatic passes before, but she had never seen one. Lord Redi-whatever must be powerful in this world as well as his own if he could give Tobin that kind of authority.

The guard didn't look at the cards, simply passing them over to his assistant who held a small card reader in one hand. He pulled a flashlight from his belt and clicked it on, moving the beam across the top of her hood.

"So," the guard began, eyes flicking down to her battered front grill and back to her. "A band tour, huh? Isn't it a bit late to try and reach Akkoy tonight?"

"We got held up," she explained.

The guard nodded, reaching out to jiggle the metal grill across the front of her bus, making sure it was connected. Margot prayed for her little bus to hold together. "I'm just going to take a little look around," he said and started walking around the front of the bus, hesitating at the obvious damage to the front end. Margot was glad none of the windows had shattered in the faeng encounter, but she bit her lip, knowing he would ask about the mangled side door. A few seconds after he passed to that side of the bus, he rapped his knuckles on the passenger window. Ash reached over and rolled it down, staring listlessly at the guard.

"You want to tell me what happened over here?" the guard asked, tapping on the mangled side door handle.

"We had an unexpected encounter—" Margot began.

"With some rabid fans," Tobin finished for her, leaning forward so the guard could see him. "Believe me, they were wild to get at us. We barely escaped with our lives."

The guard stared at them, unimpressed, but the assistant made his way around the bus and leaned over to whisper in the guard's ear. "Seriously?" he said, peering more closely into the bus as he aimed the flashlight at them. "You're with Stone Dragons?"

Margot nodded, squinting at the light. "I'm the stage manager," she explained.

He nodded, then shifted his gaze to Ash, recognition filling his face. "You're..."

"Ash Stonewall," Ash finished for him, reaching out a hand. The guard accepted it awkwardly, bobbing the flashlight until his assistant grabbed it, shellshocked at meeting a celebrity.

"I love your band!" the assistant said, waving with the flashlight as his other hand tucked the card reader under his arm and handed back their ID cards. "So bummed you didn't do more shows here." He scowled. "You didn't have any trouble with rebels, did you?" He glanced at the door. "Is that what happened?"

Ash shook his head, taking the cards. "Nothing like that. We were only in Kerva on Wednesday. As he said, just some … really excited fans."

"Occupational hazard," Tobin added. He leaned forward conspiratorially, taking his ID back from Ash, "You know how those women can get around rock stars." He glanced over at Margot as he handed her back her ID. "Thank the stars our Margot here is immune, or we would never get anywhere!"

The assistant smiled at her, clearly pleased to hear she was unattached. "Well, we're just glad to see you made it here alright. Hopefully, this business will be settled by the next tour so you can do more than one show!"

Margot and the boys nodded. "Definitely," she agreed, then waited awkwardly for them to say they could go. There was another long pause, and the border guard leaned forward, hands on the edge of the open window.

"Any chance I could get a picture with you?" he asked Ash.

"Sure," Ash agreed. "Just don't post it for a few days. I don't want those fans to find me!"

"Of course," the guard agreed, pulling his phone from his pocket. He turned his back to the bus window, ducking down to show Ash in the background. He took a few pictures, then gestured the assistant over, and the three of them spent a few minutes posing and flashing peace signs.

Margot watched in silence, feeling herself and Ash sliding back into their familiar roles. It had been different the last day, just the two of them alone in her bus, but now they were returning to the real world—the world where Ash wouldn't look at her as anything more than Baby Go again.

Will he bring a strange woman back to the Entertaining Bus tomorrow after the show? She had been avoiding the thought since last night, since she brought out the bottle of wine, but the reality of their positions slammed back into her. Her time with Ash was over. He had been hers for a brief moment—and that was all she would ever get. He had said as much, warned her over and over. And she had warned herself.

Hell, even Tobin had said it. *Guard your heart, Margot.*

But it was a battle lost long ago, and she bit her lip, looking away from the fan interaction, trying not to acknowledge the hot jealousy flooding through her.

He was never yours, she reminded herself. *Just as you were never his.*

I'm always his.

Oh, shut up. Pathetic. A warm hand on her arm roused her from her reverie. The fans and Ash were exchanging a few final pleasantries, Ash even using his rock star voice.

"Margot," Tobin said, staring at her with wide sympathetic eyes, and she knew he understood how she was feeling, however impossible that seemed. "I'm here," he said quietly, then removed his hand, settling back into the swivel seat and clipping the lap belt into place with a professional smile at the guard through the window.

"Have a great tour!" the guard was saying and waving her forward. Ash rolled up his window as they drove away, but Margot left hers down, turning up the radio and letting the wind play with her hair. She lost herself in the familiar comfort of the road at night, the glow of the dashboard dials, the smell of the night air in yet another province, the security of the next show.

Chapter 31

Back to the Real World

After Midnight, Saturday, February 21st
in Margot's Bus at the EcoDome in Akkoy, Genc

They arrived at the EcoDome a few minutes after midnight, the security guards opening the gate to the back lot and waving them through. Margot pulled up next to the other RVs, her little bus dwarfed by the modern vehicles. She put the TW in park, then leaned back in her seat, neck cracking.

Ash stirred, having fallen asleep about an hour ago, and Margot patted his thigh, trying to forget that she knew what the bare skin of his thighs felt like, tasted like. "Ash," she murmured, "we're here." If he had fallen asleep in a normal spot, she would have left him, but he was awkwardly slumped in the seat, a position that would make his neck hurt in the morning.

He yawned, then opened his eyes slowly, still very much asleep.

"Oh?" he asked, eyes closing again.

"I'll get Timothy," she said, nodding at Tobin before she climbed down from her side, the chill air biting on her legs. She had driven with the window open, so her arms and face were used to the cold, but not the rest of her body. Wrapping her arms around herself with a tiny wish for Ash's magical heat, she headed toward the RV where Nik and Timothy might be. She knocked on the door, waited, then pulled out her phone to text them. Surely, they weren't asleep?

Her phone rang a few moments after she sent the message. "Baby Go!!!" the jubilant voice of her cousin shouted, and she moved the phone away from her ear with a wince. "What's up!" There was a shuffling, a fumbling, and Timothy's quieter voice asked, "Margot?"

"It's me," she told him. "And you're at the party," she said, smacking her head. *Some manager,* she told herself. *Can't even keep a basic schedule straight. Get some dick, and you've turned into a complete airhead.*

"You coming?" he asked. "Bringing Ash?"

"Not tonight," she told him. "We're so tired. Ash is just going to bed. I'll put him in the bunk, not the back room, okay?" She didn't want to interrupt any plans Nik or Timothy had for bringing women back to the RV.

"Why are you putting him to bed?" Timothy asked suspiciously. "Something I need to know about?"

"Not tonight," she repeated. "He's fine. We're all fine. See you tomorrow."

She hung up before he could ask more questions and returned to the bus to retrieve her keys. Opening the side door with a screech of protesting metal, she gave Tobin a pleading look. "Can you help me get him inside?"

Tobin nodded, hopping up and following her out of the bus to open the passenger door, supporting his brother easily as Ash sagged out of his seat. They had made it to the door of his RV, Margot fussing with the keys to open the door, when he looked blearily from the body holding him up to her, a hand reaching out to smack her ass. "Threesome," he slurred. "Cool."

Margot froze, not turning around. She didn't want to see Tobin's face. She didn't want to have heard Ash say that. She didn't want to imagine what his sleep-addled, oxygen-deprived mind was thinking. Turning the key, she pulled the door open, sighing at the smooth give of a newer vehicle, then offered her shoulder under Ash's arm again, supporting him as she stepped up the few stairs. Ash's head lolled and tapped the cushioned wall, and Margot winced, but she had to admit that she didn't really feel too bad, not if he thought she was another groupie. They stumbled down the center aisle, between the couch and small table and the fancy kitchen. Margot slid the curtain aside from the bottom bunk—Ash's bunk. She heaved, shoving Ash into the space—bigger than her own bunk bed by far—and Tobin lifted his legs. Ash flopped, snoring lightly, and she frowned.

"I've got him," she told Tobin. "Just give me a sec."

Tobin walked back into the main area of the RV, studying his brother's living space.

Margot sighed, moving Ash's hair off his face. Leaning down, she took off his shoes, then tugged off his socks, tucking the shoes into the cubby below the bed and sliding the socks to the foot of the bed for him to deal with later. She reached for his pants and hesitated, recalling the discussion Ash and Tobin had had about providing clean underwear.

Maybe I shouldn't, she thought. *Maybe I should just leave him like this.*

She frowned, knowing she wouldn't want to sleep in jeans, but also knowing that somewhere between the mountainside and the border, she had lost the right to take off Ash's pants, especially without his consent. Sighing again, and hating the sting of tears in her eyes, she reached for the blanket balled up against the wall. She had pulled it over his legs when her eyes caught a flash of color in the corner of the bed beside Ash's head. Leaning into the bunk, she peered close, seeing that it was a photo taped to the top of the bunk, situated so a person lying on their back could look at it.

It showed the four of them at the old lake: the boys in swim trunks and her in a modest blue one-piece she had borrowed from Aunt Maddie. They were so young, that first summer she was among them, but they all looked happy, enjoying the water and the summer sun, all smiling as they hunkered together for the camera. She had the same picture on her bus, framed on the wall where she could see it from her spinning seat.

"Ash," she whispered, the bite of tears becoming somehow softer. Despite his earlier comment, and the knowledge that things were about to go back to normal, she was relieved to know that when Ash was alone in his bed, he liked to look at his friends in the old days before the band, before everything.

"Go," he mumbled, a hand reaching out to touch her, tugging her down for a sleepy kiss. Margot froze, then melted, allowing him to pull her close. "Stay with me," he murmured, his breath warm on her lips.

"I can't," she told him, feeling the space between them widening. She kissed him gently and slowly peeled his hands from her face. She tucked them under the covers and kissed him again, this time on the forehead. "You need sleep. I'm right next door," she added, sliding the curtain shut before he could say anything else. She stood next to the cubby for a moment, catching her breath and slowing her pounding heart. Tobin still stood in the living area.

"Nice." He nodded at their surroundings. "Sleek. Though I think I like yours more. Seems to have ... character."

"Character is great until you want a shower," Margot told him.

"You okay?" he asked gently, nodding at Ash's bunk behind them.

"Yeah," she said. "Just tired. I have to get the bus set up, or I won't be able to shower in the morning."

"I'll help," Tobin volunteered, and he followed her out of the RV, waiting as she locked Ash inside. They returned to her bus, ran the lines she needed to dump the water and plug into the local power. Tobin was a good partner, taking instructions easily and following her guide without any difficulty.

When they had finished, she stared at him, considering the sleeping arrangements inside her bus. When she was growing up, she and her mother had made her bed each night, dropping the planks into place so she could sleep, but when she redesigned the bus, her goal had been to always have her bed ready to go—hence the one bunk bed. Since she never brought anyone back to her bus, it hadn't mattered—and the few times Nik had spent the night, he just curled up on the passenger seat or reclined in her swivel seat. Her bus wasn't made for entertaining, though she did have two folding chairs to set up outside if she had company. "You can probably use one of the bunks in the RV," she began, but Tobin stopped her.

"It's fine," he said. "If you don't mind, and you have an extra blanket, I can just sleep on the floor."

"Are you sure?" she asked, knowing the floor was not comfortable. "It's hard!"

"Won't be the first time," he said with a smile. "Besides, it's like camping. We should make s'mores."

"Maybe tomorrow," she told him. "Right now, I'm so exhausted, I just want to curl up in my bed." She gave him a long look, thinking of his warm body, her tired mind trying to decide if her thought was manageable.

"You're wondering if you should ask me into your bunk," Tobin said. "You want to be polite, but you also don't want to imply anything."

"How do you do that?" Margot asked, plopping onto the swivel chair and taking off her sneakers. She put them on the step, then stood up, peeling off her socks and tucking them in the small laundry bag that hung on a hook in her closet. "It's like you can read my mind."

"Not my skill set," Tobin admitted, hands spread wide. "But I can read you, Margot." He nodded at the floor. "I'll be fine."

"I don't want to be alone," she blurted, not sure what she was going to say until the words came out. "But I don't want to have sex with you tonight."

"I appreciate your candor." He waited for her to continue. When she just stared at him, glancing between him and her bed, he added, "I can be a comfort to you, Margot. I will not do anything untoward."

"You sure?" she asked.

Tobin lifted a hand to his chest, one finger held out. "I do so swear, I will not offer any physical pleasure… until you ask me to."

Margot snorted, appreciating Tobin's sense of humor. Then she sobered, shattered heart throbbing. "Are you okay with this? I'm kind of using you."

Tobin shrugged, tugging off his shirt with casual abandon. Margot's mouth went dry, and she reminded herself that she was exhausted and in no mood for anything. "I'm fine with however you choose to use me, Margot, even if it is just so the bed isn't so lonely."

But I can still look, she reminded herself. *He is so fucking hot.*

Sleep, her body demanded, and she nodded, grabbing pajamas from the bin and heading to the bathroom. She changed quickly, brushed her hair and teeth, and came out into a dark bus, Tobin having turned off the lights. It didn't matter—she knew her way around, and she hopped up into bed easily. Tobin was there, his body hard and reassuring in the dark, lots of bare skin but still wearing shorts, and she snuggled against him, the two of them fitting much better than she had with Ash the night before.

"Tobin," she said, so many words wanting to escape.

"Tomorrow," he said, leaning down to kiss the top of her head. "Sleep now, Margot. I will be here."

"I know," Margot said, wrapping an arm around him, reveling in his solidity, his presence, and slipped quietly off to sleep.

Chapter 32
Morning After Blues

When Margot woke, the sunlight was streaming into her bus, and she was cuddled in the arms of a strong, warm embrace. For a split second, she wondered if she had lost a day, that yesterday had been a dream, and she was just waking up from her night together with Ash, but then she opened her eyes and glanced down at the arm around her waist, a perfectly pale arm without any tattoos. Disappointment and gratitude welled up in equal measure.

She rolled her shoulders, taking stock of her body. Considering she had been cut open the day before, she felt fine, though her hand was sore. Recalling the wound, she glanced down, seeing that the arm around her waist had pushed her nightshirt up during the night and rested above a red line wrapping across her hip bone—all that remained of her injury.

That's pretty handy, she thought, remembering how easily he had healed Ash, if not completely. *I wonder if I'll be able to do that someday.*

"You are thinking very hard for someone who just woke up," Tobin muttered, his breath ruffling the back of her head, and she looked over her shoulder at him.

"How do you know what I'm thinking?" she asked. "I didn't say anything, and you can't see my face." *Please don't tell me you can read minds,* she thought desperately. *That would be so embarrassing.*

"Your entire body tensed up," he told her, squeezing her tighter for a second before relaxing his arm. "And your entire aura shifted. Whatever you are thinking about, you're not sure if it's a good thing or a bad thing."

"What about my aura?" she probed. "You some kind of hippie?"

"Hippies may have taken a lot of drugs, Margot," Tobin said, "but that doesn't mean they were wrong. Auras are quite real."

"Is that a fae thing?" she asked. "Another one of your abilities?"

"Something like that," he said, hand tracing the air above her hip, fingers outlining something she couldn't see.

"What do they look like? Colors and stuff?"

He shrugged, the motion pressing his body against hers, and she became very aware of morning stiffness against her back. "Some of them." He snuggled his face deeper into her neck, and his hand rested on her skin. "Some are just a suggestion of an emotion. Everyone is slightly different, a code you have to learn."

"How do you understand my code so quickly, then?" she asked, moving her legs and maybe accidentally on purpose rubbing against him.

"How do you understand mine?" he asked, the arm around her waist moving so he pulled her snug against him, palm flat against her hip. "I thought this was a friendly encounter, Margot."

"It was," she insisted, not moving but not trying to get away from him either, conflicted but also perfectly content to stay right where she was. Margot rarely denied the pull of her body—she may show restraint in other aspects of her life, but she wasn't shy. "It is."

"Okay," he said, hand sliding away from her. "But I'm not apologizing for morning wood. That's to be expected, even when I'm not in bed with a beautiful woman."

Margot snorted, missing his touch but not willing to pursue him. "You're such a guy."

"You would prefer I was otherwise?" Tobin asked. "I didn't know that about you, Margot."

Margot glanced up at him. "Nah," she said, "though sometimes I think it would be easier. Men can be difficult."

"And you assume women are different?" he asked. "Shows how many relationships you've had."

"Nailed it," she admitted, turning so their facing bodies were inches apart on the bed. "I've had exactly zero relationships."

Tobin frowned. "Surely..."

"I mean, I've been with people, sure. But nothing serious. Nothing long term." She sniffed in disgust, realizing how pathetic she sounded. "I'm on the road with the guys so often, it would be hard to maintain anything unless a partner came with us."

Tobin smiled. "I've seen your crew. No doubt one of them would make an ideal partner for the road."

Margot scoffed. "No, thank you," she said. "Learned that lesson a long time ago."

"Margot!" Tobin said, feigning a scandalized tone. "How could you? And with the help!"

"He wasn't the help back then—and they aren't the help—" She smacked him. "They're the crew—but it was just for fun. We're still friends."

Tobin pursed his lips. "Let me guess. It wouldn't be the mustached fellow—Travis, is it? He's a bit too old for a youthful tryst. And John is a bit too serious for such frolicking..." he mused. Margot wondered how he already knew the crew but decided not to ask.

"Why does it matter?" Margot asked instead. "Ash asked the same thing!"

"Did he figure out your former lover?" Tobin pressed. "Did you tell him, so now he can give those daggers at the one who presumed to have you before him?" At Margot's look, he added, "You know he's jealous of anyone you touch. Did he figure out his next target?"

Margot smacked his chest again, not liking the direction of this conversation. "He did not," she said primly. "A lady does not kiss and tell."

"Of course," he agreed but gave her a pointed look, "and gentlemen do not share details of exploits, either." Margot bit her lip at the hunger in that look, the desire clear on his handsome face.

But Ash...

Ash is about to go back to rock star life with his groupies and his fan club. He told you it wasn't going to mean anything. And even if he wanted to try, what would be the point? He would never truly be with you. He can't choose you over his oath or his family.

But Tobin wants you. No games. No obstacles. He's here with you—choosing you.

Margot closed her eyes, not wanting to fall into his gaze. It would easy, she knew, to give in to the demands of her body and have sex with Tobin. He was here. He was willing. But she knew next to nothing about him. And while he may be here and willing, it had only been a few days since they met, and Margot wasn't willing to trust him, not completely. Not when she knew she was still vulnerable and hurt over Ash.

Besides, if Ash—and Tobin himself—were to be believed, Tobin was Claimed by Lord Rebinus, making anything he did a likely result of his master's bidding. And Rebinus would want to Claim her.

"Tobin," she said, keeping her eyes closed so she couldn't see his face and lose her nerve, "I'm sorry. I didn't mean to give you the wrong idea. I just—didn't want to be alone."

"You aren't giving the wrong impression, darling," Tobin assured her. "You're confused and hurt and still in your feelings. I get it."

Margot was relieved to hear the lightness of his tone. He wasn't angry with her. Of course he understood. A warm hand caressed her cheek, then let go, a brief touch.

"I can wait. I told you, Margot: I'm not going anywhere."

"Don't you have a job? Or a home?" Margot asked, opening her eyes to peer at this stranger in her bed. She recalled his white diplomat ID from last night. "And how the hell do you have a white card?" She lifted up on her elbow, watching him for any signs of lies.

"I am a vassal," Tobin explained. "That's my job."

"So you just wander around Ardon doing stuff for Lord Reginard?"

"Rebinus."

"Yeah, him." She narrowed her gaze. "What do you do, though?"

"Mostly?" Tobin shrugged. "Nothing. My lord is specific in his directives, but vague in the details, so I get a lot of time for myself."

"Why were you in Kerva?"

"I was debating if I wanted to scout the south, to find out more details for my Lord. But then I was distracted."

"Did you know we would be in the bar that night? Is Ash right about you?"

"Ash thinks everyone is out to get him," Tobin said dismissively, rolling onto his back.

"Aren't they?" She tugged the blanket up to cover her waist, suddenly cool without the heat of his body behind her.

"Not everything is about Ash," Tobin groaned. "I know he's the hero around here, but I went to that bar because I wanted a drink. And then I saw a beautiful woman alone, and I decided to take a chance."

"But why?"

He reached out to push her hair behind her ear, his touch raising little whorls of goosebumps along her arms. "Because you had such sad eyes, Margot. Too sad to be drinking alone in the middle of the week."

"You didn't know who I was?" she prompted. "Please tell me the truth."

"I didn't know who you were," he told her.

"And Ash?"

He paused, clearly thinking about what to tell her.

She nodded, tingles in her skin fading as her heart sank. "You knew who he was. Of course you did. So what is this? Some elaborate plan for your Lord to out Ash so he can get Claimed like you?"

Tobin withdrew as if she had struck him, hurt flaring in his eyes. Margot was instantly sorry as he rolled over her and slipped out of bed. He stood on the floor, his back to her, that white hair still mussed from sleep. She could see the tiny hairs on his back lit up by the late morning sunlight streaming through the windows.

"Is that what you think of me, Margot?" he asked, his voice quiet and sad. "I am my master's creature, incapable of action without some deep convoluted plan?" He chuckled, the sound empty of joy. "I suppose you're right, in a way." He bent down, locating his pants and slipping them on.

Margot shifted on the bed, guilt ripping through her, and she reached out a hand to touch his shoulder. He paused, then sank back against the edge of the bed. Margot wrapped her arms around his shoulders. "I'm sorry," she whispered, lips giving him soft kisses on the back of his neck. "I'm so sorry. I shouldn't have said that."

He turned slowly in the circle of her embrace, bending his face low to look at her, all good humor gone. "Do you really think that low of me, Margot?"

"No." She shook her head. "I don't know what I think, to be honest, but I don't think you're here to hurt me." She bit her lip, frowning. "But I don't know anything about you, Tobin. Nothing except what Ash said."

He snorted. "So you talked about me, then? I didn't think my brother would waste time like that—not when he finally got you alone."

It was Margot's turn to snort, and she pulled back, very aware of how close he was to her again. "Ash could have gotten me alone at any time," she said, flopping on her back. "I'm pretty sure he only got with me because of you."

"You think your fiery prince is jealous?" Tobin prompted, propping his head on the edge of the bed and watching her.

Margot put a hand over her face, scrubbing the last of the sleep from her eyes. "No," she said finally. "Not really. I know I'm not the one for him."

"Is he the one for you?" Tobin asked the question bluntly.

"I thought so," she admitted.

"Past tense?" Tobin arched an eyebrow. "Curiouser and curiouser, Margot."

"I don't know," she said. "I'm a mess. You should seriously think about whether you really want to help me at all."

Tobin reached out, a hand on her knee, reassuring. "I told you I'm here, Margot. Whatever you need. A friend. A teacher." He wiggled an eyebrow. "A good time. Something more. You think about it." He glanced down and to his right, scanning her little kitchen. "I assume I use the kettle to boil water, right?" He tapped her thigh. "You don't strike me as a tea woman. I'll make coffee." He moved away, opening doors and drawers, familiarizing himself with her kitchen layout. Margot rested her head on her arms, watching him, very aware of the differences between the pale angel in her kitchen this morning and the dark one who had made her coffee the previous sunrise.

Light and dark, she thought. *I wonder what their father looks like.* Tobin, probably, she decided, recalling his comment about how Ash had the look of his mother. Such very different men but also similar in some ways. Both were courteous, at times, and silly at others. Both made her blood run hot when they looked at her a certain way.

Damn, she thought, feeling the pull of her bladder but not wanting to abandon the bed. *He looks really good in my kitchen too. And we fit in my bed a hell of a lot better.*

Though I would fit fine in Ash's bed... Her cheeks flushed as she imagined sleeping with Ash in his bunk, Timothy and Nik moving around beyond the curtain as he touched her at night.

Nope, she decided. *I am not doing that. Ever.*

Coffee with Tobin in her own bus sounded a lot more appealing.

Chapter 33

Coffee and Perfectly Normal Conversation

Half an hour later, she was still drinking coffee with Tobin and chatting as if she had known him for years. Sitting in her bed, the space was high enough for her head to just brush the ceiling, and Tobin was laying on his back at the foot of the bed, her pillow bunched behind him, his glorious bare chest a distracting sight as he rested the coffee mug on the muscled planes of his abs. She had dressed in her working clothes—jeans, tank top, and staff shirt—her hoodie hanging ready by the bus door.

Tobin had helped her to find Haberson's Auto Body in Sivas, and she had an appointment for tomorrow afternoon. For only a moderate extra fee, the owner had agreed to open on a Sunday, and he had a new side door and panel held for her. He could even match the cream color.

The band manager Cayla had texted that morning to make sure everything was set for the show that night, and while Margot hadn't actually gone to check on Ash, she'd heard from Timothy that they were all fine. The on-call doctor had been by to see the lead singer, and he was much recovered; they could count on the doc's discretion, and the show should go on without any problems.

Margot had asked if they needed her for anything, and Timothy insisted she take the day for herself—showing up at 3 pm to make sure everything was set up properly. Tobin agreed to hang out with her until then, and she was grateful for the company, not sure what a day spent alone would have done for her mental state.

"Tell me more about this 'job' you have for Lord WhatsHisName," Margot said, using air quotes.

"Rebinus," Tobin corrected, seeming to never tire of her butchering his boss's name. "It's nothing, really. Boring."

"That's not an answer," she reminded him. "What are you doing in Ardon?"

"Checking in on a few people, making sure businesses are running smoothly—that kind of thing," he said vaguely.

"Breaking some kneecaps along the way?" she prompted, thinking of him shaking the faeng.

"It's not like that, Margot," he defended, taking a sip of his coffee.

"Then what is it like?" she pushed. "Hell, this is more frustrating than talking to Ash. Do you need magic wine too?"

Tobin raised an eyebrow. "So that's how you got him to crack," he said contemplatively. "I wondered how you did it."

"You say that like I drugged him." Margot didn't like the feeling in her gut.

"Didn't you?" Tobin raised an eyebrow, then reached out to touch her foot. "I don't mean that in a bad way, Margot. Fae spells are powerful. Sometimes you need a little something extra to break through."

"You knew he was under a spell?"

Tobin cocked his head. "I assumed it was something. It was more than just dumb luck and cleverness that kept him hidden from the other Lords all this time." He gave her a pointed look. "I mean, you've seen how well he fights."

"He couldn't use his abilities," she defended.

"He's an idiot. There are ways to use his powers without attracting attention. He's so hung up on playing human that he's forgotten himself." He gave her a pointed look. "That's why he's so angry with me for Awakening you, you know. You make him face his fae self—and Ash is very good at running away."

"Tell me about it," Margot said and instantly felt guilty for judging him. "I didn't mean that. If I had a good life and just had to follow a few rules, I don't think I'd jeopardize it lightly."

"You nearly died, Margot," Tobin said, his voice dark and full of anger.

"I was fine," she insisted, trying not to recall the faeng's face in the last moment before it would have climbed inside and cut her apart. "You saved me."

"I shouldn't have had to save you," he insisted. "Not with Ash right there. He chose his secrecy over your life. You do realize that, right?"

Margot hated how much his words hit home—only reinforcing the knowledge that Ash was not meant for her. "But those faeng were so strong," she tried. "You said it yourself. What could Ash do against them, even if he used his powers?"

Tobin gave her an odd look, then sat up, setting the mug against the wall. "Did he not tell you, Margot?"

"He told me a lot of things," she said defensively, not liking the way Tobin had grown serious.

"Did he tell you what he can do?" Tobin pressed.

Margot considered. Ash had shared a lot of things during their night together—his oath, the rules that bound him, his feelings for her, the reasons they could never truly be together—but no, she realized, he had never told her about his fae abilities.

"I asked him..." She remembered asking him what he could transform into, and then he had tugged her on the bed and yanked off her pants, completely distracting her. "But then I got distracted."

"Hmph," Tobin said. "Margot, you're a smart woman, but when it comes to my brother, you can be a prize idiot."

"I know," she said, putting a hand over her face. Tobin reached out and tugged it down.

"Don't be embarrassed," he told her. "Ash is very convincing when he wants to be. No doubt you were in no position to truly question him."

"But you know," she said, leaning forward and keeping his hand in hers. She put her mug aside and placed her other hand atop his, holding him near. "You know what he can do, don't you?"

Tobin looked away, clearly not liking the direction of her questions. "He's my brother, Margot," he said finally. "We grew up together. Of course I do."

"Tell me," she insisted.

"It's not my place to tell you," he argued.

"Please," she dismissed, "you can't wait to tell me everything he's done wrong. You want me to see him the way you do. You're dying to tell me what he can do."

Something in Tobin's face twitched, a flash of deep recognition, and he tried to pull his hand out of hers. "Margot."

"Tell me," she insisted, pressing harder on his hand, not knowing why, but the feeling flooding her body felt suddenly so ... delicious. She liked the uncertainty on his face, the way she could feel him about to open his mouth and share something he really didn't want to tell her— it was like breaking him open to see what lay hidden beyond his many walls.

"Ash can..." With a monstrous effort, Tobin reached out his free hand and pressed it to her cheek, leaning up and very close to her. "How do you feel right now?" he hissed, staring at her earnestly.

Margot held onto his hand, that feeling ebbing just a little, and she pressed tighter. "So good," she moaned. "Tell me, Tobin. You want to tell me."

"Do you really want me to tell you," he asked, "knowing I don't want to? Would you pry the answer out of me like a reluctant fingernail? Do you want to break my will, Margot?"

His words broke through the fog surrounding her, and the good feeling evaporated, leaving behind something uncomfortable. Margot released his hand abruptly, looking down at her hands in surprise. Tears sprang to her eyes as she realized what she had somehow been doing to Tobin—forcing her will onto him. "What have I done?"

"Nothing," he assured her. "I'm fine, darling. You just have a new ability, and you definitely need to learn how to control it." He wiped her cheek where a tear had escaped.

"That's what they could do," she whispered, remembering the corrupted face of the faeng leering over her. "It... It felt so good."

"Of course it feels good," Tobin said, wiping another tear from her cheek. "Anything bad always feels good. That's what makes it so dangerous."

"I'm so sorry," she said, reaching out to gently touch his shoulder. "I didn't mean to."

"I know," he assured her. "But it looks like influencing people is one of your abilities. You have to be aware of how much you want a thing, Margot. I can resist you for a time. A human would have replied immediately, no matter what they wanted to do."

Margot looked at her hands again. "This is an awful power. Am I already corrupted?" She ran her tongue along her teeth, searching for fangs.

Tobin smiled. "You're fine, Margot. Just don't get in the habit of doing it too often, and you'll be fine. It takes years of abuse for the darkness to manifest in fae."

"Can you do that?" she asked, voice small and trembling. "You don't have to answer me," she added quickly.

"I know," he said, then gestured for her to come closer where she collapsed into his arms, another terrible discovery adding to the stress of her new life. "And I'm going to tell you something now—and not because you are making me." He leaned down, peeking at her face. "You hear me?"

Margot nodded.

"Good because I don't tell many people this." He paused, thinking. "Correction: I haven't told anyone any of this. I'm telling you now because I think you need to know. Because now that we're in Genc, more fae will sense your power, and there will be more encounters with creatures like the faeng—but also with minor lords and ladies—and you need to be prepared."

"What am I going to do?" Margot asked, her voice tiny against his bare chest, soaking in the heat of him as he soothed her whirling thoughts.

"You're going to listen to me," Tobin told her, and Margot obeyed.

Chapter 34

Secrets, Powers,
and Connections

"When I was Claimed," Tobin began, "I already had mastered most of my abilities—inherent powers. I can fly, of course, and control the elements somewhat—though not so spectacularly as you, apparently. Like you, I can affect how people behave, but I can also sense their auras. I can change my appearance, I can sometimes move objects without touching them, and I can manifest objects or conjure them from other spaces. Those are my abilities. I also know an array of spells that allow me to travel and defend myself—and heal, as you know—those are my other powers."

He settled back on the pillow, adjusting Margot across his chest, the two of them diagonal across the bed, her right knee over his leg and his bare foot splayed against the wall next to where her head normally rested.

"Spells?" she echoed. "Like a wizard? Are those different from abilities?"

He nodded. "Anyone can learn magic, given enough practice. Abilities are unique to the individual."

"They said my mom and aunt were middle-class fae—"

"That's not a thing."

"You know what I mean. But they had one ability: air or water. Why do you have so many?"

"Because I'm the son of a fae Lord," Tobin explained. "Had I not been Claimed, I would be well on my way to being a Lord myself one day. Like Ash."

"You think Ash will become a Lord? That no one can Claim him?"

"Ash is very powerful. If he stays in hiding, he can likely live his whole life without anyone Claiming him, not that it matters in the human world. But that would shame our father if he never came back. He has responsibilities, expectations. In our world, he has gifts many covet."

"So why did Rebillard—"

"Rebinus."

"Yeah, him. Why did he Claim you and not Ash?"

Tobin considered. "Ash has power, but it's unfocused strength, especially back then. I had more useful skills."

"What did Relinus—"

"Rebinus."

"Yeah. What did he want with you?"

"I can pull items from other places. That was his favorite."

"Your backpack," Margot mused, latching onto the first power she understood, and Tobin nodded.

"If I just think about what I need, it's usually in there for me."

Margot considered how useful such an ability would be. "Except underwear, apparently," she said, thinking of his conversation with Ash.

Tobin laughed. "Oh, I can conjure anything, Margot. I was just giving Ash a hard time." He gave the top of her head a gentle kiss. "After what he did to you, he deserved it."

"He didn't do anything to me," she insisted, adjusting her cheek on his chest. Tobin cocked his head to look down at her pointedly, and she sighed, very aware of Tobin's bare skin beneath her face. "Fine," she admitted. "He definitely did things to me. And I to him. Things were done," she declared.

"Thank you for the clarity," Tobin said formally. "But this isn't about what you did or didn't do."

"Sorry," she said. "Go on. Your powers. Abilities."

"My powers," he repeated, then narrowed his eyes at her, "details about which I am currently confessing to you—a thing I have never done in all my life to another person—and yet I feel that you are barely listening to me, Margot." He sighed, his chest rising and falling beneath her. "You still daydreaming about Ash?"

"No," Margot insisted, moving her head so she could look at him. "I'm listening. And I'm grateful," she added, her face appropriately serious.

"Why?" Tobin's question was open, honest. "You shouldn't be grateful to me."

"Because I appreciate you sharing this with me. Because I understand that it can be hard to tell people things." She reached out one hand, resting it flat on his chest, enjoying the feel of him beneath her. "You don't have to tell me. I'm not making you tell me."

"I know," he told her. "That's partly why I want you to know. When more fae come, you need to know what I can do, so we can fight better together."

"Do you think we will have to fight?" she asked, voice small. "I mean, I can swing a bat, but I don't know how useful my gifts are in a fight."

"Oh, darling," he whispered. "When you master all of your abilities, you will be a force formidable to behold. I cannot wait to see you."

"Unless someone Claims me before then," she said, the fear clear in her voice. "What happened to your powers when you were Claimed?"

"I kept them, if that's what you're asking, and I can still use them at will."

"Even the darker stuff?" she prompted. "Can you ... push people like I can?"

Tobin nodded. "I can. Mine isn't with touch, not like yours, but yes, I know exactly how good it feels when someone falls to your will, when all their resistance fades away and they give in."

"Did he make you use it?"

Tobin stiffened, looking away. "Occasionally. Not very often. And only in extremity." He looked back at her. "And he's not the tyrant Ash believes him to be. He does have a plan, and it's not to make everyone miserable as some would think. When I have to use my ability, it isn't for sport or twisted joy. It's necessary."

"So says every tyrant justifying their behavior," Margot commented. "I kinda wanna check your teeth right now, Tobin."

He flashed her another brilliant smile without a fang in sight. "Feel free to check closer, if you like," he offered.

Margot held herself steady, wanting to lean over and kiss him, knowing what he could do to her body, the memory of that night in the bar flooding over her. Her toes curled as heat pooled in her belly, and she pushed her face into his chest, forcing herself to stay put. "I want to," she admitted, eyes closed as she breathed in his scent. "You know I want to, but I can't. Not now."

"Okay," Tobin said, and something in his casual tone allowed Margot to relax, tension evaporating. They were just companions talking. "Where were we?"

"You were Claimed," she reminded him, "but you could still use your powers. Is it just that you use them for him now—Lord Reminald?"

"Rebinus. Yes, something like that. But my Lord also allows me other gifts—like my strength." He leaned down to whisper in her ear. "I know you saw me, Margot, and I know it scared you. Yes, I am very strong, even stronger than Ash." He paused. "Are you frightened?"

Margot paused, considering the question. Was she afraid of him? No. Not at all. Part of her insisted that she should be; he was still a virtual stranger, no matter how many secrets he shared, and he was clearly a scoundrel of some kind, not to be trusted. Another part of her insisted everything was fine; Tobin was there for her, and he could be relied on for anything she needed.

I guess I'm just really into bad guys.

"No, I'm not frightened of you," she said finally. "Though I think I should be. Something tells me that you will never hurt me." She paused, recalling Nik and Ash's talk about her connection with Tobin. "I feel so close to you. Must be the connection."

"What about it?" he asked. "You want me to lend you some strength through it?"

Margot leaned up, eyes wide as she looked at him. Tobin wasn't kidding. "What? You talk about it like it's a real thing."

"Of course it's a real thing," he told her. "Why wouldn't it be? You think fae just Manifest without any magic at all?" He tightened his arm around her. "We're Connected now, you and I. How did you think I could always find you? Or read you so well?"

"I thought those were just your powers!" she exclaimed.

"Did I list that among my abilities?" he asked. "I can't find just anyone, Margot, and I don't immediately understand everyone's aura. Just yours."

"But—" she sputtered. "But what the hell does a connection even mean in fae terms?"

"Just what it sounds like," Tobin said, looking at her as if she were a bit dense. "Didn't Niklaus explain this to you?"

"He just kept saying we had a connection, like when two people have a lot in common or get along really well. Like when you meet someone and just know you're going to be friends. You're saying it like it has a capital letter!"

"Connections are basic spells," Tobin explained. "When two fae forge a Connection, whether physical, mental, or emotional, the magic builds a bridge between them, making it easier for them to grow closer." He looked at her, face sympathetic. "You can share my powers, Margot, and in time, when you master them and allow me, I can share yours. You can find me, and you should be able to read me once you learn how." He wrapped his arm tighter around her back. "Like I said, you're stuck with me."

"And how long do these ... Connections last?"

"That depends. Some fae are Connected for a lifetime. Some fade away after the moment of need has passed."

"How long do you think ours will last?" she asked meekly, not sure she wanted to hear the answer. A magic spell certainly explained why she felt so close to Tobin, why he felt so right in her arms, in her bed, no matter what she felt for Ash.

"How long will you need me, Margot?" he asked, and for the first time, there was a vulnerability there.

"I need you now," she told him. "But do you need me?"

He paused, considering, those bright eyes taking in her face, calculating. "I think you already know the answer to that."

She nodded, knowing she did. Tobin needed her, or he wouldn't be here. She may be a cog in his machinations, a stepping stone in his master's plot—she was still sure he was plotting—but for now, he needed her as much as she needed him.

She opened her mouth to ask the one question she still needed to know, but then closed it, knowing that Tobin wasn't the one she needed to ask.

Chapter 35

Stone Dragons at the Akkoy EcoDome

*Evening, Saturday, February 21st
at the EcoDome in Akkoy, Genc*

Margot didn't ask Tobin if he wanted to watch the show from backstage, but he came with her to the back door when it was time to go to work, and she had the guard add him to the list, tossing him a backstage pass he tugged over his neck. He had finally put his shirt back on, even adding a hoodie in deference to the chill of the Gencian winter, and Margot decided it made him even more sexy than he had been lying barechested in her bed.

She forced herself to stop staring at him, showing him the back rooms for the staff and stagehands, then abandoned him to begin her duties. Part of her worried he might be carried away by the groupies who frequented backstage, but she stopped that line of thought immediately. She already had one rock star to worry about.

She found the guys in the green room, Ash and Nik strumming their guitars and running through the set list, Timothy sitting on the couch banging his drumsticks on his thighs. "All good?" she asked, trying to sound like her normal perky self before a show. "Need anything?"

"All good," Nik chirped, his face clearly trying not to explode as he glanced back and forth between her and Ash. "You need anything, Ash?" he prompted, tapping Ash with the neck of his guitar. "Margot," he emphasized her full name, "is here for you."

"I'm fine, Go," Ash said, his voice the distant rock star she knew. And though she had fully expected it, had given him her normal employee greeting, it still hurt to be treated as the same Margot who had known him forever.

Timothy opened his mouth as if to say something, to contradict Ash, but Margot spoke over him. "Great!" she said with forced cheer, trying not to recall Ash's face as he said he loved her, the taste of his lips on hers as he moved in her. "I'll see to the crew then."

As she turned to leave, she nearly bumped into three women as they came in, each one striding purposefully toward a band member. The tall blonde sat on the couch next to Timothy, a drink in one hand and the other settling comfortably on his knee as she began talking, clearly continuing a previous conversation. The brunette settled near Nik, hand possessively on his shoulder as she eyed Margot.

But Margot only cared about the redhead, the one who casually perched on the couch beside Ash, handing him a drink with a casual, "Here, babe." Ash accepted the drink with a nodded thanks, and the woman ran her arm over his shoulder and down his arm, moving just a little bit closer. Ash took a sip, eyes glancing up to where Margot stood near the door, but he didn't move away from the groupie, allowing her to touch him. Margot stared at the stranger Ash had become for a second longer than necessary, but he said nothing, simply staring back at her. The redhead, sensing that Ash's attention had wandered, leaned close, wrapping her manicured fingers around Ash's chin, and pulled his face close to hers. Ash's eyes skipped to Margot for a split second, but then the redhead was kissing him, and instead of pushing her away as Margot expected, he put his drink down and put both hands on her instead, deepening the kiss. Timothy cut his eyes to Margot, like he wanted to say something, but the atmosphere clearly told her it was time to leave.

Margot ducked out of the room quickly, eyes burning, and hurried to a nearby bathroom, shutting herself in a stall and sitting down, her hands over her face as the tears came—hot and angry.

What did you expect? Ash was only acting the way he said he would. She shouldn't feel so hurt. She'd known what she was getting into.

"I'm such an idiot," she whispered to the empty room.

The bathroom door opened, and she froze, scrubbing her face, trying to wipe away the evidence of her broken heart.

"Margot?"

She recognized Tobin's voice, and she stood up, flinging the stall door open and staring at him. "What are you doing in here?" she demanded.

"You're upset," he said, standing in front of her like it was perfectly normal.

"Of course I'm upset!" she snapped. "But that doesn't answer my question! What are you doing in here? This is the ladies' room."

"You were upset," he repeated. "I didn't want you to be alone."

"But I am alone, Tobin," she said bitterly. "And I'm an absolute moron because I knew better, yet I did this to myself anyway."

"Love makes morons out of us all," Tobin said softly.

She leaned in the stall doorway, sniffing loudly. "Have you been in love?" she asked him, wanting something else to focus on but the pain in her chest.

"Ask me another time," he said, reaching for her hand. He led her to the sink and turned on the water, wetting a paper towel and handing it to her so she could wipe her face. She took a deep breath, then redid her hair and straightened her shoulders.

"I'm okay," she told Tobin. "And I have work to do."

"That's my Margot," Tobin declared. "Go get 'em."

She nodded, rallying, and grabbed Tobin's hand as they exited the bathroom. "Have you tried the chicken wings? Akkoy has the best wings."

"I've heard of them," Tobin said. "Apparently, it's something about the sauce."

"They have some in the breakroom," she told him. "Eat them while you're here."

"I will," he promised. "Anything I can do to help you get set up?"

"Nah," she assured him, running through her list in her head. "I'll find you when they go on. We can watch the show from the back."

Tobin nodded, and Margot headed off to the stage to see how far the crew had gotten in the setup process.

Everything went without a hitch, and Margot found her flow, Ash slowly leaving the forefront of her mind as she focused on her job. Even Travis's long smoke break didn't annoy her as the crew seemed to have everything in hand.

The opening band arrived at 6pm, and Margot got them situated, trying to ignore the sexual innuendos the lead singer of Das Leprechauns made as she walked them through the stage and setup.

"Show me again how you hold that microphone, little girl," Alby said, accent thick as he guffawed and looked at his bandmates for encouragement. "Das good," the singer moaned.

"Oh, wait," Margot told him, smiling sweetly. She plucked the normal microphone from the stand and headed over to the table where a pile of other equipment still waited to be hooked up. Grabbing the smallest microphone they had, one normally used for communication backstage, she handed it to him. "This probably feels more comfortable in your hand," she told him with a meaningful glance at his pants. "Das good, yes?" Before the singer could reply, she walked away, shaking her head.

She never enjoyed the Bacolian band, but many fans of Stone Dragons also liked Das Leprechauns, so they often hooked up for this part of the tour. This was not the first time Alby had given her crap while setting up, and normally she could just roll with it to keep the peace, but she wasn't in the mood tonight. She glanced back at the other three members of the band, gesturing to the left side of the stage. "Your guitars go there," she pointed at the racks, "and get your pedals set up. Sound check in thirty."

Without another word, she left the stage area with Alby still holding the ridiculously tiny mic and headed back to check on her boys.

Chapter 36

Heart of Stone

When Ash, Nik, and Tim went on stage to uproarious applause, Margot went to look for Tobin, spotting him across the stage near the Leprechauns' guitars. Two women stood near, both clearly angling for more attention, but Tobin only smiled and nodded politely, not leaning down to listen to them as they clearly wanted, a move that would put his face closer to their very exposed cleavage.

Margot watched the exchange for a few moments, long enough for Ash to finish their opening song, "Dragon Cry." Eyes that normally watched every second of Ash's performance drifted to see what Tobin would do next. She heard Ash start the long note opening "Breathing Fire," but she didn't look at him, didn't need to see the soulful expression as he launched into the words. Instead, she watched the groupie on the right, a tall thing wearing white leather, as she leaned up to say something to Tobin and pressed her body against his. Tobin stepped back, face polite but distant as he answered her.

The other groupie smirked, this one in a blue corset and short black skirt, clearly thinking she had won the battle for Tobin's affection, but then Tobin looked up, his eyes met Margot's across the stage, and he smiled at her. The blue groupie followed the direction of his gaze, and her face fell. She nodded at Margot, clearly recognizing her and backed off. Margot gestured that he should go behind the stage to meet her, and he nodded, stepping away from both women without a backward glance. She headed behind the stage, knowing they couldn't be seen behind the screen displaying Stone Dragons' insignia.

The sound was blasting out into the crowd, but it was still too loud for any conversation to be heard. Grabbing his hand, she led him to the side where she knew there was a short ladder leading to the lower rigging. She climbed quickly, Tobin behind her, and they emerged onto a small metal walkway just over the stage. Margot plopped down, feet dangling over the side, settling into the spot where she normally watched the show. She would work more when they wound down, seeing if they planned an encore or if they were finished for the night, but for now, she had time to herself.

Normally, she watched Ash as he sang, his entire body tight with excitement, his voice soulful as the music poured out of him. Tonight, however, she was very aware of Tobin next to her, her new companion sharing her secret observation spot, her work, her sad obsession standing front and center as he drank in the love and adoration of the crowd.

I can never replace that, she thought, watching as Ash stepped to the back of the stage for a drink, calling out his fellow bandmates with pride to a raucous cheer. They settled into their next songs, and she relaxed. "Tales of Blood and Maidens," the song featuring Timothy's drumming, started, and Ash rested near the back of the stage, sipping his water bottle. She saw him glance up into the rigging, looking around for something. When he caught sight of her, he smiled.

At her.

Margot's heart soared, unable to stop the pure joy that rocketed through her. He was looking for her. He wanted her.

Of course he knew where she watched the shows from. His face was familiar, friendly, the Ash she had known in her bus, until he caught sight of Tobin sitting beside her, and his expression darkened. He downed the bottle of water and stalked back to the microphone.

Margot felt Tobin stiffen beside her, eyes narrowing as he watched his brother on the stage below. The last notes of Timothy's song faded, and Ash strummed his guitar fiercely, a long discordant note, normally signaling the start of "Heart of Stone," their hit song, but instead of the rock song she knew, he gestured for Nik and Timothy to stop playing.

"I know this is usually a favorite," he said, that sexy voice echoing throughout the arena, "but tonight, I want you all to know that this is for someone special. You know who you are." He glanced up into the rigging again, eyes meeting hers, and launched into the opening verse. The song stretched into a lost love song more so than a rock ballad. Margot had always wondered if "Heart of Stone" was about her, spending hours dissecting the lyrics: *I know the truth when I look in your eyes, baby, but we're just not meant to be, so I gotta have a heart of stone...*

Margot listened to the words with a different world in mind, realizing most people assumed it was the ballad of the rock star singing to someone about how he couldn't drag her into his wild life on the road. Now that Margot knew he was a fae in hiding, the words made even more sense. He couldn't drag someone into his world. No matter how much he wanted to.

But I'm in your world, Ash, she thought desperately, his voice echoing through her as it always did.

No, she told herself. *It's not enough. You're not enough for him—and being fae doesn't change that.*

Sadness replaced her joy, and she looked away from Ash, reaching for Tobin's hand as she climbed down from the rigging, not listening to the rest of the song, ignoring the way Ash's gaze followed her as she disappeared into the darkness.

She let the music follow her as she headed deeper backstage, climbing stairs until a doorway opened onto the roof, letting the night air cool her heated face. She propped the brick in the door so it wouldn't close and lock them outside, then walked to the edge of the roof, Tobin lingering a few steps away. For once the fae said nothing, letting her sort through her feelings as she would. The last echoing notes of "Heart of Stone" drifting through the door faded away. The band launched into "Blood from a Stone," one of their last songs of the night. Margot knew they weren't planning an encore if they were already playing it. Nodding, she paced a few more times, trying to understand the ache in her heart.

He wants you, she insisted. *He sang for you tonight.*

But not enough, she knew. It would never be enough.

Turning, she saw Tobin lingering near the door, his short hair blowing in the wind, breath visible in the cold air as he waited for her. He was wearing jeans and a hoodie like all the guys in Stone Dragons, but he wasn't his brother.

"Am I enough?" she asked him.

Tobin narrowed his eyes, then cocked his head at her. "You are more than enough," he declared. "And you know it."

"Then why am I not enough for him?" she asked, the question shot through with her heartbreak.

"Because my brother is a fool," Tobin said.

"Are you a fool?" she asked, stepping closer.

"Apparently," Tobin said.

"Why do you say that?" She took another step toward him.

"Because you're going to break my heart, Margot," he said, "and I'm going to let you." Tobin bent his head and kissed her.

Chapter 37

Portals and Actual Beds

Normally, Margot would have checked on the guys before they headed to an after party. She liked to make sure Nik didn't bring any of the new instruments along due to his habit of gifting them to adoring fans in addition to staring at Ash one more time before returning alone to her bus and organizing the crew schedule for the drive to Sivas the next day.

Margot was a responsible stage manager. She never neglected her duties. But when Tobin kissed her, she forgot everything she was supposed to be doing, instead surrendering to the call of her body, the unfulfilled yearning he had ignited days ago when they first met. Tonight, she decided that Stone Dragons could look after themselves for one night, and she was just going to stand on the rooftop and kiss Tobin until her toes curled.

She was vaguely aware of the show ending, the music ceasing with a long shout, and the roar of the crowd fading away, but most of her was focused on the touch of Tobin's hands on her body, his warm mouth, her cold cheeks, and the air that misted between them when they broke the kiss, faces close together.

"You want me?" Tobin asked, wanting to be perfectly clear. His voice sent shivers down Margot's body.

"I want you," Margot assured him. She turned to look in the direction of her bus, so far away from the rooftop on which they stood. She could see it down there, tiny next to the huge RVs beside it. It would take too long to get down there. She considered her wings, but it was cold, and she would have to take off her shirt to call them. She was sure Tobin would be willing to suffer a little cold if it meant getting her alone somewhere private, but she didn't want to ask. "My bus—"

"I can take you to my rooms," Tobin offered, "if you want." He winked at her, and heat worked up Margot's chest into her neck at the idea of finally getting Tobin's full attention without interruption. "I have an actual full-sized bed and everything."

"Where do you live?" she asked, calculating time and distance and knowing she had to be on the road to Sivas by 10 am or she would be late for her appointment with the repair shop that afternoon. She hated to be so pragmatic, but her bus came before getting laid, no matter how badly she wanted him. Her hands were still holding his back, keeping him close, and she knew he would fit better in her bunk than Ash had. They were roughly the same height, but Tobin was leaner, a sinewy strength—she had seen—while Ash was bigger across the chest.

"Lorellon," Tobin whispered in her ear, and it took her a moment to place the name.

She put a hand out, making some space between them, but not letting him go. "Lorellon," she repeated, recognizing the name from her mother's stories. "Like the fae realm?"

He nodded. "The estate is in Demacia, high in the mountains."

"That sounds awesome," she admitted, "but I have to head out by 10 tomorrow. You don't just have an apartment nearby?"

"An apartment?" He cocked his head at her. "How do you think I live, Margot?"

"I don't know," she replied, trying to think through the lust clouding her brain. "You travel a lot, so maybe hotel rooms?"

He nodded. "Occasionally, if the need calls for it, but I do have a home, Margot. I am not some wandering vagabond."

Margot recalled the diplomatic ID. She wasn't thinking clearly. "I'm sorry," she said. "I know that. I'm just..." She looked up at him longingly, biting her lip. Tobin bent his head to kiss her again, a hand against her ass to pull her even closer.

When they paused again, she said, "Fuck it. How long will it take to get there?"

"Were you not listening, darling?" Tobin asked, grinning down at her, lips forming a wicked grin. He held out his hand next to them, and his fingers began to twist, marking out specific motions in a definite pattern. A dark purple glow formed behind his hand, the magic prickling Margot's skin. A few moments later, the magic grew, forming the shape of a door next to them. Tobin gestured at the doorway. "My Lady?"

"Of course," she scoffed, staring into the purple glow. "A fucking magic portal." She reached out to it but paused, brain finally getting in a complete thought that didn't involve what lay beneath Tobin's clothes. "Wait," she said, putting a hand to his chest. "Don't you live at his estate or whatever? Lord Refinus?"

"Rebinus," he corrected. "And yes, I do, but he isn't there now."

"How do you know?"

"Because I know," he said.

"That's not an answer, Tobin."

He paused, then sighed. "My Lord is not at the estate right now, Margot, I assure you. He will not disturb us."

"But he's the one who will try to Claim me," Margot insisted, common sense trying to overcome her desire for immediate satisfaction. "Ash said—"

"Did he?" Tobin interrupted, and she heard something harsh beneath the question. Tobin's anger with his brother wasn't limited to his own interactions with him. "Are we taking Ash at his word now?"

"He never lied to me," Margot defended, but the words were habit. She gave Tobin a skeptical look. "And your Lord has an ax to grind against Ash and his family. This feels like a trap."

"He isn't there, darling," Tobin repeated. His hand pressed hard against her back, and he brought her body closer to his, reigniting the fire inside her as he bent his head to kiss her, one hand still held out and maintaining the magical portal. "Do you think I would betray you?" he whispered against her lips.

Margot shivered, her desire warring with her common sense. In the past when she went home with someone, she'd always trusted her gut to keep her safe, that she shared expectations with her companion. Her gut insisted that Tobin was trustworthy, that time with him was well-spent. But this wasn't going to someone's place where she could just call a car to take her home when she wanted to leave. Tobin's portal magic was something he controlled. If she left with him, she was at his mercy until he let her return—or brought her back.

"Swear it," she demanded suddenly, snatching his hand from her back and pressing it between their bodies. "Swear this isn't some kind of trap."

"I swear that this isn't a trap." Tobin said instantly, kissing her fingers. "Lord Rebinus isn't there," Tobin repeated, a hand running through her hair as he bent to kiss her neck. "He will not disturb us. Did I mention the huge shower?"

Margot tugged his mouth back up to her lips, satisfied with his promise. "No, but I hope to see more of it."

"Definitely," Tobin promised and gestured for her to step into the portal.

"I'm not going to get lost in there, am I?" she asked, turning to look at Tobin over her shoulder.

"I'm right behind you," Tobin said, one hand resting on her hip and guiding her forward.

She stepped into the purple haze, not sure what to expect. Magic tingled on her skin and she closed her eyes. Her feet left the slightly gravel feel of the rooftop. As she disappeared into the portal, she thought she heard Ash's voice behind her.

"Margot!"

She ignored his call, taking another step forward into the unknown.

Chapter 38

A Night to Remember

Night, Saturday, February 21ˢᵗ at the
Palace of Lord Rebinus in Demacia, Lorellon

Margot stepped onto something soft, yielding like luxurious carpeting, and opened her eyes. She stood in a large open room, a huge bed before her covered in a thick blanket and at least half a dozen pillows. She glanced to her right, taking in the dresser and elegant chair, then to her left, a set of glass double doors leading onto what looked like a balcony. She could see the moon hanging low over a mountain range, the sky a deep purple that wasn't quite the same as the night sky in Ardon. Turning around, she watched as Tobin stepped into the room the same way she had—through an ornate mirror on a stand. The purple glow faded, and she took a step back, giving him room, then glanced at the two doors on the wall. Tobin followed her gaze.

"That's the bathroom." He gestured to the door on the right. "And that leads to the living room."

"Tobin," she breathed. "This place is ... huge."

"Thank you," he said, moving to the bed and sitting on the edge, pulling off his boots.

She took a few steps, scanning the rest of the living space through the doorway. More rococo furniture filled the other room, and she turned around, eyebrows furrowed. Nothing in the room's decoration matched what she knew of Tobin's personality.

He was a jeans and t-shirt guy, like Stone Dragons, the uniform of the late 20s man in Arillo. She had expected a room like Nik's or Ash's, a messy bed, a battered dresser, maybe a milk crate for a nightstand. Even something more mature like Timothy's matching bedroom furniture or an art print on the wall would have made sense. But this lavish assault on the senses was a bit overwhelming. "Tobin, this is your room?"

Tobin tossed his boots, then settled himself on the bed, looking sexier than ever despite the gauche decorations. "Why? Shouldn't this be my room?"

Margot shrugged, skepticism warring with her desire to tackle him on the bed and ask questions later. "I guess I just didn't think you were into this kind of ... stuff," she tried.

"You expected an old dresser and a bed made of hay?" he prompted, eyes teasing.

"No," she admitted. "I just didn't think your place would be like this. No offense."

"Fae decoration is quite different from that of the human world," Tobin explained, glancing around at the silver and black dresser with inlay of pearl around the knobs, the stylized portrait of a dark forest before a mountain range hanging over the bed. Even the doorways were surrounded by ornate molding that continued up to the filigreed corners of the ceiling. "Most of it is stuck somewhere in the 16th century."

"Yeah, this feels like something the Sun King would have had." She grimaced. "The only thing missing is fabric on the walls."

"That's in the front room," he said dismissively. "Velvet, if you're curious." At her look, he smirked. "I didn't design it, if that makes you feel better," he said. "I kind of inherited it this way."

"That helps," she said. "Gods, what you must think of my little bus? So simple and small."

"I like your bus, Margot, because it's yours. Everything there feels like you." He stood up, moving toward her, and Margot bit her lip, her body filling with heat at the sight of this man, this fae, walking up to her like that. He leaned down, putting his face against her neck and inhaled. "It smells like you."

Margot closed her eyes, loving the feel of his breath near her, his body close. "I hope that's a compliment," she murmured. She remembered the show, her hours of running around getting everything ready. "Though I probably need a shower."

"I thought you'd never ask," he said and lifted her hoodie over her head. He tossed it behind him on the bed and leaned down to kiss her exposed neck, fingers skimming the edge of both her tank top and t-shirt and lifting them as well. Margot's hair, formerly held up in a bun, began to fall down, tendrils teasing her back and hanging over her bare breasts. Tobin didn't pause, bending to take a nipple in his mouth, and Margot gasped, tilting her head back.

"You're still wearing way too many clothes," Tobin purred, then bent to unzip her jeans, sliding them down to leave her standing in her panties, denim pooled around her ankles. "Oh my," he said, kneeling before her. "I seem to have forgotten the basic order of things." Without another word, he lifted her onto one shoulder, belly down, and as she laughed, he yanked off one sneaker and then the other. Her pants quickly followed, then he set her down gently on her bare feet, the carpet silky soft against her skin. He stood for a moment, just looking at her, and Margot smiled, knowing that tonight was going to be a very good time.

She took her time undressing him, savoring the sight of him as he had her. "You are so hot," she told him. "How in the world are you still single?"

"I have particular tastes," he said, leading her into the huge bathroom and turning on the water. "And high standards."

"Particular tastes, huh? That sounds like something someone says before talking about handcuffs and whips."

Tobin shrugged, hand held under the stream of water as he tested the temperature. "I'm amenable, if you like," he considered. "Though I'd rather your hands were free to wander at the moment." He reached out for her, pulling her into the shower, then spent a long time touching every inch of her skin, wringing pleasured cries from her lips. After her very loud shout near the peak, she had clapped a hand over her mouth, embarrassed. Now settled again, she glanced around, judging the acoustics of the room.

"No one can hear us, darling," Tobin assured her, rubbing shampoo into her scalp. "You yell as much as you like."

She closed her eyes, relishing the feel of his hands on her body. "In any other context, that would be super creepy, Tobin."

"Like, no one can hear you scream?" he asked, moving close to press himself against her, hands sliding down to bury his fingers between her legs. "Let's test the theory, shall we?"

He brought her over the edge again a few moments later, and she slumped against him, body warm and wet and wilted with pleasure. "Oh, darling," he whispered against her neck, "how I love to hear you sing for me."

Margot sighed, a slow smile crossing her face as she turned to face him, pushing him back until he hit the wall of the shower. Kneeling, she took him in her hands and her mouth, demanding the shout that matched her own. When she had him gasping her name and shuddering, his legs gave out, and he slid down to sit on the floor. Caught up in her own desire, Margot moved forward, climbing atop him and claiming him in one swift movement. Tobin opened his eyes wide, watching her find her own pleasure, only releasing her from his gaze when they neared the edge of ecstasy. Tobin yanked her head down to kiss him, their joined shouts echoing in the huge room.

Chapter 39

Huge Beds and Promises

After Midnight, Sunday, February 22nd at the Palace of Lord Rebinus in Demacia, Lorellon

Hours later, Margot let out a huge yawn. She was sprawled on her belly in the huge bed, blankets and pillows mounded around them both, Tobin still resting half atop her, both of them gasping for breath as they recovered from their latest exertions.

"Need ... drink," she managed, hand flopping around as if she could find a water bottle hidden in the bed. To her surprise, her hand touched something cool and plastic, and she dragged it closer, opening an eye to peer at it. A water bottle rested in her hand. She glanced over her shoulder where Tobin was limp against her back. "Handy little gift," she said, popping the lid and taking several long swallows. When she had downed half the contents, she tapped him with the bottle, ordering, "Drink."

"Mmph," he managed, but the body atop hers slowly slid to the side, and she heard him drink as heartily as she had.

Margot adjusted her body so she rested on her side, looking at Tobin who turned to face her as he finished drinking. Without looking, he tossed the bottle aside. Margot expected to hear it land somewhere on the floor, but there was no sound. Margot's eyes widened, realizing he must have sent the empty bottle to wherever he had gotten the full one. She wondered where it had come from and where it had gone. Did fae water bottles resemble the ones in the human world? She had so many questions and not enough answers. "Show off," she said, rubbing her face with a hand.

"All that, and the thing that impresses you is the water bottle? Darling, I assure you I have more impressive gifts."

"I know," Margot assured him. "I enjoy all of your gifts." Her head flopped, body exhausted. "You are absolutely amazing, Tobin."

He reached for her, pulling her boneless body close to him so she fit with her back against his chest. "You are exquisite, darling," he said, leaning down to kiss her neck. "Now rest. You are exhausted."

"The best kind of exhausted," she mumbled, snuggling against him, body sated and mind quiet. "This bed is perfection. I like my bunk but being able to spread out is really nice." She opened an eye to stare at one of the pillows, many of which they had put to good use throughout the night. Tobin adjusted the blanket, tugging it up and over them, and Margot sighed, glad to be with him in his giant bed. "I have to say, Tobin, I had my doubts when I saw this room, but you definitely know your way around a woman's body."

"I know your body," he told her, hand sliding down the length of her waist, over her hip, and down her thigh. "I know you."

"You know what I want," she agreed. "Is that the Connection spell, you think?"

Tobin paused before answering, hand coming to rest against her thigh as he contemplated. "Do you remember our first kiss?"

Margot thought back to the night they met, shocked to realize it had only been a few days ago. "We were sitting at the bar," she recalled, "and I don't know why, but suddenly I wanted to kiss you more than anything in the world. So I did."

"A boldness I very much appreciated," he admitted. "But we weren't Connected yet. Not until later—when your wings Manifested. Everything before that was just..."

"Chemistry," Margot finished for him. "Attraction." She remembered the rest of the night, reviewing the memories in her mind. "You knew exactly how to touch me," she said, voice low as she recalled the feeling of his hand between her legs.

Tobin's hand slid down the outside of her thigh and slipped between her legs, fingers gently pressing as they had that first night. "Like this," he said, voice low.

Margot groaned, skin both sensitive and battered, rebelling and longing for the caress. She felt him stiffening against her back.

"You wanted me just as much then as you do now."

"Are you sorry," Margot asked suddenly, "to be Connected to me?" She recalled Ash's tone as he replied to something Tobin had said, words that she hadn't understood then: *I will not be forced into a foolish Connection.* "Am I a foolish Connection?"

"Darling," Tobin said, pulling her tight with one arm as his other hand lazily stroked her.

"You said you were a fool," she reminded him. "For being with me."

"Not for being with you," he assured her, pressing his lips to her neck as his fingers pressed deeper. "I'm a fool for wanting you the way I do." He kissed her neck gently, then suddenly bit her, marking her skin. "I know you don't love me," Tobin continued. "I know you love him. So that makes me the fool for wanting more than you can give me."

Without a word, Margot rolled over, tugging him atop her. His body pressed into hers, slowly, gently, but moving with a rhythm that dragged them both into bliss yet again.

Moments later, still gasping, Margot kissed him long and slow, relishing every touch of his skin. "Why can't you Claim me?" she whispered, heart aching as she stared at him.

"Oh, Margot," Tobin promised, as lost in the moment as she was. "Even if it kills me, someday, I will."

Chapter 40

Misrepresentations and Alarm Clocks

Morning, Sunday, February 22nd at the
Palace of Lord Rebinus in Demacia, Lorellon

When Margot woke, she spent some time studying the room, fingers searching the blanket for a tag—none—as she listened to Tobin's steady breathing next to her. Though they had snuggled most of the morning hours, she had woken with only his hand resting on her hip as he lay on his side, pillow crunched beneath his head and that white hair covering part of his face.

Handmade blanket, she decided, then slowly slid off the bed. She dipped into the lavish bathroom first, body heating as she recalled the fun they had in the shower and later in the huge bathtub, then returned to the bedroom, hunting for her jeans. She found them on the floor, and she dug her phone out of the pocket, flipping it open to check for messages. The screen was dark, and after a long press to reboot it, the phone only spent some time searching for a network before shutting off again.

Note to self: Fae realm doesn't have cell coverage.

Movement jarred her still sore hand, and she flexed it, finding it was much better than it had been. She glanced out the window, trying to judge the hour. Not wanting to go outside to the balcony naked, she snagged Tobin's shirt from the floor and shrugged it on, automatically twisting her hair into a fat braid. She had lost her hair tie, but it would stay for a bit if she didn't move too much. Moving quietly across the thick carpet, she slid the door open, carefully stepping onto the stone outside.

The view was spectacular, mountains and the sun still low in the sky. Margot hoped that meant it was still morning. Her internal clock said it was still early, but she had an appointment that afternoon in Sivas. Turning around to face the building, Margot stepped to the far edge of the balcony, trying to see as much of the house—palace?—as she could. White stonework decorated the outside with detailed work around the windows. Margot could make out a winged man in armor fighting a dragon—and winning—along the edge of the closest casement. The palace continued in both directions, ending in turrets and wide towers. She considered her wings, knowing she could fly up and see the whole place but that would mean taking off Tobin's shirt, and she didn't want anyone seeing her naked and flying around. Having wings was cool, but not practical in terms of modesty. She wondered if she should swap out tank tops for those weird fae shirts.

Shaking her head, Margot glanced down instead, trying to determine how tall the building was. Without leaning too far over, she counted five windows below the balcony.

Your rooms, my ass, she thought, recognizing a penthouse when she saw one, and headed back inside. Tobin still slept, and she used the few moments of privacy to rifle the drawers in the dresser. The top ones held some kind of silky shorts—what she assumed passed for underwear in this realm. The middle row held bottoms in varying lengths and fabrics: velvet pants ending below the knee, silk wide-legged pants, tight black material that would hug every curve of ass and thigh. She moved to the lower drawers, finding a wide assortment of socks in all heights, materials, and colors.

If this was Tobin's room, he regularly dressed like a fae prince, something out of a fairy tale book in her world. She could see him in it, as ridiculous as it seemed. Tobin could pull it off, barely. Unbidden, the image of Ash in the same style flashed in her mind, and she knew he seemed better suited for those clothes. Maybe it was because she had seen him in so many different outfits—regular clothes, rock star clothes, cover model clothes, music video clothes—of course he would wear these clothes well if they were in dark colors, reds and blacks, not all this silver and white.

Feeling guilty for imagining Ash in Tobin's clothes, if they were his clothes, she banished the singer from her mind, continuing her examination of the room. She wondered if she should feel guilty for rummaging through his stuff, then decided not to feel bad. He had lied to her. Well, not lied, but certainly misrepresented. She thought Tobin might misrepresent himself a lot. A quick peek in the closet—long robes, cloaks, platform shoes—only proved her suspicions: this was not Tobin's room.

And if it wasn't his room, it could only belong to one other person: Lord Rebinus.

Margot wandered back over to the full-length mirror they had walked through the night before. She ran her hands along the edges, having seen enough movies about magic mirrors to think there might be a switch, something to activate it, but she found nothing. So the mirror may be a convenient exit for the portal, but she needed Tobin to create the magic.

Why does his portal exit in his Lord's room? Frowning, she wondered if Tobin was allowed so many liberties because he and Rebinus were lovers, then discounted the possibility. Tobin had assured her he wasn't with anyone else.

He also assured you this was his room.

No, actually he didn't, she reminded herself. What he had said was: *Why? Shouldn't this be my room?*

As she thought about his words, she also remembered his reply to her question about him being single: *I have particular tastes,* he had said, *and high standards.* Again, not an answer.

"Oh, Tobin," she whispered, staring at her reflection in the mirror, her tousled hair hastily bound in the braid, his shirt covering her body to her upper thighs. She wondered if Lord Rebinus used the mirror as some kind of spying device, if he could see her now. Her skin prickled, and she wrapped her arms around herself, rubbing her forearms to remove the sudden chill.

"Darling," came a lazy drawl from the bed, "you look wonderful in my shirt."

Margot turned to face him, less annoyed than she thought she should be. "What time is it?" she asked him. "My phone doesn't work here."

"Oh," he said, clearly not expecting the question to be the first words out of her mouth. He rolled over to the edge of the bed, revealing a lovely bare ass, and opened one of the nightstand drawers. He retrieved something that looked like an ancient wind-up clock and rested it on the top of the nightstand. Rubbing his eyes, he peered at it, then announced, "Half-past 8. No worries. You won't be late for your appointment today."

"Is that some kind of alarm clock?"

He nodded, abandoning it, and rolled back over to lay on his back, hands folding under his head as he looked at her.

"Why is it inside the drawer?"

"I'm a sound sleeper," he quipped. "I'm more likely to smash it than wake up, so it's safer in the drawer."

"Did you set an alarm for this morning?" she pressed, wondering how much he had planned and how much he was making up as he went along.

"No," he admitted. "I hoped you might wake me up." Margot stared at him, the silver god naked in what must be his master's bed, surrounded by silky blankets, his hair mussed, his eyes wicked, his body clearly eager for her, and decided that there would be time for questions later.

Chapter 41
Coffee and Oaths

"So, do you have coffee in this magical palace?" Margot asked, sliding on her sneakers. She was dressed in the clean clothes Tobin had conjured for her— yoga pants and a tank top, though not actually hers—and her hoodie from the night before.

Tobin finished pulling on his own boots, fully dressed in a fresh pair of jeans and shirt that he had conjured at the same time, and pursed his lips. "We do, but I know you need to get back. We can have coffee on your bus."

"Really?" she asked, wanting to push him a little bit and test his boundaries. "You don't want to show me your fancy kitchen?"

"Fae kitchens are ancient compared to modern human conveniences. Your coffee will be ready much sooner," he explained dismissively, reaching for her hand to tug her close. Margot let herself be moved, enjoying the feel of his treacherous lips despite herself.

She glanced at the dresser and the unmade bed. "So," she tried again, "you don't get dressed out of your dresser, and you don't make your bed."

"You judging me, darling?" he asked, giving the bed a cursory glance. "I didn't think you were a make-the-bed girl."

"You're just going to leave it like that?" she pushed. "Won't someone see?"

He shrugged. "And?"

Margot recalled the smooth blanket when they arrived, the undisturbed room. "Tobin," she said, putting a hand on his arm, "this isn't your room."

His eyes widened, and he looked around, clearly waiting for the punchline. "It's not?" he asked.

"This is the top room in what seems to be a palace," she told him. "The furniture I can ignore but not the clothes." She eyed his jeans and shirt, then pointed at the dresser. "You're telling me that when you're here, you wear the clothes in there?"

His eyes narrowed, something like excited pride and desire rushing through his face, and he brought her chin up with a finger. "You went through my things?"

"No, I didn't go through *your* things," she said, "because this isn't your room."

"So whose room is it, then?"

"It must be Lord Rebimart—"

"Rebinus."

"Whatever. Why would you bring me here? Is this some kind of game—bedding me in your Lord's sheets?" She grabbed at his hand, fear slicing through her. "Is this some kind of weird Claiming?"

"Margot, listen to me," Tobin tried. "I meant what I said—if I could, I would Claim you this instant."

"Why do you do that?" she whispered. "I believe you, but I don't know why." She gestured at the room again. "This is clearly a Lord's room, Tobin. And last I checked, you're not a Lord. I don't care how close you two are—a vassal doesn't get the penthouse." She forged ahead, wanting it out in the open. "Are you sleeping with him?"

Tobin's eyes widened, then he burst into laughter. "Oh, darling, you have no idea what you're asking me right now."

"Is that part of it—your Claiming? You said it was different because you were a child, but you're a man now—"

"Margot," Tobin soothed, putting both hands on her cheeks and staring into her eyes, "I am not fucking Lord Rebinus." There was something else in the words he said, but his meaning was clear. His relationship with his Lord wasn't sexual.

"But why then?" she uttered, peering into his eyes, feeling their Connection, trying to find the truth of him at the end of the tether. "Why would you bring me to his room?"

"It has the biggest bed," he said simply. "And the best shower, and I wanted you all to myself."

He leaned down to kiss her, and Margot felt something deep within answer his call. "How did you know he wouldn't come home?" she mumbled, the question still unanswered, her own mouth eager against his.

"Trust me," he coaxed. "I knew we would be safe here."

"Safe from what?" Margot's head spun. She did trust him—and she knew she was an idiot. Everything Tobin said was a shade of truth, not a lie, but not exactly what it seemed to mean. "From you?"

"Exactly," he told her and pushed her back onto the bed, landing atop her with her arms pinned above her head, his hard body pressing her to the mattress. "I want you, Margot," he growled. "I need to have you."

"You have me," she told him, body surrendering to the pure lust between them.

"Not yet," he insisted, his free hand working the waist of her pants and sliding them down. "Dammit, woman, you need to wear more dresses!" Margot giggled at the frustration in his voice, then he was ripping the pants, sending her shoes flying as he pressed his body into hers, demanding satisfaction. "So you went through my things?" he said, moving fast and hard. "You like seeing my dirty laundry?"

"They're not your things," Margot insisted, hooking her legs around his hips and meeting him thrust for thrust. "Tell me I'm wrong."

"You're wrong," he said, kissing her hard enough to bruise her lips.

"I'm not," she argued, trying to free her hands and failing. Instead, she hooked her leg and shoved with her body, rolling them to the side. "You're hiding something from me." They fought for dominance, teetering slowly one way and then the other, neither breaking pace. She kissed him again, harder, and he lost his focus, hands releasing hers. Margot moved immediately, pushing him flat and climbing atop him, leaning down to press her forearms across his wrists on either side of his head, trying to pin him down. "You're lying to me."

Tobin's eyes opened, suddenly wide and clear, and she saw the hurt in them, the fear that she would see whatever secrets he was hiding. His body relaxed, no longer pushing for dominance, and he let himself be held down. "I'm not lying to you, Margot."

"But you're not telling the truth, either," she said, and he said nothing. Slowing, her ardor cooling, she reached a hand up and fisted a chunk of his hair. "I can accept a lot of things," she told him. "I can accept your secrets. I cannot accept your lies."

"That seems a fair bargain." His voice was quiet.

"Promise me," she demanded.

"Promise you what?"

Margot didn't reply, slowly moving her body again, trying to find that place where they could meet as equals. When he arched against her, clearly wanting more, she leaned down to whisper in his ear. "I need your word."

For a moment, she was sure he would pretend to misunderstand her, to twist her demand into something else, but then his hand was free, pressing hard against her chest. "I swear to serve only you, Lady Margot."

She started to object, to say that she didn't need his complete servitude, but it was too late. She felt the magic spill over them both, and she lost herself to the power.

"What have you done?" she managed a few moments later, collapsed on his chest. "I felt it."

"You wanted an oath, so I swore one," Tobin said mildly.

"An oath?!" She recalled Ash's explanation. "But—your Claiming? Your Lord?"

He tilted his head, eyes narrowed. "Ash told you about oaths, did he?" He nodded. "I expected as much. I assure you, his situation is very different from my own. I can swear to you without compromising my Claiming. If oaths could overcome a Claiming, everyone would use them that way."

"It only works the other way, then? Protecting the sworn until they are Claimed?"

Tobin shook his head, sitting up a little and moving her with him. "Oaths aren't wonderful protection, either. Ash is only safe because the others fear our father."

Margot wanted to ask why they hadn't feared his father enough to refrain from stealing Tobin, but she didn't. Maybe Lord Novus had grown more powerful since then.

"So what does it mean for you? You swore to serve me just now, but what if serving me conflicts with something Lord Rebinuts—"

"Rebinus."

"Yeah—What if he wants you to do something that hurts me? Which will you do?"

Tobin smiled, a look of pure delight crossing his face. "I truly cannot wait to find out," he told her. "In serving you, I have a chance to test the oath's power—the limits and possibilities." He kissed her quickly. "Thank you."

Margot shook her head. "You are ... mind boggling."

"You love it," he assured her, then lifted her bodily off him and set her down on the bed. "Now, we have to go or you are going to be late."

Margot looked down at her destroyed pants, collected her discarded sneaker, and waved it in one hand. "Hey," she began, "about that cool conjuring thing?"

Chapter 42

Harsh Words Before Breakfast

Later Morning, Sunday, February 22nd
in Margot's Bus at the EcoDome in Akkoy, Genc

Margot stepped through the mirror into her bus, nearly stumbling as she hit the small counter of her kitchen. Tobin followed close behind, the burst of purple magic fading as the portal closed behind them.

"Mirror travel," Margot commented. "Pretty cool! Another ability?"

"Anyone can learn portal magic." Tobin wiggled his fingers, the digits suddenly snapping into perfectly designed triangles and squares. "Given enough time."

Margot shook her head. No wonder he was so good with his hands. "You say that like it's easy. Like anyone could just study a book or something and never have to take an airplane again."

Tobin shrugged. "It is easy, Margot. Controlling your other abilities is much more complicated. Magic like this is memorizing what your fingers should be doing. I can show you."

"You'd better," she said. "Though there are other things I would learn first." She kicked off her sneakers, shaking her head as she caught sight of the skirt Tobin had conjured for her, very aware of her naked body beneath the flowing bottom. Glancing at the clock in the dashboard of her bus, she headed for the kitchen, pouring water into the kettle and getting the coffee ready.

Tobin had settled into the swivel seat on her floor, and she was pouring the hot water into the carafe when someone banged on her side door. "Margot!" Ash's voice was loud and bordering on angry.

Margot took a deep breath, set the kettle down, leaving the carafe on the small counter, and walked to the side door. She glanced at the clock again, noting she had exactly five minutes before she needed to be on the road toward Sivas. She pushed the door open without a word, the metal screeching loudly, and stood in the doorway expectantly. Ash was standing a few feet away, just beyond the reach of the door, his chest heaving.

"You're here," he said simply.

"Of course," Margot replied, voice neutral. "Where would I go?"

"You went somewhere," he snapped. "No one could find you last night." His gaze skipped behind her to where Tobin sat.

"Did something happen?" she asked, moving so she stood between him and his brother, blocking his view. "Did you need me?"

"Well, no—" he began.

"Then it's none of your business," she snapped.

"Margot," he gritted, "we're in Genc now. Other fae—"

"I was perfectly safe," she insisted, gesturing to herself, "as you can see."

"You could have let me know—Let us know," he corrected quickly. "You're usually there after the show. Everyone was asking for you."

"Who was asking for me?" she demanded. Behind her, Tobin stood, heading to the counter where the coffee had finished. He busied himself in her kitchen, making their coffee.

Ash blanched, struggling for names. "Alby!" he managed finally and crossed his arms. "They didn't know where the afterparty was."

Margot stared down at him. "You're telling me that Das Leprechaun couldn't find their way to the afterparty without me giving them an address? Are you kidding? They were drowning in groupies last I saw them. Those girls always know where to go." Margot paused, then added, "And with who." She thought of the redhead again, the casual way she touched Ash, and felt her resolve harden. Tobin took that moment to lean down next to her, retrieving the small container of half and half from the fridge. He winked at Ash on the way back up, his upper half disappearing from view.

"Why is he here?" Ash demanded.

"Why shouldn't he be here?" she retorted. "You said it yourself—We're in Genc. There could be fae around. At least Tobin can protect me." The words came out before she thought them through—and she watched the hurt spread across Ash's handsome face.

"I see," he gritted.

"No," she sighed. "You don't see. And it doesn't matter. What matters is that I have an appointment in Sivas to get my bus fixed, and I don't want to be late." She reached out to grab the door as if to swing it shut, but Ash didn't move out of the way. "What?" she asked him.

"I didn't know if you were safe," he said quietly. "I was ... worried."

"Were you." She turned to Tobin, accepting the mug of coffee he held out to her and took a sip. "I'm surprised you even noticed I was gone. You seemed to have plenty of company."

"Go..."

"Don't Go me. As I said, it doesn't matter." She took another sip, relishing the sweetness. "Get back on your RV, rock star," she told him. "I'll see you in Sivas tonight." She reached for the handle, but he held his hand out, preventing the door from shutting.

"At least take Nik with you," Ash said. "Please."

Margot rolled her eyes. "Whatever." She left him at the door. Handing Tobin her mug, she yanked off her hoodie, warm enough inside her bus, despite the open door, then accepted the mug and headed to the driver's seat, dressed in her conjured tank top and skirt. She heard Ash's sharp intake of breath and couldn't help but look at him. His gaze lingered on her shoulder—on the mark Tobin had left earlier that morning.

Good, she decided, *let him see. Let him know how it feels*. She regretted the thought, but the redhead from the couch swirled into her memory along with the casual way he had dismissed her. Margot sat down in the seat. Resting the mug in the cupholder, she reached for what she called her driving socks. Glancing over to where Ash still stood in the doorway, she yanked on the thicker socks. "I'm leaving in one minute. With or without Nik."

"Go..." he began.

"If he's coming, he needs to get here now," she told him, swapping out her other sock and shoving the abandoned pair into the laundry bag hanging in the closet. She swung her legs around into the footwell, then took another sip of coffee before adjusting her mirrors. "Thirty seconds," she announced, glancing at Tobin. He took his cue, grabbing the carafe and emptying the contents into their mugs, then quickly rinsing it and tucking it back on its shelf. Twenty-five seconds later, he settled into the passenger seat.

"We should travel together. It's safer!" Ash insisted.

"You didn't seem to care so much about my safety yesterday," she said, not looking at him, "while you were busy entertaining your many fans."

"Go, that's not fair, and you know it."

"None of this is fair, Ash," she told him, turning to look at him again—which was a mistake. His face was sad, earnest, the Ash she knew from those early days— and that night on her bus—her Ash.

Nik popped into view behind the lead singer, shoving him aside and jumping onto the bus. He turned to face Ash, gave him a one-fingered gesture, then reached for the door. "Go has to go!" he shouted and slammed the door in Ash's face. Whirling around, he leaned down to lift the swivel seat and snapped it into place for driving. He gave a quick glance to their coffee mugs and gave Margot a pleading glance.

"Is there more?"

"Sorry," she said. "I can swing through a gas station."

"It's cool. I can wait until lunch," Nik said, buckling himself in and sitting up, clearly ready for road trip mode. She saw that he was wearing a different t-shirt today, but it still had a picture of him playing drums in high school.

"Thanks," Margot said, checking her mirrors one more time. She could see Ash, still standing along the passenger side door, face crestfallen. As if sensing her gaze, he glanced up, meeting her eyes in the side mirror.

His mouth opened, closed, and he simply watched her. Margot sighed, hating how the look tore her heart, and put the bus into gear, leaving Ash behind.

Chapter 43

A Look in the Mirror

Afternoon, Sunday, February 22^(nd)
at Haberson's Body Shop in Sivas, Genc

Nik waited until they were waiting for the repairs to ambush her. "Go," he began, his casual tone letting her know the conversation was anything but, "you going to tell me what happened?"

Margot glared at him across the picnic table. The three of them had settled in a park nestled next to the repair shop, claiming an old table by an ancient swing set—the shop's attempt to entertain clients and their children while they worked. Tobin had wandered over to the swing, slowly drifting back and forth, long legs dragging dirt devils in the air, leaving her alone with her cousin to have a much-needed discussion.

"You know what happened," she told him.

"Do I?" he asked. "Because to me, it seems like you're being a complete bitch."

Margot raised a hand to her chest. "Me? Are you kidding me?"

"Tell me how I'm wrong," Nik said, cocking his head at her. "You finally hook up with dream boy, and the second he turns his back, you disappear with New Guy."

Margot gasped, the sound coming out of her without thought. She felt her face grow hot. "Nik," she managed, "the second we got to Akkoy, Ash went right back to being Ash. What was I supposed to do?"

"He sang 'Heart of Stone' for you!" Nik defended.

"After he spent the afternoon with a redhead hanging all over him!" Margot exploded, her voice loud. Tobin looked over at them from his swing, but he didn't get up, returning to his slow back and forth movement without comment. The wind picked up, a slight chill in the air.

"Go," Nik began, "that's just—"

"Don't you dare tell me that's rock star stuff, Niklaus Hodges," she warned him. "If Ash was serious about me, he wouldn't have let her do that. He wouldn't have treated me that way."

"They were only there looking for passes to the after-party," Nik said after a moment. "They didn't ... stay."

"Uh huh," Margot said, looking up at the pale blue sky. She tucked her arms close as the breeze blew, chilly despite her layers—a tank top and leggings, long-sleeved shirt, and heavy hoodie. She had given up on the skirt at the gas station, changing clothes as Nik grabbed coffee, much to Tobin's dismay, though he had promised to undress her the first chance they were alone.

"Nik, you know that if I meant anything to him, anything at all, they wouldn't have been there in the first place."

"The girls are always there," Nik defended. "You know that."

"She wouldn't have been there—not like that. He wouldn't have kissed her like that." When Nik only looked away, she narrowed her eyes at him. "You mean to tell me that if you met someone you truly cared about, someone you loved, you would be in the green room before a show with another woman calling you babe and rubbing on you?"

"It's just how it is," Nik said with a shrug. He stretched, long arms above his head, and zipped his hoodie, shivering a little. "But I guess you're right," he finally admitted. "It wasn't cool to do that to you."

"It wasn't, and the song just made it worse." She looked down at her hands on the table, tears suddenly blurring her vision as the old pain sliced across her chest. "He gives me whiplash, Nik. One moment he swears he loves me. The next he's talking to me like a stranger and letting other women kiss him. I don't get it."

Nik reached out to touch her hand, his skin only slightly warmer than her chilled fingers. The temperature had dropped dramatically in the last few moments. She looked up at the sky, wondering if a storm was rolling in. Dark clouds loomed overhead. "I didn't realize how it looked. Ash is ... complicated," Nik said.

"Excuses, excuses." She grinned, letting the ache go again. "Besides, if anything is complicated, it's my life the last few days. The only one I can rely on has been Tobin. At least I know where he stands."

"You were with him?" Nik prodded, eyebrows raising. "Last night?"

"That's none of your business," she said primly, reclaiming her hand. The breeze had warmed, the chill abating slightly.

Nik chuckled, glancing over at Tobin and back at her. "Look at you, Baby Go," he mused and shook his head. "Good for you, actually."

"Why?"

"You're finally doing something for yourself," he said. "It looks good on you."

Margot marveled at how quickly Nik's alliance had shifted from his bandmate back to her. "Please," she told him. "A few minutes ago I was a cold-hearted bitch."

"You didn't see him last night, Go. He was a wreck." He took a deep breath. "Honestly, he was off all day. Getting up like he was going to leave but sitting back down. I think he was going to—maybe talk to you—but then the doc arrived, and he had to stay in the RV until right before we headed inside."

"I'm sure he was fine," she snapped, not liking this new image of Ash—one who had agonized over her all day. She changed the subject. "You had fun at the after-party? No issues with Das Leprechauns?"

Nik gave her a stern look. "He didn't go to the party, Go. He spent the night looking for you."

"Why would he do that?" she asked, hating the simultaneous jolt of excitement and pain that shot through her. "He knew I was with Tobin. He knew I was safe." She paused, then added, "And why does this feel like you're trying to make me feel guilty?"

"That's not it, Go," he insisted. "I'm just saying—"

"Saying what?" she demanded, angry. "Spit it out, Nik."

He took a long breath, clearly gathering his thoughts. "You aren't exactly the most welcoming person, Go," he said finally.

"What?" she asked, feelings hurt. "What the hell does that mean?"

"It's true!" he insisted. "You may judge Ash for his hot and cold thing—which you're right, it's fucked up—but look at yourself for a moment, huh?"

"What about me?" she asked. "I think I've been doing pretty well considering my life turned into a fairy tale a week ago!"

"I'm not talking about this week," he admitted. "You've adapted very well." His face lit up, and he held up a finger. "We are totally talking about your new abilities after this—don't let me forget."

"I won't," she promised. She gave him a little shooing motion with her hands. "Continue."

"Where was I?"

"Telling me how unwelcoming I am."

"Exactly. I mean, I can tell you're longing for Ash, but you keep yourself pretty closed off in general—even from us."

"Closed off?" she echoed.

"Think about your bus," he suggested. "You have a twin bed, Margot. A bunk bed. You're 23. Clearly, you're not interested in entertaining."

"I'm closed off because I live on a bus?" she countered.

"No, you're closed off because you designed a bus that has literally one spot to sit in that's comfortable: your seat. Anyone else is an intruder—sitting on the floor, perched on the passenger seat. There's no room in your life for anyone else."

"Are you really lecturing me about my bus layout? I wanted a full shower, and it made more sense for the water to be at the back with the kitchen. I gave up my back doors to make it fit!" She remembered designing the bus layout with Ash so many years ago, both of them arguing the pros and cons. In the end, she kept the windows but abandoned the back doors as an exit point. They still opened, but only to access the water tank, though she supposed she could climb out over the counter in extremity.

"I'm asking you to look in the mirror, Go. You have plenty to say about Ash and his habits, but you're not the most open person in the room." He sighed. "Hell, did you actually tell Ash how you felt?"

"Of course I did!" she snapped. "And it didn't matter. None of it matters because..." Her voice fell away as she recalled the many obstacles between her and Ash. "It wouldn't have mattered—groupies or no groupies," she admitted. "He was never for me."

"Or you were never for him," Nik observed.

"What does that mean?"

Nik cut his eyes to Tobin, then back at her. "You let him in, Margot. Way more than I've seen anyone else in your life—and I'm going back to the Benjamin days."

"Shut up!" she hissed. "I have no idea how you even know about Benjamin." She shook her head. "I can't explain it," she said finally. "But I just ... trust Tobin."

Nik nodded, giving the fae another glance. "I hope he deserves it," he said finally. They sat in silence for a long moment, Margot digesting his words. The air warmed again, the biting cold finally fading away as the sun came out from behind the clouds. Nik looked around, nodded, and leaned in close. "Do you want to know something?"

"Know what?"

"How I knew about you and Benjamin."

Margot leaned in close, excited despite herself. "Tell me."

"I could smell him on you—and you on him."

Chapter 44

Scents and Changes

Margot ran through the possibilities, immediately returning to the long ago afternoon with Benjamin. It had been fun and awkward and nice enough, but she wasn't particularly sweaty afterward. Nothing like the marathon she had shared with Tobin.

"Smell him?" she asked, wondering if Nik thought she didn't shower enough. "What—like an animal?"

A slow grin crept across Nik's mouth. "Got it in one!"

"Got what?" she asked. "You some kind of animal, Nik?" She tried to imagine what kind of fae creature Nik could be. Definitely something yippy, like an eager puppy, she decided.

To her surprise, her cousin nodded. "Yep." He let out a breath. "That was so much easier than I thought it would be. Wow." He laughed, hands reaching up to the ballcap on his head. He took it off, ran a hand through his hair, and plopped it back down in one smooth motion—Nik's way of showing he was relieved when a tense situation was resolved. "I really should have told you years ago."

"What the hell are you talking about, Nik?" Margot asked. "You're some kind of fae-shifter animal?"

"Not a fae," Nik said immediately. "I told you. I'm not one of them. I didn't inherit any of my mom's abilities. Just pure human like my dad. Sexy human," he added, tilting back so she could appreciate his handsome face.

"Yeah, you're perfect," she assured him. "But ... animal?" she prompted.

"Oh yeah," he said, then slid up the sleeve of his hoodie, pointing to a scar on his forearm. Margot had seen it before.

"Your skateboarding accident?" she asked, recalling the story of how a young Nik had broken his arm skateboarding. The line was jagged, and she had always wondered just how bad it had been to leave a scar like that. Margot had never broken a bone, so she didn't know if scars always looked like that—but she had never gotten on a skateboard just in case.

Nik snorted. "Hardly." He held it closer to Margot's face, fingers tracing the lines. "I got bit, Margot. See the outline there?"

Margot studied the scar. She could make out what might be a line of top and bottom teeth. She raised her eyes to meet his. The world contains many creatures, she recalled Ash saying. "Werewolf?" she whispered, the word strange to say outside of a fantasy novel. Nik nodded. "But how...?"

"Just like the stories say," he told her, rolling his sleeve back down and leaning back. "I was in the woods at night, being an idiot and not listening to my parents, and a wolf bit me. I didn't think much of it at first, but I got really sick. My parents took me to the hospital. They treated me for rabies. A day later, the swelling went down and I was fine again. Problem solved." He paused, rubbing the back of his neck, lifting and replacing his hat a second time. "But a few weeks later during the full moon..." He laughed. "Well, let's just say my dad had a great sense of humor—and he knew how to roll with the punches. That first time, he just sat with me all night, rubbing my belly."

Margot tried to imagine her reaction if she had a child who suddenly turned into a wolf. She didn't think she would have been nearly as calm about the situation. Then again, Maddie had been fae. Maybe she had suspected there was a chance it had been more than a normal wolf.

"You literally turn into a wolf?" Margot asked, trying to imagine her cousin as an animal. "Like a regular-sized wolf?"

He tilted his head, displaying his broad shoulders. "I'm a bit bigger than a gray wolf, but yeah, you get the gist."

"But you're still you?" In some of the stories, the bitten forgot themselves completely, turning into the monster, but in others, it was just another shape for the same consciousness to occupy.

"I'm always me," he told her. "I just get really hairy once a month."

"Can you control it? Like can you wolf out on command?"

"Command like a dog?" Nik asked, slightly irritated. "No. I change when the moon rises, and I change back when the moon sets."

Margot nodded, trying to think of other werewolf rules. "Does it hurt?"

Nik shook his head. "Not really. I get a bit ... emotional the day before I change."

Margot thought about the tour schedule, the way they had extra days off every month or so. "Wait, does Cayla know?"

"Hell no!" Nik exclaimed. "We complained that we need a break, so when she posed our first schedule, we massaged some of the days."

Margot did the quick math, recalling some of what Ash and Timothy had said about Nik seeing his old friend a few days ago. "So Tomas..." she began.

Nik nodded. "Yes, Tomas helped me adjust. Now we're good friends."

Margot considered. "If the full moon was Thursday of last week and the next one is the 18th of next month..." She recalled the tour dates. "Taflah," she breathed, naming the capital city—shows that Cayla was flying in to attend—and the gala afterparty. "And then Denham Island. It's that week between!" She shook her head, doing the math. "So you can't play the Wednesday..."

"I could probably play Thursday," he admitted, "but it wouldn't be my best work. Besides," he added, "we're taking the ferry over to Denham. We wanted enough time in-between to be sure."

"You're going to turn into a wolf while we're on Denham Island?" Margot asked. Then she blurted the first thing she recalled about Denham, a suspicion, a wild theory that didn't seem so wild anymore. "Aren't there dragons there?"

Nik laughed, a true belly laugh that caught Tobin's attention. "You," he said loudly in Tobin's direction, "are awesome, brother."

Tobin stopped swinging, taking the invitation and wandering back to sit with them, hopping atop the table and sitting cross-legged between them. "And why is that?" the fae asked.

"Thank you for properly educating Margot here. I'm glad someone finally told her something."

"You're welcome," Tobin said and glanced at Margot. "What topic have I stumbled into?"

"Dragons," Nik said with a wink.

Tobin coughed but caught himself in time. "I see," he said, giving Margot a long look. "My Lady wishes to hear more about dragons?"

"I imagine she already knows enough," Nik continued, "if she knows they live in Denham." Nik gave Tobin an appraising look. "You're fae. You probably know a few of them yourself."

"Hold up," Margot said, lifting her hands in the time out gesture. "Are we talking about actual dragons?"

Nik cocked his head. "I doubt we'll see them in their true form," he said casually. "Most of the time, they're human. Right, Tobin?"

Tobin nodded slowly. "That's right," he agreed. "They are notoriously secretive about showing their true forms—unless there is a specific need." He pursed his lips. "Of course, they are huge creatures, so I imagine transforming has to do with planning. Can't have a banquet set up for a shifter ambassador who arrives and doesn't fit inside the venue. They would take offense."

Margot blanched, trying to imagine a creature that wouldn't fit inside a banquet hall. *And Ash,* she thought, pulling the pieces together, *uses fire and takes after his mother, who is from Denham Island.*

"Oh my gods," Margot breathed. "Is Ash a fucking dragon?"

Chapter 45

Digging for the Truth

Nik's eyes widened, and both he and Margot turned to stare at Tobin. The fae said nothing, simply watching until finally Nik exploded, "Well?!"

"Well what?" Tobin replied, face perfectly blank.

"Is it true?" Margot pressed. "Is Ash … a dragon?" She recalled Ash standing next to her, a small flame flickering on his palm, his cryptic words about transforming. She had asked him directly, but he had used the moment to distract her. When Tobin didn't reply, she continued, "All the things you both said—about his mom." Nik gave her a confused look but said nothing, watching their exchange with great interest.

"I was annoyed," Tobin said dismissively. "I don't believe any of that."

"About Ash's father?" Margot asked, knowing Tobin was trying to change the subject. "You think Lord Novus is his father. But his mother…"

"Lady Abigail is more than I can comment on," Tobin said diplomatically. "I didn't know her very well."

"You were ten years old," Margot insisted, determined not to let the topic go this time. "Ash would have been eight. You spent eight years living with her as your mother—"

"She is not my mother," Tobin interrupted, voice cold.

"No," Margot agreed, realizing she was pushing a tender point. "But you were young. You must have spent some time with her." She waited. "She was a dragon, wasn't she? Is a dragon?" she corrected, recalling that Ash's mother wasn't dead—just gone—maybe back home.

Tobin looked away, uncomfortable. Nik looked between them both, unsure if he wanted to jump in. Nik seemed about to speak, probably to ask if they wanted him to leave, but then Tobin broke the awkward silence. "And why is this relevant?" Tobin asked finally, voice still cool with distance. "You planning on learning more about the dragons, Margot? Joining them on their island?"

"No," she said, "but this is about Ash. You said I needed to know what you could do. Shouldn't I also know what he can do?"

"Perhaps you should ask him," Tobin quipped. Nik pursed his lips, looking over at Margot now.

Margot narrowed her eyes. She glanced over at Nik, who was watching both of them like a tennis match. "Hey cousin, can we have a minute?"

Nik nodded, taking the hint. "Yeah, sure. I'll just ... take a walk." Instead of heading to the swing where he could probably hear them, Nik headed the other direction toward the shop where they could hear the faint sounds of the mechanic working on her bus. He had removed the old doors easily enough, but making the new ones line up with her old bus was more challenging. She heard some metallic banging, then a grunt of effort followed by a short shriek of metal on metal. Nik disappeared beyond the fenced area into the mechanic's yard.

"Something on your mind, Tobin?" Margot said bluntly, turning to face him.

He flashed her a disarming smile. "Whatever do you mean, darling?"

"Don't darling me," she told him. "You've been touchy since the topic came up. What gives?"

"Perhaps I don't enjoy constantly talking about my brother," he admitted with a sigh. He seemed surprised to say it, but he didn't contradict his words.

"Jealous?" she prompted, raising an eyebrow.

"No," he grumbled, hands sliding along his jeans, flattening invisible wrinkles.

Margot sighed, reaching for his hand. "Don't do that," she told him, feeling the Connection between them. "Don't shut me out."

"What do you want me to say?" he asked, running his free hand through his hair as he looked at the sky. The temperature had dropped again, and Margot squeezed his hand.

"Is that you?" she asked. "Changing the weather?"

Tobin looked around, as if realizing that it had grown colder. He closed his eyes for a moment, took a deep breath, and Margot felt the breeze lose its chill. "Sorry," he apologized. "I am not myself."

"You want to talk about it?" Margot prompted. When he said nothing, she added, "Seriously, Tobin. I'm here for you. I know it's been all about me for days, but if something is bothering you, you can talk to me. That's what friends do."

He leaned closer, looking at her. "Are we friends, Margot?"

She felt her cheeks heat, recalling the taste of him on her lips, the feel of his body against hers. "More than friends," she said, smiling up at him as she felt the familiar heat between them. "We're Connected."

"But you remain Unclaimed," he said quietly. He looked away, shaking his head. "I cannot believe he spent the night with you and didn't Claim you. My brother is either the strongest person I know ... or the biggest idiot in the world."

"You wanted him to Claim me," Margot said, realizing how much Tobin had pushed for it. "Why?"

"He could protect you," Tobin insisted, eyes trying to tell her something she couldn't see. "He's strong enough." Margot remembered Tobin's strength, the easy way he moved her around, the way he had held the faeng out with only one hand.

"Protect me from what, Tobin?" she pressed. Tobin's mouth opened, but he didn't speak. "From your Lord Rebinald?"

"Rebinus," Tobin replied automatically, frowning.

"And you can't protect me from him, can you? Is that what this is about?" She watched him bite his lip, clearly conflicted. "You swore to serve me, whatever that means, but when it comes down to it, you have to obey your Lord. You think that Ash is safer because he isn't Claimed."

"He is strong," Tobin admitted. "Foolish, but strong enough."

"Because he's a dragon," she continued.

"He's not a dragon!" Tobin blurted. "I mean—"

Margot cut him off, a finger across his lips. As whatever he was about to say faded away, she watched his eyes grow wide, then he closed them, wincing as if something hurt. Margot felt something ethereal happen to the

Connection she shared with Tobin, and she furrowed her eyebrows in confusion. "He's my brother," Tobin continued after a moment, face back to normal, as if she had imagined the magical interruption. "He's strong, and if he would just Claim you, then all of this would be over!"

"All of what, Tobin?"

He gave her a desperate look, words failing him for once. "I didn't know," he said finally, shaking his head. "I didn't know it would be like this."

"That what would be like this?" she pushed. She didn't want to use her ability to force it out of him, but this was closer than he'd been to telling her whatever secret he had buried. Even those powerful moments in his bed hadn't brought him this close to her. "Tobin, what have you done?"

"Oh, Margot," he said, face strained, "I want to tell you everything. Everything."

"But?" she asked, sensing a huge reluctance. She wondered if she needed more of Maddie's magic wine to break the secret loose.

Tobin didn't answer, head jerking to look across the small playground. Margot followed his gaze to see Nik hurrying back from the direction of the mechanic.

"Margot!" Nik said breathlessly, eyes cutting to Tobin as he scanned the opposite direction, beyond the swing. "You sense it too, right?"

Chapter 46

Fae Godmothers

Tobin nodded, and Margot focused on the spot in the trees the men were studying, a gasp escaping her as a tiny woman in a formal brocade dress stepped out from the woods. She held the dress up in small hands as she took delicate steps, lips curled in a frown as she tried not to step in any frozen mud marring the path to them.

Nik took up a position behind Margot's back, and Tobin scrambled off the table to stand between them, body executing a perfect bow before the newcomer.

"My Lady," he greeted.

Margot stood, awkwardly stepping from the bench, not wanting to be sitting for this new encounter.

"Oh, my dear!" the newcomer squealed. "You are the very picture of my Penelope." She shook her head. "Margot Tanner, you are a hard woman to find," the woman continued, her normal voice deeper than Margot expected from such a small person. The dress was huge, dwarfing her small form, making her seem both delicate and terrifying. The woman's hair was tied into multiple tiny braids twisted into an elaborate bun, and she wore a small golden tiara woven into her hair. She gave Tobin a dismissive glance. "Though I did not expect to find you in such company. Curious."

Margot said nothing, noting the way the woman's speech pattern matched the way Tobin spoke—but not Ash. The woman glanced over at where Nik stood behind her. "Oh, and you brought a little wolf! How adorable!"

The woman took the last few steps to stand directly in front of Margot. Tobin stayed where he was, body ramrod straight, hands behind his back, a perfect servant staring straight ahead.

"You knew my mother?" Margot echoed, wondering if she was supposed to recognize this woman. "May I ask who you are?" Margot asked, not wanting to offend her given the obvious respect Tobin was showing.

"Of course I did!" the stranger snapped, ignoring Margot's second question. "She was mine, after all. Well," she frowned, "until she ran off." She rolled her eyes. "Young love," she drawled. "How tedious." Her eyes cut to Tobin. "I do find it odd that you are here, vassal. No doubt doing your Lord's ... business." She glanced around the small space. "Where is Ashton? I did not think he would leave your side with you ... still Unclaimed."

"Who are you?" Margot demanded, tiring of the way the woman spoke circles around her.

"I'm Lady Drina," the woman said. "I Claimed your mother." She gave Margot a knowing smile. "But she was never meant for me, nor for our world. She was much happier roaming about Belsune, mingling with the humans."

"Like my father," Margot said, wondering how much the woman knew about her family.

"Oh, please," Lady Drina cooed. "We both know your father was no mere human." She gave Margot another appraising look. "You mostly favor your mother, but I can see him in you." She cocked her head. "Can you move through the worlds as he can?"

Margot shook her head. "You mean with portal magic?"

Lady Drina scoffed, giving Tobin another look. "Oh, Margot, you've been lingering too long with the riffraff. Portal magic is used by those with no other means. True fae can step through worlds."

"Can you do it?" Margot asked, forgetting how rude it was to directly ask about powers from her frank discussions with the boys, but she didn't like the way Drina had dismissed Tobin.

"I'm merely a Lady," Drina replied, her previously friendly tone fading a bit. "Such lofty abilities are beyond me." She gave Margot a long look. "But you…"

"I can't do that," Margot told her flatly. She didn't add, *Not yet*. "Look, can I ask why you're here? Are you here to Claim me?"

The woman tossed her head back and laughed, the sound loud and obnoxious. Margot hated the way it crept under her skin. "As if I could, my dear! You are far too powerful for the likes of me," Drina exclaimed. "No," she assured Margot. "I'm not here for that."

Margot didn't know why, but she believed her. She resisted the urge to put a hand on her hip. "So why are you here?"

"I can't come to see Penny's daughter?" Lady Drina asked. "You're practically my godchild, if we still did things like that. I wanted to check up on you, my dear, especially after hearing what happened with those … creatures back in Armav."

"How do you know about that?"

"Everyone knows about that!" Lady Drina said. "You're all anyone can talk about these days. Everyone wants to know who will Claim you."

"Everyone who?" Margot demanded, imagining some gaggle of fae ladies gossiping about her. "And why do they care?"

"You're powerful," Lady Drina explained, answering her second question. "Whoever gets you will gain acclaim and praise. It will probably shift the balance of power among the Lords." She gave Tobin another dirty look. "I see Lord Rebinus already has his hand in play." She sniffed. "Your father will not be pleased about that."

"Tobin is here as Tobin, not for his Lord," Margot said. She knew immediately it was the wrong thing to say.

Lady Drina laughed, the sound a magical tinkle that grated on Margot's nerves. "Oh, dear!" she cooed. "Your mother was a smart girl—at least until she fell in love. Please tell me you inherited some of her sense."

Margot gave Tobin a nervous look, but he didn't look at her, face blank as he stared straight ahead in perfect servant mode.

Is this how he behaves around other fae? Where is the Tobin I know?

Margot reached for that Connection, used to sensing his mood, but to her surprise, she couldn't find it. Frowning, she wondered if Lady Drina's presence was affecting the spell. Her words were certainly having an effect on Tobin.

"Please leave my mother out of this," Margot said. "She's been gone a long time now."

"Exactly," Lady Drina said, angry. "We have his Lord to thank for that, don't we?"

Margot's mouth fell open. "No..." she said softly, recalling her mother's last few weeks, the sickness growing in her. "My mother was sick."

Lady Drina nodded, face grim. "A spell, dear girl. More of a curse in the end," she explained. "Of course he wouldn't have told you." She grabbed Margot's hand, tender now. "Lord Rebinus was playing another of his games, trying to wheedle something from Lord Tennere. The easiest target was your mother. She was supposed to come back to Lorellon, but instead, she kept running. I imagine she meant to keep you hidden."

"Curse?" Margot repeated, trying to understand what Lady Drina was saying.

"It killed her, obviously, and devastated Lord Tennere. Lord Rebinus had very little love from the high Lords before then, but after, he certainly lived up to his reputation." She gave Tobin another dark look. "No doubt his vassal has hidden much of this from you."

Suddenly, her glance at Tobin shifted to sympathy. "It's not his fault, dear boy." Her face transformed into friendliness, as if her previous judgments hadn't occurred. If Margot hadn't seen how she treated Tobin earlier, she would have believed her concern was genuine. "Tobin, your mother would like a visit when you finish your duties here. She says it's been too long since you've been by." Margot recalled that he had said his mother was Claimed by Lady Drina, a forgiving mistress who allowed her to come back home to live with her after her marriage with Lord Novus ended.

If she is a forgiving mistress, I don't want to know what the other fae are like.

"Yes, my Lady," Tobin said, voice distant.

"Margot, dear, you look a little pale," Lady Drina continued, guiding Margot to sit on the bench. "Are you unwell?" She glared at Nik who stood behind her. "You need to take better care of her, little wolf. She will need all of her strength for what's coming."

"What's coming?" Margot managed, mind whirling.

"Your Claiming, of course!" Lady Drina exclaimed. "Others think it will happen somewhere in Bacoli, but I bet it wouldn't be until Taflah. After the Dragon show, everyone will be at the gala at the Aerie." She frowned. "What was it again—something for the fans? An exclusive party? Whatever," she dismissed. "It doesn't matter. Everyone will be there." She lowered her voice. "Do try to stay Unclaimed until then, dear. I can't wait to see the look on Lady Sylvia's face when I win. She thinks you'll be Claimed in the next few days."

Lady Sylvia. Tobin's mother. The fae are betting on how long I will retain my freedom. Lord Rebinus ... killed my mother. Tobin...

She looked up, barely nodding in Lady Drina's direction. "Thank you for your confidence," she said formally, "but I intend to remain Unclaimed."

"Ooh!" Lady Drina exclaimed, clapping her hands together. "We haven't had a new Lord in a very long time. I would love to see it, my dear." She gave Tobin another look, shaking her head. "Look, I know he's charming," she told Margot in a low whisper, "but you know who he belongs to. You can't trust him."

"Tobin has told me nothing but the truth," Margot defended, cheeks heating as she rose to her feet. If this was how the other fae treated Tobin, no wonder he spent so much time in Ardon among the humans.

"Well, of course he has!" Lady Drina exclaimed. "He has to. We fae can't lie to one another without losing our abilities. The price of power, I suppose." At the look on Margot's face, she put a hand on her hip. "Didn't tell you that either, did he? Not surprised. He may not lie to you, Margot, but he will twist his words and leave out convenient information." She nodded at Nik. "You're better off with the wolf."

Margot hated how much Lady Drina's words stung. She straightened, determined not to lose faith in Tobin, no matter what the woman said. "Is there anything else I should know?"

"Oh dear," Lady Drina said, "The first thing you need to work on is asking better questions. You'll never last among fae with such open-ended liberties." She reached out, patting Margot's shoulder. "I do wish you luck." She leaned down, examining Margot's hoodie and yoga pants. "And do dress more appropriately for the gala in Taflah," she urged. "You have a reputation to uphold."

"Oh," Margot said, not sure what the appropriate reply was, but Lady Drina was already walking back to the trees where she had appeared.

"Don't make it so hard to find you next time!" she trilled. "I'm rooting for you, dear!"

She was gone, a swish of skirts in the greenery. Margot felt a pop, something magical echoing in the atmosphere that tingled her skin.

"Holy crap," Nik said quietly. "That woman was beautiful ... and terrifying."

"I guess she knew my mother," Margot said, not sure what else to say.

"Some fairy godmother!" Nik exclaimed and grimaced. "Sucks for you, Go. You better wear something nice to that party. You don't want her to get mad at you."

"Because that's what matters right now," Margot commented.

"Yeah," Nik said, looking back and forth between her and Tobin, recalling their interrupted conversation, "so you probably need a moment, but right before I came back, they finished the bus. We need to settle up and get going."

Margot nodded at him, then gave Tobin a long look, still sorting through her swirling thoughts. She had known he was shady, was feeding her half-truths, but she had wanted him anyway. Her damn libido was always making terrible choices—first the unattainable Ash, now a scoundrel who definitely had ulterior motives.

I have a pseudo fairy godmother. Does that mean I end up with the prince?

Chapter 47

Working It Out

Evening, Sunday, February 22nd
in Margot's Bus at The Hive in Sivas, Genc

The drive to The Hive was silent, all three of them lost in their thoughts, no one daring to break the mood and open a discussion. Margot turned up her music and sang along, forgoing her angry girl music for more traditional driving tunes, the window down despite the chill in the air. When they wound through the back lot of the arena later that night, the security guards waved them on to park next to the two huge RVs and crew bus. Margot sat in the driver's seat for a long moment, not in a rush to face Ash after the long day.

"Hey," Nik said, typing on his phone, "they have dinner on the Party Bus if you're hungry." He glanced between her and Tobin. The fae hadn't moved from his spot in the passenger seat either. "I can bring you something." Undoing his seatbelt and standing up, he stretched and gave Margot a pointed look. "Though I don't know where you both would eat in here."

"We'll manage," she said, answering for Tobin. "Let's not talk about how emotionally closed off I am again, Nik." Tobin's head moved at that, giving her an appraising look. "There's plenty of room in here for someone willing to compromise."

Nik snorted. "Very subtle, Go. Cute." He shook his head. "What am I telling the guys then? We'll see you tomorrow at 3?" When she nodded, running both hands through her hair and shaking it out of its bun, he tilted his head. "You okay, Baby Go? I can stay."

"No," she told him. "I'm fine. Tell them I'm fine. I'll see you all tomorrow. Just…" She twisted in the seat, not looking at Tobin at all. "Just give me the night, please."

Her cousin nodded, reaching for the door, which opened without a sound to Margot's relief. He hopped down and turned to face them, hand on the new door-frame. "Look, I'm rooting for you two. I hope you can work it out." He gave her a grin and a cheesy thumbs up, then shut the door. Despite the force he used, the door shut quietly, evidence of the decades of new technology in the new piece. The repair shop had done great work. Even the color of the new panels matched the cream exterior.

The silence in the bus was palpable, but Margot didn't break it, simply waiting for Tobin to say something. Anything.

Finally, he turned to face her, body still facing forward. "I will leave," he said quietly. "Just tell me to go." When she didn't speak, his head tilted back to hit the headrest, eyes filled with anguish. "Make me go away, Margot."

"Do you want to go?" she asked quietly, voice neutral as she watched his face, this fragile Tobin she had glimpsed in small snatches before.

"Don't ask me what I want," he told her. "I don't deserve that. Tell me what you want me to do." He closed his eyes. "Or just let me go."

"I'm not keeping you here, Tobin," she reminded him. "You can leave whenever you want. You owe me nothing." She thought of his oath but said nothing.

"I should go," he whispered, looking away. He raised both hands to run through his hair, looking up at the ceiling of her bus.

"Because of Lord Rebinus?" she asked, for once saying the right name.

"Yes." He nodded. "But it's more than that now." He sighed. "I understand why Ash couldn't let you go."

"Because I'm powerful," she said with a long-suffering sigh. "Or I will be. I'm an important pawn in fae politics. I get it."

"No," he said, twisting to face her fully, hand reaching out to touch her. "Not for that." Their hands met, loosely gripped in the space between the two seats. "No one has ever stood up for me before," he said. "No one ever defended me to them."

Margot frowned. "You mean Lady Drina?" She rolled her eyes. "I deal with bitches all the time. I can handle her. Besides, she was really rude to you." She paused, then asked, "Is that how they treat you?"

He shrugged. "Mostly. I expect it though. Lord Rebinus is..."

"Not real popular, yeah." She pursed her lips. "Is he as awful as they say he is? Be honest, Tobin."

Tobin considered, face running through an array of emotions. "He's ... not great. But none of the Lords are. You think your rock stars are selfish and greedy? They are nothing to fae Lords. They crave power and obedience—and it's never enough." He paused. "He's not particularly kind to me, but he's not awful, either. I have my freedom, mostly, so long as I accomplish my goals. He lives a life separate from my own."

Margot raised an eyebrow at the odd phrasing, but she shook her head. "I'm going to ignore that—like I ignore every red flag from you—and ask you one question. Just one."

"Okay," he said, sitting up straighter, obviously preparing for something awful.

"Do I have anything to fear from your Lord Rebinus?"

"No." The word was out immediately, and she felt the truth in it, though it was a thin connection, a human gut reaction, not the full-body certainty she normally had with Tobin. She reached for that magical Connection but found emptiness.

"What happened, Tobin?" she asked, her newly magical senses tingling with the missing spell. "Why can't I feel you?"

"I..." His voice trailed off, and he closed his mouth.

Margot watched him, this sexy stranger she had invited into her life, and realized that while she still longed for Ash, had worshiped him for years, her feelings for Tobin were somehow more ... real. Loving Ash was like appreciating fine art or exquisite food or a great night of sex.

Her relationship with Tobin was comfortable, based on mutual interests and physical attraction. She didn't love him, nothing like that, but she liked him—and she didn't want him to leave.

"You don't have to tell me," she said. "I know I keep badgering you with questions, demanding answers, but you don't have to tell me. I'm here, and I'll be here, and you don't owe me anything. No promises. No oaths. Just you and me and a good time. For as long as we can."

"But your mother—" he said.

"Is that what this is about? Lord Rebinard—"

"Rebinus."

"Yeah, he did that. Not you."

Tobin's face fell. "I didn't stop him."

"How could you? You were what 18, 19?" She paused. "Tobin, how old are you?"

"29 in three months."

She did the math. Tobin was five years older than she was, and her mom died when she was 15. "Okay, so 20 then. Besides, how could you have stopped him? He Claimed you."

"I stopped him," Tobin said quietly. "Just not in time."

Margot quirked an eyebrow, confused at his words. Before she could ask, Tobin released her hand and stood up, moving to stand in the space between the door and her bed. "Margot," he began, "do you really want me?"

"That's a dumb question," she replied, watching him carefully. "You know I want you."

He smirked, but it was fleeting. "I mean me." He tapped his chest. "Myself. Do you want to know me, really?"

"I have no claim on you, Tobin. I release you from your oath. I want you to be here because you want to be. You choose to be. But if you're asking what I want, the answer is yes. I want to know you. I like you. And I know that you're hiding things from me, but it's okay. I can live with some secrets."

"What if you don't like what you find?" he asked.

"Why don't we deal with that as it arises?" she suggested. "I'm sure you won't like everything about me." She stood up, meeting him where he stood. "Isn't that what couples do? They work it out?"

Chapter 48

Fae Lords

"You want us to be a couple, Margot?" he asked, hope sparking in his bright eyes as he tugged her closer.

"The thought crossed my mind," she said. "I mean, you are beautiful—and you know it. And you're insanely good in bed." She reached up, brushing his hair out of his eyes. "And you're funny, too. And charming, not to mention clever and witty." She smiled at him. "You're pretty amazing, Tobin." She narrowed her eyes at him. "Don't look so surprised."

"No one appreciates me like that, Margot," he told her. "I mean, you saw Lady Drina. She knows my mother, and she still treats me like a servant."

"Because of Rebinus?"

He nodded. "They don't treat Rebinus with disdain. They're all afraid of him." Something cruel twisted his lip, and instead of being turned off, Margot felt herself drawn closer to him. Lady Drina was awful—she needed to be afraid of someone. It was good for her.

"Can't say I'm sorry to hear that," Margot said. "Fae society sounds terrible. I understand why you might linger here instead."

"It is terrible," Tobin agreed. "But it doesn't have to be, not if you're strong enough."

"Is that what this is about?" she asked, rolling her eyes. "I know. You want Ash to Claim me so I'm protected by someone strong. What if I don't want to be Claimed by anyone?" Tobin turned aside, and she saw the same defeated look she had seen on Ash's face when she spoke of remaining free. She caught his face between her hands. "You don't think I can do it?"

He sighed. "I think you can do anything you want, Margot. I want—" He paused, leaning down so his forehead met hers. "I want to tell you something."

Margot pushed down the urge to tell him he didn't have to. "Why?" she asked instead.

"Because I think you'll understand." Breaking free from her embrace, he rummaged through her fridge and stood, holding the bottle of magic wine.

"You need magic to tell me?" she asked.

"No," he said, pulling out the temporary cork and downing the rest of the bottle in one go, neck working as he swallowed the contents. He set the bottle down on her counter and moved back to her. "I just needed a drink before I say this."

She smiled at him, unable to help it. Tobin was weird, and she loved it. "Let me guess," Margot said. "You've never told anyone this before."

"You might want to sit down," he suggested, motioning to her seat.

"Well that sounds ominous." She obeyed and settled into her swivel seat.

"I—" he began, stopped, turning around to pace the few feet to her kitchen and back again. "Lord Rebinus..." He stopped himself again. "Maybe I should just show you."

"Okay," Margot said, not knowing what to expect. With her feet on the floor and hands braced on her knees, she prepared for a new bombshell. "Whatever you prefer."

"Yeah," Tobin said, then turned around again, his back to her. She felt the prickle of magic against her skin, and as she watched, Tobin's form began to shift. His body filled out, growing more muscular and taller. His simple jeans and hoodie faded away, replaced by dark velvet pants that hugged his body and a silver brocade vest over a white long-sleeved shirt. His hair spilled over his back, long and white and wavy.

The man in her bus turned around slowly, and Margot took in the stranger who had been Tobin. His boots matched the ones she had found in Tobin's closet that morning, the tight pants accentuating thick thighs, and the poet's shirt matched other clothing she had seen in his dresser. This was definitely the man whose room they had been in. Her gaze roamed up his broad chest, the strong arms, the blunt fingers, and settled on his face. The chin was wider, the cheekbones more pronounced, everything about the face older, more mature, but the eyes were the same pale blue. The hair was longer and fuller, adding another level of majesty and glory to what was already an imposing figure.

He looked like Tobin, only aged up and bigger, with more lines on his face. Margot stared at him, trying to understand, something deep inside already making the connection.

"My Lady," the stranger said, bowing deeply, a move she had seen Tobin make. "Allow me to introduce myself. I am Lord Rebinus."

Heat flooded Margot's body as she stared at him. He was imposing, every inch the Lord Ash had told her to fear, but he was also handsome, and his domineering presence was doing odd things to her insides.

If all fae Lords look like that, she thought, *I am doomed.*

"But..." Margot tried, shaking her head to clear it, then she swallowed hard, finding her voice. "You're Tobin."

"I am," he said, his voice deep and rich, making her toes curl. "And I am also Lord Rebinus."

"Why..." She rallied. "Why would you pretend to be a vassal?" Her eyes widened in horror. "And what happened to the real Tobin?"

"You're asking the wrong question, Margot," Lord Rebinus said, leaning down to kneel before her, that huge body folding with impossible grace.

She stared at him, running through everything she knew—Ash's comments about Rebinus, the obvious connection between the brothers despite their differences, Tobin's casual freedom, the bedroom of a Lord, and finally, Tobin's words: *He lives a life separate from my own.*

"You're Tobin," she whispered. "Where is the real Rebinus?"

"I killed him," Tobin replied. "Seven years ago."

"You live as both?" she asked, trying to wrap her head around the logistics. "You play Lord Rebinus back in Lorellon?"

He stood, shrugging, the massive body moving with ease. Margot had never felt that her bus was small, but with Lord Rebinus inside, she suddenly understood what the guys had been telling her.

"It's not a game," he said, then paused and laughed, the sound rich and deep in his chest. Margot's toes curled despite herself. "Though I suppose maybe it is. Politics often can be a game of strategy and cunning."

"If you're him, or he's you," Margot struggled with her words, "then why are you here? Is this still part of some plan to use me to get to Ash? To Claim him?"

"That was the original plan, yes," he admitted, reaching out to touch her face with his big hand.

"But what?" she prompted, skin shivering at the touch despite herself.

"Then I met you," he said, "and I couldn't do it." She reached up to hold his hand against her face, studying his features. "You are more than a pawn, Margot."

"Why do you look so much like Tobin, though? Are you related?"

He nodded. "Lord Rebinus is—was my uncle."

"Oh," Margot said, pieces falling into place. "Your uncle stole you from your father, and you killed him. Tobin, you have a really fucked up family."

He laughed again, the sound changing as he shifted, Tobin's lean features emerging from the mature mask. "Truth," he agreed, the clothes hanging on his slimmer frame.

She reached out to touch the material of the vest. "I think I prefer your face," she said.

"Your body says otherwise, Margot." Tobin arched an eyebrow. "You want me to change back?"

His face began to shift, and she shook her head. "No," she insisted. "He's a bit ... intimidating." To her relief,

Tobin remained Tobin. "Your clothes," she prompted. "You're leaving them?"

He frowned, still peering at her. "Ah," he said awkwardly. "That."

"Gods," Margot said. "There's more? Please tell me this new thing doesn't trump the fact that you are fucking Lord Rebinus!" She paused. "Oh god. I'm fucking Lord Rebinus!"

Tobin grinned. "Margot, I already told you: I am not fucking Lord Rebinus."

"Only when you jerk off, I suppose," she muttered. "So how does this work with Claiming? I mean, are you Unclaimed?"

"When I'm Lord Rebinus, I am. When I am Tobin, I am Claimed."

"But your Claimer, or whatever, is dead! I thought that broke the deal."

"Claims don't fade like that, Margot," he explained. "If they did, everyone would try to kill the Lords."

"I got the impression that they do that, anyway."

He frowned. "Well, yes, they try, but the Claim simply passes to the next strongest member of the family."

"That would be you—since you managed to kill Lord Rebinus. That's why no one noticed a shift. But how do they not know it's a glamour? Ash made it seem like fae can tell if someone is glamoured."

"It's not a glamour, Margot," Ash told her. "I *am* Lord Rebinus. One of my abilities is to shapeshift."

"You can change your physical body?" she asked, recalling the feel of her hair while seeing the short blonde spikes in the mirror. "That's so cool!" She paused, thinking. "Wait, so can you just be Rebinus, or can you be anyone?"

"I can be anyone," he said, face shifting to Nik's, silvery hair darkening to brown. "Is there someone you want to see, Margot?" Nik's face shifted to Ash's, eyes lightening to the honey she knew and loved.

"Stop it," she said quickly, touching his cheek. "Don't."

"You don't want to see me, Go?" Ash's voice asked her. "I can be him, if that's what you want."

Margot dropped her hand. Something dark and ugly welled up inside her, and she fought it down fiercely, forcing herself not to speak.

"It's okay," not-Ash whispered, leaning close. "He doesn't have to know what you truly wish. We can pretend, and he'll never know."

Margot reached out and fisted his vest, yanking him toward her.

"I'm tired of pretending," she growled at him. "I want you—whoever you are." She reached for the Connection, surprised again to find it missing. "Where are you?" she demanded, shaking him a little bit. "Why can't I feel you anymore?"

Ash's face dissolved back into Tobin's familiar features. "I broke a thing," he said meekly.

"Tobin Fetch," she snarled his name, "what have you done?"

Chapter 49

Lies and Negotiations

"I lied to you," Tobin said quietly. His body shifted, sinking into himself, and her arm extended as the fabric stretched between them. "When a fae lies to someone, we lose any magic we shared with them."

Margot stared at him. "Centaur's Balls, Tobin," she said, the fae curse coming easily to her lips, "why would you do that?"

"I had to," he said, body still bowed.

"How do we fix it?" she pried. "How do we get the Connection back?"

He looked up at her. "Like this. Now you know—and can render judgment. When it's over, the magic should return... if you want it to."

Margot stared at him, at his posture, his complete submission before her. She wasn't sure how she felt about having him clearly under her power, waiting for her vengeance. "What did you lie about?" she asked, keeping her tone light.

"I ... can't tell you," he gritted.

"Can't ... or won't?" she demanded, tone a bit sterner as she pulled him closer again.

"Won't!" he exclaimed. "I will not tell you." He widened his eyes, opening himself to her. "Punish me as you will, my Lady."

Margot released him, and Tobin stumbled back a little, catching himself and crouching on the floor of her bus, eyes down, refusing to look at her. She hardly recognized this Tobin, his subservience and broken will. *Is this how other Claimed fae behave?*

"You really expect me to punish you," Margot said, staring at the stranger in her bus. Her heart went out to him, this wild abused boy who had become a Lord. "What the hell did he do to you?"

Tobin glanced up, eyes dark with remembered pain but said nothing.

Margot shook her head, hatred surging through her at that look—at the idea that someone would hurt Tobin. "The more I learn about fae society, the more I hate it," she spat. She could understand why someone would fight against such a system. "Tobin," she said finally, sadness leaking into her voice, "I forgive you. Whatever you lied about, it's fine. I've been forcing you to do all kinds of uncomfortable things."

He stared at her without blinking for a long moment before the words burst out of him. "How can you forgive me?" Tobin asked, face incredulous. "I'm Lord Rebinus, the man who essentially killed your mother!"

"Did *you* kill my mother?" she asked.

"Well, no, but—"

"Then it doesn't matter," Margot told him, calm filling her as she reassured him, her broken man. Strangely, the idea didn't make her yearn to fix him, as she sometimes wished with Ash, that she could change the rock star into a man who would be content with just her. Instead, she could accept Tobin as he was: cunning and twisted but also loyal and sweet. She recalled Nik's words about how she had let Tobin into her life immediately. He was right. There was something about the fae that spoke to her deep inside, and it was more than a magical Connection that he had broken.

Can't I just like him? She remembered Ash commenting that he liked that option because it meant she could change her mind. Well, Ash had been right. Margot could change her mind. She could choose Tobin. He may be a scoundrel, but he was her scoundrel—and he had always been kind to her. As for his treatment of others, especially as Lord Rebinus, that was something she would deal with another day. This one had already been filled with too many surprises.

"Look," she began, "I know that I'm only beginning to scratch the surface of your world, and that you've had a hell of a life, but let me tell you something about the humans here on Ardon: we forgive each other."

"You truly want my company, despite everything I've told you?" Tobin asked, disbelief obvious in his tone.

"Tobin," she sighed, running a hand over her face and standing up, "I want you more than anything right now." She gave his clothing another glance. "Although I have to say the outfit doesn't suit you at all."

He stood up, meeting her eagerly. "Suited Lord Rebinus, didn't it?" he asked her, a sultry grin crossing his lips, the Tobin she knew back in that look.

"Maybe," she admitted, leaning into his arms. "Definitely feels like an acquired taste," she told him. "But only because I know it's you."

"Keep telling yourself that, darling," Tobin said, voice dipping into the Lord's low voice again. "Fae Lords are said to be irresistible," he bragged.

"What if I don't want to resist you?" Margot bit her lip, unable to deny the chills running through her. She gave him a sharp-eyed look. "Wait—if you're Lord Rebinus, why can't you Claim me?"

Tobin stroked a hand through her hair, gently tracing the line of her chin. "Because I want you to remain free."

"But you kept saying you wanted Ash to Claim me, to keep me safe. Was that the lie?"

Tobin shook his head. "No, actually, I do—did—want him to Claim you."

"What changed?"

"Now that I know you, I've grown rather fond of your freedom. But I wanted Ash to Claim you and reveal himself to fae society."

She nodded, suddenly seeing the plan as easily as if it had been her own. "So you could then Claim him," she mused. "And he would know what it was like." She took a deep breath, sorting the possibilities. "But now? What is your plan?"

"Perhaps I will just marry you instead, darling," he said, and Margot felt something swoop deep in her chest—fear or excitement, she couldn't tell.

"Wait," she said, a thought surfacing amid the chaos. "Does Lord Rebinus have a wife?"

Tobin shook his head. "No one is brave enough to approach him as a partner, though plenty are willing to entertain him here and there."

"Tobin," Margot said seriously, "if we're a couple, there will be no entertaining here or there."

"Ah," Tobin said, leaning down to peer into her eyes. "Monogamy, is it? You realize that is not a norm in fae society." He gave her a long hard look. "Darling, you really think that when my brother grows a brain and tries to get you back, you won't go running into his arms?"

Margot glared at him, not liking the burst of hope in her chest at the possibility. "No," she said quickly.

"No?" Tobin asked, staring intently at her. Margot could feel the Connection sparking again, metaphysical butterflies in her stomach, and she felt his skepticism—but not his judgment. She tried to understand his society, wondering how she felt about such rules—or lack thereof.

"You mean that you wouldn't mind if I run around fucking whoever I want?"

"Fucking is fun," Tobin reminded her. "Pleasure is a good thing. I would never deny you joy."

"Why would anyone ever get married in the fae world?" Margot asked. "What about commitment?"

"We're not talking about commitment, darling. We're talking about sex. The humans get hung up on both." At her darkening expression, he held his hands up. "Look, I'm all for monogamy, if that's what you want—but I've seen how you look at Ash. You truly believe if he crooked his finger, you wouldn't go running back to his bed?"

"What about you?" she asked, trying to redirect the conversation. "Am I going to walk in a room and find you with some groupie's tongue down your throat?"

He shrugged. "I wasn't going to discount the possibility, but judging by your face right now, I assume the correct answer is no."

"Have you been with other people?" At his look, she added, "Since you were with me?"

"Margot." He reached out to touch her face and tuck her hair behind her ear. "I haven't left your side since we've been together."

"Oh." Margot felt her cheeks heat up. She was being unfair, acting like a jealous girlfriend, when she couldn't honestly answer his question about Ash. Margot had never been shy, enjoying casual sex when she got lonely, but her connections with both Tobin and Ash had long surpassed the casual stage.

And he's a fae Lord, she reminded herself. *No doubt he has a reputation to uphold.*

"I have a proposition for you, Margot," Tobin offered. "Care to hear it?"

"Sure," she said, moving away from him to slump down in her seat again, trying not to picture Tobin kissing someone else, whispering in someone else's ear, sharing secrets with another.

"We are Connected," he began, "and that is a commitment of a sort, an emotional and spiritual link. In this regard, I would prefer your loyalty." When she opened her mouth, he held up a hand. "I know you still love Ash. That's a given. But no one else," he demanded, kneeling down to take her hand. "Not until we know what lies between us."

Margot nodded. "Okay," she agreed. "That seems fair." She frowned. "But the sex thing..."

He nodded, contemplating. "Let me offer you this: if, the next time you see my charming brother—and believe me, you will see him again, and probably soon—and you do not want to disappear into his arms, we can discuss more restrictive terms."

"Is that a thing among the fae? Monogamy?" she asked.

He nodded. "Oh, yes, but it's not the norm. We fae are a sensual people, Margot, and we live a very long time. We enjoy getting lost in the moment."

"I enjoy getting lost in the moment," Margot said, "with *you*." She brought his hand to her mouth, kissing the back and looking at him. "I don't want you to be with anyone else. Not now."

He grinned, his other hand stroking her chin. "How very human of you, darling. I understand. Jealousy is a terrible thing."

"You wouldn't be jealous if I slept with Ash?" Margot asked, trying to understand his perspective.

"If you didn't ask me to watch," he admitted. At her scandalized expression, Tobin laughed. "Relax, darling. I don't expect you to adopt all of our ways immediately."

Margot heard the subtext. "But you would expect me to adopt them eventually?" she prompted.

He gave her a broad smile, and she caught the hint of the fae Lord hidden within. "Oh, Margot. I expect you to always do exactly what you want to do, and I look forward to seeing what that is." He stood up, lifting her easily to her feet. "Now, are we done negotiating the rules of this relationship?"

"I think so," Margot said, a thrill running through her at the word relationship. "Why?"

"Because I want to kiss you again, and I need to know we're done talking," he declared.

"Oh," she said, heat spilling through her again at the words. "We're definitely done talking."

Chapter 50
Sunrises and Coffee

Morning, Monday, February 23rd
in Margot's Bus at The Hive in Sivas, Genc

The next morning, Margot crawled awkwardly out of her bed, Tobin's arm around her back as she slid off the bunk, feet thumping on the swivel seat. She nearly fell as the seat moved out from under her, spinning freely, and Tobin's arm tightened around her back. She looked over at him. His eyes were still closed, but he held her tight for another second, waiting for her to catch her balance.

"Please don't kill yourself before breakfast, darling," he said, opening sleepy eyes to peer at her.

"I blame you," she quipped. "My legs haven't recovered."

"Glad to be of service," he said, releasing her and rolling over.

"You in coffee mode yet?" she asked, enjoying the feeling of a new routine: Tobin in her bed, the two of them spending the morning before the show together.

"Soon," he mumbled, pulling the blanket back up over his shoulder.

Margot smiled, then headed to the kitchen for her morning routine. By the time the coffee was ready, Tobin was asleep again, snoring softly, and Margot decided to take her mug outside. She dressed in layers, noting that many of her clothes were less than fresh. She would have to do laundry soon, and if she didn't want to find a laundromat, that meant facing the guys on their RV. Normally, she just hung out with them while washing her clothes, but lately, the idea seemed awkward and intrusive.

Maybe I can ask Nik to do it, she mused. *He certainly owes me for not telling me he was a werewolf.* She recalled the years at Maddie's when her pleading cousin had cajoled her into doing his laundry alongside her own. Smiling at the pleasant memory, she opened the side door of her bus, reveling in the quiet hinges. The air outside was chilly but not too cold. The back lot of the arena was quiet this early as she stepped down, sliding on her boots and shutting the door behind her. She walked to the back of her bus, eyeing the ladder rungs running to the roof. It had been a while since she sat outside, even longer since she sat atop her bus, enjoying the small flat space. Balancing her mug carefully, she hopped onto the bumper, easily pulling herself up and settling cross-legged on the wooden platform. The sun was up, but barely, the sky still waterlogged with night, and she sipped in silence, soaking in the peace.

Not even a week, she realized, running through her schedule. *I've been fae less than a week.* Well, she supposed, she had always been fae, but she hadn't known about it. *Six days,* she mused, *and how many new abilities?* The wings, for one; then the glamour; the weather had been third; and lastly, the terrible push power. If Tobin and Ash were right, and she was as powerful as her father, she should have a new ability very soon. She wondered what it would be: elemental control like her mother and aunt? Maybe traveling, the walk-through-worlds ability Drina had mentioned, like her father? She could have something more like Tobin's powers: conjuring items or moving things with her mind.

Or fire? The thought came with the image of Ash, and she sighed, good mood evaporating.

It doesn't matter, she told herself. *You're with Tobin now. Ash can do whatever the hell he wants, per usual.*

Despite her resolve, and her determination to explore her feelings for Tobin, she knew that seeing Ash again would only hurt her. It wouldn't matter what he did or said. He was an open wound, one she feared would never truly heal.

"Margot?" For a second, she wondered if Tobin had woken up and was fucking with her, but Ash's wild curls peeked over the edge of the roof. The lead singer climbed up and sat next to her as if he had every right to be there. "Can we talk?"

"Apparently," she snapped but regretted her tone. She may be with Tobin and putting her obsession with Ash behind her, but she still had to work with him for the rest of the tour—and beyond, unless she planned on getting a new job after this was over. The thought was odd: *Am I really thinking about leaving the guys?* She peered at Ash, trying to see him as he could be. Her friend, an old crush. *Like Benjamin,* she told herself, picturing the cheerful crew member who never gave her any trouble, not even hinting that they had once been together.

Can I have that with Ash? she wondered. *More importantly, can he have that with me?*

"What is it?" she prompted when it seemed like he wasn't going to speak.

"I'm sorry," he blurted. "I was an ass."

She nodded, heart singing at the words she had longed to hear. Well, part of her heart. The rest was still angry at him, still broken. "You were," she agreed.

"I just..." He held up his hands. "I don't know how to do this," he explained lamely.

"How to do what?" she asked.

"Be with you," he replied. "You know, for real with you."

"Ash, are you really telling me that you don't know how to be loyal to someone?" He flinched, and part of her rejoiced, enjoying his discomfort. She remembered that Ash was raised in a world where monogamy wasn't the norm and tried not to blame him for his promiscuous ways. "Look, it's fine. I knew what I was getting into."

"And what was that?" His eyes were big, his face soulful, and Margot could feel the pull of him, of her need for him. But she pushed it away, knowing that Ash came with so many restrictions and guidelines—and a life that was never going to be shared with her. She thought of Tobin still asleep in her bed below them, and she smiled. At least with him she knew what she was in for. Mostly. Sort of. Ash would always be unpredictable.

"I'm not the one for you," she reminded him. "I know that. You don't owe me anything, Ash."

He reached for her hand, and she let him take it, cataloging the differences between his grip and Tobin's. "I could be," he tried. "I love you, Margot."

She took her hand out of his, heart shattering at the words she had longed to hear for so long. Having heard them, they only made the ache worse. "I know, Ash," she told him, surprised that her voice held steady. "But not enough—and I understand that."

"What does that mean?" he asked, soft tone twisting slightly as he realized she wasn't falling right into his arms.

"It means that you have obligations, and I understand that they will always mean more than I will. It's okay," she reassured him. "I mean, I think part of me will always love you—will always wonder what could have been—but we don't have to pretend this is anything truly possible."

Ash stared at her, eyes wide, and as she watched, a tear slipped free. "But things are different. I can explain—" He broke off, staring. "You really don't want to be with me?" he asked, voice thick with emotion. Margot couldn't believe it—Ash was actually crying—and for her.

"I think you made the choice for both of us, don't you?" she said softly, not wanting to hurt him, but knowing it had to be done. Ash never seemed to suffer the consequences of his actions. "And it was the right thing to do. I know that. Now we both have to live with it."

She thought of Tobin in her bed, wondering how different this conversation would be if he wasn't there. *But I wouldn't be having this conversation at all if it weren't for Tobin,* she realized. *Ash would have never been with me if there hadn't been competition for my affection.*

"Ash," she said finally, "tell me something."

"Anything," he blurted, wiping his face. "I mean, yeah, sure. What?"

"Why did you stay with me that night?"

"Because—"

She held up a hand. "Tell me the truth," she said, careful not to touch him and accidentally use her push ability. "I deserve the truth."

Chapter 51

You'll See

"You don't believe that I love you?" Ash asked.

She could hear the heartbreak in his words. The handsome rock star was finally vulnerable, the rising sun highlighting the riot of colors in his dark hair—brown, black, red—he looked like he had a halo.

More like the devil, she thought. *A charming devil.*

"I believe that you love me in your own way," she told him finally, knowing it was true, "but I also think that you would have been perfectly content not saying a word, just letting me love you." She paused, thinking of all the time she had spent watching him, wanting him. "Did you think I would always be there—waiting for you?"

Ash looked uncomfortable, squirming a bit as he wiped his face again. "Go, you know why I couldn't tell you before—"

"Oh, I know," she assured him. "Believe me, I get it. I've seen enough of fae society to understand why you wouldn't want to upset your situation." Ash cocked his head, opening his mouth to ask what she had seen, but she cut him off. "Look, if you care about me at all, just let me go." She didn't mean to say it, but the words felt right.

"Let you go?" Ash echoed. "What the hell does that mean?" His face was tense, bordering on angry.

"I have to figure all this out—without you," she told him. When he didn't seem to get it, she added, "Since you won't Claim me, I need to figure out another way to get through this."

"Go," he began, "you know—"

"I know," she repeated, thinking of Tobin and how he had shared himself with her despite the obstacles, had trusted her with his secrets and respected her as an individual. "I'll be fine," she said, seeing his expression and hating herself for causing it.

"You're Unclaimed," he reminded her. "I can help keep you safe."

"Tobin can help keep me safe," Margot said.

"Tobin?" he asked. "My brother is still around?"

"He's asleep," Margot said. Ash winced, and while she didn't want to relish the pain on his face, her heart recognized the jolt and was glad to know he shared her heartbreak.

"Oh," he said quietly. "So it's him, then?"

"I like him," she said.

"He has just as many restrictions," Ash warned her. "Remember his Lord will want you for himself."

"I know," she told him, thinking of Lord Rebinus in her bus the night before. "But he wants to be with me."

"I want to be with you!" Ash said, voice heated.

"Oh, Ash," she said, reaching out to touch his face. "Eventually you'll figure out what you do want—and I know it won't be me."

"So that's it?" he asked, more tears streaming down his face. "You're just ... leaving me."

"We were never together, Ash," she reminded him. "It was one night, and it was amazing, but you were never truly with me. If you were, things would have changed when you went back to work." She gave him a hard look, and he squirmed a little.

"I panicked," he defended. "You left me alone in my bunk!"

"After you almost died because you didn't use your powers!" she whisper-shouted, very aware of Tobin below her. Their conversation had been subdued, but the rage inside would not allow her to remain calm. "You chose your secrecy over my life!"

"That sounds like Tobin talking," Ash replied. "What I mean is, it sounds like Rebinus talking. Tobin is his Lord's creature, Margot. Never forget that."

"I won't," she said, "but it doesn't change the truth." She gave him a hard look. "You would have let us both die for your precious oath."

He had the grace to look ashamed. "Go," he tried once more, "you don't understand. You don't know how fae society—"

"Oh, believe me," she snapped. "I'm learning." Part of her hated this, hated to have such venom between them, missing the ease with which they had always interacted before their night together—before he insisted on giving her whiplash. "Look," she said finally, "I am sorry. I didn't want it to be this way. But this is how it is. You made it this way. We both have to live with it."

"I was wrong," he said softly. "I did everything wrong."

"You did," Margot agreed. "But it's done. And honestly, Ash, it's probably better. How long would we have lasted?"

"I wanted to try," he said.

"Seriously? You think you would be happy giving up this life?" She gestured at the RV alongside her bus. "No more groupies? No more random threesomes?" He gave her a wide-eyed look at that one. "Oh," she said. "You thought Tobin and I were groupies when we brought you home that night."

"I'm so sorry," he mumbled.

She shook her head, though part of her still yearned to reach for him, to soothe the ache in his eyes, to meet him where he was and do anything so long as she could still be in his life, in his orbit, in his world. "I can't," she managed to say. "I just ... can't ... do this anymore."

"Margot," he whispered, and it took everything in her not to fall under the spell of his voice, "don't leave me."

"I'm not leaving you," she promised, hating the concession as she said it. "I'm still here. But I can't do this with you anymore, Ash."

"We're good together, Go," he insisted, Margot tried not to think of his lips against her, their bodies moving together. "Let me make it up to you. I screwed up. I know that. Please let me make it right."

Margot bit her lip. Tobin's face flashed in her mind, but more than that, she recalled her relationship with Ash over the years—her always watching him, him always with someone else, giving her just enough attention to string her along, to get her hopes up, only to dash them immediately when he moved on to someone else.

"I have loved you since I first saw you, Ashton Stonewall, that night in Maddie's bar when I was fifteen years old. Since then, I've been here, Ash, for eight years. Eight years. The whole time, I've been here." She shook her head. "Then we finally get together, spend a great night together, you confess that you love me—and the next day, Ash, the very next day, you shove your tongue down a groupie's throat and treat me like the hired help!" She glared at him. "I will always love you, Ash, but I'm done with this. I'm done being your Baby Go."

His face had grown more and more pale as her words hit home, but when she finished, he only nodded. "Okay, Margot," he said softly, "but know this: I will wait for you."

"Don't wait for me," she told him. "Don't."

"Don't tell me what I can or can't do," he snapped. "I failed you. I know that. But I'm here, whatever you need, and I won't fail you again."

"Don't make promises like that," she told him. "Just let me go."

He shook his head. "You didn't let me go," he reminded her. "Not for eight long years. Now it's my turn."

"You're being ridiculous," she said, rolling her eyes.

"You'll see," he said, standing up and heading to the back of the bus. "I'm here, Margot, whatever you need."

"I don't need—" she began, but instead of climbing down the ladder, Ash simply leapt off the bus, flipping in the air and landing solidly on the ground below. Margot gasped, leaning over to see him, upsetting the remains of her coffee in the process. "Ash!" she yelled.

"You need me," he declared, giving her a smile that nearly succeeded in melting her heart.

"I don't," she insisted. "Go be a rock star."

"I will," he assured her. "Your rock star." Without another word, he walked back to his RV, leaving her on the roof to stare after him, heart pounding wildly.

Chapter 52

Stone Dragons at
Riverside Theatre

Evening, Friday, February 27th
at Riverside Theatre in Mineo, Bacoli

"How many passes did they give away?" Margot griped, walking past the long line of eager fans waiting to meet the band before the show. Normally, there were a dozen people backstage, but the Bacolian radio station seemed to have given away more than twice the amount they'd volunteered.

Margot glanced behind her, making sure none of the VIPs were using her as a way to sneak by the line and into the green room. A tall man with blond hair and a pleasant smile caught her attention. In the past, Margot might have returned the look, possibly lining up some evening entertainment, but those days were behind her.

I'm in a relationship, she thought dazedly. She thought of Tobin, missing him immediately. While he rarely left her side, he did have work to do as himself and as Lord Rebinus, and he had headed back to Lorellon for a few hours. Margot guessed he didn't like watching the shows anymore, not now that Ash dedicated "Heart of Stone" to her each time he sang it.

She pushed through the clumped fans at the head of the line with a brusque "Coming through!" Turning around at the door, she put a hand to her mouth to amplify the sound.

"Listen up!" she began. "VIP Meet 'n Greet in five minutes. Get in a single line and have your badge ready. If you're getting a photo, have your phone ready too!" Seeing she had their rapt attention, she brought down the drill sergeant and added some sweetness. "I know you all love the guys, but please remember that they have a show to perform in a little bit—and they need enough time to see all of you!"

The first few fans nodded, eyes wide with excitement. This was their chance to meet the band—the members they idolized. Margot let their eagerness wash over her, recalling those early days when any fans were a welcome sight. She had a responsibility to make sure the experience was positive. Doing mental math, she judged that each fan had about one minute with the band.

She opened the green room door, slipping in without opening it fully, and turned to face the band, her hand ready on the handle. Ash was sitting on the couch, guitar in hand, singing a new song:

"*—and dream I could be with you.*" He stopped singing, though his voice echoed in Margot's ears for a moment. Timothy stood up, tucking his drumsticks in his back pocket, and Nik put down the guitar he had been strumming along with Ash's singing.

"New one, huh?" Margot asked, scanning the wall for the clock she knew was somewhere in the room.

"Yeah," Nik said, getting to his feet. "It's coming along." He gestured at the door. "How is it?"

"Busy," Margot told him. "Polite so far." She found the clock leaning against the wall behind the arm of the couch and picked it up. Luckily, it was still ticking. She set it atop the small bookshelf next to the couch so she could watch the second hand move and keep the line going. She pointed at the wall covered in graffiti to her right. "Greetings where you are—Stand up, Ash—then pictures against that wall. I'll grab one of the crew to take the pictures." They nodded, and Margot walked back to the door, squaring her shoulders and taking a deep breath.

"You ready?" she asked the band's leader.

Ash got to his feet, tugging the guitar strap over his shoulder. Margot knew it was his new way of greeting fans, the body of the guitar putting physical space between his body and any eager fans. It was another way of trying to show Margot he had changed—both Nik and Timothy insisted he hadn't touched a groupie since the redhead back in Akkoy. She stared at the trio, her boys, and smiled. "This is a far cry from opening at the Palace Hotel Ballroom," she said, remembering their first show, the guys nervously excited, the crowd there to see another band.

"Definitely," Nik agreed. The guys shared a look, bringing Margot into the connection, and for a moment, everything was fine again—the world she knew and loved returned to normal. But then Ash winked at her, and the image fizzled away—leaving a dull ache behind.

Those days were gone now. Though part of her missed them, a bigger part was excited about what lay ahead ... after they survived this fan backroom experience. "Let's do this," she said, then opened the door and stepped outside, scanning the crowd for a crew member. She had texted Travis, but Margot wondered if he was on yet another smoke break.

Sensing the crowd's eagerness slowly building into annoyance, Margot caught the eyes of the pleasant blond near the front and walked over to him.

"Hey," she said, "you know how to take pictures?"

He nodded, eyes wide as he stared at her.

"Good enough," she said and crooked her finger. "Come with me." Without watching to see if he obeyed, she headed back to the door, opened it, and moved aside to shove him through.

"Guys," she said, gesturing at the newcomer, "this is—" She studied his badge, but it just said VIP Access—no name. "What's your name?"

"Lawrence," he replied nervously.

"Larry, meet the guys of Stone Dragons," she told him, sweeping her hand at the band. "Guys, meet Larry. He's our photographer today."

Larry eagerly approached the band, shaking hands excitedly but without making it awkward. "So glad to be here!"

"Larry," Margot interrupted, "take at least three pictures, but try for five if you can. We get a minute per person, so use your judgement based on group size."

"Got it, my—" He stumbled a bit, then added, "Ma'am."

Facing the room, she gave everyone a thumbs up. "We ready?"

Ash nodded, Nik returned her thumbs up, and Timothy said, "We are ready, Go. Let them in."

The next thirty minutes flew by with Margot letting in groups of twos and threes and the occasional singleton. Larry was an adept photographer, adjusting to each new phone with ease, never letting them time out or needing a code or face recognition to re-load. When the last fan had finished, Margot eased them out the door and directed the large group to follow the lines on the floor to the VIP area in front of the stage, relieved to see that Travis had returned and was herding them out.

Checking the clock, she saw they had about ten minutes before Das Leprechauns started their set. "Need anything before the show?" she asked, trying to ignore the obvious desire on Ash's face as he stared at her. The lead singer said nothing.

"We're all good," Nik told her. "Why don't you show Larry here to the good seats in VIP? Man just started a new career as a photographer tonight!"

Margot laughed. "Thanks, Larry. I appreciate it." Turning to the door, she added, "Come on. The guys need some time before they go on."

Larry's smile, big to begin with, grew even more emphatic, making his face almost creepy. "Yes, ma'am," he said, following her.

"Don't ma'am me," she said, leading him out of the room and ignoring the slow frisson of warning that slid up her arms. "I'm hardly older than you are." The door shut behind them, and she led the way through the backstage area.

"My apologies, my Lady," Larry said instead, and Margot didn't miss the fae title. Whirling, she faced him, a hand on his chest.

"Who are you?" she demanded, pushing him against the wall of the narrow corridor. "Actually, I don't care. Why are you here?" she asked instead. She had thought it odd that he hadn't wanted a picture of his own with the band, but now she suspected it was because he wasn't there for them.

"You know why," he said, voice silky, and Margot felt something slide out of him, slow and seductive, and start to pool around her, starting at her feet. She could almost see it, the cocoon of magic, but it was so slow that she had time to react, kicking a foot out to break the formation.

"You are mine," he whispered, and Margot looked up, seeing the expression on his face slowly twist from starstruck excitement to demented possession.

Her first instinct was to laugh at him—at the idea that this boy could try to Claim her. And at that thought, Margot suddenly understood how to defeat him. With startling ease, she reached down and scooped up his power—his tiny power compared to what she could feel burning within herself—and threw it at him, coating his body and freezing him in place. She added her own power on top, building an unbreakable barrier, and pushed the magic forward, deeper, inside of him.

Oh, she thought dazedly. *This is how you Claim someone. It's so easy!*

A moment later, the magic fizzled, and Margot could see way more of Lawrence O'Malley than she ever wanted to. She could see all of his actions—the journey to the show, his acquisition of the VIP badge by seducing some poor girl who was high on fae magic in her car in the parking lot, his orders to Claim the troublesome new girl and move the game along. She knew he had come with the intention of Claiming her but not of his own accord.

"Lord Kristoff," she whispered the name out loud and understood she had just broken any Claim Kristoff had on Lawrence—ensnaring Kristoff's servant without any effort at all.

Is that even possible? I thought Claims were unbreakable... Looking at Larry's face, she knew it had worked. *How strong am I?*

"Oh, Larry," she breathed, "you are going to tell me everything."

He looked up at her, bright eyes filled with love and devotion. "Of course, Mistress. Anything for you."

Something in Margot recoiled at the look—at his words.

Oh fuck, she realized, guilt spilling over her. *I Claimed him. I took his free will. What have I done?*

"No," she said suddenly, putting up a hand as Larry moved closer, clearly intending to smother her with his new affection. He grabbed her hand and kissed the back of it, a slavish echo of the courtly manners Tobin had shown her. She pushed him away. "Stop," she ordered.

Larry obeyed immediately, stepping away and squatting on his haunches, eyes gazing at her with complete adoration.

He's waiting for his next order, Margot realized, her gorge rising. *Will that happen to me? If Rebinus had Claimed me, would I look at him like that?*

Staring at Larry's face, Margot decided that it didn't matter what she had to do—she was going to make sure that Claiming as a general practice was stopped.

"Lawrence," she said softly, holding out a hand, "stand up."

He obeyed instantly, taking her hand respectfully and staring at her. "Can you do something for me?" she asked, hating herself as she said it but not knowing what else to do. She knew if she got too upset, Tobin would sense it and come running. Ash was only a few yards away and would soon come out of the green room to watch the opening act.

"Anything," Larry breathed, entire body straining to please her.

"I want you to leave this place. Leave your Lord's home, if you can do that safely, and hide. Don't let anyone know you have been Claimed by me. This is our little secret, okay?" Larry nodded, her words sinking in, and he waited for the rest. "I need you to be yourself, Lawrence. Don't think about what I would want. Think about what you want."

He nodded but opened his mouth. "May I ask a question, Mistress?"

"Of course," she told him, soul aching at the way he asked.

"Give me a task," he pleaded. "Something to focus on while I am in hiding."

"I want you to listen," she told him suddenly. "Listen to the other fae. What are their plans? What is the gossip? What news can you find out?"

"I can do that," Larry said, nodding. "I can do that while I take their pictures."

"You like taking pictures?" she asked.

Larry nodded. "I'm good at it," he admitted. "But how long, Mistress? When can I see you again?"

Margot thought about time, the tour, when she would be back home in Arillo again. "Four months," she told him. "Come find me in four months."

"I can do that," Larry agreed. "Leave, hide, listen."

"Larry," she said, needing to know, "do you have someone special in your life? Like a girlfriend? Boyfriend?"

"Oh no," Larry said. "No one but you, Mistress."

"I'm not your Mistress," Margot told him. "After the four months, you're free to do as you wish. Live your life."

"Thank you, Mistress," Larry said, some of that fanatical adoration leaving his face. "I will not disappoint you."

"I know," Margot told him, feeling the magic Connection that allowed her to see everything within him. "Now go."

Larry walked away without a look back, intent on his new mission for his Mistress: hide, listen, report in four months.

Margot put her face in her hands, deep breathing for a few moments, and gathered herself. By the time the door to the green room opened and Stone Dragons filed out, Margot was already hustling Das Leprechauns on stage, distracting herself from the sick feeling in her gut.

Chapter 53

An Unfortunate Encounter

Afternoon, Tuesday, March 3rd
at Thessaly Stadium in Vada, Bacoli

The Bacolian leg of the tour was wilder than the previous shows, the Das Leprechauns fans adding a level of crazy that Margot struggled to contain. The hordes of screaming music lovers camped along the entrance to the venues—bodies pressing up against the RV and bus windows as they arrived—made Margot uncomfortable. They'd had some energetic crowds back in Arillo at the start of the tour, but these Southerners were something else.

Margot hoped security was able to keep everyone in line. She had enough to deal with as it was. Alby, the lead singer of the Leprechauns, had decided her little stunt with the microphone meant she actually wanted him, and he spent his time making crude comments and "accidentally" rubbing against her. Margot endured his attention in silence, gritting her teeth and soldiering on.

She knew she could make it stop with a word to Ash or Tobin, but she didn't want to get them involved in band problems.

Besides, she could handle Alby. That was, until their final show in Bacoli. Security had disappeared to handle a group of fans who had pushed down a fence into the back lot. Alby got her alone, behind the stage. Margot had been listening to the updates on her headset, and she didn't see him approach, so when he pushed her into the corner, swiping the headset off her head, she was startled and allowed herself to be shoved behind the speakers. His hand moved fast, flicking the switch to turn off her headset and microphone.

"Finally alone," Alby said, smiling in a way that she assumed he thought was charming.

"Alby," she sighed, "I have work to do." She tried to reach for her headset on the ground, but he moved again, his body blocking the way. "Stop fucking around, Alby," she gritted, fumbling for the pack at her waist and dragging the headset back by the cord instead.

Alby stepped on the cord and grabbed her face. "Look at me," he demanded.

Margot's lips pursed, pushed together by Alby's fingers. She narrowed her eyes at him.

"You never fucking look at me, Margot," Alby sneered. "You think you're too good for me?" His other hand reached out as if to grab her breast, but Margot caught it in mid-air, pressing it back to his chest.

"Alby," she said, words distorted as he gripped her harder, "let me go." She felt the power go out of her, and Alby's hand fell away from her face. His expression flickered, rage and confusion, as he watched his hand lower without his consent.

"Bitch," he mumbled.

"Bitch?" Margot echoed, pressing her hand harder against his chest. "You want to see a bitch?" She felt the rage grow in her, not just at Alby and his casual misogyny, but at everything that had happened the last few weeks. She leaned in to speak softly, her words barely audible. "Let me tell you this. *Everyone* here is too good for you." She watched the rage on his face shift to fear—and joy filled her. "You are scum, and you will not look at me ever again," she ordered him. "You don't deserve to look at anyone!"

"I don't deserve anyone," he mumbled, nodding, a tiny bit of drool gathering in the corner of his mouth. "Scum." His hands reached up to cover his eyes, fingers pressing deep into the eyelids.

"You may be a halfway decent singer, but your band would be better off without you. You only drag everyone down," she continued, part of her relishing the sadness and fear emanating from him.

"Better off without me," Alby muttered.

Margot stood there, soaking in the joy of the moment, of Alby finally subdued and subservient. She was wondering what else she could tell him when a voice caught her attention.

"Margot, what are you doing?"

She glanced up, only half aware, the dazed smile still on her face. Ash stared wide-eyed at her. He seemed to understand immediately, and he reached out, pulling her hand from Alby's chest. The singer slid to the ground, knees pulling up as he rocked in a fetal position. "Scum," he mumbled. "Not worthy. Don't look."

Margot blinked, slowly returning to herself. "Ash," she breathed. "What—?" Alby moved, and his foot caught the cord of her headset, jerking her hips toward him. She looked down and saw a broken mumbling man instead of the cocky lead singer she had known.

"What did I do?" she asked, but she knew.

I pushed him. I told him terrible things. I broke him.

Margot wanted to deny the thrill of pleasure that burst through her at the idea, and then she was too busy throwing up. She was aware of movement beside her, low voices, and then a hand was pulling her loose hair away from her face and another was rubbing her back. Someone handed her a bottle of water, and she drank it eagerly, allowing herself to be led away. When she looked around again, Tobin and Ash stood next to her. Behind them, Nik and Tim heaved Alby to his feet and led him away from her.

"I—" she stuttered. "I—"

"It's okay, darling," Tobin said.

Ash gave him a surprised look. His expression said it was most definitely not okay. Or maybe he didn't like that Tobin had called her darling. Margot's disjointed thoughts couldn't connect any ideas.

"We talked about this, Margot," Tobin continued speaking to her in a gentle voice, and again Ash gave him another shocked look, gaze flicking between them. "Humans can't withstand that power. It breaks them."

"I didn't mean—" Margot tried, realizing that her face was wet. She reached up to touch her cheek, half expecting to find blood on her fingers, but it was just tears. She didn't finish the sentence because she knew it was a lie. She did mean it. At the thought, she began to sob in earnest, chest hitching as she tried to catch her breath. Ash leaned down and pulled her into his arms, the warmth and comfort making everything fade away.

"Shhh," he whispered in her ear. "Just breathe, Margot. Breathe." He tapped a slow rhythm against her back, guiding her to slower breaths. After a few long moments, she could feel her lungs expanding, body somewhat returning to her control. "That's it, baby, just breathe. In and out. You can do that. Good girl."

Closing her eyes, she surrendered to the calm of his voice. *Ash just called me baby.* The thought was disconnected from anything else, an observation in the void, and Margot surrendered to the emptiness. Time passed, but she wasn't in it, only vaguely aware of a hissed discussion about the show and how it must go on. She grew aware when the warm circle of Ash's arms disappeared, replaced by the strength of Tobin's.

"I've got her," Tobin was saying. "You deal with the rest."

"I can keep her calm," Ash argued.

"So can I," Tobin insisted. "This is your world. You know how to fix it."

There was a pause, and Ash mumbled agreement. He leaned down, breath warm against her forehead, and gave her a quick kiss on the cheek. "Keep her safe," he told his brother.

"Always," Tobin replied.

His hand moved, marking symbols in the air, and then they were moving in a purple haze.

Chapter 54

Fear and Consequences

Morning, Wednesday, March 4th at the
Palace of Lord Rebinus in Demacia, Lorellon

The next time Margot opened her eyes, she lay in the big bed in Tobin's room. *Lord Rebinus' room,* she corrected herself, looking up at the ceiling and recalling the last time she had been in this bed. She turned over, searching her surroundings. "Tobin?"

"I'm here, darling," he said, and she realized that she had been resting against him, what she had taken for a pillow was actually his leg. Before she could say anything else, he plucked a mug from the nightstand and put it in her hand. "You need to drink."

Margot sniffed, moving her dry tongue inside her mouth and pulled herself up. Her body was light, languid, satisfied and filled with the echoes of a good time. She gave Tobin a look, glancing down at herself. She was wearing a plain nightgown, not her own, but the ease in her body wasn't from sex. Taking a sip, she winced at the flavor.

"This isn't coffee," she said frowning.

"I told you that fae coffee was terrible," he reminded her.

"I thought you were just saying that to get us out of this room before someone discovered us," she said, peering at the brown liquid in the mug.

"No one will discover us, darling," he assured her. She took another sip, thirst winning out, and winced again. "That said, there's a reason we spend so much time in Ardon. Food is so much better there."

"I always thought fae food would be delicious, a temptation to stay here forever," Margot said, recalling the stories her mother had told her about the fae world, stories Margot now knew were probably true.

"Some food," Tobin admitted. "Coffee is not one of them. That's a human thing."

"Oh," Margot said, taking another sip despite the bitter taste. A flash of Alby's face reminded her of what she had done, and she took a longer sip, wanting the bitterness to quell the lingering calm within. "I..."

Tobin placed a hand on her leg. "You don't have to," he told her. "It happens. Mistakes are made. You aren't the first and you won't be the last to break a human."

Margot shivered at the coldness in his tone while something inside her rejoiced at his words. "Did I break him?" she asked.

"Oh yes," he assured her.

"Maybe I can undo it—" she began.

"It can't be undone," he told her. "Humans are fragile. Once broken, they rarely come back." He gave her a long look, half admiration and half frustration. "I don't know what he did—though I can imagine—and I wager he deserved it. That said, I don't want you to forget this moment." He jerked his chin at her body. "You still feel it?" he asked. "Inside?"

Margot bit her lip, then nodded slowly.

"It feels good," Tobin said. "So good. It's very easy to get addicted to it. Trust me, I know."

"Did you ever make mistakes?" she asked, voice small in the big room.

He quirked an eyebrow. "None that I admit," he replied. "My mistake was in feeling the way you do right now—wracked with guilt."

"I pretty much killed a man," Margot said. "I should feel guilty!"

"A pitiful excuse for a man," Tobin argued. "A human who no doubt molested many other people before you. You saved future victims, Margot." He shook his head. "And no doubt that band will find a better singer. You've likely improved their fortunes as well, darling. It all balances out."

Margot stared at him, wanting his words to make less sense, wanting to lose herself in her guilt. "I think he was going to hurt me," she said quietly, trying to justify her actions. "I was afraid—"

"Oh, darling," Tobin interrupted, "don't."

Margot stared at him, not sure what he meant. "Don't what?"

"Don't convince yourself that way," he said. When she stared at him, not following, he leaned forward, putting a hand to her cheek. "I found you, Margot, because you were excited. Honestly, I thought you had decided to take Ash back. It took me a moment to recognize what you were doing." His hand tightened, fingers clenching her jaw. "Margot, I know all the emotions you were feeling.

Fear was not one of them." He released her, leaning back against the headboard, assessing. "You really going to tell yourself you pushed him because he threatened you?"

"He did threaten me!" Margot exclaimed, but her mind spun back to that moment, recalling her emotions. What had she felt? Annoyance, mostly, and that had quickly exploded into anger. Now that she thought about it, she had never been afraid. She never thought Alby could hurt her. She looked down, taking another sip of the bitter drink, then nodded, breath exploding out of her. "Fine," she admitted. "I wasn't afraid. But I hurt him. I ... ruined him. He may have been a shit human being, but he didn't deserve that. Or at least, it shouldn't have been my choice to judge him."

"Why not you?" Tobin asked.

"What kind of question is that?" she prompted, hating that she had already begun to unwind the logic. Who else had been in the position to stop Alby? Who but her had known how dangerous he could be?

Was he dangerous?

Margot sighed, brain struggling to process the various emotions. She knew part of it was justification, her morality desperately trying to find a reason to make her actions acceptable. It was going to be a long time before she could unpack the good and bad consequences. Sighing, she stretched, glancing at the light outside. "What time is it?" she asked.

"It's almost noon," he told her. "I know you don't want to think about this now, but the band has already started back to Genc. You have a few days off before the show in Dikmen on Friday, but they don't want to stay in Bacoli after what happened."

"You've been talking to Ash," Margot said, trying to get back into work mode. "How did they handle it?"

"It's unfortunate," Tobin said. "The lead singer for Das Leprechauns suffered a stroke. Happily, Stone Dragons and the remains of the band were able to perform the final show together and sate the fans, though I will say, I did not enjoy their rendition of 'Heart of Stone' this time."

Margot narrowed her eyes. "Why not?"

"Das Leprechauns doesn't sing love songs," Tobin reminded her, "not without the clever addition of the word 'bitch' to the end of each line." He shook his head, dismissing the show. "They won't be continuing with the tour. Stone Dragons will hook up with Devil's Play for the rest of the Gencian shows."

Margot stared at him. "When did you start doing my job?"

"When you were too sick to continue last night," Tobin replied. "I can text as well as you, and Cayla said to rest up during the break." At her expression, he added, "Margot, I'm a vassal. Organizing things is what I do." He patted her leg. "You need to rest."

Margot nodded, the idea of rest very appealing. She wanted to close her eyes and sleep for days. "Oh no," she groaned, an idea hitting her. "My bus. I need to drive to Dikmen by Friday."

"Margot," Tobin said, "you are in no shape for driving."

She nodded, trying to recall how many times she had zoned out during their conversation. "I know, but I can't leave my bus there, not with angry Bacolian fans breaking down fences."

"Margot," Tobin said softly, gray eyes gentle, "I know it's a boundary. I know you have rules."

She watched his face, part of her wanting nothing more than to surrender to his care and let him take care of everything. "Will you…" she tried, but the words wouldn't come out.

"Yes," he replied, answering her unspoken question.

An hour later, they sat in her bus, Margot dressed in her yoga pants and a soft sweatshirt and sitting in the passenger seat, adjusting to the awkward view. She watched Tobin move her mirrors, the fae fitting in her bus perfectly, knowing where everything was almost as well as Ash. He started to set the music and Margot reached out, intending to play her Road Trip playlist. Dikmen was two days away.

Tobin slapped her fingers away playfully. "Rules, darling," he reminded her. "Driver picks the music."

Margot bit her lip and let the smile cross her face as she surrendered to him. "Passenger shuts her piehole," she finished.

Chapter 54
The Person Within

Morning, Saturday, March 14th in
Margot's Bus at the Willis Center at Beau Lake in
Taflah, Genc

The next two weeks flew by as Margot tried to fall back into her routine. The tour was still running smoothly, Devil's Play meshing much more with Stone Dragons, and while Ash had continued his reformed rock star pursuit of her, Margot had been spending most of her time away from the band.

Tobin explained more about fae society, filling in the gaps that Ash would never have shared, and Margot realized that he had as much disdain for his people as she did. She learned that her father, according to the rumors he had dug up, had been forced to let her mother go since she was not powerful enough to be his Lady. Margot thought of her mother, always so carefree, so hellbent on not putting down roots, on being able to leave at a moment's notice, and saw how much that attitude was also hers.

Margot had worked in a few subtle questions about Claiming, learning that Lord Kristoff probably didn't know that Margot had stolen his servant, not if Larry had obeyed her and left. Claims were strong enough to see into a person but only if they were physically present. They faded with distance. Margot wondered if that was how Tobin managed to plot against Rebinus, by keeping away so his Lord wouldn't be able to see his thoughts. The only other way would have been spontaneous, and Margot didn't think Tobin did much of anything without forethought.

Except maybe his oath to her. So far, that hadn't conflicted with any of Rebinus's needs that she knew of.

As they arrived in Taflah for the three nights at the Willis Center on Beau Lake, Margot tried to prepare herself for the Fan Gala and VIP performance on Sunday night. The fae were waiting, Tobin explained, to see how she would conduct herself among them. The odds of her remaining Unclaimed through the weekend were fairly low, according to the latest estimates. Margot thought they might be underestimating her, especially since she had two new abilities manifest: creating illusions and altering light, though Margot thought they might be two applications of the same thing. She could control the ability enough to make something invisible from a certain angle, and Tobin was convinced that with time, she would be able to make herself invisible.

"You really think I'll be able to disappear?" she asked in her bus Saturday morning, lounging with Tobin in her bunk. She held her hand up, playing with the light around it, seeing her fingers and then somehow through them.

"Of course," Tobin assured her, moving so he could look at her. "You thinking of hiding out tomorrow night, darling?"

"The thought crossed my mind," she admitted. "But I have to go. Cayla is here." While she had been texting the band manager the entire tour, Cayla only came to what she considered the important shows. The Fan Gala tomorrow was one of them, but Cayla was here for the show tonight as well. Margot flopped onto her back, staring at the ceiling of her bus. "I need to be there—to put on a good show." She twisted to stare at Tobin. "You're invited to the gala, of course, but I'll have to spend most of the night with the guys. I have a pass for you."

Tobin smirked. "Margot, while I appreciate your efforts to get me in, I won't be going to the party."

Margot sat up, turning to look at him. "You won't? Why not?" she demanded, trying to ignore the jolt of fear at facing all those people without Tobin nearby.

"Vassals do not attend galas, darling."

"You're my date," Margot insisted. "I don't care what the fae say."

"Oh Margot," Tobin said, leaning over to kiss her gently, "words like that start revolutions."

Margot stared hard at him, her dislike of fae society increasing with every new detail she learned. "Maybe some things need a revolution," she told him. "Maybe some things can't be fixed by going along with things as they are."

Tobin chuckled. "Oh, my fiery darling, I adore you," he drawled, kissing her properly. "I can't wait to see you there."

"But you said you weren't going?"

"Tobin Fetch isn't going," he explained, winking at her.

"Oh," Margot said, feeling stupid for not catching on sooner. "But Lord Rebinuts—"

"Rebinus."

"Yeah. He'll be there, making an appearance to evaluate the new Unclaimed fae for himself." Margot pursed her lips. "Are you going to be a jerk?"

He shrugged. "Maybe. It depends on what the situation calls for. Sometimes, Lord Rebinus can very charming." At this, he moved, flipping her so she lay beneath him. Margot giggled, a hand against his chest.

"Tobin Fetch is quite charming," she insisted.

"Truth," Tobin agreed, kissing her gently, claiming her in all the human ways he knew she valued. "But," he told her, "you will officially meet Lord Rebinus." He gave her a wicked look. "I expect you to be properly impressed, Margot."

"What?" she asked lightly. "You think now that I've seen you naked, I won't be cowed by the glory that is Lord Rebinuls?"

"Reb—Margot, why do you never say his name properly?"

She snorted, running a finger down his cheek. "Because of that look right there," she admitted. "You correct me every single time, but you never seem to mind. At first I did it because I was actually afraid of this mysterious powerful Lord that Ash seemed so certain would Claim me against my will—you should probably work on that part of your reputation, just saying—but after a while, it became a habit."

"Lord Rebinus would never take someone against their will. His reputation is fine," Tobin defended.

"He Claimed you," Margot pointed out.

"Oh, he would Claim someone, especially a useful someone, but he—I—would never abuse someone that way." Tobin's face was searching, honest, needing her to believe him.

"Ash said that when it came down to it, I wouldn't mind because the Claiming would have taken my will to resist." She hesitated, then forged forward, needing to know. "Have you used that willingness when it presented itself, knowing it wasn't there before?"

Tobin narrowed his eyes at her. "Are you asking me if I've ever abused my power and position as Lord Rebinus? I assure you, the answer is yes." Margot swallowed hard. "Now, if you are asking me if I bedded someone who didn't want me before I Claimed them, the answer is no. I cannot say the same for the other Lords."

"I'm not asking about the other Lords, Tobin. I'm asking about you. You ... as him."

"Tobin the vassal does all right for himself, darling," he assured her, face dipping to kiss the line of her neck. "I don't need to bed unwilling partners. As for Lord Rebinus, he too finds plenty of ever-willing company."

"But it sounded like everyone is afraid of him."

"They are," he assured her with a rakish grin. "You would be amazed what an aphrodisiac fear can be. They can't help themselves!"

"I don't want to hear about your exploits," Margot said, ardor fading.

"Sometimes you are so prim, darling! I love it." Tobin laughed, leaning down to kiss her nose.

Margot frowned at him. "Don't patronize me."

"I'm not," he said. "I truly find it adorable how shy you are. Positively puritanical! I can only imagine your reaction to a fae party."

"Just because I don't go around fucking anything with a pulse doesn't make me a prude," Margot grumbled, annoyed now.

"I don't go around fucking just anything, darling," Tobin assured her, body solid around her as he refused to let her up. "I told you I have high standards."

"And particular tastes," she gritted, pushing against his chest, though she knew it was pointless. Tobin was still stronger than her. "Is bullying one of your kinks? Prepping for the party?"

Tobin's face grew serious, and he grabbed her hands, holding them both in one hand just above her head, the other sliding down her body. "Oh, darling," he crooned, and Margot tried to ignore the fire he ignited with his voice, his touch, "don't pretend you don't like my past." His fingers ran over her thigh, slipping between her legs and touching her the way she liked. "You love that I know how to touch you," he whispered.

Margot bit her lip, trying not to groan.

Tobin stopped his movement, watching her face as she opened her eyes to meet his. "You don't like me talking about it because it reminds you of Ash."

"This isn't about Ash," she said, moving her legs, trying to coax his hand back.

"Honesty, Margot," Tobin demanded. "Everything with you is about Ash. That hasn't changed, despite what you tell yourself."

"I want you!" she exclaimed.

"Of course you do," he said smugly, running a line of kisses along her neck. "But part of you will always wish for him. Don't ignore that part. Don't let it die."

"What are you saying? You want me to love Ash?"

"I want you to be yourself, whatever that is," Tobin said, fingers drifting lower. "That means admitting what you want when you're with me. Just let go, Margot. I want you. Just you. All you."

"Tobin," she moaned, his words sinking into her, releasing the part of herself she kept hidden. She opened her eyes, not aware she had closed them, and watched him closely, a glint in her eye. "My Lord," she whispered.

Tobin chuckled, then bent down to suck hard on her collarbone, marking her. "Not yet, darling. Not yet."

Chapter 55

Meeting the Manager

Afternoon, Saturday, March 14th
at The Willis Center at Beau Lake in Taflah, Genc

Margot sat in the green room with Stone Dragons and Cayla. Their manager wore what she called her working clothes—a leather jacket and tight jeans. No one would mistake the middle aged blonde for anything but what she was—a serious badass who didn't take any crap and expected the best performance from her band. They had run through the set list for the night, and Cayla was reminding everyone to be on their best behavior at the gala tomorrow.

"This is bigtime," she said, giving each of the guys a look in turn, every inch the mother prepping her boys for an important event. "Niklaus, I expect all of your charm and none of your shenanigans."

Nik nodded. "Yes, ma'am. Charm loaded. No shenanigans."

"And your suits?" she prompted.

"All pressed and on the RV," Margot told her. "They can shower on both RVs and get ready on the Party Bus."

Cayla nodded. "What about you?"

"Me?" Margot echoed.

"Yeah, you have a dress somewhere in that tiny home of yours?"

"It's a bus, Cayla," Margot reminded her yet again. "And yes, I have a dress. It's blue," she added lamely. She didn't explain that Tobin had acquired the dress for her after a heated discussion where he insisted she could not wear silver or white; they were Lord Rebinus's colors. Nor could she wear red or black, Ash's colors, and those of the house of Lord Stonewall, without upsetting the other fae and making them think she was already Claimed and this was a sham. She had asked if blue was anyone's special color, and he told her that blue, dark blue, was appropriate, the color of Lord Tennere.

When she asked if Lord Tennere would attend the gala, Tobin said, "All the Lords will be there."

Margot took a deep breath, trying to decide how she felt about meeting her father. Deciding that topic was better explored another time, she turned her attention back to Cayla and her speech.

"There will be big players at the show tonight," she told them all. "And even bigger ones at the gala. Play this right, and you can tour to your heart's content." She frowned. "You know we can afford to fly and get hotels, right?" Glancing at Margot, she added, "Even you can live out of a few suitcases for a few months."

Ash gave his band mates a look, and they all grinned. "We like driving, Cayla," Timothy said for the group. "If we can keep touring, let's do it this way." Margot wondered if they would ever tour Belsune—and if she would go back there with them if they did.

Cayla shook her head. "Whatever." Expression softening, she reached out her arms. "You crazy kids," she said. "Give me a hug!"

Margot laughed, stepping close to join the group hug. As the arms came out to tug her close, she smelled the familiar scent of Ash on her right, his body pressed against hers, and the warm comfort of Cayla on her left. Sometimes it was hard being the only woman on tour who wasn't a groupie. Though her days of touring were over, Cayla understood that isolation and would no doubt pull her aside at some point during the show for a full rundown of the tour events. While the manager would never replace Penelope or even Maddie, Cayla did have maternal moments Margot appreciated.

"Tonight is going to be wonderful," Cayla said, releasing them. "Now go out there and make everyone dream about dragons!"

Timothy nodded at her, "Ma'am," and grabbed his drumsticks from the couch where he had left them. Nik blew Cayla a kiss and followed after the drummer. Ash lingered a moment, nodding at Cayla but giving Margot a longer look and a tentative smile. Margot smiled back, hating how much she enjoyed this new Ash who went out of his way to acknowledge her, to speak to her, to be the friend she recalled from the days before the band took over their lives. Since that morning on the roof of her bus, she hadn't seen Ash in the company of a single groupie. Part of her wanted to think he was just more careful about hiding his entertaining from her, but Nik and Timothy insisted that Ash had been celibate for weeks.

Ash was trying to be good enough for her. His words, of course.

"Have a good show," Margot said lamely, watching the lead singer as he strode from the room, already embodying his rock star persona.

Ash had barely passed through the door before Cayla slammed it shut, spinning to put her back against it. "Dear gods, woman," Cayla said, eyes wide, "whatever did you do that boy?"

"Nothing!" Margot insisted, but Cayla's skeptical gaze made her backpedal. "Well, we kind of..."

"Kind of what?" Cayla exclaimed. "I need to get your version of this because your cousin does not know how to tell a story."

Margot held a hand up to her chest. "What has Nik told you?"

Cayla shook her head. "First he said that you and Ash finally got together." At Margot's reluctant nod of agreement, Cayla squealed, then calmed herself. "But he fucked it up with some groupie." This time, Cayla's face was somber at Margot's nod. "Now he says you have some new beau, but Ash is trying to get you back. That's the part I don't understand."

"Nik is right," Margot confirmed. "I am seeing someone. Not Ash."

"This is the one who texted me when you got sick?" At Margot's nod, Cayla continued, "I like him. Efficient and goal-oriented. He'd make a good manager."

Margot smiled. "He's pretty amazing."

Cayla abandoned the door and moved to the couch, patting the seat beside her. "Tell me everything, Margot.

I imagine you've been dying for a woman's perspective." She sighed. "You know, I worry about you with these boys."

"I'm fine," Margot assured her. "It's just the guys. I know them."

"Some better than others, hmm?" Cayla laughed, raising an eyebrow. "I don't need to know the details about everyone's favorite heartthrob but just tell me one thing."

"What's that?"

"Is he as good as they all say?"

Margot slumped on the couch. "Better," she sighed.

"Oh, honey," Cayla said, leaning back to slump beside her. "Those are the worst."

"I'm just trying to forget about it," Margot commiserated. "Trying to move on."

Cayla tilted her head to face Margot. "That may work on someone else, but have you seen the way he looks at you? He's not going to forget." Cayla winked at her. "Well done, girl! You may have tamed that man for good."

"Ash doesn't want to be with me!" Margot burst, tired of the same old argument. At Cayla's expression, she added, "Okay, he wants me. But not enough, Cayla. Not enough."

"Would you give everything up to be with him?" Cayla asked.

Margot sighed. "If you had asked me that a month ago, I would have said yes. No hesitation. But now..."

"Now you have someone else," Cayla finished for her. "That changes things." She turned, facing Margot. "Tell me about this new fellow of yours. I assume I'll meet him at the gala?"

Margot grimaced. "Actually, no. He can't come."

"You know we can get him in, right?" Cayla asked.

"Oh, I know. He just has ... something else going on. Work stuff."

Cayla frowned. "Too bad. He's going to miss you in your fancy dress!"

Margot ducked her head, not wanting to tell Cayla that Tobin had seen her in the new dress—and out of it—earlier that day.

"Well, he's not getting through this weekend without meeting me in person," Cayla insisted, giving her best manager/mom face. "You tell him that. He's not seeing my Margot without meeting me."

"Of course," Margot agreed.

Chapter 56

To Family

Late Afternoon, Sunday, March 15th
at The Aerie in Taflah, Genc

When Margot stepped off her bus in the dark blue dress, she wished Tobin was by her side. He had left earlier, heading out to take care of fae business before the party, and she missed him. She knew she would see him again soon—though not as the Tobin she knew. Margot took a deep breath, straightening her back, and headed to where the guys were getting ready on the Party Bus.

She opened the door without knocking, hearing them inside, and entered the bus to catcalls from Nik. "Baby Go!" her cousin exclaimed, nodding. "Damn!"

"I guess that's a compliment?" she snarked, lifting her dress to step up into the living room. She felt a bit like a princess with the flowy layer of tulle around her legs, though the plunging neckline and off the shoulder top definitely belonged on a woman. She had braided the front of her hair to keep it out of her face, but left the rest down, a nod to the braided style she had seen on Lady Drina, but also a reminder of her mother's always wild hair.

"You look lovely, Margot," Timothy said, striding into view and fixing his bowtie. He grabbed his jacket from the edge of the couch, shrugging it on and smoothing the front. Timothy cleaned up well, the black tuxedo accentuating the lines of his shoulders and arms toned by years of drumming.

"And you," she said, meaning it. Turning to Nik, she crooked her finger. "Get over here," she told him, grabbing the dangling ends of his bowtie as he obeyed. "You look great," she told him, fixing the bowtie in place and running a hand down his shirt sleeves to smooth them. "Cayla will approve."

"Ash will approve of that dress," Nik whispered, winking at her, and headed to the back room to get his jacket. He passed Ash in the small hallway, the lead singer still buttoning up his white shirt. Margot caught sight of the lines across his chest and arms, heat rising up her cheeks as she recalled running her fingers across the bare skin.

Get a grip, she reminded herself. *Keep it together.*

Ash finished the top few buttons, and Margot thought he took his time with it, letting her gaze linger on his bare skin. He lifted his hand, the limp length of the bowtie held out to her. "Margot," he said, "will you tie mine?"

Margot sniffed, trying to regain her composure, and took the fabric from him. "Sure," she said, gesturing him closer. He stood before her, watching her as she first wrapped it around his neck, then began twisting it into shape. She was aware of her fingers grazing the skin of his neck as she folded the collar down. She rested her palms flat on his chest for a second, to check the balance, she told herself, trying not to let her hands linger. Pulling her hands back, she gave him a weak thumbs up. "You're good," she said, turning around to check the rest of the boys.

"You look lovely, Margot," Ash said to her back, and she felt her cheeks heat, the compliment running deep.

Stop it! she told herself. *You're being ridiculous!* But she knew it was useless. If she could have made herself stop loving Ash, she would have done it years ago. Even now, knowing they had no future, that she was with Tobin, that his words didn't matter, she couldn't help the fierce joy his approval raised in her.

"Thank you," she managed, not turning around, and stood by the door. The guys finished putting on their jackets and grabbing their things. Margot's phone pinged, and she glanced at it, glad her dress had hidden pockets. "The limo is here," she told them. They filed off the bus, and Ash glanced around, walking next to her as they headed to the stretch limo parked by the gate.

"No Tobin?" he asked her.

Margot shook her head, glad she wore sensible strappy sandals as they crossed the wide lot. Her dress was long enough, she had decided. No one would be looking at her shoes—and if they did, fuck them. "He's ... busy," she said vaguely, not wanting to lie to Ash. She thought he may be able to tell.

"Right," Ash agreed in the same tone and gave her a searching look. "That's all you're going to say?"

"What do you want me to say?" Margot asked, watching Nik and Timothy's backs as they walked ahead of them.

"I want you to explain why my brother, who hasn't let you out of his sight for three weeks and five days, has decided not to accompany you to a gala that will likely include all the members of fae society."

Margot nearly stumbled but kept walking when Ash grabbed her elbow. "How do you know about that?"

"I'm in hiding, Margot," Ash reminded her. "I'm not a fool. My father will be there. No doubt the other Lords will also be there, hobnobbing with the human elites." He paused, then added, "Lord Rebinus will be there."

Margot nodded, biting her lip. She wanted to reassure Ash, to tell him that she was in no danger from Lord Rebinus, though she still didn't quite understand why Tobin wouldn't just Claim her and end the game. There was something else she didn't know. She hoped tonight would reveal more of his plans.

"Go," Ash said, hand warm on her arm, "where is my brother?"

"He's busy," Margot said, reaching out to remove his hand, but he only held her in place with his other, escorting her the few final feet to the waiting vehicle. "I promise you, Ash. I'm not in any danger."

"You aren't," he said, releasing her arm and putting a hand on her lower back, "because now I can protect you." He pushed her gently inside after Nik and Timothy, and Margot didn't get to ask him what he meant with the sudden change in motivation.

The drive to the Aerie passed with Nik messing around with every possible button inside the limo and shoving his hands through the open sunroof.

"Why don't you just howl while you're at it?" Timothy griped, and Nik replied by lowering the barricade between them and the driver yet again.

"You don't know how to have a good time," Nik complained, reaching out to study the contents of the small built-in cooler. Finding bottles of Gencian beer, Nik grabbed four and handed them to everyone. "A toast!" he insisted, popping the cap on his and Margot's beer and wiping the foam with his hand so none got on Margot's dress. When everyone had an open drink, he raised the bottle. "To old friends," he began. "To music and to the ties that bind us together. You are my favorite people, my family, and I can't imagine doing this with anyone else." Ash and Timothy nodded, Margot smiling at her cousin. "To family!" he shouted.

They all raised their glasses to the center of the limo, clinking them together.

Margot drank, feeling more a part of Stone Dragons than she had in weeks. She remembered this feeling, the connection between her and the guys, the bond forged on the road, the muscle memory of years spent together. Tobin's arrival may have sent her life on a different path, but she would also have this: the guys—even Ash—would always be part of her life.

Chapter 57
The Aerie in Taflah

Evening, Sunday, March 15ᵗʰ
at The Aerie in Taflah, Genc

Margot had always heard that the Aerie in Taflah was the most beautiful venue for any event, but she had never been. The last time Stone Dragons passed through the capital, she had retired early to her bus, not wanting to watch Ash and his harem of gorgeous women take in the exquisite views. Standing atop the stairs, Margot finally understood what Tobin had meant when he promised to show her sometime. The Aerie was a glass building, open to all sides to showcase the mountains surrounding Beau Lake, the dark water glistening in the light of the nearly full moon.

Margot glanced at Nik, reminding herself that the full moon wasn't until Wednesday—her cousin seemed fine—no pre-shifting PMS or anything. Taking a deep breath, she lifted the edge of her gown and descended the stairs. She was halfway down when Ash appeared at her side, gathering her arm and escorting her the rest of the way. They entered the main ballroom together, people turning to point and whisper at their arrival.

"Real subtle," she gritted. "I was trying to keep it quiet."

"There is no keeping you quiet, Margot," Ash quipped. "Believe me, I remember." Cheeks flaming, Margot elbowed him and pasted a fake smile on her face.

At the bottom of the stairs, Ash paused, bowed formally to her, kissed her hand, and stepped away, joining Timothy and Nik on the small stage in the corner of the room. The crowd drew close, and Margot was very aware of the voices around her, hushed whispers and conversations, mostly including "Is that her? Did you see her with Ashton Stonewall?"

Margot didn't join the general flow moving to watch the show, instead lingering near the back. When it seemed like the crowd near her had lost interest, the group made up of last-minute arrivals eager to get a good spot for the show, Margot stepped back, looking for a quiet place behind the stairway. She found a wide pillar in a corner opposite the show and settled against it just as Ash let out the opening notes for "Dragonfire." Margot knew Cayla would be near the stage, no doubt plotting with the record company executives for the next tour, the new album they would record over the summer. No one would bother her for a little bit.

Margot's solitude lasted exactly four songs.

"My Lady," a voice said from behind her, and Margot turned to see a tall man standing to the right of the pillar she leaned against. He was dressed in a tuxedo like the rest of the men, but he held a short black cane and wore a top hat, his eyes sparkling with excitement as he stared at her. "May I introduce myself? I am—"

"The lady is already engaged," a deep voice said from her left and Margot and the stranger both turned to see Lord Rebinus. He was dressed in a tuxedo like the others, but his long white hair was glossy and smooth, covering his shoulders and running down his back like liquid. Margot brought a hand to her mouth, unable to stop herself. Lord Rebinus was startling standing in her bus—seeing him in full formal Ardon dress was jaw-dropping.

The stranger took one look at Lord Rebinus, dropped into a bow, and stepped away. "My apologies, my Lord."

Margot watched him go, then frowned at Rebinus. "Does everyone react that way to your presence?"

Rebinus stepped closer to her side, his breath brushing against her bare shoulder—right over where he had left a love bite she had covered up with makeup. "Not everyone, Margot. You're still here."

Margot stayed still, forcing herself not to look at him and fall under the hypnotic spell of a fae Lord. On the stage, Ash was finishing the last lines of "Breathing Fire." Next, they would play "Tales of Blood and Maidens" and then finish with "Heart of Stone." She wondered if he would dedicate it to her as he had for every show since Akkoy.

After the short show, the band would circulate among the guests, taking photos with fans and press, showing everyone what great guys they were—Cayla's orders. Margot's job was to look pretty and answer any technical questions if the record company asked.

"I thought we weren't going to meet until after the show," she said to Rebinus, enjoying their time alone among so many other people.

He laughed, the sound rich in her ear. "None of the Lords will wait," he told her. "They are all eager for their chance to meet you. But while I'm here, they will not approach."

"That fearsome reputation at work?" she asked, still not looking at him. "Will anyone try anything tonight?"

"Perhaps," he admitted, "but I am here, darling. No one will succeed."

Margot tried to repress the smile on her lips, knowing that others were probably watching them. "Am I to be seduced by you, then?" she asked, turning to face him as the pounding of Timothy's drumwork synced with her heartbeat.

"That's up to you, Margot," Lord Rebinus said, turning to look at the stage. Margot followed his gaze.

"Tonight, this song is for Margot," Ash said, then launched into a slow sultry version of "Heart of Stone." Her mouth fell open. Ash had been dedicating the song to "a very special lady," never saying her name. She glanced around, seeing her name ripple through the crowd as some people—no doubt fae—turned around to point at where she stood in the back with Lord Rebinus close to her side.

"Interesting," Lord Rebinus commented. "It seems I'm not the only one trying to seduce you tonight, darling."

Margot made a strangled noise, unable to deny the rush of longing and heat running through her at the sight of Ash on stage, dressed in his fine tuxedo, wavy hair wild around his face, eyes closed as he sang the chorus. As he finished, his eyes opened, and he stared right at her, eyes piercing the crowd to stare deep into her soul.

When she turned to reply to Lord Rebinus, he was gone. She stood awkwardly where she was through the closing song, "Dragon Cry," and when the show was over, she made her way through the crowd to Cayla, the manager stunning in a red sheath dress. She smiled politely and shook a few hands, falling into her role as stage manager easily, laughing in the right places and reassuring when any doubts about the band's ability to continue touring came up. Cayla gave her a surreptitious nod a few times, signaling how pleased she was with Margot's performance. Margot may have doubted a lot of things in the last month, but she was good at her job, and tonight only reinforced it.

An hour later, the photo ops had ended and the band was circulating freely among the guests. Ash found Margot standing near Cayla and three record executives.

"Can I steal this one?" he asked, winking cheerfully at the group.

"Don't let her go!" Cayla reminded him. "You need that girl."

"Oh, I know," Ash agreed, taking Margot's hand and leading her away from the group.

"What are we supposed to do now?" she asked, glancing around at the scattered clumps of people, some of whom were dancing to the music now being piped in.

"It's a party, Go," Ash said, leaning down to say it close in her ear. "It is customary to dance."

"With you?" she asked, letting him lead her to the center of the room. Other couples were already swaying to the music, but too many heads shifted to watch them as they passed.

"Of course with me," he said, turning around to bow formally to her. "Who else would you dance with?"

Margot dipped her head, not knowing the proper response. In the old movies, women dipped in a curtsy, but she didn't want to try that in front of so many spectators. His hand grabbed hers and held it up, while the other slid familiarly around her lower back, holding her close.

"Doesn't this send a message?" Margot asked, following his lead and allowing him to move them around the floor. She recalled that he had named her during the show. "What are you doing?"

"It does send a message," Ash said, leaning down to speak, the move bringing his face near hers, marking her even more as his partner.

"What does it say?" Margot asked, a bit breathless at the spectacle of dancing with Ash, his full attention on her, everyone staring at them. "You can't be with me, Ash. This is bad for you!"

"They don't care about me," Ash told her.

"But you're supposed to be in hiding!" she squealed. "Isn't this a bit obvious?"

"Yes," he said. "It's okay, Margot. My exile ends tonight. I don't have to hide anymore."

"What?" Margot's questions were muffled against his shoulder as he moved her more vigorously, careful not to linger too long in one spot lest anyone overhear their conversation. "What the hell does that mean?"

"It means I'm free," Ash told her, spinning her out and tugging her back. "I will not fail you again, Go." Margot tried to ignore how natural it felt to dance with him, how well her body moved with his, the two of them in concert. "My father has an announcement," he whispered the next time she drew near.

"That's ominous," Margot said, trying to follow this new confident Ash. "What announcement?"

Before Ash could reply, someone was moving alongside them, delicately tapping Ash on the shoulder. "I insist on cutting in," a tall man with light brown wavy hair said. "You don't mean to occupy all of her attention this evening?"

"Lord Kristoff, of course." Ash dipped his head respectfully, but Margot could see the reluctance in the move. "May I present Lady Margot?" He transferred her hand to the stranger and stepped neatly aside.

Margot stood awkwardly, remembering to close her mouth as the new man began to move her around. Lord Kristoff, she recalled, a fae Lord. He was tall, elegant, imposing, maybe mid-30s, with a stiff bearing that made her think of the prince the princess runs away from in every fairy tale.

"How delighted I am to make your acquaintance," Lord Kristoff said politely, but something dark skittered across Margot's skin. This Lord was not delighted by her presence at all. She wondered how he managed to lie to her, promising to ask Tobin more about how the fae truth thing worked.

"Charmed," Margot replied, the word falling out of her mouth. She was not charmed.

"You must know how eager we are to see you properly sorted," the Lord continued.

"Properly sorted, huh?" she echoed, unable to keep the annoyance from her tone. "You make me seem like a piece of property."

"Aren't you?" Kristoff replied, gaze cutting across the room to where Ash stood, already surrounded.

"I am not," Margot snapped, releasing his hand and freeing herself from his grip. She stood on the floor, not moving, glaring at him.

Lord Kristoff smiled, and it was cold, twisting something in Margot's gut. He bowed graciously, said, "You will be," and headed into the crowd.

Margot stood on the dance floor for another moment, gathering her wits, then headed toward the nearest wall. She wanted to wash her hands, not liking the residue of Kristoff on her skin.

Why isn't everyone afraid of that guy? she wondered. *He's awful.*

She was standing alone for ten seconds before another man approached her, the same one who had tried earlier, except now he didn't have his top hat or cane. He had dark hair neatly tied back and the same regal bearing Margot was starting to recognize as a fae Lord. He was distant, cordial, and he bowed before speaking. "My Lady Margot, I presume?"

Margot nodded, not sure what to say. She didn't want another interaction like the one with Kristoff.

"I am Lord Alick," the stranger said. "I see you have already met Lord Kristoff." He tsked, shaking his head. "Please forgive his impertinence. He can be difficult."

"Why are you apologizing for him?" Margot asked. "Is he your Lord?"

"No!" Alick said, scandalized by the thought. "I was only trying to say that he is not representative of fae society, something I fear you've seen precious little of in Ardon."

"You're right about that," Margot agreed. "I haven't seen much of the fae." She didn't add that she hadn't enjoyed anything she had seen yet.

Well, except maybe Lord Rebinus.

"But you will," Alick assured her. "Once you have a place, you will see—"

"See," Margot interrupted, shaking her head, "there you go again, talking about me like a possession. I don't know if you know this, Lord Alick, but women raised in Ardon take offense to that kind of thing."

"But you weren't raised in Ardon," Alick replied smoothly.

"I—" Margot stopped, not sure what to say. If Alick knew about her childhood on Belsune, what else did the fae Lord know about her? "I was raised by my mother," she said finally, "and she taught me to value myself. I don't need a place among the fae."

Alick laughed, and it was charming, light and airy, a sound Margot had heard at afterparties before, the carefree sound of a man with no skin in the game. "Oh, my Lady, you are a delight! I cannot wait to see what you achieve."

"How long did you give me?" she asked abruptly, recalling Lady Drina's comments about her odds of remaining Unclaimed.

Alick's laugh settled into a chuckle. "I never gamble on Claimings, my Lady." He lowered his voice, friendly now. "Though if I had to wager on you, I'd say you just might outlast us all." He dipped his head respectfully, then backed up. "I wish you a good evening."

Margot said nothing as he left. Alone, she used the reprieve to scoot over to the glass wall, back to the room, hoping no one else would recognize her from that direction. She could see her silhouette in the window, bodies moving back and forth behind her.

I should find the band, she thought. *I should see Cayla again.*

But her encounter with the two fae Lords had unnerved her, and she needed a moment to collect herself.

Are they all here? Margot started to turn, to look around, but stopped herself. *Is my father here?*

Chapter 58

Politicking with the Fae

Margot hadn't thought much about the elusive Lord Tennere. Tobin had told her the rumors surrounding her father—how he grieved her mother and swore vengeance on Lord Rebinus—a revenge that had yet to occur. Margot had a brief spike of fear for her lover, afraid that someone would attack Lord Rebinus and kill Tobin instead.

No, she assured herself. *They need Lord Rebinus. Five Lords. A balance of power.*

Is that why they're so eager to see where I end up? Am I powerful enough to tip the balance of power in the fae world?

It seemed a pretty weak world if she alone could change it. Alick and Kristoff both seemed to think she would join one team or another—though maybe Alick hoped she didn't—but neither had tried to Claim her themselves. Other than Kristoff's lame attempt in sending Lawrence, no one had tried to Claim her since the faengs back in Armav. She recalled both Ash and

Tobin's warnings—she had expected fae to be constantly attacking her. But that hadn't happened.

Am I already too strong for them? Or are they afraid of my father? Or Ash? She recalled Ash's mysterious announcement and turned around, scanning the room for him. Part of her wished Tobin was there, but she forced herself not to look for his white hair, knowing she would only find Lord Rebinus.

Instead of finding Tobin's alter ego, she found herself staring at an older version of Tobin, a striking man with the same shock of short white hair, fine features and an aristocratic bearing. He met her gaze from across the room and gestured slightly with his chin, calling her to him.

That's Lord Novus, she realized, *Tobin and Ash's father. No wonder everyone thinks he's not Ash's father.* She lingered by the window a moment, not allowing herself to be summoned by a chin, then slowly headed his way, finding Ash standing among the throng around Lord Novus.

As she drew closer, she noted similarities with his younger son. The eyes were the same shape, though not the same color, and the jawline—Ash was swarthy, his chin often dark with stubble while Lord Novus's face was smooth, serious and blank, a look she had seen on Tobin's face more than once. Broody rock star that he was, Ash smiled a lot more than the rest of his family.

People moved aside to let her pass, clearly getting the message that the Lord wanted to meet her. Margot made a point not to lift her dress as she walked, sure that this man would notice her simple sandals and judge her for them.

It doesn't matter what he thinks, she told herself, but she knew it was a lie. *He's Tobin and Ash's dad. Of course you care what he thinks.*

Swallowing, she stood in front of the white-haired fae, dipping her head in greeting and hoping it was enough. "Lord Novus," she said, "pleased to meet you."

The Lord looked her over from the hem of her dress to the crown of her hair, a slow perusal meant to unnerve her. Margot had been dealing with this kind of ogling since she first started touring with Stone Dragons. She waited patiently, meeting his gaze firmly when he reached her face. He seemed surprised at her boldness but pleased. "The Lady Margot, I presume."

Margot said nothing. *How long until he comments about me finding my place?* She pressed her tongue hard against her bottom teeth to keep herself silent. This was the fae Lord's show—she was just part of the entertainment.

Ash looked between them, clearly waiting for his father to speak again. He didn't disappoint.

"So you're the one who caused all this uproar?"

Margot's hands raised, lifting to her chest. "Me?" she asked. "I've done nothing."

Novus said, "I hear you slayed two faengs on the road after calling down a hurricane."

"Oh," Margot said uncomfortably. "That." She glanced at Ash, whose face revealed nothing, and wondered why Ash didn't tell his father the truth about who really saved them.

"Yes," Novus repeated. "That." He gave Ash a suspicious look. "I imagine she's done far more in the last month." He sighed. "You are what I call a disturbance,

Lady Margot. Best to have you settled to stop all this excitement."

"You don't enjoy excitement?" Margot challenged, her anger rising. "Your sons didn't inherit that quality." Novus's eyes widened at her use of the plural.

"Tobin?" he asked, the name barely above a whisper. He looked at Ash, who remained silent. "You have seen your brother?"

"He's been helping me with my abilities," Margot told him, not caring if that was a secret. "Since Ash was otherwise occupied."

"Your Claimer will help you with your abilities," Novus snapped. "Tobin has no business meddling—"

"He Awakened her," Ash said, finding his voice at last.

"Tobin Awakened her?" Novus repeated. "That is not what I heard."

"What did you hear?" Margot asked, stepping into his space, her normal manner asserting itself.

"Ash!" Novus exclaimed, peering at his son. "Ash Awakened you."

Margot scoffed. "Please. Ash is too afraid of disappointing you to even touch me."

Novus's expression darkened as her words landed, and he watched a few nearby guests soak in the new information. Margot tried to restrain herself, knowing that in this world, knowledge was power. Fae society was slow and subtle, Tobin had explained. Margot was anything but. "Listen," she said, "I know everyone here wants me sorted so life can go back to normal—that would be lovely, you know, if my life could go back to normal—"

"Just let someone Claim you, and your life will settle into what it was meant to be," Novus interrupted.

"Just let someone Claim me?" Margot echoed. "Do you even hear yourself?" She shook her head, anger rising again. "You know what? I don't care. I don't care what anyone," she turned to face the spectators, "thinks about what I should or shouldn't be doing. I have no intention of being Claimed. Ever. End of story."

"Margot," Ash tried.

"I believe the Lady Margot has spoken," a deep voice interrupted, and Margot turned to see Lord Rebinus standing behind her. He was tall, much taller than Tobin, and bigger, but standing near Novus, she could suddenly see the family resemblance.

Tobin's uncle, she reminded herself, seeing the resemblance in the long white hair, the light eyes. Something dropped deep in Margot's stomach at the sight of him in the light of the room with the night sky and moon behind him in the windows, and she bit her lip, reminding herself that it was only Tobin, an older, mature, ruggedly handsome and domineering Tobin whose voice did odd things to her insides.

"Margot," Ash tried again, reaching for her hand, but she pulled it back, stepping away from Ash and his father to face the newcomer.

"Lady Margot," she said simply, dipping into an awkward curtsy, wanting to show Lord Rebinus the respect his fearsome reputation required.

"You reputation precedes you," Lord Rebinus said and bowed formally, taking her hand as he stood up. "I am Lord Rebinus." If she wasn't so awed by his presence, she would have scoffed at the pretense. Many people had seen them talking already—knew they had already met—but everyone pretended this was the first time.

Margot watched him as he brought her hand to his lips, gently kissing the back before releasing her. She became aware of the room again when Ash's warm hand grabbed hers, tugging her back a few steps.

"You heard her," Ash said. "She wishes to remain Unclaimed."

"So she says," Rebinus agreed, glancing down at Ash and Margot's entwined hands. He gave Ash a knowing look. "Sounds like you may disagree on that, young Ashton."

"Stop it," Margot snapped, not liking the way he spoke to Ash. She recognized her mistake the instant she said it, the chorus of gasps from the surrounding patrons, all of them silently watching to see Lord Rebinus's reaction.

He stared at her for a moment, eyes narrowing, and then he burst into laughter, a sound the crowd awkwardly mimicked. "Oh, you truly are a delight!" he roared. "For once, the rumors are true!" He held out his hand to her. "Please, Lady, grant me the courtesy of a dance. I see you have already satisfied Ashton, Kristoff, and Alick. I assume I warrant the same consideration."

"O-okay," Margot managed, peeling her hand free from Ash's to take his. As she stepped away, Ash grabbed her other hand, fingers slipping across hers. She turned to meet his gaze, and he mouthed, "Be careful."

"I will," she replied softly and let Lord Rebinus pull her away from the Stonewalls, following him to the dance floor. The other dancers moved aside, giving Rebinus plenty of space, and Margot reminded herself that she was dancing with Lord Rebinus, the most feared fae Lord. She could not forget that again. He may have been able to laugh off her earlier mistake, but another would be suspicious.

"My Lady," Rebinus said in that deep voice, "you seem nervous."

"I am properly awed, my Lord," she replied, accepting his hand on hers and the other against her back, their bodies moving easily around the floor as the music continued.

Rebinus chuckled, the sound pleasant as he pressed against her. "As you should be."

"You look pretty great in a tux," she commented. "Much better than the other stuff."

"You love that other stuff," he said, dipping her low.

Margot bit her lip, stifling the thrill he raised in her. "Maybe a little," she admitted. "But this is nice."

"This is familiar," Lord Rebinus said, spinning her out and back again. "It's easy to appreciate the known."

"Is this the part where you lure me into the unknown?" Margot asked, tone a little too flippant but definitely in keeping with the way she had addressed the other Lords. "I've heard all about your persuasive tactics."

"I would never charm you into doing anything you didn't want to do, my Lady," he assured her.

Margot smirked. "Never," she agreed. "You are a perfect gentleman."

"I am," Lord Rebinus assured her and released her from the dance. "Thank you, Lady Margot," he said loudly, "for the pleasure of your company." Bowing once more, he abruptly turned and left, people giving him a wide berth.

That's it? she wondered. A few hesitant people tried to catch his attention, but Margot decided his brief appearance was far more effective. She left the dance floor, done with dancing with strange men for the night.

Chapter 59
Actual Fae Politics

Late Night, Sunday, March 15th
at The Aerie in Taflah, Genc

The gala settled down after Lord Rebinus departed. Margot hovered among the rest of the band and Cayla, Ash finally leaving his father's side to join them. By the end of the night, Margot's nerves had settled enough for her to have a good time. She had met what she assumed were more fae, including a judgy Lady Drina who had tsked at her sandals, but none were so imposing as the Lords who commented about her finding her place in the world.

As the people started leaving, Margot found herself alone with Ash, and he used the moment of freedom to tug her out of the main room and down a hallway, out of sight of the remaining guests.

"Ash!" she exclaimed softly. "What?"

He held a finger to his lips, pulling her along and through a doorway into a small room where the glass windows showcased the mountains in the distance. She let herself be pulled, echoes of watching a teenage Ash lure other women away from the parties flooding her memory. Margot paused as the door closed, sealing them in silence and semi-darkness. The moon had set, the night late, and Margot studied the still water of Beau Lake in the darkness, soaking up the sight.

"It's so beautiful," she whispered, then remembered he had said to be quiet. She turned to face him.

"Margot," he said, quietly pulling both of her hands to his chest, "I was so worried for you."

"Why?" she asked, trying to reassure him, though her heart had started to pound. She hated how much her hands wanted to stay there, touching him. "Those fae Lords were nothing." Grimacing, she added, "Though your dad is plenty scary."

"He's just protective of his legacy," Ash said dismissively.

"That's you, right?" Margot asked. "His legacy? Was tonight your official fae coming out? I don't understand any of this, Ash. Why bother to hide you if he was going to show you off anyway?"

"I've been protected before, but now, no one will dare challenge me."

"What changed?" she asked. "A few weeks ago, you couldn't even use your powers."

"I know," he said, "and I will never forgive myself for what happened. I nearly lost you!" His grip tightened on her hands and he moved closer, body almost pressed against hers. "But we don't have to worry about that anymore." He brushed a hand against her cheek, tucking an errant strand behind her ear. "It's partly because of you,

Margot," he said. "They are all scrambling to see where you will end up. They have lost interest in me entirely."

Margot didn't like how much Ash sounded like his father. "What happens when they remember you again? Especially now that you've reminded them?" she pushed, her gut warning her that something was wrong. "Ash," she asked, "what is your father's big announcement?"

"The dragons," he said proudly. "My mother's people are allying with my father. That's what she's been doing all this time—securing the alliance. No one will dare Claim me now or oppose my father." He gave Margot an excited look. "And if we can keep you Unclaimed, you can be free too!" He raised an eyebrow. "The only thing we need to figure out is how to get Lord Rebinus out of the way. He's crazy enough to challenge the dragons."

"How do you mean to do that?" she asked, cold settling in her stomach. "Get rid of Lord Rebinus?"

"He has enemies, Margot. So many. Eventually, one of them will be successful. His death would even free Tobin—"

"No!" Margot yelled, her voice loud in the small room. "You can't kill him!"

Ash released her hands, narrowing his eyes as he gave her a long look. Finally, he said, "It was one dance, Go. I know everyone says Rebinus is charming, but I didn't think you'd fall for him after one dance."

"I haven't fallen for anyone," she snapped, not liking the jealousy in Ash's eyes. "I'm objecting to your casual discussion of murder, Ash."

"It's not like that," Ash defended.

"It's exactly like that, Ash," she reminded him.

"Lord Rebinus is a monster," he said. "He's done terrible things."

Margot nodded. "You mean like what happened to my mother?"

Ash took a long breath. "My brother needs to learn how to keep secrets," he said softly. "There are some things you don't need to know."

"And you're the one to decide that?" Margot asked.

The look he gave her was pure possessiveness. "If it's going to hurt you, yes," he said decisively.

"Dammit, Ash," she said, smacking his chest. "This is your problem. You decide all by yourself what the rules are, no matter what anyone says!"

Ash turned the heat of his gaze on her. "He told you what happened to your mother, yes? Did it help, Margot? Did it make you feel better, or did it only add to your anger and frustration?"

Margot looked away. Ash wasn't wrong. Her mother was gone. Knowing the details only made her hate the dead man more. Ash didn't know about Tobin. He thought the target of her hatred was still alive and well. "At least he told me the truth," she said grimly.

Ash laughed. "My brother has a very loose relationship with the truth," he said.

"You think you're better? Just making all my decisions for me because you know what's best?"

"Centaur's Balls, Go. It is going to be better! Isn't this what you wanted, a way to be free? With Rebinus gone—"

"Murdered," Margot interrupted.

"Gone," Ash repeated. "You'll be safe. No one else can even try to Claim you. You can stay with me and my father, and we will keep you safe."

"Oh Ash," she said, "I doubt very much your father would have me anywhere near you, Claimed or not."

When he said nothing, she added, "And Tobin? Where is he in this plot?"

"Tobin always manages to figure it out," Ash said dismissively. "No doubt he'll work a new angle."

"With Lord Rebinus gone?" she prompted. "What about the people under his protection?" She wondered how secret this plot truly was, if Lawrence may have heard of it while listening for her.

"Protection!" Ash scoffed. "Hardly. They will be glad to be free of him!"

"Except they will only answer to a new Lord," Margot said, recalling Tobin's explanation of how the magic worked. "Whoever kills Lord Rebinus will Claim his people." She glared at him. "Is that your plan, then? To steal his household?"

"Margot, what are you talking about? This is Lord Rebinus. He's the villain. Taking him down is a goal, not a tragedy."

"Who are you right now?" she asked. "I hardly recognize you!"

"I could say the same!" he spat. "You spend so much time with Tobin, I can hear him in your words!"

"At least Tobin sees this for what it is—fucked up!"

"Tobin only sees what his Lord wants him to see!"

Margot was about to scream something else at him, though she wasn't sure what, when their phones rang. Breathing hard, Ash reached into his pocket and pulled out the phone. "Timothy," he said.

Margot looked at her phone. "Nik," she said. Sighing, they both answered. "What?" they asked, holding both phones out on speaker.

"Where the hell are you guys?" Nik asked, voice a bit loud. He must have been drinking.

"Still at the Aerie," Ash said. "Why?"

"Is Margot with you?" Timothy asked, much more subdued.

"Yes, I'm here," Margot answered.

"You both need to get back to the Willis Center," Timothy said. "There's been some kind of water main break, and we need to move the RVs. I know that Margot—"

"It's fine," Margot insisted, swiping to text Tobin. "Just tell him where to put it."

"Him?" Timothy and Nik asked at the same time.

"Tobin," Margot said, then looked up at Ash's shocked face, his open mouth. "He has the keys." At the long silence, Margot rolled her eyes. "Nik," she said into her phone, "you were the one who told me to let someone in. I took your advice."

"I see," Timothy said. A long pause, then, "Ash, call me when you get back."

Ash said nothing, just turned his phone off. Margot told Nik to get back to the RV safely and ended the call. Ash was still staring at her.

"You let Tobin drive your bus?" he asked finally.

Margot narrowed her eyes. Surely, he knew she and Tobin were together. Why this odd reaction to him driving her bus?

"But ... no one drives your bus ... but you."

Margot shrugged. "I needed help. Tobin was there. We've grown close, Ash. You can understand why your little murder plot against Lord Rebinus may concern me." Ash raised an eyebrow at her use of the Lord's proper name. She had always said it wrong before.

"I see," he said, turning away, his back to her.

"Oh hell no," Margot said, reaching out to grab his shoulder. "You don't get to play the hurt jealous guy."

Ash said nothing, and Margot continued, "We aren't together, Ashton Stonewall. You said we couldn't be together! Don't blame me for moving on."

His shoulders slumped, but still he said nothing.

"Ash," she said gently, "you have to let me go."

"No."

"What?"

"I said no." He turned around slowly, an unearthly red glow around his face, eyes blazing with fire. "I will never let you go, Margot."

Ash grabbed her, yanking her close as his mouth claimed hers. The sudden wave of magic swallowed her whole, knocking her flat with its intensity, and Margot had no choice but to surrender to it.

Chapter 60

Claimed and Reclaimed

After Midnight, Monday, March 16th
in the Old House in Sorne, Arillo

At some point during the magical onslaught, Ash sidestepped, moving them both through space, mouths still connected in a soul-searing kiss.

Margot's ears popped, body protesting the sudden elevation difference between the Aerie and the low-lying lands of their old house in Sorne. She recognized Ash's bedroom, the small bed with its worn blue blanket pushed against the wall, the faded posters of other rock stars, the empty guitar stand in the corner, his brown dresser, the top covered in a layer of dust. Beyond the wall next to his bed lay her old room, her bed pressed against the same wall.

Sometimes, when she slept, Margot felt like she could reach through that wall and touch him. Now, there was no wall, only the overwhelming force of Ash's will surrounding her, smothering her. It covered her in an instant, and she felt the bond snap into place, feeling at once whole and completely shattered, everything she was reforming into a new Margot, one who was completely and utterly Claimed by Ash.

Oh no, she thought, tearing herself away from him, gathering her own will. *You will not Claim me without consequences.* Without thinking or knowing how she did it, Margot copied what Ash had just done, enjoying his wide eyes as she slammed her own magic into him, the blow making him fall to his knees in the old room. She felt him fighting it, fighting her, more aware and able to defend himself than she had been, but Margot was persistent and angry. Her rage made her magic stronger, and she could feel his resistance fading, ebbing.

<Surrender to me,> she demanded, looking down at him. *<You know you want to.>*

<I can't,> she heard him think. *<I won't.>*

<You will,> she demanded. pushing even harder. If Ash was going to Claim her, then she was going to Claim him right back, keeping them on even ground. If they were ever on even ground.

She pulled him up to her, a hand twisting in his hair as she pressed her body against his, feeling the attraction between them, the wild desire spilling free.

<Mine,> she heard Ash say in her head as his arms wrapped around her. *<Always Mine.>*

<Yours,> she agreed, *<but also Mine.>* Her fingers worked frantically at the front of his tuxedo, needing to be closer. Ash stepped back, sitting hard on the bed and yanking her atop him, one hand freeing his pants as the other shoved her dress up, both of them crazed with the magic, the push to complete the connection. Margot

found him just as he jerked her forward, filling her, and everything in Margot lit up.

Ash opened his eyes, really seeing her, and then he ducked his head, chin dipping as he let the magic flow over him, surrounding him and encasing him, the Claim settling into place.

For a long time, they stayed that way, Ash inside her, chest heaving from his exertion, Margot atop him but not moving, her own heart pounding in her ears. When she finally returned to herself, feeling her body again, she stared at him, truly seeing him with her new eyes.

He was beautiful.

Of course he's beautiful, she reminded herself. *You knew that.*

But the Ash before her was glowing, a soft red flame outlining his body, and she could sense the raw power within him, power that was now at her disposal, should she want to call on it. Transfixed, Margot held out her hand, palm up, and imagined a small flame dancing in her hand as he had shown her. The fire was warm, tickling her skin but not painful, though she knew that it could burn anything down if she wanted it to.

"Wow," she breathed, her voice loud in the empty house, and Ash looked up at her. For a second, Margot wondered what he saw, but then she could sense it, could see herself through his eyes, and the image was frightening.

She was a fae creature with wild dark hair, eyes glowing bright blue as she crackled with electrical energy.

Taking a cue from her, he held out his palm, a tiny ball of lightning appearing. "Go," he said quietly, "when did you learn to conjure lightning?"

"I didn't," she told him, but as she watched him, she suddenly knew she could, targeting the bolts here and there as she liked. "But I do now."

Ash looked up at her, into her. "I see you," he said quietly. "All of you."

"I see you," Margot whispered. "All of you." She paused, and though it was obvious, she asked the question aloud. "Did we just Claim each other? We're so fucked."

Ash nodded, fingers flexing as he played with the light around his hand, testing another of her abilities. "I think ... I know what you know."

"And so do I." She peered at him. "Though I already thought you were a dragon." She could see Ash in his memories, a huge black dragon the size of the house they stood in, leathery wings spread wide as he followed the wind, exhilaration flooding him as he flew above the clouds, diving and spinning in the air currents. "You can see the wind."

"Half-dragon," he reminded her. "And not only full dragonborn can see it."

"So that's what he lied about," she mused and knew Ash was seeing the conversation with Tobin in her memory. "He was protecting your secret."

"Interesting," he said slowly. "I didn't think he would defend me." She watched as he saw more of her memories, pulling the secrets from her without any effort at all. He blanched as he saw Lord Rebinus in her trailer.

As the memories of Tobin played before them both, Margot remembered where she was, literally sitting atop Ash.

"Um..." she said awkwardly, moving forward and sliding over to sit on the bed next to him. Ash adjusted his pants, putting himself to rights again. "That was ...

intense." She laughed softly, emotions raging through her. "You did say it would involve sex, though I didn't think that's what you meant."

"Claiming may involve sex," Ash said, "but that's not what it means."

"Love then?" Margot asked.

Ash reached out to stroke her cheek. "If love made a Claiming, you would be here with him," he said softly, "wouldn't you?"

"What is it then?" she asked, feeling the magic all around them both, but not understanding it.

"Can't you see?"

And Margot could see—everything in him. It was amazing, and also horrible, knowing she was just as exposed to him.

"Is this what Claiming means? Knowing everything about someone?" Margot asked. She remembered how easily she had seen into Lawrence—and the way his interest had morphed into slavish devotion. *Will that happen to me? Has it already happened?*

"The Claimer knows everything. The Claimed only knows their side, the loyalty, the fealty, the need to please their Lord." Margot took that in, adding it to what she already knew about Claiming.

Lord Rebinus knows this about everyone beneath him. No wonder it's so easy for him to cow the others— and why they fear him—while longing for his approval.

"Is that what you feel?" she asked, enjoying the feel of him next to her on his bed, years of longing to be with him echoing from her to him. "You yearn to please me?"

"Just as you want to please me," he replied, turning to face her. "I shouldn't have hesitated, Margot," he said bluntly. "I should have protected you from the start."

She could see his regret, but she didn't expect to see him approach his father after the faeng attack, after that disastrous moment in the green room where it had been easier to fall back into old habits than face the possibility of a life with her. He had demanded the right to defend her next time, the right to reveal himself to the fae, even if it put him at risk.

Lord Novus had agreed, sharing his news about the dragon alliance, provided Ash remained Unclaimed and on his way to becoming a Lord.

A promise Ash had just broken to be with her.

She could see it all: his desire for her, his internal struggle between loyalty to his father and his people and the temptation she represented, the powerful magic he kept hidden from everyone.

"Oh, Ash," she said, seeing a young boy covered in soot, eyes wide as he stared at Tobin, his older brother picking him up and promising him that the secret of Ash's power would die with him.

She sighed, seeing Tobin in her mind, wondering how he would react to what she had done. "He knew," she told Ash, "and he never told anyone. I don't think even Rebinus truly knew. Tobin kept that loyalty to you. Held onto it. He even lied to me about it."

Ash nodded. "I never knew how deep his loyalty to me went. I assumed it all vanished with the Claiming." He peered at her, and she knew he longed to kiss her again, to feel her body against his. "What about your loyalty, Go? You still choosing my brother?"

Margot considered his words. She could talk about Tobin's loyalty, but she had just broken her word to him. Though he had insisted he didn't expect her to resist Ash,

Margot still felt guilty for that moment—and the desire for more still tingling under her skin.

It's just sex, darling. She could practically hear Tobin say it. But it wasn't.

"I think I love him," she said, the words falling from her lips despite herself.

Ash nodded, but she could feel the flinch of pain within him. "And me?"

"I'll always love you," she said, the truth heavy between them. "But I think I resigned myself to never being with you." She frowned, the outside world struggling to get back in. "What happens now?" she asked. "We Claimed each other. Doesn't that fuck up your precious fae hierarchy?"

"It does," he admitted, turning the full force of his honey gaze her way. "Right now, I don't care. We can sort it out later."

"Later?" she prodded, feeling his need for her just as her own rose to match it. "This is insane, Ash," she mumbled, a hand reaching out to meet his, palms pressed together. "It's ... too much."

"I just need to kiss you," Ash said, voice low and husky. "Please kiss me."

Margot closed her eyes, feeling the pull of the magic between them, passion swirling around them both. For a moment she hesitated, just to see if she could, but then she leaned forward, meeting his mouth with a hunger fueled by years of frustration. Lust rose in her belly, hot and demanding, and Margot climbed back on his lap, straddling him on the edge of his bed, the old blue blanket dipping under their combined weight. She Claimed him again with her mouth, her hands, consumed by the pull of their bodies, his excitement only spurring her on. They kissed for a long time, truly feeling one another, finally connecting as equals.

Chapter 61

In Big Trouble

Wee Hours, Monday, March 16th at the Stronghold of Lord Novus in Folamour, Lorellon

A new pulse of magic broke their kiss, and Ash moved instantly, pushing Margot behind him as someone stepped through the air into the room. For a split second, Margot wondered if it was Tobin, but there was no telltale purple haze, the mark of portal magic. This person was simply stepping through space, like Ash had done to her.

A true fae, she recalled Lady Drina's words about the ability to fae step or teleport. *I can do that eventually, once I learn how.*

The man who stood in Ash's old room was another white-haired fae, clearly another relative of theirs, but this one older, more stern as he stared at both of them on the bed, an eyebrow raised. Margot knew from Ash's thoughts that this was Clifton Ward, his father's vassal, just as Tobin served Lord Rebinus—or had. Clifton was mercenary, executing his Lord's wishes without mercy.

Ash had spent his childhood annoying him at every opportunity.

"Ashton," he said coldly, "your father wishes a word."

Ash sighed, annoyance flitting through him. *Can Father not leave me alone for five minutes?* Margot caught the thought, but she said nothing.

"He will not be kept waiting."

"Yeah, yeah," Ash grumbled, shaking his head, dismissing the command with the air of a spoiled prince ignoring a summons. "Calm down, Clifton. He can wait a few minutes."

"He cannot," the man snapped and gave them a pointed look. "Besides, I think what you have planned will take more than a few minutes. Come, my liege," he repeated. "The Lords await."

"Lords?" Margot repeated, glancing at Ash. "What Lords?"

Clifton deigned to answer her. "All of them, Lady Margot. You two have transgressed every possible law. There will be consequences."

"Of course," Ash sighed, but Margot knew he wasn't worried. His father's consequences had never truly affected him. This mutual Claiming was unexpected, of course, but no doubt his father already had a plan. He held out a hand to Margot, helping her up off the bed. He glanced down at his wrinkled tux, shirt and vest hanging open, Margot's disheveled blue dress and her wild hair. "Can we at least change?"

Clifton shook his head. "That can wait. It's time to face the music, my liege. You've done enough running away."

Margot knew the barb hurt Ash, tapping into his insecurities about his connection to his family, his fae responsibilities warring with his love of singing and being with the band—and with her. She glared at Clifton, not only for interrupting what was promising to be an amazingly good time, but because he had the nerve to judge Ash for something he had no control over—Ash wasn't running away; he was hiding on his family's orders. Margot ran a hand down her dress, attempting to smooth it, then yanked her hair into a quick bun before taking Ash's offered hand.

"Go," Ash said, gripping her hand tightly, "do not let go of me. No matter what happens."

"I won't," she promised.

They stepped through space again, this time to the fae realm, to stand together in a wide room with high ceilings. Margot could feel the hardwood floor beneath her sandals, arms prickling at the cooler air, and she studied the space. A throne room, she realized, spotting the fancy chair atop a dais a few feet away. A tapestry with stylized silver and black eyes set above a ragged mountain range, the Stonewall crest, covered the back wall. No one sat on the throne, though. There were five men in the room, all standing in a loose circle on the floor before the dais. She recognized all but one.

Lord Novus stood with his back to the dais, clearly commanding the space, face dark and angry. Lord Alick and Kristoff stood to the right, across from where Ash, Margot, and Clifton had appeared, both watching the proceedings with great interest. When they arrived, Clifton moved to stand just behind and to the left of his Lord, making room for the two men.

Margot met Lord Rebinus's gaze for a split second, wondering how Tobin would react to her new status. He gave her a wink. Warmth flooded her at the reassurance, and she felt Ash's burst of jealousy at her reaction.

This is going to be complicated, she thought, and turned to study the last person in the room. He was lean and dark-haired, his face blank as he stared back at her with eyes she had seen in the mirror her entire life. A small smile curled the edges of his mouth, and he nodded at her, a slight acknowledgement.

"Daughter," he said. The rest of the room watched them.

"Father," she said, the word awkward but not awful. Staring at him, she knew she had seen him once before—when he had delivered her mother's bus to her all those years ago. This was Lord Jasper Tennere, the man who had loved her mother enough to set her free, only to have her murdered by a fellow fae Lord in a bid for advantage.

"We have much to discuss, but I believe there are more pressing matters at the moment." He nodded at Lord Novus. "The floor is yours, Novus."

"I appreciate that, Lord Jasper. I know you must be as eager as we are to have this matter sorted so you can enjoy your reunion." Jasper nodded deferentially, but Margot sensed an undercurrent of resentment, her father disliking the formalities. Maybe her disgust with fae society didn't originate with her after all.

Lord Novus addressed the room. "As you all know, my idiot son decided to throw away his future tonight."

Margot gasped at the words, unable to stop the sound of indignation from escaping. Lord Novus ignored her, though the other Lords noted her reaction.

"Instead of adding another to our ranks and revisiting the allocation of power in this realm, we must decide how to deal with him." He glowered at Margot. "And her."

"Is it true, then?" Alick asked, peering at both Margot and Ash. "Did you Claim one another?"

Margot glanced at Ash, felt his resolve harden as his hand tightened on hers. "We did," he said.

"Well, that is problematic," Lord Kristoff commented, cocking his head. "What shall be done with you now?" He looked at Lord Novus. "No doubt you have a plan?"

Novus nodded, and for a moment, Margot could sense the pain in him. She knew it was Ash's insight that allowed her to see it. He knew his father very well, could read him easily enough. Whatever he was about to say, he didn't want to condemn his remaining son, but he had no choice. Ash had seen to that. Margot felt the guilt surge in Ash, and she held his hand tight, trying to soothe him with her presence. So what if these fae Lords kicked them out? They were perfectly content living in Ardon among the humans. They didn't need this world.

But she could feel Ash already slipping away from her, his loyalty to his family surging, and suddenly, she was aware of the oath, the spell binding Ash to his father. *If he goes into exile,* Margot realized, *his father will have no remaining sons.* In fae society, that seemed to be a big deal, not having an heir to marry with the other children of the Lords. Lord Novus would lose his status. He may be Unclaimed, but without an heir, such status hardly mattered, not without someone to pass down his Claims to.

"I have treated with the dragons," Lord Novus announced, and Ash looked up quickly. He knew the previous arrangement had been an alliance to stand against Lord Rebinus long enough for someone to succeed in assassinating him. But now? From the look on his father's face, Margot knew something had shifted—something that Ash wasn't prepared for.

"They have agreed to accept Ashton as a partner to Lady Iphega," Lord Novus said, "formally joining fae and dragon society at the highest level."

Chapter 62

Official Alliances

Ash's mouth fell open. The possibility had never occurred to him that his father would force him into an arranged marriage. He had heard of Lady Iphega, the eldest daughter of the dragon queen Shomentu, but he had assumed the dragon alliance was political, not a marriage. Margot felt the rage in him at such a thing, but she also felt his acceptance, knowing this was the only way for his father to save face.

"What?" he managed to say.

<See?> she thought at him. *<It sucks when other people determine your choices for you.>*

<This is way beyond that,> she heard, but their connection was hard to follow—the bursts of insight overshadowing anything else Ash might have thought.

Margot didn't think it was any different than him insisting she accept a Claim from some stranger. It seemed like exactly the same thing to her, but she already knew what Ash would do, could feel him falling back into his oath.

Really? Margot sighed, trying to use her Claim to pull him back to her, but Ash dug in, resisting her call. Margot didn't have much experience with Claims, but she hadn't fought with Larry like this. Something about the Claim with Ash was different.

"But the Claiming?" Alick was speaking now. "The dragons do not share their mates."

Novus dismissed this concern. "The dragons care nothing for Claims, so long as their partner is loyal to them alone." He gave Ash a look shot with meaning: expectation, threat, desperation. Margot felt it hit home with the power of a lifetime spent trying to please his father. She had never been on the receiving end of such a look, but she could sense the power there, more than just the oath sizzling along Ash's nerves, forcing his hand. "My son knows his duty," Lord Novus announced. "When the time comes, he will do the right thing."

Margot felt the words pierce both her and Ash with a sense of finality, Ash's will falling before his father's command, regardless of the cost. Not only would he marry some stranger, but that woman would demand his loyalty, Claim or not. Ash's hand loosened on hers. Margot could feel the war within him fading as he succumbed to his father, replaced by a deep melancholy she had never seen but should have guessed dwelled within the elusive lead singer.

"Seriously?" Margot burst out. "An hour ago, you were hell bent on Claiming me. Now you're just going to cave and do what daddy wants?"

Ash winced at her words, but he could only sigh. "It's my duty," he said softly. "I have to."

Margot's rage rose, black and tangled and ugly, and she addressed the fae nobles. "I'm really tired of people telling others what they can and can't do around here. How about you grow a backbone?" She stared at the three Lords, waiting for a reaction. Kristoff was beaming, certain her latest outburst would force Novus to punish her, and Alick was pensive, but she could sense a hint of excitement. He was very curious to watch it play out.

Lord Novus was angry, a lovely shade of red creeping up his neck as he stared at her.

She turned to assess the others in the room: her father was watching her, a tiny smile on his face. Because Ash understood the power dynamics in the room, she also knew that Lord Novus was in charge here. Her father had no say in this game—not yet. Not until Lord Novus had finished with them. Lord Rebinus's face was thoughtful, no doubt running through the possibilities.

"My son has a backbone," Novus said. "He will use it to continue his family line and represent the fae among the dragons."

"What if I don't want him to go?" Margot asked bluntly.

"Your wants are of little import to me," Novus dismissed.

"Okay," Margot said, stepping forward and placing herself between Ash and his father. "What if I don't *let* him go?" The Lords didn't like that, and Margot continued, "He's mine now, right? Claimed. You have no authority at all over him." She lifted their hands. "We can do whatever the hell we want."

"That is correct," Novus gritted, "but you should consult with my son before making such rash declarations. As you have seen fit to Claim each other and break with our laws, you are exiled. No Lord will shelter you. You will be alone."

"You say that like I should care," Margot snapped. "I've been alone most of my life. Ash and I will be just fine back on Ardon. We don't need you or your stupid fae laws. We're free."

"Oh yes," Novus agreed. "You are free." He looked at Ash. "Why not ask your lover what that means?"

Margot didn't need to ask with words. Ash's mind filled in the gaps—a life of being hunted by other fae, always in danger, never able to trust anyone, never knowing where the next strike would appear. When Margot didn't understand why that would happen, he reminded her that because they didn't have anyone else under them, the person who killed them would inherit their powers. Any fae would take a chance to Claim either of them, earning power and freedom in the process.

That's why he's considering giving in, Margot realized. *This path offers protection ... for him.* She knew it wasn't cowardice, but it was the easiest reason to latch onto, something she could resent instead of his loyalty to his father.

"Okay," she said slowly. "What about me?" When no one replied right away, she added, "Am I part of Ash's property now, lumped in as dowry when you marry him off to some stranger?"

Novus snorted. "Oh, no, my dear. The dragons would never accept you."

"Why not?" she demanded, slightly offended.

"Because you Claimed Ashton. They would assume you are a spy, there to report back on all his doings to the fae. It would undermine the treaty." It was Lord Jasper who spoke, her father explaining the situation succinctly.

"This is how you treat your powerful fae?" Margot asked. "Just fuck Margot and leave her all alone?"

"You are too dangerous to be left alone," Lord Novus said. "We've all tried to tell you! Don't worry. Someone will take you in as a precaution." Margot thought that being taken in might actually mean imprisoned in this world.

Scoffing, she glanced at her father to see if she would find support. He seemed about to speak, but Lord Rebinus beat him to it.

"Very well. I will accept Lady Margot under my protection," he said formally.

Her father blanched, and he snarled, "No!"

"You?" Novus exclaimed. "Why would you do such a thing?"

"Because you are selling your son to the dragons, no doubt to plot ways to twist the balance of power. What better way to keep myself informed than through the one who has Claimed Ashton?"

"No!" Ash shouted, hand suddenly tight on hers again. She could feel the fight raging in him again—family and duty vs his desire for her. Family had been winning, but with the prospect of giving her to Lord Rebinus, his brother in disguise, his possessive nature was back in control. "Margot should go with her father." He glared at Rebinus. "She will not be another of your whores."

"Of course not!" Lord Rebinus said, shock infusing his voice as he raised a hand to his face. "I fully intend to marry her."

Chapter 63

Bargains

There were several angry outbursts at Lord Rebinus's bold declaration, not the least came from Lord Jasper.

"The hell you will," her father growled. "Over my dead body!" His face was red, the observant stranger she had seen vanished in the ace of this enraged fae Lord. "I will never agree to this!"

"You are changing the game by inviting the dragons to our affairs," Rebinus reminded them, specifically Lord Novus. "The consequences are tempered by Ash joining them, but I still face the risk of a conspiracy. Having Lady Margot join my family alleviates the risk, as she would know what her Claimed was up to." He cut his gaze to Ash. "You would never risk the life of your Claimed by betraying fae laws and engaging in a coup." He looked at each of the Lords in turn, settling for the longest on Lord Jasper. "This is the best possible outcome, and you all know it."

Lord Novus nodded, followed by Lord Alick and Lord Kristoff. Her father took longer, clearly struggling to contain himself. Margot decided that she must have gotten her temper from that side of the family—her mother never had such outbursts. The difference was that Lord Jasper knew the rules here. If fae society could be considered a loose democracy, he was outvoted. Going against Rebinus now would mean he had no support, and for whatever reason, he wasn't ready or able to declare outright war, if that was a thing here. Margot was shocked by how easily she understood the undertones in the room, knowing it was because of her Claim on Ash.

Ash.

Her heart melted as she looked at him. She could feel the war within raging—and she didn't think it would stop any time soon. By Claiming her, he had set these events into motion, ensuring the end of the rock star life he loved. In one moment, he had given it all up for her.

No, she realized, *not for me. For jealousy over me. He wants me, but not at the risk of everything else he holds dear. The only time he will risk everything is when he thinks of me with someone else.*

Oh, Ash, she thought. *You idiot.*

She knew she wasn't being fair. Ash loved her—she could feel it. But the same reasons that had kept him away from her were still there. Ash didn't know how to fight against his family. Margot didn't know if she would have fought if she were in his position. She tried to picture her mother demanding she stop seeing Tobin and imagining her response, but the image fell flat. Penelope had always encouraged Margot to follow her heart, to chase adventure. She would have adored Tobin Fetch.

"Lady Margot," Lord Rebinus was speaking, pulling her out of Ash and back into the room "what say you?"

"I..." She paused, thinking. A vague notion of a plan had begun to form, a way to buy some time for both of them. "I have my own proposition," she said, recalling Tobin's language when he had done the same. "Will you hear it?"

"I am listening," Lord Rebinus said, eyebrow raised in curiosity.

"If I—" she stumbled, steadied herself, and forced her voice to sound normal. "If I agree to marry you, will you swear to consider my thoughts and feelings on matters which concern me?"

Ash's head whipped around to stare at her, hearing her complaint against him in her request. His hand tightened on hers, as if trying to pull her back from some invisible ledge.

"What an odd thought," Lord Rebinus mused, eyebrow raising in a way that reminded her of Tobin. "You wish to be treated as an equal?"

Margot nodded. "I do. I can consider your proposal, assuming you agree, and for my part, I will let you know if the dragons start planning anything you should know about. That should keep everyone here happy, right? Keep your little status quo?" She glanced around the room, trying to gauge the atmosphere through Ash's perceptions.

"Margot." It was Lord Jasper who spoke, "you do not have to do this. You can live in my household, under my protection if not my Claim." Part of her wanted to agree, to spend time with this man who was her father, but a bigger part had more important issues to consider first. Her father would be there. He had apparently known where she was for the last 23 years and hadn't made any effort beyond the TW to have a relationship with her.

He only cared now because she was fae. Powerful fae. A powerful fae who had Claimed the son of a rival.

That last part wasn't Ash at all, she realized, but Tobin.

Margot turned to face her father, seeing the lines of her face in his cheeks, his eyebrows, his thick dark hair. "And what of Tobin?" she asked.

"Tobin?" Lord Novus repeated, clearly not expecting to hear his son's name at this meeting. "What of him?"

"He's your vassal," she said, looking at Lord Rebinus. "Claimed by you. If something happens to you, he would be affected."

"Why should you care about him?" Rebinus asked, voice deeper now, the hint of a threat. "I know my vassal has been spending time with you, but I do hope he hasn't overstepped his boundaries."

"He Awakened me," Margot said simply, "and he was the only one—the only fae—who cared enough to help me with my new abilities. Without him, I wouldn't be here. Nor would Ash. Those faengs would have killed us."

Lord Novus narrowed his eyes at her and Ash. "But my sources—"

"Were wrong," Margot told him. "Tobin saved us that day. I hope that doesn't get him in trouble. But I thought you needed to know that while I have Claimed Ash, and he is mine just as I am his, my first loyalty is to Tobin Fetch. I will not give him up."

Lord Rebinus stared at her for a long time. As the darkness gathered in the depths of his eyes, Margot felt heat stir deep within, an attraction she couldn't quite explain.

"How ... curious," Lord Rebinus said finally. "But your loyalty pleases me. My nephew is an excellent vassal, and he has never given me reason to question his motives.

I will indulge this little friendship of yours. Are you satisfied?"

Margot nodded, though part of her ached at the thought of Ash being so far away. "This isn't an immediate thing, right?" she asked suddenly, hoping this part seemed like an afterthought. "We have a show on tonight. Ash has responsibilities back on Ardon. The tour runs another six weeks."

"Very well," Lord Rebinus agreed. "I propose a six-week engagement to see if this will work out." He looked up at Lord Novus. "That will give you enough time to secure everything with the dragons?"

Ash's father nodded.

"Good," Rebinus said. "Lady Margot, I look forward to our next encounter. We can get to know one another more intimately, I hope."

Margot shook her head, but Rebinus was gone, stepping back into nothingness. There was silence for a moment, and Alick spoke. "Well, my dear, you certainly know how to keep things exciting."

Turning to face her father, Margot watched Lord Tennere's cold expression as he studied her, any warmth between them doused by her recent betrothal to her mother's murderer. She opened her mouth to speak, to say anything to the stranger who was her father, but Lord Jasper stepped away into nothingness before the words could come out.

Chapter 64
Love Shall Set You Free

Morning, Monday March 16th
at The Willis Center at Beau Lake in Taflah, Genc

Margot stared at Ash across the empty room. The remaining Lords had fae-stepped away, and Lord Novus was giving them a few moments of privacy. She was exhausted, body aching as she stood in her blue party dress, but she knew it wasn't over yet.

"Ash," she said, finally breaking the silence. He hadn't spoken since his father had left them, but she could feel the whirling maelstrom within. His loyalty and resignation warred with his Claim on her and his possessive nature. Sighing, she shook her head. "Look, do you have to be such a dragon right now?"

He whirled on her, eyes narrowed, and she knew he didn't think they were alone. His father may have left the room, but there would be eager ears nearby. They couldn't speak freely here.

"Home," she told him, knowing he would understand her request.

Without a word, Ash grabbed her hand and pulled her through the world. They stepped out in front of her bus, the night sky beginning to lighten with dawn.

"I..." Ash began, letting her hand drop. "You can't marry him, Margot. You just can't."

"Why?" she asked. "Because he's Lord Rebinus?" She moved closer, lowering her voice. They were alone, but apparently it never hurt to be cautious. "Because he's your brother?"

"He's not good for you," Ash gritted.

"And you are? Last I heard, you're engaged to a dragon princess. You're not in a position to tell me what to do." As she spoke, she could feel Ash running through her, using his Claim to see her thoughts, feel her emotions. "Oh, Ash," she said, voice sympathetic. "You really are an idiot."

"What would you have me do?" he demanded, heat rising as he felt the walls closing in. "Betray my family?"

"I'm going to stop you right there," Margot interrupted, "because as I recall, my father is just as outraged that I would consider marrying Rebinus." Before he could interrupt, she continued, "That's my problem to deal with, Ash, and I will deal with it." She shook her head. "But you—you have some serious daddy issues that need a lot of work."

"We all have issues," he said, admitting the truth of her words.

"True," she agreed. "Right now, I just want to go to sleep and think about all of this another day."

"Stay with me?" he asked gently, and Margot could feel the pull of his need for her. "Just for a little while?"

Margot stared at the handsome face she had dreamed of, longed for, ached over, cried about, and underneath, she could see the boy she had met so long ago. Before all this, she would have loved nothing more than to hear him ask her to stay with him.

But not now.

"Oh, Ash," she said again, and she could feel that pull inside her slowly fading. She watched it go, not understanding what was happening. Since Ash had Claimed her, she had been waiting for the slavish devotion to hit her, to overwhelm her desires and transform her into a mindless follower.

It hadn't happened yet. She understood him now, but she didn't have to please him. She knew what he wanted—which wasn't that far from what she wanted, if she was honest with herself—but she was still enough of herself to refuse him.

Is it because I've spent years feeling this way? Is Claiming just magical love? And if I already love him, then what is a Claim except a deeper connection?

Margot had a Connection with Tobin, a relationship built on mutual respect, but she hadn't lost herself in him. She wanted him, but it was her choice, not a foregone conclusion.

I don't think this is what a Claim is supposed to be like, Margot thought. She watched Ash, but he had disappeared inside himself, mulling over the possibilities. He wasn't listening to her. No doubt Ash would do what he always did—push her away. And Margot would do the same to him.

But I'm not pushing him away, she realized. *I'm pushing his Claim away. Pushing him out of me. Freeing myself.*

A spark of pure delight raced through her at the thought, but she pushed it down, shoving a wall of reluctant acceptance in Ash's direction. He focused, looking at her again. "Go, what is it?"

"Is this what it's supposed to be like?" she asked. "I can feel you, but I'm still pretty sure I have my free will."

"Kiss me," he said suddenly, and she stepped forward without thinking, the magic jerking her close, but then he put a hand on her chest to stop her. He raised an eyebrow, seemingly proving her point.

But I could have stopped, Margot thought. *I would have stopped.*

"Kiss me," she demanded, testing her own hold on him, and Ash bent without objection, mouth ravaging hers in a way that made her toes curl.

When they parted a moment later, breathless, Ash chuckled. "I thought you would stop me."

"So did I," Margot mused, "but I can't seem to help myself around you." *Nothing new there,* she thought. It may take a little while, but Margot was fairly certain she could refuse Ash in the end if she wanted to.

"I love you," Ash whispered, eyes glowing, face everything she dreamed it would be.

"I know," Margot replied, knowing it was true. He did love her in his way, but it would never be what she felt for him. And that was okay. It gave her some breathing room inside the magic, a small space of separation to keep herself true. "I..." She gave him a gentle kiss, a quick meeting of their lips. "I need a moment, Ash. Just give me some time."

He nodded, but she could sense his reluctance. "With him?" Ash asked, and she heard the bitterness in it, felt the jealousy screaming through him at the idea of his Go in Tobin's arms.

"I think you have other questions to be asking right now," she reminded him. "I'd start with that arranged marriage your dad is so excited about." She gestured to her bus. "I'm going inside. Let's get through the show tonight. Then we have to head to Denham for the next show—and help Nik deal with his issues. There is more going on here than just us."

Mentioning Nik had been a good idea, and Ash nodded, jealous rage fading as he began to plan his next moves. "Be careful, Go," he told her, and he meant it.

"I will," she promised him. She turned around and entered her bus, never so glad to be home.

Tobin laid in her bunk, her latest romance novel in his hand, and glancing down at her, he replaced her bookmark. "Of course, you show up right as they're about to kiss."

Margot grinned up at him, heart lightening at the sight even though she knew they had a lot to talk about. "I know that book. It's not the kiss you're excited about." She racked her brain, trying to remember the order of the courtship between Hannah and Klauden. "Is it the boat ride? That part in the hold is pretty hot."

He raised an eyebrow at her. "Darling, you know I'd take you on a boat ride any time you want." Dropping the book on the pillow, Tobin slid off her bed, all grace and glorious fae sexiness. Once he hit the floor, though, his face was serious. "I didn't know if you'd come back here," he told her. "You can still go after him."

"He wants me to," Margot said, kicking off her sandals.

"Then go," Tobin said, voice perfectly neutral. "I understand how it is."

Margot snorted, turned around, and presented her back to him. "Unzip me, please. This dress is great, but I'm dying to get out of it."

Tobin obliged, hands professional as he undid the dress, helping her lift it overhead. Eyeing her lacey bra and panties, he said, "That's a new one. He'll appreciate it, but it's a bold move to walk across the parking lot in that." He eyed her feet. "Wear the boots."

"Tobin," Margot said, freeing her hair and attempting to fingercomb the snarls and unbraid the remaining front. She faced him. "I'm not going to Ash."

He furrowed his brow. "But ... you said he wants you to come to him."

She shrugged. "Yeah, so what? He's wanted me to come to him since he learned I was with you. This isn't new."

"You know he wants you."

"Yes," she replied, not understanding Tobin's confusion, "and I'm ignoring him—just like yesterday, and the day before that, and the week before that. What gives? You want me to leave so you can get back to my book? I didn't know you were such a fan of vampire romance."

Tobin reached out and gently spun her around to face him. "Margot, he Claimed you."

Margot bit her lip and looked away from him. "Yeah," she began, wondering how to explain what had happened, "about that..." She took a deep breath. "We had sex. I'm sorry."

Tobin eyed her curiously, a slow grin quirking his lips. "Sex during a Claiming?" He put a hand to his mouth. "How shocking!" At Margot's expression, he put a hand to her cheek. "Darling, I told you I don't mind. I know how you feel about him." He frowned. "Though I am disappointed I didn't get to see it."

Margot smacked his arm. "Perv!"

"I just have very different ideas about sex, darling." He leaned forward, running a hand across her collarbone. "Last I heard, you didn't mind."

"I don't mind," she told him, meeting his eyes boldly. "I want you."

His eyes narrowed. "Let me get this straight: you know Ash wants you right now. You can feel his need for you. And you're staying here with me? How ... curious."

"I don't understand it," Margot said. "I mean, I know he Claimed me. I felt it. And I Claimed him. But I can say no. I can walk away. I know how he feels about it—but I can do it." She looked up at him. "Did we do it wrong somehow? Can you fuck up a Claim?"

"There's only one thing that would make the Claim allow such freedom," Tobin explained, "and I didn't know if it was possible. I've only seen it once before I did it. It was just a theory." He paused, then added, "I hoped I was right."

"What are you talking about?" Margot asked. "Before you did what?"

"Broke my Claim."

"With Rebinus? How did you do it?"

"How did you do it?" Tobin countered.

Margot frowned. "You think I broke my Claim with Ash? But I can still feel him over there thinking about me. That's not broken."

"But you can act according to your will," Tobin said. "That part of the Claim is broken." He peered closely at her. "Margot, I know you love Ash, but do you believe he loves you?"

"I think so?" she replied. "In his own way."

Tobin nodded. "You are both fools. Why go through all this and Claim one another if you're only going to set each other free?"

"You think that's what we did? That we broke part of the magic because we love each other?" Margot considered. It did make a kind of sense. "Do you think Ash knows it's broken?"

"He probably doesn't," Tobin told her. "Rebinus certainly didn't notice."

"Wait," she said, putting a hand on his shoulder. "Is that how you did it? I wondered how you could have killed him if he had Claimed you—he would have known everything you thought or felt or wished. But you broke free by loving him?"

Tobin shrugged, the move dismissive. "He was my uncle. It wasn't hard, once I figured out what I needed to do."

She cocked her head. "How did you figure it out? I didn't realize anything except that the Claim wasn't working the way you said."

Tobin's hand stroked her arm, as if assuring himself she was really with him. "When I arrived, there was an old woman in the palace. She had been the one to raise him when he was a child. You could call her his nanny. He Claimed her when he was very young, of course, much like Ash Claimed Timothy, but over time, I saw her behavior shift. I guessed his Claim wasn't as strong because she already loved him—couldn't help but love him—even when she didn't want to."

Margot nodded, thinking of how Timothy was able to argue with Ash despite the Claim. "Is that it? If you love the one who Claims you, you can break it? Or it doesn't work the same way?" It made a weird kind of sense, especially since Claiming seemed to enforce a false love of sorts, an adoration or flattery. Margot recalled Lawrence's fawning eagerness to please her and dismissed the image. She had plenty of time to deal with that—and tell Tobin what she had done. "Wait," she said, looking up at him, "this whole time you kept pushing Ash to Claim me. Was it because you knew he loved me? That it would ultimately set me free?"

The man in her arms shrugged, this time uncertainly. "Like I said—I hoped. It seems like that worked for us, but I don't know. It's hard to tell since so few couples Claim one another. I need more information." He reached out to touch her hair, slowly pushing it behind her shoulders to reveal her strapless bra. His finger traced the red line under her arm where the bra had dug in after so many hours of wear.

"Darling," he drawled, "let's get this off." Margot smiled at him, lifting her arms so he could reach around and unhook the back. He tossed the bra atop the dress she had thrown on the passenger seat, eyes bright as he took in her nearly naked body.

"You really want to stay here with me?" he asked her.

"Oh yes," she assured him, wrapping both arms around his neck and leaning close. "Darling," she said, "we are going to have such a good time." By the expression on his face, she knew he understood she was talking about more than just this night.

It would take some time to wean herself from Ash. She would never be completely free, but now that she was Claimed, she was safe from other fae's attempts to control her abilities. Margot would learn to use her new powers and see just how strong she was. And when she was ready, she wouldn't stop until she had broken every last Claim.

Epilogue
Selling Your Soul

Afternoon, Monday, March 16ᵗʰ
at the Estate of Lord Kristoff in
Beauraton, Lorellon

Tobin met his mother's gaze across the table, the tea implements laid out between them as if this was a civilized discussion.

"Son," his mother began, snapping the napkin across her lap and protecting the white lace decorating her silver dress, "you want to tell me why you've gone and lost your mind?"

"Mother," Tobin began, settling his napkin the way she had taught him, "I have not—"

"Years of planning," she interrupted, hand gesturing in magical motions to encase them in a spell of secrecy. "Years of tedious and excruciating details, carefully moving all the pieces into place, and you go and ruin it all within a few weeks."

"It's not ruined," Tobin insisted. "Plans have simply been rearranged."

His mother frowned, lifting the teapot and filling one of the delicate cups on the table. Tobin helped himself to a sugar cube, watching it dissolve in the hot water as his mother continued to exude anger from across the table. "I see," she said finally, "and Lord Rebinus's new engagement is a part of this plan?"

"Margot is ... useful," Tobin argued, knowing this would be a hard argument to win. His mother was as stubborn as he was sometimes. She wouldn't like the addition of a new person to their plans, not when it had been the two of them for so long. Before Margot, she had been the only one who knew he was Rebinus. "Her Claim on Ash gives us insight into the dragons."

"And his Claim on her? How does a new wife who has been Claimed by another further our aim?" Her voice was tart, his words cutting, as usual. "You were supposed to let Ash Claim her, then Claim him. That was the plan, son."

"I think," Tobin began, "their bond may also be an asset."

"How?" his mother demanded.

Tobin took a sip, enjoying the flavor of the fine tea, a drink only found on Lord Kristoff's estate, the Lord who ultimately owned his mother. "It remains to be seen," he admitted, "but it will be seen. I believe she will be the key to everything—to all of our plans."

Lady Sylvia scowled. "Spoken like another idiot in love," she dismissed. "Trying desperately to convince me this woman has value beyond the obvious. Don't be a fool, Tobin."

"Mother," he said, knowing it was probably useless to argue but unable to let the insult slide, "you haven't met Margot. I think you'll like her."

"I think I'll like her powers," Lady Sylvia commented, taking a small sip of her tea and dabbing her mouth with a delicate napkin. "Much like you, I imagine."

"Mother," Tobin argued, setting down the teacup to stare at her, "I like Margot. For herself. If you give her a chance—"

"I am not giving chances to anyone Claimed by a Stonewall," his mother declared, and Tobin frowned.

"Now who is being foolish?" he cajoled. "Don't let your prejudices blind you. Margot is an asset, Claimed or not, and I fully intend to marry her."

His mother took another sip and set her cup down, the glass clinking against the saucer. "Oh, Tobin," she sighed, giving her son a sad look, "you've never been in love before."

Tobin rolled his eyes. "Not this again," he insisted.

"You don't understand, but you will," she told him. "She's Claimed now. She's in love with Ash. You'll see it in her eyes all the time, just beneath everything she says." She held out a hand to pat his wrist where it rested beside his half-drained cup. "It will eat you alive."

"I am not you, Mother," Tobin told her.

"You are my son," she reminded him. "I know how you are."

"So you say," Tobin muttered, immediately regretting the comment as his mother's gentle hand darted up to smack his arm, a reminder not to dismiss her words.

"You think I don't know what you're about to encounter?" his mother asked. "You think I don't know what it is to watch the one you love pine over another?"

"I think your life and mine are very different," Tobin observed, finishing his tea with a long swallow.

"I don't think they will be so different when you find yourself wondering what your precious Margot is like when she is with the one she truly loves."

Tobin's eyes snapped to hers, not misunderstanding her intention. He had always wondered if his mother used her shapeshifting ability to impersonate Lady Abigail before she was sent away. Her own experience with the ability was one of the reasons why she had immediately known he was not Lord Rebinus. She had told him later, much later, that the other reason she knew Rebinus was gone was in the truly polite way he treated her. The real Lord Rebinus had propositioned her when she was living as Novus's wife and again when she was newly exiled. Tobin hadn't asked whether she had taken him up on his offer, not wanting to know that much about his mother's sex life.

He put the cup down, pushing the chair away from the table. "Margot loves me," Tobin declared.

"Maybe," he mother agreed, "but not the same way you love her. Someday you will wonder what it is to be held by someone who really loves you."

Tobin shook his head, lifting the napkin from his lap and standing, annoyed, as he often was when he left a visit with his mother. "It's lovely to see you, Mother, as always."

"Don't let your lust get in the way of our plans," she scolded him. "Don't forget who you are—Who *we* are."

"Of course, Mother," he said, bowing briefly in her direction. "How could I ever?"

"Women have a way of changing things," Lady Sylvia commented. "I'd hate for all this to be for nothing."

"I wouldn't have sold my soul to undo Lord Novus if I didn't intend on following through," he assured her. "Having a wife won't change that."

Without another word, he left her room, fingers forming the symbols for the portal spell that would bring him back to Margot and her bus. He tried not to think of it, but his mother's words lingered as he stepped through the mirror and into the small space of Margot's kitchen.

His fiancée sat cross-legged in her swivel chair, a glowing ball of electrical power hovering above her palm. She gave him a broad smile, closing her hand and releasing the magical energy in a display of light and power.

Tobin returned the smile, part of him wondering just how powerful Margot would be—and if fae society would survive when she figured it out.

Cast of Characters

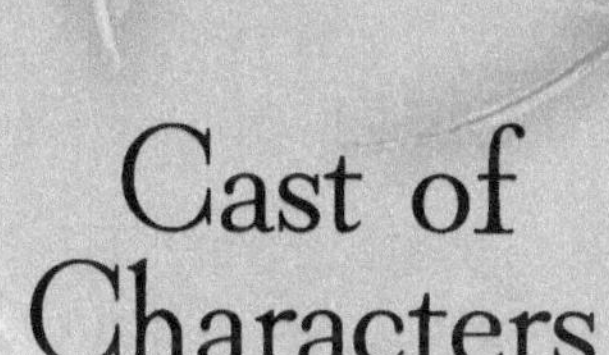

<u>Fae</u>

Lord Novus Stonewall: Fae Lord. Father of Ashton and Tobin. Currently married to Lady Abigail.

Lady Abigail Stonewall: Current wife of Lord Novus. Mother of Ashton Stonewall.

Ashton Stonewall: Second son of Lord Novus. Lead singer and guitarist of Stone Dragons.

Lady Sylvia Stonewall: First wife of Lord Novus. Mother of Tobin (Stonewall) Fetch. Claimed by Lady Drina Atherton.

Tobin (Stonewall) Fetch: First son of Lord Novus. Claimed by Lord Rebinus Stonewall.

Clifton Ward: Vassal of Lord Novus.

Timothy Green: Claimed by Ashton Stonewall. Drummer for Stone Dragons.

Lord Kristoff Daglorin: Fae Lord.

Lady Drina (Feston) Atherton: Claimed by Lord Kristoff. Widow of Lord Josef Atherton. Current Host of Lady Sylvia.

Penelope "Penny" (Atherton) Tanner: Deceased. Mother of Margot Tanner. Claimed by Lady Drina Atherton.

Madelyn "Maddie" (Atherton) Hodges: Deceased. Mother of Niklaus Hodges. Claimed by Lord Josef Atherton.

Lawrence O'Malley: Formerly Claimed by Lord Kristoff. Currently Claimed by Margot Tanner.

Lord Jasper Tennere: Fae Lord. Father of Margot Tanner.

Lord Alick Feston: Fae Lord.

Lord Rebinus Stonewall: Fae Lord.

<u>Dragons</u>

Queen Shomentu: Queen of the Dragons on Denham Island.

Lady Iphega: Daughter of Queen Shomentu. Princess of the Dragons on Denham Island. Betrothed to Ashton Stonewall.

Humans

Marcus Hodges: Deceased. Human. Father of Niklaus Hodges. Married to Maddie (Atherton) Hodges.

Niklaus Hodges: Former Human. Current Werewolf. Guitarist for Stone Dragons.

Alby: Lead singer for Das Leprechauns. Ruined human.

Cayla Menard: Band Manager for Stone Dragons.

Travis: Road crew for Stone Dragons.

Dustin: Road crew for Stone Dragons.

Ben: Road crew for Stone Dragons. Ex-boyfriend of Margot Tanner.

John: Road crew for Stone Dragons.

Alex: RV driver for Stone Dragons.

Jeff: RV driver for Stone Dragons.

Book Club Questions

1. Margot accepts both her fae heritage and the super-natural world without much difficulty. Why do you think she reacts this way to her new experience of the world around her? How would you react to wings exploding from your back?

2. Tobin insists he met Margot by accident, simply noticing a beautiful woman alone at the bar. Do you believe him?

3. Margot has pined over Ash since she was 15. Do you believe such young love can last the test of time?

4. Ash says he has kept his distance from Margot because of his family obligations. Do you believe him? Would you make the same choice in his position?

5. After their night together, Ash immediately falls back into old patterns, a mistake he regrets bitterly. Should he be forgiven for his behavior in the Green Room? Why or why not?

6. Tobin lives a double life as Lord Rebinus. Were you surprised to find he killed his lord and replaced him?

7. Margot learns a bit about fae culture and society and decides she dislikes most of what she sees. Do you agree with her assessment?

8. Margot "accidentally" uses her powers to hurt two people: destroying Alby and Claiming Lawrence. She feels some kind of guilt for her actions, but she also justifies her behavior. Do you agree with her actions and/or justifications? Would you have done the same?

9. The story ends with Ash engaged to a dragon princess and Margot engaged to Lord Rebinus. What do you think will happen as the story progresses?

10. You knew it was coming. Which one should Margot be with: Ash or Tobin? Why?

Author Bio

Author of the Klauden's Ring Saga and the Conjuring Fascination series, JM Paquette writes fantasy and paranormal romance novels. When she isn't writing, she can be found teaching English to college students as Dr. Paquette or watching her favorite Russian shifter romance movie, *I Am Dragon*. Her areas of expertise include the history of the English language and the intricacies of grammatical rules, but her favorite class to teach is on *Lord of the Rings*. (If you've ever wondered why English is a crazy language, watch her video series on YouTube under Editor JMPaquette!) She enjoys editing manuscripts for academic and creative writers alike, and she adores tabletop roleplaying (THAC0, anyone?) where her halfling ranger/Twi'lek adept/vampire wizard/[insert race and class here] is often underestimated. You can also find her guest co-hosting the podcast Drinking with Authors--even though she doesn't drink, she loves getting to know fellow authors! Check out JM Paquette at authorjmpaquette.com and 4horsemenpublications.com and as Author JM Paquette on Facebook and Instagram.

Discover more at
4HorsemenPublications.com

10% off using HORSEMEN10